I0699407

BUTTERFLY *effect*

OTTAWA REGENTS, BOOK TWO

RUBY RANA

*For those who lost a part of themselves too young and spent
years trying to feel whole again.*

CONTENT/TRIGGER WARNINGS

This book contains explicit language, graphic depictions of various sexual activities (including oral sex, anal sex, mutual masturbation, use of sex toys, rimming), mild BDSM acts (orgasm denial, pegging, consensual forced orgasms), mild recreational drug use, and alcohol use.

While this is a romantic comedy, grief, death/loss of a parent, and abandonment are key themes. One main character has lost her parent to suicide at a young age and another is estranged from his father and both discuss how it affects them in adulthood.

There are also brief references to a cheating ex-fiancé, past bullying (verbal) and otherwise mature themes.

If any of these topics are a trigger for you, please refrain from reading or proceed with caution.

PLAYLIST

Ruin My Life - Zara Larrson

Jolene - Dolly Parton

Fidelity - Regina Spektor

Please Please Please - Sabrina Carpenter

Love at First Fight - LANY

Apple - Charlie xcx

Mirage - Sabrina Carpenter

The Walls - Chase Atlantic

Maps - Yeah Yeah Yeahs

Beggin' - Måneskin

Your Soniya - KAYAM, OfficialD8

War of Hearts - Ruelle

Pull My Heart Away - Jack Peñate

Snooze - SZA

I Wear My Roots Like A Medal - Dhee

Navrai Maajhi - Sunidhi Chauhan

CHAPTER 1:
FLAILING ON THE BED WITH A HAND DOWN MY PANTS

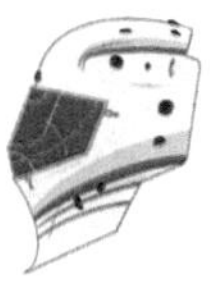

WADE

ONE NIGHT WITH GABE FINCH RUINED ME.

You'd think my dick would get over it after a year, but you'd be wrong. It wants nothing to do with anyone but her. With the exception of my hand.

What a shame. A waste, really. Someone so good at sex unable to perform.

For as long as I'd been having it, sex was enough. It worked fine to stave off the loneliness of an empty bed, a temporary distraction to fulfill the lack of true intimacy. I mean, how much closer could I be to someone other than physically inside them?

But no one stayed beyond the night, if that. They'd move on, so I'd move on.

Until last summer. Until Gabe Finch.

I'd never met someone so easily able to command a room without overtly demanding attention. Someone so unafraid to put me in my place. Being pursued was normal, but being challenged by someone so unbothered and unimpressed? Never happened before. And damn, if I couldn't stop vying for her approval.

Glass squeaks under my fist as I clear a circle from the shower steam, frowning at the brown curls sprawling across a pillow and over my date's face. The second pint of dark beer had Vanessa yawning in the taxi to the hotel, and she was more than happy to accept the bed for a quick nap instead of its intended purpose.

She's pretty. Sweet, easy to talk to. And unlike Gabe, she wants me around, if only for the time being. Our expectations for what this is are set and limited. The mask I've spent so much of my life under stays on.

But the mere thought of a certain gorgeous sportscaster with eyes like daggers and a mouth that could only be described as Heaven—*despite hurling insult after insult at me for the past twelve months*—has the mask melting away. It probably means something that I enjoy being challenged by her, but I have no idea what that is.

God, I'm fucked.

I post a hand onto the tiled wall of the shower while revisiting the beginning of that perfect night, eyes screwed shut and my free hand fixed around my rock-hard dick.

Nothing could've held my attention except her. By far the hottest reporter covering the NHL, Gabe stood out from the rest of the wedding guests. She was over six feet in heels, and the navy beaded dress hugging her lean figure would've made Daisy Buchanan cry with joy.

A champagne flute rocked in her slender fingers before tightening around its stem. My cock stirred, self-inserting in her grip.

Our alternate captain, Landon Radek, and his new bride, Indi, smiled and swayed in the background, not at all in sync with the upbeat melody. As if nothing and no one existed but them. Sickening.

I straightened from a pillar at the perimeter of the white marquee. The one and only Fletcher Donovan, the reliable Ottawa Regents center but my unreliable wingman, glugged a beer.

Was it his fifth or sixth? I'd lost count.

"Slow down, buddy. You're gonna piss your pants at this rate."

"Shut up," he grumbled.

I shoved him forward to Bea, the short, curvy bridesmaid he'd been fixated on for months. "Ask her to dance already."

"Easy for you to say. Fucking look at her."

Bea threw jet-black waves of hair over her shoulder before accepting another offer on the dance floor.

"Lost your chance." I tsked.

The bashful shit reddened and fled stage left. I refocused on eavesdropping.

"I thought a wedding would make me emotional, but damn…"

A sip of super smooth Scotch rolled over my tongue and down my chest as I neared the not-so-hushed voice, hoping to catch the rest of the sentence.

"…I'm just horny," Gabe said to no one, taking a sip and hugging those long arms around her torso.

"Me too," I replied from behind. "Want me to fix it for us?"

She cursed under a breath, eyes fluttering shut as she dropped her head to one side.

"Whaddya say?"

"Crap," Gabe lamented in the opposite direction before gazing at the tent above as if addressing a universal power. "Is this a joke? It's like you want me to make a bad decision."

"Bad? Never." I took in some floral scent from her skin and held up two fingers. "Goalie's guarantee."

Her body stilled for a moment as if lost in thought. Those freckled cheeks tinged pink.

Oooh, she's considering it. God knows I've fantasized about it for too long.

Slowly, she placed her drink on the table to her left and backpedaled.

Was that a yes?

I downed the rest of my glass and went after her, slinking away from the reception in the same way. Gabe bolted up the hill to the estate's large farmhouse and skipped multiple porch steps so fast I had to catch my breath in the foyer.

Stretching my chest only did so much to recover from the short sprint. A hand yanked at my jacket before slamming my back against the inside of a closet door. My heart thudded under her palm as she loosened her grasp.

"Don't. Say. Anything."

I nodded, mouth parted.

"I'm gonna regret this," she said through a sigh. "But I'm gonna kiss you now, okay?"

I nodded rapidly again, like a dope.

The tart sweetness from her champagne mixed with the Scotch's leftover malted vanilla as Gabe's lips covered mine. It was a hungry, desperate kiss, as desperate as the fingers fumbling to open my button-up.

She moaned before releasing with a frustrated noise. My belt clanged onto itself at the force of becoming undone. I reached for the *back of her neck and rejoined our mouths, tongue angrily swiping across hers. Gabe broke us apart once more, her lips coasting across my jaw and below my ear. The teasing nibbles and sucks had me clenching her body to mine and replying with a groan.*

The mask slipped.

"Fuck, Gabe. I haven't been able to stop thinking about you since New Year's."

Or the way she squeezed my neck while yelling at me. And the fierce, heated kiss that followed? It branded itself deep into each wrinkled ridge of my brain.

"Ugh. What part of 'Don't say anything,' do you not" —she interrupted herself by pressing me to the door by the throat— "Wait, what?"

Shit. Put the mask back on!

"I mean, what? Pfft," I backtracked. "I've forgotten about it. I've made out with, like, dozens of women since then."

Gabe scoffed from the corner of her upturned mouth. "Um, cool?" Her palm met the covered tip of my upright cock. "You have a condom, or what?"

"Yeah-yeah-yes." I fished one from inside my suit jacket and tore it open. "Okay. It was a dozen. Maybe."

You chump.

"Shut up and put it on." She shimmied her dress up.

The boxer brief band was tugged down enough to roll it over my length. Gabe's scowl shifted to surprise. I smirked back.

"Holy shit, you're" —her eyes widened at my size— "You're..."

Shocked at her verbal trip-up but impatient with the back and forth, I spun us, pinning her to the door with a hand on the dip of her waist. She wasn't the only one who could be a fucking tease.

"I know. I'm big." The glass beading on the fabric bit the skin of my palms as I bunched it higher over her bare torso, my free hand reaching between those long legs. A slick warmth brushed my fingertips through her panties. "And you're not wet enough yet."

"That's 'cause you don't have any idea what—"

She swallowed her words when my mouth swept down the column of her throat, tasting more and more of the delicate skin. Between how soft she felt and getting hit with that damn flowery smell, I felt dizzy.

I swiped the strip of fabric covering her aside, pushing her up the door until her knees hooked over my hips. When I circled her clit, she squirmed and whimpered.

"What's that? Not so mouthy now, huh?" One finger prodded into her little pussy, gliding in and out until her arousal coated me down to the knuckle. "There you go." I rubbed and tapped the sensitive spot inside her until she clamped and pulsed around me. "We're gonna make it fit."

Gabe bit back a pleasured hum and tore at the hair on my nape in response, notching our faces together and forcing eye contact. "Get inside me. Now."

The swollen head of my cock rested at her entrance, waiting for one last reply. Her cheeks burned with a rising flush.

"Do you like it rough, Gabe? Or do you want me to hold back and ride you in slow-fucking-motion?"

"Jesus Christ." She threw her head back, annoyed. "The speeches are on soon! Let's fucking go." Her wiggle spread those legs wider in an attempt to get herself off.

Not on my watch. If anyone gets her off, it'll be me.

"Rough, it is."

She agrees silently with a nod.

"Say it."

"Go rough."

We gasped together as I drove in the first time and again when I started moving. In and out, in and out, her dripping cunt wrapping me so tight, I could hardly breathe.

I moaned her name into the crook of her neck, a needy plea for confirmation that she felt what I did.

The door rattled with the increased speed, unraveling the rest of my restraint as her quiet whines got louder and louder with each subsequent thrust.

"Oh, God," she panted. "Wade."

The mask might as well have disintegrated into thin air.

"You feel so fucking good," I whispered into her mouth. "Kiss me."

She repeated a moan in response but didn't kiss me.

"Kiss me so we can both come," I grated out with another slam, then slid a finger over her swollen clit. "Good girls listen. You're a good girl, aren't you, Gabe?"

"Don't you ever shut up?" The question contrasted the needy pull that drew our lips together.

A hum vibrated between us, the harsh sweeps of our tongues tipping us over. We let go with a shared scream as I bottomed out, dick pulsing inside her. My hands roamed, caressing every inch of her within reach, absorbing every sensation of the moment, not wanting it to end.

Gabe tapped my shoulder to be released, and I obeyed, removing myself and the condom.

"Fucking incredible." I sighed.

She inhaled sharply, a lopsided, unimpressed smile coloring her face. "I've had better."

Outrageous.

"The fuck you have."

Her dress hem returned to its place above her knees. "It was too fast. You could use some endurance training."

"Whatever." A haphazard tucking of my shirt back into the suit pants made a louder rustle than intended. "This isn't the last time we do this, eh, Finch?"

"Oh, Pretty Boy." Gabe patted my face with enough force that it could've been confused for three slaps. "This is absolutely, one hundred thousand percent never *happening again."*

Fuck, I'm gonna come.

My toes curl over the wet marble, knees and thighs shaking. The steady speed of my hand syncs with the beat of Dolly Parton's "Jolene," and I mutter the namesake lyrics before coming in my fist, vision white and Gabe's name on my stifled breath.

"Wow." A yawn sounds out. "Jolene's a lucky lady."

I huff out a laugh at Vanessa's comment while recovering from the high. A few splashes from the cascade rinse away the filth. "Not really. It's that song. By Dolly Parton."

"That's what you beat off to?"

"Hey, good rhythm is good rhythm."

I step out to dry off, then throw my boxers and slacks on before leaning on the counter. Vanessa continues to battle a tangled bobby pin as I guide her between my knees.

"Here." I reach for the knot of hair. "Let me."

Vanessa turns, her back to my chest, hands on her legs in wait. The pin relents, and I display its defeat in her sight line.

"Thanks, Wade." She returns the pin to a twisted strand while glancing at me. "You're boyfriend material, you know that? If you wanted to be."

I trill my lips and stroll to the bed. "Nah. I'm a good fuck, though."

"Are you? It's been so long, I've forgotten." She tosses a sarcastic smile my way.

Air hisses past my mouth. "Sorry about that."

"Eh, it's my fault, too." Vanessa shrugs. "We'll blame the chocolate stout."

So she didn't notice my cock was uncooperative.

"But don't underestimate yourself."

"Me? Never." I lie back, tucking my hands behind my head, giving her a complete view of the goods, flexing my biceps, and curling up to show off my abs. "I'm the *best* fuck. Is that better?"

"That's not what I meant, but..." She trails off, taking the bait and eyeing my torso. My tongue pokes victoriously through my teeth. Vanessa ahems and straightens her sweater. "Thank you for that. And thanks for letting me crash." She salutes weakly from her brow. "Wade. Always a pleasure."

"Likewise. And Vanessa?" I jump up, breaking into a jog to meet her by the door. "Remember, *uh*, not to...?"

"Yeah, yeah, I know. '*Tell no one what you're actually like.*'" She imitates the deep timbre of my voice and shakes her head. "'*Gotta protect the rep.*'"

"Thanks."

"See you next time you're in L.A.?"

"Sure. I'll text you."

She winks. "Sounds good."

I stare at the pale blue wall for a split second after the door claps shut.

Then I'm back to the mental disarray, flailing on the bed with a hand down my pants, replaying the rest of that night with a woman I'll never get to touch again.

This feeling can't last forever. I haven't slept with anyone in a year, but it has to happen sometime, right?

Soon, I vow to myself. Soon, I'll be inside someone else and forget all about Gabe Finch.

CHAPTER 2:
WHERE ARE THESE MEN IN REAL LIFE?

GABE

I WANT TO STICK THIS SALAD FORK DIRECTLY INTO my eye.

Or maybe I'll stick it into the eye of Dr. Dan Briarstone, Ottawa's Most Eligible Bachelor and orthopedic surgeon for the city's professional athletes. It'll be the most interesting thing to happen on our date tonight.

Hidden from view, I set a timer on the phone in my lap. If he talks about anything—*literally, anything*—other than medicine and his daily skincare routine in the next five minutes, I will give him a blowjob right here, in the middle of this packed restaurant.

The countdown begins as I force an unladylike yawn. Doesn't seem to translate.

"I used to have spots on my cheeks and nose like yours" —oh, how nice, he finally said something about me— "not as many, of course. But I started using this Vitamin C serum and, *poof*! Gone. Turns out they were melasma. Highly recommend it to everyone with blemishes."

Blemishes? Time's up.

The relationship I have with my freckles is as complicated as the one with my mother. Freckles and the color of my eyes are all I have left of her. I'd cut all the other parts away, a necessary amputation in an effort for self-preservation, but it still aches like a phantom limb.

A deadpan look shot at him doesn't seem to register, either. So much for being a genius. This dude is dense as lead.

I go for a tried-and-true tactic: groaning while scrunching my stomach. "You know what? I'm actually not feeling so hot."

"Oh?" He grimaces, looking at my picked-at greens. "I bet it's that dressing. Gotta watch out for those rich sauces. They're so fatty."

My eyes roll. Dan raises an arm to call the waiter over for the check, and I retrieve a card from my wristlet.

"We'll split it."

"Please, Gabe. Don't insult me." He passes my card back across the table. "I'll take you home, too."

Great.

This has got to be one of the Top 5 Worst Dates I've ever been on. Right below Mr. Drank-Too-Much-He-Pissed-Himself.

To others, Dan would seem a gentleman. Offering to pay for dinner, opening and closing the car door. But everything he does and says prickles my skin. He's smug, self-involved, and borderline controlling. Barf. And how much should I bet that he's still gonna try to get in my pants?

I pay absolutely zero attention to him on the drive through downtown, fake nausea slowly turning into real nausea with every swerve and screechy stop at busy intersections.

When we pull up to the curb, he jogs around to the passenger side, helping me out from the low ground clearance of his fiery red Mercedes. My bare arms prickle with goosebumps from the touch. His grip is too firm, a creepy, unspoken sort of persuasion.

"Let me walk you up."

It's a step beyond comfort. An uneasy noise hums out.

"I don't know if that's a good idea." I hug my torso, milking the stomachache some more. "I'm still not feeling well. It won't be a fun time."

"I don't mind." He shrugs. Pushy bastard. "You might feel better in a bit. We could watch some Netflix, get comfortable..." His eyebrows waggle suggestively.

Yuck. No.

"...See where the night takes us."

Cold fingers connect with the arch of my hip over the black fabric of my dress. I shrink away.

"I need to rest, actually. I'm traveling for work tomorrow, and I can't be sick on the road."

The doctor laughs with a shake of his head. "You might as well have said you don't like me."

"*Heh-heh*," I titter, taking a step back toward the lobby doors. Enough to be in camera range and view of the security desk. "Good night."

"Holy shit." He stalks forward, eyes squinting as his smile drops from his face. "You *don't* like me?"

"I didn't say it. You did."

"*Wow*, Gabe."

His steps halt, thank God.

"You know there are literally hundreds of women in this city who do, right?"

Seriously, where do I find these guys?

"How nice. Maybe one of them will go out with you, but it won't be me."

Dan's jaw ticks before he scoffs and turns to the street.

"Prude," he mumbles.

I wait until the car door slams and the engine roars to life.

"I hope that Botox seeps into your bloodstream and paralyzes your face!" My insult strikes as he peals away, flipping me his middle finger.

"And another thing! Your balls are the size of peas!" I continue before retreating to the corridor. It earns me raised eyebrows from the security men seated in the lobby. Olawale and Jawed have been witness to many sad nights.

"You alright, ma'am?" Jawed's kind eyes crinkle in worry. He's always so polite.

I grumble. "Yeah."

"Was it a bad date?" Olawale adds, curling his hand against his cheek.

"Isn't it always?"

"Maybe these days." Olawale shrugs. "But nothing lasts forever, eh?" The way he says *eh?* in his Nigerian accent makes me smile.

Jawed agrees with a nod. "Sorry to hear that, ma'am."

"Me, too." There's an awkward lull. "I'm gonna get going. Early morning flight tomorrow."

"What time shall I have the taxi wait?"

"4 a.m., please. And thanks, Wale."

They wave me off as I enter the elevator and slump into the back wall. My belly growls.

"I know," I reply. "You deserve a grilled cheese."

The lights click on as I kick off my heels and drop my clutch onto the sideboard in the foyer, pausing to swipe a hand across the herringbone wood pattern on its cabinet doors in admiration.

I'm desperate for something grounding, and head to the last door on the right, the one to the corner room. It creaks as I peek in and ends with the faint buzz of the humidifier and black lights. Scents of sweet gardenia and tart hibiscus fill the space. My collection of tropical plants sleeps peacefully. I rub a few lush green leaves between my thumb and index finger. No matter how hard I try, I don't feel anything in response to nurturing them. These plants thrive here regardless. I wish I could say the same for myself.

I sigh and leave, feeling just as empty as when I returned home.

While the grilled cheese sandwich crisps on the pan, I shed the bodycon dress and replace it with a white tank and loose gray joggers, satisfied with the handiwork of my new cleaning service.

Constant travel during the season makes it hard to keep tidy. The apartment is simply a place to crash, eat, dump used clothing, and pack for the next trip. I've got the basics and a fancy gadget or two, but I don't spend enough time here to make it my own. Wondering if Dottie's Cleaners did the laundry, I wander towards the machines in the closet. They did, thank God.

Plush athletic socks retrieved from the dryer keep my feet warm. My hair goes into a high ponytail while I smoothly skate back into the kitchen, then plop down on the couch with possibly the best sandwich I've ever made. Angels would sing if they saw this beauty.

The cozy vibe calls for a comfort watch. I flip the TV on and stream a favorite: the one in the quaint little town in the northeastern United States where everyone knows everyone's business, quirky side characters are always up to no good, and the mom and daughter talk way too fast.

A dark-haired dreamboat who talks out of the corner of his mouth and reads on park benches throughout the aforementioned quaint town appears on the screen, leaving behind his book to follow around a girl like a puppy.

"Damn," I say through a cheesy bite. "Where are these men in real life?"

I frown at myself, gushing over an on-screen teenager. Google confirms he was twenty-four when they started filming his part, which makes me feel a little better. A little.

"Twenty-four? That's way too young for you, Finch. Been there, rode that. Never again."

At thirty-one, there's no more time to waste on immature jerks and mediocre dick. Or on immature jerks with excellent dick.

Especially not when they're irritatingly hot goalies. Or named Wade Boehner. The man loves making my work life hell by being unprofessional any chance he gets. It'd been a mistake to kiss him at a New Year's Eve party, but the night we'd spent after Indi's wedding surely cleared our systems once and for all.

Like answering a distress signal, a text notification from my best friend pings my phone.

INDI

Text me SOS if your date sucks, and I'll call to bail you out.

INDI

Or the kitty cat if it's going well.

ME

How much wine have you had?

INDI

Enough hehe

Hehe? Marriage has truly changed her.

ME

Isn't it 2 a.m. in Italy?

INDI

Never too early for wine in this country!

ME

Oh boy.

INDI

Don't judge us! We're on vacation and haven't gone back to the hotel yet from dinner

ME

You're right, you should be having fun!

ME

And I'm already home, watching Gilmore Girls.

INDI

Ouch. That bad?

ME

Worse.

INDI

Fly here! We'll find you a gorgeous Italian man who'll beg to eat grapes off of your body.

ME

I'll settle for a man in Ottawa who'll beg to eat me out properly.

INDI

Cin Cin!

INDI

ahahah, but seriously, they're out there.

She'd know. Indi Davé married her dream man, Landon Radek, the poster boy for the NHL. She's off canoodling with the alternate captain of the Regents during the end of European Summer before the season kicks into gear.

ME

Stop rubbing it in.

INDI

That's what she said.

ME

Landon is a bad influence.

INDI

Absolutely. Thank God he has a big dick
to make up for it.

ME

This is where I'd like the conversation to end.

INDI

I love you!! Call you soon.

ME

Love you, too.

My plate makes its way onto the coffee table as the Netflix app glitches and switches to live TV.

"What now?" I ask the remote, pressing a few buttons to troubleshoot.

When I casually glance over the screen, anger builds toward the star of the athletic wear ad. Kurt Vaughn, a Toronto Towers center and my ex-fiancé, dunks on an undefended basket. He looks like he always does: angled jaw, broad shoulders, toned arms. Six feet and six inches of pure strength and speed.

I turn the TV off.

I want to scream, but I don't. No tears come, either. Instead, the hollow ache of lost love settles in my chest.

It's been almost four years since I broke off our engagement, but grief is sneaky. It lurks below the surface like a shark. And when I stop paying attention, presuming the anger is gone for good, it breaches the barrier and engulfs me in an uncontrolled wave of loss.

It wasn't my fault. I shouldn't care. *He* was a cheating bastard. But why wasn't I enough? Was I really that hard to love that he had to stick his dick wherever he could?

I take a sinking seat in the pit of self-loathing; I grab my phone and send a message to my neighbor, Brett. He's not the best fuck, but it's better than thinking about Kurt.

ME

You home?

BRETT

Yep. Be there in 5?

Twenty minutes later, I'm on my back with Brett's cock inside me. A drop of sweat from the tip of his nose lands on the pillowcase next to my ear. He spews profanities as he finishes, then deepens the wrinkle in his brow.

Don't say it. Don't say it. Please don't say it.

There's a curious, quizzical gleam in his eyes.

Crap, he's gonna say it.

"Did you come?"

My throat clears as he pulls out.

There can't possibly be a worse question.

"Uh…" I'm about to lie, but he catches it.

"Shit. You didn't?"

"Sorry, I think it's me."

"That's bullshit, Gabe." Brett swipes the condom off and climbs off the bed to get rid of it. He kneels below me upon his return. "Let me try at least."

His hands pry apart my legs, but I push his face away. I'm grateful he's willing to learn, but it's too exhausting to have to walk through this with someone I don't care about. Or trust fully.

"It's okay, Brett."

"Are you sure?"

"Yeah, I think it's stress from work or something. I should probably sleep it off. Thanks, though."

We take turns peeing and get clothed again. There's a flash of regret in his smile when he leaves, and I sorta feel bad.

It *is* me, after all. I'm the jerk in this situation. Beggars can't be choosers, but I'm simply not in the mood to teach Pussy Eating 101 to a grown man.

Toys never disappoint. They don't run out of steam or change the pace when you're about to come. They don't try to spell the alphabet on your clit because they read about it in a magazine article. Most of all, they don't cheat or leave you heartbroken after seven years.

"Thank you," I whisper to the baby blue silicone clit sucker tucked in my nightstand drawer, sated after an orgasm. My lip turns up.

I'm talking to inanimate objects again.

"I gotta stop doing that." The warm comforter tucks under my chin as I curl in. "Makes it seem like I'm super lonely or something."

Who am I kidding? I *am* super lonely. I am also super sleepy.

Maybe I should get a dog. That's what lonely people do, right? Yeah, a sweet, loyal puppy is exactly what I need.

CHAPTER 3:
WOULD A DRUNK PERSON BE ABLE TO DO THIS?

WADE

"WELL, YOU CAN BEH-TENNE-TENNE-TAH-TAH-TAH-DUNNA woman's man..."

I straddle the urinal, bunching the bottom of my tee under my chin while riffing the Bee Gees's timeless hit, "Stayin' Alive."

The rest of the team boo from the other side of the wall, where they get dressed. Guess they don't like today's song choice.

"How can you hate disco?" I call.

"*You suck!*"

"No, *you* suck!"

Blake Szeczin, one of the starting forwards, scoffs two urinals away.

"Really?" He motions to my up-tucked shirt. "What are you, five?"

"Whatever, Szecze. At least I'm not walking around with a pee-pee shirt."

Pee-pee shirt? I facepalm internally, disgusted with how easy it's become to pretend. But there's no point in showing the world who you are when they're perfectly content with the part you play.

I flip him off and turn away. Should probably use the toilet anyway. Sitting backward on it had been good luck the past few seasons. Would be a shame to mess up the streak by letting Winnipeg score. I emerge from the stall and wash up, then bump my shoulder into Szecze while walking by.

"Sorry, didn't see you there, pee-pee shirt."

Again, with the pee-pee shirt? Get a grip, Wade.

It's a cheap dig on the 5'8 forward. The other starters are all above six feet.

I pinch his cheeks and talk in a baby voice. "You'we just so wittle."

He elbows me. "Hands off, douche."

Jaeger, our captain, and the team's resident grouch, glares at me behind his bench. "Wade," he intones. "Grow up."

My arms fly up in surrender and get to my locker, emptying my mind of every violent thought. Everything except wanting to cut the arms off Jaeg's suit between periods. That'll show him.

After trailing the rest of the team onto the ice, my first stop is to the goal. I leave a kiss on the T-bar and stroke it from habit and superstition. "Good girl," I murmur. "You're gonna be a good girl for me this game, eh?"

Its metal pings in reply, and I skate back to the boards for warmups.

The backup goalie, a trade from Vancouver named Sullivan, and I stretch together, smirking at one another at the groups of women fawning over our splits. We run through a few quick edgework drills before he goes to the bench, and I return to the net.

Landon hits a puck over, and I scoop it up on my paddle, popping it against the blade. The section behind me *oohs* and *ahhs* as I throw the puck higher and higher.

"When the puck hits the screen, like a tray of poutine, that's *amore*," I sing, imitating Dean Martin. No one can hear how good I sound over the blaring stereo system, which is unfortunate.

Getting a signal for the start of the game, I toss the puck over the glass at an adorable, bespectacled kid wearing my jersey.

We're at the top of the league, having won the Stanley Cup twice in the past three years, so tending the goal means stretches of downtime between explosive stints.

I fill the lulls the only way I know how: the steady entertainment of my own mind.

"Here comes the puck. Here comes the puck!" My excited chant echoes in the helmet. "Can I block it?" The opposite team's center slaps a shot my way, and I knock it away. The crowd roars. "*Ooh, I* blocked it. Take that!"

Landon claps and points. "Atta boy, Wade."

"I gotchu, dawgy."

A minute later, in the middle of my falsetto version of "Single Ladies" by Beyoncé, Winnipeg makes a breakaway.

"Look sharp, Boehner." I trill out a Tarzan yell, diving to the side to stop the goal.

Jaeger finally catches up and rounds the net.

"*Now* you show up. We got a bunch of dusters on the ice today. Damn."

He lightly smacks my helmet for that comment and taps away the next shot before it gets to the crease to make it up to me.

"*Aw*, thanks, Jaeg! Love you, Jaeg."

During the last intermission, I strip the pads from my torso and scarf down half a burger and a Red Bull. Jaeger's reviewing plays with Coach. It's the perfect opportunity.

There's no rhyme or reason for antagonizing Derrick Jaeger. He's married to Skylar, my childhood best friend, and the closest thing I have to a sister, practically family. I can't stop myself.

"Hey, Peter!" I shout to my PA. "Find me a pair of scissors, will ya?"

I unzip the suit bag hanging in the captain's cubby and chuckle. Can't wait to see the look on his grouchy face. Two snips and the sleeves are off, their remnants stuffed into my duffle.

Third period, my men go hard. Must be all the Coke they guzzled. The game's been a shutout, and Winnipeg is visibly tired. One attempt to get the puck through my five-hole is unsuccessful.

"Your shot can't repel a butterfly of that magnitude!"

I growl and puff my chest, lifting my arms in victory for the arena as half of it cheers and the other half looks grossly disappointed by their hometown team.

Fletch gets the assist to Landon's last goal before the buzzer, and we pull together in a huddle, exchanging laughter and congratulations.

"Nice one, Fletch." I tip my helmet up before my paddle circles his neck. "That's gonna get you laid tonight."

"Fuck off." He pulls away and steps through the boards.

"Fine. Be like that. Maybe you won't, but I sure as hell plan on it."

Or die trying.

Press appears in one corner of my vision when I turn to check on Jaeg.

Gabe Finch smiles into the camera and says something in the mic before offering it to our captain to answer. My dick doubles. Shit.

I head down the hall to undress and cool down, grumbling curses at my luck, wishing there was a way to scrub a meaningless one-night stand from my brain in this locker room shower.

———

All the puck bunnies in town followed us to Byzantium tonight.

Landon disappeared after team dinner, probably to meet Indi. Jaeg isn't here either, thank God. Sky unknowingly saved my ass from a beating after our captain found his newly-cut sleeveless suit. It's not like he can't afford another.

Most of the guys scatter throughout the carnival-themed club's bar area, but Fletch, the nervous Nelly, sits on a stool and nurses his drink like it's the last one on Earth. He jolts upright when my hand claps his back.

"Bottoms up, Fletchy boy. It'll put some hairs on your chest."

I take a long gulp of my beer and order another.

"It's too strong," he complains, stirring the gin and tonic. "And I already have hair on my chest. Can we go back to the hotel yet?"

"You're the most emo wingman I know."

He rolls his eyes. "Pick a girl so I can go read my book."

My palm meets the back of his head with a *thwack*.

"That's not how this works. I have standards."

"Oh, please," he says through a sneer. "You'd bed anything with legs."

He's not totally off. Good-looking people are good-looking people.

"Now, c'mon. Throne of the—"

"Seriously. Stop with the book talk."

"Hey, you like them, too—"

"*Shh-shh-shh*!" My hand silences his yappy mouth. "Will you shut up?"

A rumble rolls through his chest, and he goes back to sipping from the tiny mixing straw.

"Excuse me, *hi*." A voice interrupts.

I straighten and glance over my shoulder at a petite blonde with big brown eyes and a rack to match. Her low-cut shirt barely contains her chest.

"Hey, what's up?" I tip my chin up.

"That was *such* a great game."

Fletch winces. I kick him.

"*Aw*, thanks...?" My raised eyebrow cues her to go on.

"Kyra."

"Thanks, *Kyra*." I flash her a smile. She smiles back, biting her lip, pitting a sole dimple in her cheek. Cute.

Her finger twirls the end of an intentionally messy braid. "*Um*, here."

She pulls a pen from her purse and scribbles on the corner of my coaster. "If you ever, y'know...call me."

Kyra strides off.

I tap on the coaster, then wave her number at Fletch, who groans.

"What the *fuck* was that?"

"I call it 'the butterfly effect.'" A gloat stretches across my face.

"'The butterfly effect?'"

I lean in, divulging the secret.

"Once they see me drop to my knees on the ice, they can't help but imagine my face between their thighs."

Fletch scoffs. "You're pathetic."

"Says the guy with his head in a book and hand squeezing his dick every night."

A routine in which I am very experienced.

He glowers and punches me right on the pec.

"*Ow.*" I rub the sting away. "You should try eating pussy. It'll make you feel better, I promise."

His entire face flushes deeper than the copper shade of his hair. "Can't you be normal for, like, one sec?"

"Normal? I *am* normal."

He scrunches his nose. "Aren't you gonna go talk to that girl, *Kyra*?"

"Oh, yeah." My shoulders turn, but my feet stop.

Suddenly, I don't want that girl, *Kyra*. Sure, she seems okay. She's not bad to look at. But my eyes fix across the space at a pair of bowed lips, a set of freckles topping high cheekbones that won't escape my memory.

They belong to the only woman I can't have.

Damn it. Why is she here? It's throwing me off. I should be taking shots from between Kyra's tits right now, not drooling over Gabe's long ass legs and the curve of her pretty mouth. Or her ass.

Christ. That ass.

Fletch is right. I *am* pathetic. Not for the reason he thinks, but still pathetic. I shouldn't go over there, right?

Though she's alone. My heart pangs. Where are her friends? Where's her camerawoman sidekick?

She frowns while finishing her drink, pushing the empty glass away. It joins a handful of other fallen brethren.

Going over there would be a bad idea. I exhale sharply through my nose. "Fuck it."

The bottle and Fletch are both abandoned at the bar as I dodge everyone between me and her.

Asshole #1 beats me there.

"Gabe."

Ugh. It's that little-pricked bastard, her ex. I caught Kurt Vaughn cheating on her at a dive bar in Montreal mid-season a few years back. And for some reason, she's hated *me* since.

She glances up before rolling her eyes shut. "I'm not cool enough for this."

I'm tempted to step in, but Gabe Finch can handle her own shit. I'm a few inches taller, at least forty pounds heavier, and *she* nearly strangled me when I confronted her one New Year's Eve. But she also kissed me after. And I'm not sure what I liked more.

It's all very confusing.

My chest pounds as Vaughn gets in her face.

"It's too late!" she says loudly, moving his hands away. "I don't care if you're sorry, and I *don't* forgive you."

Atta girl.

Vaughn takes a step toward her. It doesn't take me a split second to be right there with him.

I wrap an arm around her waist as she teeters backward. My heart races at the surprised hazel of her eyes. She doesn't shrink away. Instead, she melts into my hold. I savor how good it feels. Inadvertently, my nose nudges her hair.

"This guy bothering you, *baby*?"

Baby? Where did that come from?

Her lips part and reconnect as she studies me. Gabe hardens her gaze at Vaughn.

"Yeah. He *is* bothering me."

Vaughn's jaw drops. "You're with *this* guy?"

"Sorry?" I interrupt. "Do I know you?"

That should take him down a peg.

He sneers. "No, but I know *you*."

I think the fuck not.

"C'mon, Gabe. Be real now. He's like the fuckboy of all fuckboys—"

Gabe throws up her hands with a sharp scoff of disbelief, stepping out of my grasp. My palms twitch, and I reach for her but recede. The skin there tingles from the loss of contact.

"Unbelievable!" She sways and jabs a finger into his sternum. "*You* have the *nerve* to say that to *me*? After sleeping with, like, half" —she hiccups— "of the women in North America while we were engaged and, more recently" —she points to someone behind him— "sticking your tongue down that poor woman's throat?"

Vaughn runs a hand through his hair. "Shit."

"Yeah, *buddy*. I saw that!"

This dude is scum.

"Listen up, ladies!" Gabe calls, cupping her hands around her mouth. "I have something to say about our boy Kurt Vaughn here."

A curious audience creates a circle around the three of us.

I'll let her have this, then we gotta go.

"He leaves behind pubes on bar soap, the toilet seat up, and won't kiss your mouth after eating you out. His ego is so delicate, he gets jealous of vibrators."

I choke on saliva while calling an Uber on the app. It's only a few minutes away. The crowd breaks into sputtered laughter.

She makes herself appear taller, raising finger guns to the ceiling and swinging them like a rogue cowboy. "That's right! A real *man's man*, this one. I feel bad for whoever has to sit on his crooked penis tonight."

"*Oh-kay.*" I swoop in before we garner any more attention. People are already taking pictures and videos. "Let's go, baby. That's good. They get the point."

I hate how easily that second *baby* slid through my lips.

She *hmphs* with pride and lets me usher her away, looping her arm around my neck and using me for support.

"Mouthy cunt." Kurt coughs out.

I pause, positioning myself in front of Gabe. My jaw ticks.

The fucking audacity.

"That's enough," I bark, stepping close to him, then drop the volume to a low threat. "If the next words out of your mouth aren't, 'I'm a disgusting excuse of a human with a tiny, limp dick,' I'll jam a foot so far up your ass, my toes will tickle your throat."

A girl behind Vaughn tugs him away. Gabe's arm returns to my shoulder and tightens around my neck as we shove through the horde toward the exit.

"You can let me go now." She twists.

"Me? *You* boa-constricted around *me*."

I wave to the Uber, grabbing her just in time before she nearly face-plants onto the sidewalk.

"What're you doing, Boehner?" She fights the help.

Great. Gabe Finch is a belligerent drunk.

"You're hosed. I'm getting you back to...wherever you're staying." I swing open the car door. "Come on, Freckles."

"Freckles?" Her tongue sticks out. "*Ew*. Don't call me that. Like, *ever* again."

"Get in the cab."

"No. You're not the boss of me!" She stomps a foot and almost loses her balance again.

"It wasn't a question." I bring her hand gently through the hook of my arm. "Now get in the damn car."

Gabe grumbles but finally listens.

"Alan?" I confirm the driver.

"That's me."

"Alan, do you mind changing the destination?"

He shrugs. "Sure, where to?"

I look at my angered company. Her arms cross her chest.

"Gabe?"

"The Fairmont."

"You got it." Alan nods in the rearview and resets the map.

She doesn't say anything for the rest of the ride. She won't even look at me.

But when we exit the car, Gabe clasps my hand and doesn't let go while we rush through the lobby.

In the elevator up to her floor, she breaks the silence. "I *really* hate you."

I nod. "I know. That's why you're holding my hand."

She peers wide-eyed at the intertwined grasp, then releases it.

"Dick," she grits out.

The elevator doors separate, and she tears down the hall. She's a runner, too? Fuck my life.

I yelp when she pulls me with her through the open doorway of her room. "The hell? You gotta stop doing that."

Another harsh shove has my ass sat on an armchair across from the bed. "This is what you wanted, huh?"

"What?" Her hand flattens on my crotch. "Whoa, *hey!*"

"When you came over to '*save me.*'"

I keep her away by palming her wrists. "Excuse me?"

"It's what you do, right? Take drunk women home and—"

"Listen to me very carefully." I split her words and force eye contact. "I don't fuck with women who can't say yes."

She wets her lips and lowers her head to hover over mine. "And what if I'm saying yes?"

I hold her at a distance. "You're not remotely sober. It doesn't count if you say yes."

"No?" Gabe backpedals three stumbling steps and clumsily kicks off her heels. One would've taken me out if I didn't duck.

"No."

"Would a drunk person be able to do this?" She drops her pants, then pulls off her shirt, revealing all that gorgeous skin, her gait going predatory as she comes back to me. Her knees press into either side of my thighs, pinning me in place.

I gulp. She's trying to kill me.

Her hands drag mine up her bare legs and over her hips.

"I want you to touch me. *Everywhere.*"

"Fuck," I mutter, resisting any movement, but she's surprisingly strong.

"Yes." She hisses and sways forward. "I wanna be fucked."

"Stop it. I" —my torso reclines from her— "we can't do that. You said it yourself."

Her nostrils flare. A ruby-red sear blazes across her skin.

"Know what? You're full of shit, Boehner. You don't wanna keep me. Kurt didn't either." Hurt quivers her voice. "You're no different, another egomaniac fuckboy who sweet talks his way—"

I cradle her neck with a firm grip and pull her to my mouth so she hears me loud and clear.

"You really believe that, Gabe? Go ahead. Hope it helps you sleep at night. And you're right, I don't want you. Not like this. Drunk and cloudy. I want you so sober you feel every inch of me, feel how I fill you up completely."

Her breath hitches.

"Want you to feel me hit every spot deep in that tight pussy until you can't forget it. Just like me."

My eyes drift down to the panties pressed against my groin. "You think I can't feel how warm and wet you are right now? Any other time you're sober, I'll fuck you senseless and then fuck you some more for the road. I'll bury my tongue inside and eat you out until you can't come anymore. But not when you're like this. *Never* like this."

My hold loosens when she scrambles to stand. Tears gather in her lower lids. "Get out."

I sigh and pivot to leave. This woman makes me want to rip my hair out.

"Whatever happened to 'thanks for getting my drunk ass to bed safe, Wade?'"

"Fuck you."

I linger at the threshold. "You're welcome."

She slams the door shut.

———

It's 2 a.m., and I'm aggravated beyond limit.

In my defense, it's not only because Gabe's on my mind. Jaeger, the old fart, is snoring like a freight train.

The team got rid of room sharing, but tonight's hotel booking snafu has us paired up. I don't know what I've done to deserve this cruel and unusual punishment, but it couldn't possibly be less than premeditated murder.

A stack of pillows on my face muffles an irritated groan. Smacking him with one does nothing. Smothering him would be actual murder. Then, his wife would murder me out of revenge. It'd start a Titus Andronicus string of revengeful murders. We can't have that. I pinch the bridge of my nose.

"Plan C."

"*Kwaaahhh,*" Jaeg replies.

I dig the heels of my palms into my eyes before throwing on some socks and slides to jog down the hotel hallway for backup.

Landon Radek sleepily grumbles while opening the door. The left half of his hair swoops up and inward, unintentionally styled like A Flock of Seagulls.

"What the fuck, man?"

I take out an ear plug. "We gotta get Jaeg a sleep study or a CPAP or something. I can't deal."

He yawns. "Just roll him over."

"I tried. He's unmovable."

Landon scratches the back of his ear and squints an eye. "Alright, let's gather the troops."

Eight of us circle the bed where Jaeger putters snore after snore at the most annoyingly consistent cadence.

"This is ridiculous."

Landon keeps his hands on his hips.

"At least he's got rhythm."

My palm smacks my forehead.

"Check this out," Szecze adds, standing across from our oafy d-man, Theron Olsen. They mime the push-and-pull of a saw cutting a huge log in time with the grating noises coming from Jaeg.

I snort.

"Wait, watch." Landon giggles and pretends to start a faulty lawnmower.

The sleep deprivation is getting to me because by the time four of the guys sit down on the floor and form a rowing team oaring in tandem, tears prick at my eyes from stifling laughter.

They keep going while I record on my phone.

Eventually, the team stops, helps me roll the beast to his side, and the room quiets. We breathe a collective sigh of relief.

Ear plugs reinserted, I salvage the remaining hours of sleep before we move on to the next city and pray Gabe Finch isn't there to ruin more of my nights.

CHAPTER 4:
I'M GONNA BE SICK

GABE

A LOBOTOMY SOUNDS GOOD RIGHT ABOUT NOW.

I squint through the eye that burns slightly less, which isn't saying much, and groan at the source of incessant knocking on my hotel room door. The hallway light creates bright halos around my unexpected and unwelcome guests.

"Put some pants on, Finch." Mel, my producer, circles a hand around my arm and pushes through the entryway. Jordan, the station's PR rep, follows behind, shaking her head. "You're a mess."

Shit.

Goosebumps wake over my bare legs, an oversized tee barely covering my underwear. I swear I put on pants. Where did they go?

I seek them out while Mel pores through my suitcase.

"Looking for these?" Jordan points to a desk chair. It's wearing my sweatpants.

Oops.

"What're you waiting for?" Mel claps. "Let's go."

My head splits as I struggle to balance and push my legs through the appropriate holes in the joggers. "Ouch. You're being too loud."

"Come on, come on. We gotta put this fire out ASAP."

"What? There's a fire?" The ringing in my ears continues as we enter the elevator. "Are we allowed to be in here? Shouldn't we be taking the stairs or something?"

"It's not a *fire*-fire." Jordan gives me a once over and frowns, retracting her hand from the half of my hair that resembles a rat's nest. "But otherwise, it's real and will grow unless we take control."

I clench my eyes shut. "I have no idea what you're talking about." Re-opening them is a serious wake-up call. They've led me into a conference space on the lobby level of the hotel.

Wade Boehner, flanked by Jules Tryon—*the Regents' GM*—and the team's PR guy, Elliott-something, waits at the far end of a long table.

The four staffers huddle upon meeting, leaving Boehner and I to fend for ourselves. My vision isn't blurry enough to ignore how the sleeves of his black tee hug his bulky, defined arms.

Oof. Something in my belly twists.

Stop it, Finch. Get yourself together.

"What are you doing here?" I say under my breath.

"No idea. Why do you smell like you crawled out of a whiskey barrel?" he whispers back.

"Shut up."

"Ladies first."

"You two," Tryon commands. "Sit."

We do as we're told and drop our asses into the empty chairs.

My head throbs harder as Jules flips through a carousel of pictures from the night before on his tablet. The Daily Times site is one tab of fifty on the open browser.

Double shit.

It's all there. Wade and Kurt's near-fight in the club. His arm around my waist. Me practically hanging from his neck while leaving. And why was I snuggled close and smiling all googly-eyed like that?

More photographs show us getting in a cab together. A few zoom in on our interlaced hands while entering the Fairmont.

Oh, *ew*. I held his hand?

I have never been so embarrassed in my life. It's never a good time to be in the tabloids, but at least the last time was bearable, with them vilifying Kurt while I hid away. But this? After throwing myself at the NHL's resident playboy in a drunk, desperate stupor? Humiliating.

And the hangover is making everything worse.

"Anything to say for yourselves?" Jules raises an eyebrow. "The paps are having the time of their lives."

Boehner sniffs and chews at a nail.

"From him, this is expected." My boss points to the unbothered dope to my right.

"*Hey*," Wade whines out his defense.

"But you? I'm shocked. You don't do this sort of thing."

"You're right. I didn't *do* anything because nothing happened."

Wade's eyebrows bounce as he clears his throat. I threaten him with a side-eyed glare.

The staff murmurs.

"It's not what you think," I explain. "Okay, I...wasn't sober. I'll admit it. But Vaughn was being inappropriate and—"

"We're lucky I stepped in and got her outta there before she tried to beat the living hell—"

"What! I wasn't gonna—"

Wade gazes ahead, as blank and unfeeling as I've ever seen him, and lets out a barely audible mutter. "He would've deserved it."

Before I get a chance to question why any of this matters to him, Mel holds up a hand for us to stop.

"You realize what this looks like, though, right?" She moves her hair so it drapes over one shoulder.

"We didn't sleep together!"

A rebellious smirk stretches the corner of Wade's lips. "Not last night, anyway."

Jules groans.

I kick Wade's shin.

"Are you an actual idiot, or do you really not know when to shut up?" I say through my teeth.

"No, no. This is good, guys." Jules nods and motions for us to calm down with his hands. "The more we know, the better we can manage...*this*."

Mel and Jordan agree. So does Elliott what's-his-face.

"Boehner, this couldn't have come at a better time. The press catches you with a different girl every night."

Excellent. Now, I'm one of the many.

My stomach lurches. Wade slides over a mini water bottle. I scowl but accept.

"So?" He shrugs.

"*So?*" Jules parrots in a mocking whine. "Hockey is a family sport, buddy. I get you're young, the team's young, but there's a reason Radek and Jaeger are the most popular in the franchise." He taps the gold band on his left ring finger.

"Being popular isn't everything," Wade retorts.

"Fine. But it took us two years to recover sales after Radek's scandal—" Elliott adds on, his voice warbling and trailing off as the ringing in my ears flares.

Boehner looks bored. For once, he's right. Elliott is a bore.

"Can't we deny it? Tell the truth and move on?"

"You could, but they'd turn it against you," Mel argues.

"Exactly, Langley. Might as well lean into it." Jules posts both hands onto the tabletop on Wade's side. "Being with Ms. Finch will be good for your image. Your redemption story. The beautiful, successful journalist who's caught the playboy's attention. Fans are already eating up the possibility of your relationship. When we confirm it—"

I choke on a sip, causing the water to dribble from my mouth and down my chin. "*Excuse me?*"

Jordan snaps. "Yes! That's perfect."

"It's not perfect!" My tone rises an octave. "How is that *perfect*?" I switch glances between her, Mel, and Jules. "You can't be serious!"

"Wait." Wade's brow wrinkles as he rubs a hand across his chin. "What are you saying?"

"You two," Jules waves a finger between us, "are dating."

I guffaw, tossing my head back and whisking my brain into scrambled egg consistency.

Ouch.

"We are doing nothing of the sort."

"The fuck we are," Wade says over me.

"You're *exclusively* dating each other," Mel adds, to the delight of Jordan, who claps and gasps.

"No," I protest with a vigorous shaking of my head. The rattling worsens the ache.

"It doesn't have to last *forever*," Jordan intones. "A few months, *max*."

"A few *months*?" I scoff. "No one would believe it! Me? Dating this... this *pubescent*?"

"You'd be so lucky," Wade finally pipes up. "And I think you know I'm fully grown." His pecs bounce as he flexes his arms and chest.

Jules runs a hand down his face and groans again. Mel and Jordan widen their eyes at my grimace.

"Yuck. Not in your wildest dreams, Boehner. Come on, guys." I turn to the schemers and plead to their sense of reality. "He's way too...young for me."

Jordan beams with a sinister smile. "Age is just a number when you're in *love*."

"*Love*? Please stop." Elbows resting on the table, my fingers massage circles into each temple. "This can't happen."

"Oh, it's happening. We gotta get this out properly, and everyone wins. The Regents fan base and ticket sales will see some growth, and we get a boost of views when you cover the games. So here's the story." Mel twines her fingers together. "You've worked together for the past four seasons and have kept a friendly rapport."

"Friendly?" I sob out a series of laughs, remembering how unprofessional he was at my first press conference with the league.

"Gabe, you've been single since your breakup with Kurt Vaughn, but Wade's...youthful enthusiasm has been a breath of fresh air."

"More like I need a breath of fresh air." I curl against the table. "I'm gonna be sick."

Wade's shadow hovers over me but retreats when I snarl.

"And getting to know you better has changed Boehner's bed-hopping ways," Jordan finishes.

Wade slow-claps and lazily chuckles. "*Ha. Ha. Ha.* This is hilarious."

"It's not funny, Boehner!" My head pops up. "You may not have a reputation, but—"

"Hey, I have a reputation!" On his feet now, Wade towers over my seated position. "I don't date. Dating someone means I can't—"

He doesn't scare me. I'm not scared of a manbaby.

I get up, too, bracing myself on the edge of the table. "You can't...what, huh? Sleep with whoever you like, whenever you like? *Please*, don't let me stop you."

"Alright!" Jules barks. "That's enough." He sighs and comes to stand between us. "All you have to do is pretend to date through the end of the year. Go places, do things together whenever you're in the same city. Take pictures to feed the vultures. Make it believable, and they'll get bored and go away. Once the spotlight is off you, you can go back to your old lives."

Wade exhales, defeated. "How long?"

Jules looks to Mel, who confirms with a silent nod.

"'Til New Year."

My mouth gapes. I don't even want to be near this clown. And I'm supposed to fake-date him for the next four months?

"I'm not thrilled about it either, Freckles."

I bare my teeth to him. "I told you not to call me that."

"*Aw*, see?" Jordan juts her lip out in a sardonic pout. "You already have cute nicknames and everything."

Blood burns the tips of my ears.

I'm not beneath tackling another woman.

"Here." Sheets of paper hiss over the table surface as Mel glides them in front of Wade and me. "Sign at the bottom."

"What is it?"

She hands us each a pen. "HR statement. Saying you won't let your personal relationship affect your professional one. Unbiased reporting stands. No partiality in coverage, interviews, etc. And there's an NDA for all of us. This agreement doesn't go beyond the room. No PAs, no friends, no teammates. The less they know, the better. It's too risky otherwise."

I peer up from the documents and blink rapidly at my producer, who has clearly lost her mind. "It's a *fake* relationship."

Looking to Wade for help is useless. He's already signing.

God help me. What is wrong with him? Never mind, there's too much to unpack there. But why is he agreeing to this so quickly? A second ago, he was up in arms about not being able to stick his giant prick anywhere he likes.

"To *you*." The unpolished nail of her index finger taps on the signature line. "To everyone else, it's as real as you can get. We can't have any loose ends. Go on. Sign." She nudges the pen closer. "You've made your bed; now lie in it."

Boehner's mouth twitches, visibly fighting back the urge to smile. I don't know what he's so happy about. He's about to live a celibate life until New Year.

What other option do I have?

So I sign.

Mel and Jules collect their copies and shake hands, exchanging smug expressions.

I need an Advil.

It's the first thing I search for when returning to my room, but instead, I find a phone full of manic messages and voicemails.

"Christ," I huff, scrolling through the multiple concerned texts on the girls' group chat.

INDI

UMM HELLO??

BEA

GO OFF SISTAH

INDI

WHAT

SHEENA

IN

BEA

TARNATION

INDI

GABE FINCH

BEA

Aw, man. I wanted you to use her full government name!

INDI

THERE'S TIME YET FOR THAT, BEHRAZ

SHEENA

The baby's up from his nap, catch me up later

INDI

Which one? Akhil or the actual baby?

SHEENA

Actual

INDI

Aw give him a big kiss for me!!

INDI

Back to business

BEA

If you were wondering, and I know you were, I'm now singing "Business Time" by Flight of the Conchords, and it's gonna be stuck in my head for at least a week

INDI

ANSWER ME, FINCH

I'll deal with that later. Dad's voicemail awaits. The speakerphone icon lights up white when I press it.

"Hi, bala…"

My nose crinkles at the nickname.

"It's me. So, uh…I was at the grocery store and saw your picture in one of those magazines they have out by the cashier. Looks like you had a good night." A nervous laugh sounds on the line. "A hockey player, eh? I had no idea you were dating anyone. Thought you were done with athletes. Maybe you told me, and I forgot. Sorry about that." He sighs. "Anyway,

I'd love to meet the guy sometime. Bring him home some—"

I tilt the phone away to pause his message and roll my eyes.

"Meet him?" I say to the air, turning towards the washroom for the much-needed Advil. "He's fake, Dad."

"I'm as real as it gets, Freckles."

At the deep tone of his voice, my heart plummets to my ass, and I trip while rounding the mattress corner.

Wade Boehner catches me in the broad, square surface of his chest. Those rounded biceps strain under my palms, warm and firm, the skin smooth and taut and...*no.*

"Do you usually talk to yourself?"

"God damn it." I escape his grip. "The hell? You followed me in here?" Like a lost puppy.

Are you there, God? This is not the kinda puppy I asked for.

"I'm your *boyfriend*, remember?"

I harrumph while pushing past him. Where's that Advil?

"*Fake* boyfriend."

"Uh-huh. Anyway, we have a situation on our hands."

"No shit, Captain Obvious. My friends are losing it. And my dad—"

"The team, too." Wade waves his phone at me. "Jaeg called an emergency meeting." The sugar coating of the twin pills melts on my tongue, dissolving down my throat as I down the rest of the bottled water. "I said we'd be there soon."

Second spit-take of the morning. "*We?*"

"Yes." The cool, calm finality of his reply sends a shiver down my spine. "And you're not the only one getting confused phone calls from family." He taps on his screen.

A woman chatters in French without pausing for breath. I should have paid more attention in school because I can't tell if she's angry as hell or super excited.

It fades out, and so do I. The combination of a hangover and shaken nerves draws a fog over my mind, but when I close my eyes and take a long breath to calm down, I've somehow navigated through the haze. There's no racing pulse, no panic.

There's only Wade Boehner and me facing an unfamiliar door.

My glance shoots over to him. He's as serious as I've ever seen him, but the line of his mouth softens. Something strokes my palm.

It's the pad of his thumb. I gasp softly at our hands, woven inexplicably between us.

How did we even get here?

"Ready?" The browns of Wade's eyes melt as his hand squeezes mine. A roguish smile pops a dimple in his cheek, and my heartrate plops to the pit of my stomach. "It's *showtime*."

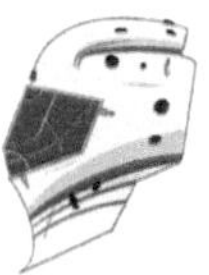

WADE

SOMEONE PREP MY OSCAR.

My years of theatrical training are being tested. The dumb jock routine is a piece of cake, but pretending I wasn't excited to have Gabe Finch all to myself took everything I had. Though faking a relationship will require more finesse.

Indi's frustrated whisper toward her husband isn't much of a whisper. "They're holding hands, Landon!"

A significant portion of the Regents roster ends their conversations to stare. Jaeg, Skylar, Landon, Indi, and Fletch await us in the suite's seating area.

Gabe focuses straight ahead, but a swallow travels down her throat. Her slow, defeated blinks set off a pinching pain in my chest. I recognize that look. It's the same one she wore last night when Kurt Vaughn got too close.

Won't be me. I never want her to feel uncomfortable in my presence, no matter how awkward the situation.

My thumb draws a hidden circle in her palm, a repeat of how I got her attention before we entered. She sucks in a quick breath.

"*Heyyyyy*, guys," I start. "What's up?"

Skylar's eyebrows shoot to the middle of her forehead. "What's. *Up?*"

They stand in various states of confusion. Hands on hips, arms akimbo. A couple of them sneer and narrow their eyes. I extend a hand to the empty couch in silent offering. Gabe accepts.

When I lower to join her, the soft seat cushion gives in and squishes our bodies together. Her warmth hits my bare skin. The thumping in my chest climbs to my ears.

Stop that, heart. It's fake.

"Cut the shit, Wade."

Leave it to Jaeg to ruin the moment.

"This *cannot* be happening." Indi bends and inches forward to Gabe as if approaching a skittish animal. "Gabe, sweetie? If you're being held against your will, blink three times."

Call me a caveman because a primal need to protect Gabe has my adrenaline rushing. I straighten and meet her at eye level. "Indi, I like you. But you have three seconds to back away from my girlfriend."

"*Girlfriend*?" Fletch asks.

Gabe shrugs and confirms with a silent nod.

The red-headed bastard throws up his arms. "You were literally flirting with that Kyra girl last night. And now Gabe Finch is your '*girlfriend*?'" Air quotes taunt me.

"*Kyra*, huh?" That wakes Gabe up. Her glare could shred flesh. "Who's Kyra, *sweetheart*?"

I don't miss the knife-like stab hidden under her sweet tone.

"*Baby*," I say through my teeth, "we talked about this." Now to face the accusers. "That was *before*."

"Before what?"

Fletch is a rascal.

"Before we talked about it."

Indi's confusion is blatant. "*It*?"

"You know, the undeniable attraction between us." My arm tucks behind Gabe, squeezing us together by the shoulders. "We got tired of fighting it."

Fletch scratches his head like a cartoon.

Indi re-crosses her arms, her mouth flattening, unimpressed with the explanation. "Oh, yeah? When did *it* all happen?"

"See, a few years ago, your husband blew the playoffs."

Indi's eyebrow rises in Landon's direction.

"*Hey*," he snaps. "Don't bring me into—"

"*Anyway*, we were drowning our sorrows at a club called Persepolis. I didn't know who Gabe Finch was but thought she was hot as fuck. Landy told me she was engaged, so I kept my distance but couldn't stay away. Remember when I said you were beautiful in front of everyone at your first press conference?" My head turns to Gabe.

She bats her eyelashes coyly, rage brimming in those pretty hazel tones. "I do."

"You hated that!" Indi addresses her.

"You did?" I ask.

I hurt her?

"I had no idea."

"Don't worry, *baby*." Her hand squeezes my thigh, too harsh for forgiveness. "It was kinda cute."

"You said it was embarrassing and unprofessional! And that you loathed him."

"I was fighting my true feelings." Gabe smiles, faker than some women orgasm—*not that I'd know*—and pats my knee. "Like he said."

"Yep, and then we kissed on New Year's Eve."

Gabe pales. So does everyone else.

"You *kissed* her?" I don't know if I can handle any more of Indi's shrieking. The pitch keeps getting higher and higher.

"Which New Year's Eve?" Landon holds out questioning palms.

"The one where Indi looked sexy as hell, and you told me to pretend to be blind."

Landon hides his eyes while Indi gapes. "When she told you off and choked you?"

Gabe goes red. Her grasp on my knee tightens.

"Yep." A sheepish grin splits my face in half. "And I liked it."

My fake girlfriend's eyes widen. Her pulse drums every place we touch.

"Oh, my God," Indi laments.

"Also, we had a quickie in the stairway closet before your wedding reception."

Those thick lashes of Gabe's flutter closed as she pulls her lips into her mouth. Oops. I'm so fucked.

"What!" It's the highest I've ever heard Indi's voice.

"Radek knew about it." I point.

If I'm going down, they're all coming with me.

She slaps Landon's shoulder with a loud, sharp sound. "You promised me they didn't!"

"*Dude!*" The alternate captain winces while rubbing the spot where her hand landed. "Why are you tryin' to screw me over?"

"Jaeger knew, too."

Sky also smacks her husband's arm. "Derrick!"

He doesn't flinch, the refrigerator. Instead, his eyes hone in on me, thumb motioning across his throat. "You're dead," he growls.

"It's not my fault you lie to your wives. I have nothing to hide." My chin juts up. "Gabe had such a great time; she spent the night with me."

"I think I'm gonna be sick." Indi hugs her belly. She looks more than a little green.

"*Baby*." Landon searches her body. "You okay?"

"No! Your manwhore friend is—" Her cheeks puff mid-sentence, and she runs toward the washroom. Landon runs after her.

Skylar shakes her head. "I don't get it. What happened last night? The pictures—"

"What's not to get? Vaughn showed up, was a dick to Gabe, and I straightened him out. I took my girl back to the hotel."

My girl? Shit. The words taste too good.

"We talked about it, and the rest is history."

"Sure, *the rest is history*." Fletch breaks his silence, still bemused. "There's been so many women, and you've never—"

I stand. "What are you trying to say?"

"I'm saying...I have no idea what you're trying to pull, Wade, but I'm not buying it."

Landon and Indi return. She looks a little better. "She's fine," he affirms softly. "Must've eaten something funky."

"I'm not trying to pull anything, Fletch."

Lie.

"You don't even know each other," Indi cuts in.

"We know each other well enough. Like, *biblically*."

Her eyes roll. She does that a lot. It's warranted because I'd be rolling my eyes at myself if I could.

"Don't remind me. I meant, like, you don't know anything about her."

"Sure, I do," I retort.

Indi's beady little lawyer eyes narrow, seeking out the truth. "When's her birthday?"

Crap.

"Oh, it's in..." Gabe offers no clues. I have no idea what her expression means. April's as good of a guess as any. "Ayy," —she clears her throat with a forced cough, creating an *o* with her mouth— "Ahh-October."

I know it's not real, but Gabe beams. Something inside my gut somersaults.

Indi responds with a pursed mouth. "Lucky guess."

"False. I knew! In fact, I had a surprise planned for her birthday. Thanks for ruining it. Nicely done." I give her a golf clap. She rolls her eyes again. "Not that it's any of your business, but it's been, what, twelve hours since we got together?" I peer over my shoulder. Gabe agrees. "Everything I know so far I like."

Where the lie ends, and the truth begins is a blur.

"Gabe is smart, we have similar interests…" I continue, "Not to mention she's gorgeous. Almost as gorgeous as me. And I don't think it hurts that I have a huge dick."

Groan after groan bellow out as they swat the comment away. Can't have them thinking I'm too serious.

"This is what I'm talking about." Indi motions to me. "Gabe, come on. Tell me what's going on. You can't possibly be dating this…this…"

Gabe's height nearly matches mine when she rises. "Go on."

"You've said it before. He's young and immature and has problems with…commitment."

Her left eye twitches. "You mean he sleeps around."

"Well—"

A set of Gabe's fingers delicately thread through mine. They tense around my knuckles, firm and protective. The flitting movements in my stomach return.

What's this?

"That's such bullshit, Indi. Yeah, he's younger than me. And okay, he can be immature, but the same goes for the rest of these guys. Doesn't mean he doesn't have good qualities. And it doesn't give you a right to slut-shame him. Hell, you once told me he was sweet and was growing on you. I'm surprised, Skylar. I never thought you'd stop him from wanting to be with someone."

Sky's mouth pops open and closed.

Gabe tugs me closer. "You guys are supposed to be his team? His brothers, his best friends? Aren't you ashamed? You're supposed to be happy for us. We're together. You don't have to like it, but you have to respect it."

Every word is more convincing than the last.

It's not real, I remind myself. It's not real.

Indi tilts her head. "*Gabe.*"

"Unless you're apologizing, I don't wanna hear it." We pause in wait. No apology comes.

Gabe harrumphs and leads me to the door. "Let's go, *sweetheart.* These hypocrites don't deserve our time."

As we leave, I crinkle my nose and stick my tongue out at them. "Right behind you, Freckles."

We march down the hall to my room, and before I can properly process how incredible it was to be defended like that, I've sandwiched Gabe between my chest and the door, my mouth latched onto hers.

CHAPTER 6:
SOUNDS LIKE A DATE TO ME

GABE

"FUCK," WADE MUMBLES BETWEEN ROUGH KISSES. "What are you doing to me?"

His big, stupid, soft lips crush mine again, the slithery tip of his tongue greedy in its swipes. An unintentional pleasured noise hums between us. My mind melts from how our hands wander over each other until something *else* of his that's big and firm digs into my thigh. It brings me back to my senses, and I push him away by the chest, propelling off the door to get as far away as possible.

"Me? What are *you* doing?"

The smartass huffs out a series of chuckles. I don't know what he thinks is so funny. "I think the technical term is 'French kissing.'"

"Well," I fumble through the words, arms flailing while heading to the opposite end of the room, "stop doing that!"

"I will when you stop liking it."

Unbelievable.

My teeth clench. "I didn't. Like it."

"That's funny. I coulda sworn it was you moaning into my mouth."

"*Excuse me*? I did not moan—" When I spin around to face him, he's shirtless. How'd he do that so fast? "What the fuck, Wade?"

"Oh, *uh*—are we not..." —the grasped tee flaps between us, drawing attention to every cut of his insanely chiseled chest— "...doing this?"

"No!" I screw my eyes shut. "Put your shirt back on. For fuck's sake."

"My bad." The black fabric returns to his torso, falling over it like a closing curtain. Show's over. And good riddance. I don't need the temptation. He shoots me a double-finger gun with snaps. "You were awesome in there, though. Was really cool of you to stick up for me."

"It's called *acting*."

"Right, yeah. Me too." His fancy hand flourish accompanies a deep bow. "You're welcome for that brilliant performance."

"Brilliant? You brought your dick into the conversation!"

"A penis is just a body part, Freckles." He catches me staring while his hand adjusts the crotch of his jeans and smirks. "My best body part, *as you already know*. And hey, it's nothing they haven't seen before."

I snort. "I get it. You have a reputation. But not everyone has seen your penis."

"Nah, not everyone," he says through a yawn. "Though, now that I think of it, every person in that room has."

"Everyone?" I'm positive he constantly peacocks around the lockers naked. But in front of the wives? Doubt it. "Skylar?"

"She's my best friend. Of course, she's seen it."

I have a hard time holding back my surprise. It's embarrassingly tinged with jealousy. "You slept with her?"

"*Ew*, no!" Wade gurgles out a vomiting noise and shudders. "She's like my sister. I had a hernia when I was seventeen and didn't know what was going on, so she took a peek and helped me out."

Fine. I can't let him have the point so easily.

"Indi was in there, too," I argue.

Wade lets out a lopsided smile. "Like I said, *every person* in that room has seen it."

My smug expression drops. "Indi's seen your penis?"

"Yep."

No way. She never told me.

"Does Landon know?"

That man's possessive at a toxic level. I once heard from another journalist that he threatened to shove a hockey stick up an ex-teammate's ass for touching her, and they weren't even dating yet.

Wade nods with excitement. "He was there. It was the first time we all met. She came into the locker room, and Landon and I were..." Wade makes a *clang* and wields an invisible sword from his crotch.

"I'm sorry." My eyes narrow. "Am I supposed to know what that means?"

Wade answers with a childish grin. "Sword fighting."

"I thought that's when you try to" —I mime the action of aiming a penis— "hit each other's streams of pee..."

"That's the twelve-year-old version."

"So you were..." I cross my index fingers, "...with your..."

"What can I say? I'm comfortable enough in my sexuality that it doesn't bother—"

"*Christ*," I grumble, face hidden behind my hand. I'll ask Indi about it later. "But was it necessary to tell everyone we slept together after their wedding?"

"It's one of the only true parts of this conjured-up scenario. They already suspected something." He shrugs. "I had to think fast."

We share a sigh.

"I can't believe we lied to our friends." I crumple onto the bed. Wade's bed. In his hotel room. That we're alone in.

White sheets cool my sweaty palms as I smooth their wrinkles away from me. They're nicer than the ones in my room, the mattress plusher. Plush. Like his lips. The reminder has my eyes searching for them, and it doesn't take long. They're within reach from where he sits next to me. Raised veins on his propped arm shift under flawless, taut skin.

A swallow descends the column of his neck, reminding me how good it looked under my palm. The night from a year ago returns in a flash.

Aged wood and the vintage gold plate fitted with the assigned number contrasted with the high-tech black box surrounding the hotel room's door handle. I unfolded my right hand to reveal its matching black fob on a keychain, hot and clammy from sitting in my grip.

Nerves kept me from knocking.

I should not be doing this. What if someone's in there with him? No one can know.

Ear pressed to the door, I waited for some sort of indication that it was okay to enter, but only a muted buzz came through. Without a chance to rethink, I accidentally brushed the key too close to its lock while resting a hand on the wooden surface.

It clicked and creaked open to an empty foyer. The door clapped shut, and I winced, each cautious step taking me closer to the bed, which was also empty.

I followed a sliver of light from the floor to its source—the wash-room—at the same time as Wade appeared in its entryway. Naked except for a white towel tucked low on his hips, their arches tapered to a defined v below a nearly perfect set of abs and pecs wide enough to sleep on. I gulped.

His saunter stalled, large hands pausing from drying his hair with another towel. Darkened brown strands fell across his forehead. Wade's gaze softened as my lower lip pinched between my teeth.

"You're here."

Two of his long strides closed the short distance between us. My pulse pounded. A shaky breath exited my nose.

"I have no idea why."

Girl, please. You know exactly why.

He dropped the towel in hand to the mattress, a lust-sparked expression relishing the gentle stroke of his warmed knuckles over my cheek. Calloused fingertips drew a line down my throat to the collarbone before curling around it with his palm. Goosebumps trailed behind.

"I do." The light pressure of his grasp had my legs buckling beneath me. A sparse strip of chest hair trailed down his stomach and directed me to the massive bulge behind his towel.

My mouth watered.

"On your knees, Freckles," Wade demanded, guiding me to the low-pile carpet below. "Need you to undo what you've been doing to me all night."

"I didn't like that part either." The hoarse whisper of his voice blurs the memory away and pulls me back to his focus on my mouth. I inhale the mint on his breath. His gaze lifts to mine, the deep umber tones swirling like melted chocolate. "We can tell them the truth after it's over." A wild rhythm climbs from my heart into my throat. The pink tip of his tongue breaks through the seam of his lips. "We did what we had to."

Oh, God. It's his I'm-about-to-kiss-you face. Run!

I leap up, evading the attempt. Wade forces out an airy laugh and runs a hand through the mussy wisps of his hair while glancing at the ceiling.

"Okay, first things first." My legs lead a manic pace across the room despite the uncomfortable, growing wetness between them. "We are *not* actually sleeping together."

"*Pfft*, duh." One of his broad shoulders lifts and drops. "I didn't wanna do that with you anyway."

One eyebrow shoots up. "You wanted to a second ago."

"Only 'cause I thought *you* wanted to." He drops back to his elbows, dragging his eyes down my frame. "Who am I to deny Gabe Finch?"

My eyes roll closed. The Advil is effective, but a brand-new headache in town brews. He's named Wade Boehner. The man is testing me.

"Then let me make it crystal clear. At no point will we be sleeping together. That's not part of this fake dating...*deal...thing*." Words evaporate as Wade rises and stalks toward me, eyes unwavering. "Can't make that... mistake. Again."

"Who are you trying to convince, Freckles?"

Valid question.

No, not valid!

"No one," I lie.

"Whatever, *baby*." He keeps saying it like that, all snippy. "But if we want to make this believable, we have to do better. I hate to admit it, but Indi's right. I don't know you well enough. Your birthday, your preferences. If you were my girlfriend, I'd know everything about you."

"If I were your girlfriend, I'd have to be sedated—" My phone alarm interrupts the tirade with a notification for my upcoming flight. "Shit. I have to get to the airport." And get back to my room to pack. I scramble toward the door. "We'll have to schedule something..."

Wade's mouth explodes into a smirk. "Gabriella Finch, are you asking me out?"

He's only a few inches taller than me but somehow appears bigger as he nears.

"That's not my name, and no. We're...meeting up."

His hand reaches the overhang by the door and leans forward. "Sounds like a date to me."

"Shut up." I glower and wave my phone. "When are you back in Ottawa?"

"Wednesday."

"*Great*. I'm back Thursday. Put it on your calendar."

"*Oooh*, direct. I like your game." He reaches into his pocket to retrieve his phone, but my patience wears thin. I snatch it from him.

"Here's my number."

His tongue clicks. "Nothing turns me on like a bold woman."

That'll do it. I'm definitely not attracted to him.

"Do you hear yourself? There." I hit save on the created event and hand the phone back. "Thursday at 5 p.m."

"It's a date."

"You wish. It's an interview. I'll have questions ready. You do the same."

"Sounds good, Freckles. I'll pick the place and text you."

"You're a terrible listener. Didn't I say not to call me that?"

"False! Your boyfriend is a *great* listener."

"Get away from me." I scowl over my shoulder on my way out.

His hand cups one side of his mouth. "Miss you already, Freckles!"

I grumble and ignore his ridiculous behavior while mashing the elevator button.

And I'm supposed to keep from murdering him for the next four months? Lord, help me.

———

The crew socializes with the Winnipeg Blazers as we wait for the charter plane to arrive. I settle into a quiet corner of the lounge in prep for my pre-flight routine.

Dad's picture pops up while the FaceTime call rings. It's from four years ago, after the first NHL game I covered, his goofy, gaping smile pretending to use my held-out mic while we half-hug.

The top half of his head answers. "*Balaaaaa.*"

My heart twinges at the nickname my mother used. No matter how long it's been since her passing, the word always comes out in her voice. Will it ever stop doing that?

"Daaaaaad," I whine.

"What? Kai jhala?" Concern wrinkles his brow.

The wound of her absence deepens when he speaks to me in Marathi, too.

"Move the phone down." I repeat myself when the screen skews. "*Dad.*"

He adjusts to show his body going lax and his head lolling to his chest.

"Dad! What are you doing?"

"You said 'dead!' I thought it was a command. I played dead."

"Very funny."

Dad snickers. "I thought so."

"Can we stick to English, please?"

Mouth pulling into a frown, he tilts his head. "I miss the days when my little girl called me Baba."

Shame fills my breath. I avert my eyes off-camera. It's been ages. Dad lets out a long-winded breath and changes the subject, thank God. The sweet man shakes off his disappointment. "What's up?"

"I'm at the airport, about to board."

"Very nice. Appreciate you always calling before. Where are you headed?"

"Vancouver." Metal clinks in the background as he sets the phone down. "How's the nursery?"

"It's alright." Dad steps aside and extends an arm. "The mums came in. Hoping to sell lots of fall foliage and hay bales before cuetlaxochitl season."

"What about staffing?"

He hisses. "Dicey. It's hard to find reliable help."

"You mean you want to do it all yourself."

"It's easier this way."

"*Dad*. You're supposed to be slowing down."

"And do what? I love being in the greenhouse."

"I know, and I'm not trying to keep you from it, but" —my fingers find a tense spot between my eyebrows and press— "I wish you'd get someone to do the heavy lifting at least. How about when I come home for Thanksgiving—"

"*Ah*, tut-tut-tut." He waves a hand to deny me. "Home is for rest. Will you bring that new boyfriend of yours along?"

No way.

"I wasn't planning on—"

"Come on, bala. Why not?"

The genuine excitement in his pale blue eyes is hard to crush.

"Can't promise anything. I don't know if he's playing that weekend or not—"

"Details. You'll figure it out. Man, he must be something special for you to—"

Something special, alright. A special pain in my ass.

"*Hey, Tez!*" Someone calls in the background. "*I've got the truck out front.*"

"Be right there!" His eyes furrow with apology. "I gotta go. Crowley's here to get some new tree saplings. We'll talk later?"

"Yep. Love you, Dad."

"Love you, bala."

He disappears from the screen. It darkens to reveal my pathetic reflection in its wake.

Wade Boehner is gonna meet my dad.

I am so fucked.

CHAPTER 7:
YOU HAVE DADDY ISSUES

WADE

"I'M SERIOUS, WADE. NO SCREWING AROUND "

Maddie, the team's new social media manager, glares from across the plane. The previous one was fired at the end of last season after a fan had an unhinged reaction to some posted thirst traps of Landon. It became a whole thing and now we all have to tone it down.

No more fun choreo. No more slo-mo sultry walks from the bus to the locker room.

I'm already on her bad side. Hey, she was the one who asked, 'Who wouldn't you sit next to while on the road?' for a video. I answered honestly, 'Hands down—Theron. He farts *a lot*.' How was I supposed to know they're cousins? Eh. She'll get over it. If she ever sat next to him, she'd know I was right.

"So what do you need me to do?" I lean into the aisle. "Run my fingers through my hair? Slowly button my suit?"

Maddie's nostrils widen. Her eyes go flat. "Hold your coffee cup. Answer whether you like it hot or iced. Take a sip. Smile."

"That's it?"

"That's it."

"Bo-ring," I sing. "I'll add a little pizzazz."

She sighs. "We talked about this. Tim Hortons is sponsoring the video, and it needs to go well. No. Screwing. Around." Maddie pops on her over-the-ear headphones and taps on her tablet as her threat ends. I straighten to give her a dramatically serious expression and an exaggerated salute.

"Stop antagonizing her," Jaeg grumbles. "She's just trying to do her job."

"Buncha party poopers."

My attention redirects to my phone, and to Gabe's latest one-word response.

ME

We still on for Thursday?

FRECKLES

Yep

How enigmatic. I can't figure her out, but I can't forget either. And I'm not sure I want to.

My face tilts toward the ceiling, eyes fluttering closed. I sweep the tip of my tongue across the seam of my lips and back, remembering, savoring. It's been days, but the traces of stale whiskey from Gabe Finch's warm mouth linger.

A text notification scares my stirring dick into hiding.

SKYLAR

I need to talk to you.

ME

Now? I'm in the air

SKYLAR

Not now, you twit.

ME

Tonight?

SKYLAR

Nope, Jaeg, Doug, and I are having
a family night.

My mouth twists. It's strange how childhood friendships evolve. One day, you're pinky-swearing loyalty, and the next, your best friend has a husband

and a dog that are both a higher priority than you. A piece of your heart is now someone else's, while they get to keep whichever part on which they staked claim.

ME

I'm not family?

SKYLAR

You know that's not what I meant.

Get over yourself, Boehner. Too needy.

ME

I know I was kidding

ME

You wanna bone, I get it.

SKYLAR

Hell yeah, I do! I'm ready to be used
like a rag doll.

ME

Okay yuck. I was trying to gross
you out but now I'm grossed out.

SKYLAR

Maybe next time you'll think twice.

SKYLAR

How about tomorrow evening?

ME

I have a date with Gabe tomorrow

SKYLAR

When?

ME

5

SKYLAR

Perfect. I'll head over to yours after work, around 4.

—

Thursday's my only day off in the next couple of weeks, and I take full advantage. I sleep in until 6 a.m., get a decent workout in, and finish up the last chapters of Kerri Maniscalco's *Kingdom of the Cursed* so Fletch will leave me alone about it. But none of it—*not even a forty-five-minute shower or the fifteen-minute pep talk in the mirror*—quiets my nerves.

By the time Sky arrives, I've worn down a path in the rug spanning the bed with my pacing.

"Wade?" She calls from the foyer, hand over her eyes. "You're not naked, are you?"

"Why, you want me to be?" I yell back.

Her guffaw makes me smile. "Please, *no*."

"I like my balls where they are, thanks." I emerge from the bedroom to meet her in the living area. "Jaeg would chop 'em off, slice 'em up, and force feed 'em to me."

"He's sweet like that." One side of her straightened blonde hair gets tossed over a shoulder before she opens her arms as wide as they can. Wiggling fingers beckon me into an embrace.

I accept, squeezing her small but solid frame, then nuzzle the top of her hair. The distance created by marriage shrinks, if only for the moment.

Once again, we're teenage Wade and Sky, frantically rowing across Lac Ste. Anne, in an attempt to evade that curmudgeon Monsieur Bertrand after knocking him out of his rickety fishing boat or diving deep into the lake to see who can hold their breath the longest until our moms shout for us to act our age. Just two best friends getting each other into and out of trouble, time and again.

She hums upon release and sits, patting the spot on the couch next to her. "You okay?"

Not really. My brain tangles itself in knots, feeling nervous but having to pretend like I'm not, but also that I am. This is probably the stupidest situation I've gotten myself into.

"Why would I not be?"

Her polite smile dips in concern. "I wanna preface this with...I am not being judgmental, and I support you fully. Promise. But Gabe?" She pauses while searching my eyes. "You understand why we're all confused, right?"

"I don't, actually. I thought you liked her."

"I do! I think she's great. Smart, funny, *so* gorgeous—"

"Then? What's the problem?"

"She's not really...your type."

"What's my type? I don't have a type. I like all sorts."

"Okay, but they're flings. You've...never dated anyone."

I sniff. "So? I'll try anything once."

"Wade," she chides. "Don't make me say it."

"Say what?"

Skylar makes a throaty, rumbling noise before her arms fly up. "You have daddy issues!"

"I do?"

"Don't play dumb with me, mister. You're a sweet, charming guy—"

"Thank you." I accept the compliment by bowing my head. "But I knew that already."

"Hush." Sky elbows my ribs. "You didn't let me finish. You're worse than Doug; you need all sorts of attention from lots of people. And don't get me wrong, I wholly accept your choices around sex—"

My lips purse while I let out a whine. "This kinda sounds like you're calling me a slut."

"I didn't say that. You use sex in place of anything real."

Why she gotta call me out like that?

"Hey, I get exactly what I want from sex."

Her brow quirks, exasperated. "You'll do anything to keep your heart safe."

"My heart's safe with Gabe." Safe? She'd keep it under lock and key and have it for breakfast.

"Yeah? What about hers?"

While it is fun to irritate her, one thing I'll never do is break Gabe Finch's heart.

"Her heart's safe with me, too."

"You're serious?"

I seriously can't stop thinking about her.

"Yeah."

"How serious?"

Serious enough that I haven't been able to sleep with anyone else since her. I won't admit it to Sky, though. She'd never believe me.

Quick! Make something up!

"She...keeps clothes here."

Idiot. Of all the things, why'd you say that? Gabe is gonna have your left nut. This is a dangerous fucking game you're playing, Wade.

"Whoa." Her eyes go wider, blues thinning to rings around her dark pupils. "You're sharing a closet?" Sky flops into the back of the couch. "This is *major*."

Academy Awards, here I come.

"To be honest..." A hand scrapes through the side of my hair, my knee bouncing. "I'm trying to keep it together, but I'm freaking out. I have no idea what I'm doing."

The manic look on my face is convincing enough. Skylar goes upright and softens against me. "Aw, *Wade*." Her arm hooks through mine, and she rests her head on my shoulder, free hand palming my knee. "Dang. I knew you wanted to sleep with her, but look at you." She switches to a baby voice and pinches my cheek. "All grown up and in a relationship."

"Yeah, yeah." I slap her hand away before we share a long exhale. "I mean, obviously, she's beautiful, but beyond that, we've got this...connection." Mostly bickering and hurling insults. "I can't seem to stay away from her."

My best friend squeals and kicks her feet. "Jaeg said something like that to me when we started dating. Most people think we're too different. That I'm too social, and he's a grouch. He might be gruff to everyone else, but he has never once raised his voice at me." Her thumb wiggles her engagement ring and wedding band from the underside of her palm.

I knock my knee into hers, breaking her from the spell of focus on her hand. "That's why I like him."

We share thankful smiles as an alarm goes off on my phone.

"*Oooh.* Is it time for your big date?" She shoves my shoulder. It's cute that she thinks she can move me. "*Hup hup!*"

I fake falling sideways and roll off the couch before jumping to my feet. She stands and offers another hug. "Love you, Walty." I don't protest my most hated nickname. "I'm proud of you."

"Get out of here. You're a menace."

Sky blows a kiss my way as she leaves.

I get another message from Gabe. There's no point fighting the urge to smile.

FRECKLES

Where am I meeting you?

ME

You mean for our date??

FRECKLES

Answer the question.

ME

It's a surprise

FRECKLES

Tell me anyway.

ME

If I tell you, it won't be a surprise

FRECKLES

I don't care for surprises.

Of course, she doesn't. Surprises are fun.

FRECKLES

Just tell me so I know what to wear.

ME

I was thinking something lowkey,
like the Meltwich on Orleans

FRECKLES

Meltwich? I can make grilled cheese at home.

ME

Not like these!!

FRECKLES

Grilled cheeses are the easiest sandwiches.

ME

Are you saying you can make it better than them??

FRECKLES

100%

ME

Challenge accepted and holding you to it

FRECKLES

Whatever.

FRECKLES

Tell me now, or I'll show up wearing this.

Three little dots flicker on the screen before a bathroom mirror selfie appears. Full brown waves lead to a lacy, black bra and tiny matching panties covering her smooth, tan skin. My jaw drops. My eyes bulge. A thread of drool drips from where I'm practically frothing at the mouth. I suck it back in.

Temptress. No one gets to see her like that but me.

Before I can save it to jerk off to later, she unsends it.

Nooooo. Come back!

ME

Cafe Jardín

ME

Wear clothes or else

FRECKLES

Good boy.

My cock responds by swelling.

Oh. I like that?

ME

Is it too much to ask for you to wear that underneath??

FRECKLES

Yes.

ME

Yes, you'll wear it??

FRECKLES

Yes, it's too much to ask.

FRECKLES

And don't pick me up. I'll meet you there.

ME

A gentleman would pick his girlfriend up

FRECKLES

Too bad you're not a gentleman.

FRECKLES

It's around the corner from my house.
See you in 30.

ME

Okay, girlfriend

She reacts to my last text with a thumbs-down emoji and a Meryl Streep GIF captioned "*Boooo!*" I laugh. What is wrong with me? This girl has me so twisted.

As I stuff the keys to the Lambo in my pocket and put the finishing touches on my hair, another text dings.

LANDY

You're so screwed

LANDY

What did you do??

ME

What do you mean?

LANDY

Gabe swung by to drop off two dozen
lemon raspberry cupcakes

ME

Sounds delicious

LANDY

They are, but that's beside the point

LANDY

I get that you two are new, but here's a fun fact
about Gabe: she bakes when she's stressed out

ME

Ohhhhh.

ME

Why is she stressed out??

LANDY

I dunno, man! She's your girlfriend, you figure it out!!

LANDY

And these are her favorite. The only reason
she'd give them away is if she was out for blood.

ME

I'm not scared of her

LANDY

You should be. Indi told me in vague terms that
Gabe *may* have done some things to Vaughn's
car after they split.

LANDY

With a bat

ME

Wel , shit

LANDY

Don't tell anyone I told you

LANDY

Now fix it and save your Lambo!! Good luck

———

I fiddle with the collar of my hoodie while leaning against the brick facade of Cafe Jardín. Paparazzi wait at the window, across the street, and down the block, failing to be inconspicuous.

Leeches. Every last one.

Their clicking starts before Gabe turns the corner. Enormous, dark sunglasses cover her eyes and freckles. Her straight-cut tan peacoat billows with every long stride, framing the lean lines of her legs in those black jeans. Classy, cool. All the flashes in my periphery couldn't pull my focus from her.

If they want a show, I'll give them one.

As she nears, my hand reaches for hers, drawing the ridge of her bare, chilled knuckles to my mouth. Genuine shock replaces her unnerved expression, the fog of her breath quickly retreating mid-air as I pull her close.

"For the cameras." My lips graze and warm the plane of her cheek. I pause the kiss to address the paps between our shoulders. "Do you mind? This is a private moment."

She hisses as I usher her into the bustling restaurant with an arm cinched around her waist. "You're a douche."

Her words mean almost nothing because the way she eases into the hold? It's that night last summer all over again. That Gabe was so different, so...open, willing.

We both were.

My pulse gallops in my throat.

A hostess leads us to the reserved table in the back, private and far from prying eyes and eavesdroppers. The short walk is a tease, the close contact with Gabe gone too soon as we take our seats across from one another. Frustrated fists form in my lap. Her hands disappear below the tabletop as the waiter approaches, introducing himself as Paul and listing the specials. I accidentally ignore him, too hypnotized by her pink-tinted lips, and he has to repeat the question.

"And for you, monsieur?"

"Sorry. I was too distracted by my girlfriend's beauty." He and I exchange cheery glances. "I'll have the same."

"You're gonna have a harvest salad and cranberry juice?" Gabe asks.

I throw an oversized grin at Paul. "It's my favorite."

He nods and scribbles, saying he'll return with our drinks.

"That was a bit much," she says, docking her sunglasses atop her head. Her makeup mutes the splatter of dark brown freckles across her nose and cheeks.

"Gotta give them something to talk about." My elbows rise and rest on the white tablecloth as I lean in. "You never know if the staff is in cahoots with the tabloids."

She rolls her eyes. "I meant all the PDA out front."

"Oh, I did that because you love it."

The corner of those pretty lips curls into a sneer, eyelids drooping to deaden her glance. "Why are you like this?"

I recline into the woven back of the French bistro chair. "Devilishly handsome? Effortlessly charismatic? Ottawa's number-one heartthrob? You'll have to be more specific."

"An unbearable asshole."

I swear my heart soars at the idea of getting under her skin.

"It's payback for sending me a nude and then unsending it."

Gabe's teeth grit. "It wasn't a nu—"

Paul quietly sets our drinks down. My date thanks him and lifts the glass to her lips. I stare, tracing the rim of my glass with my index finger, circling and circling and circling while imagining it's that soft spot inside her pussy instead.

I almost knock it over when she notices and sputters, clearing her throat while a strawberry flush floods her cheeks. As if the same filthy thought is crossing her mind.

She likes me, after all.

"*Anyway.*" Gabe retrieves her phone from her coat pocket. "I brought notes and have questions."

"You came prepared?"

"I'm a journalist. I do my research."

My chin bobs in her direction. "Whatcha got so far?"

"Wade Boehner—*full name, Walton Boehner*—" Her lips wrinkle, a stifled smile teasing at their edges. "Twenty-four years old, 6'4, 210 pounds, first round, number five pick, drafted from Harvard to the Ottawa Regents in his sophomore year. Originally from Lac Ste. Anne. Only son of Naomie Boehner, former Olympic rower and fitness model."

"Not bad."

A hum buzzes against her curled finger. "Though I couldn't find anything about your dad."

A twinge in my chest burns, but I douse it. "I don't have one."

The last rays of dusk meet the copper hues of her eyes as she looks up from her screen. I can't tell whether it's pity or sympathy, but I don't need either.

"He's not around, okay? Any more questions, or is it my turn yet?"

The waiter serving our salads breaks the conversation.

My knee is bouncing again. I have no interest in talking about that son of a bitch. The tips of my ears heat, and I attempt to take a relaxed pull of the cranberry juice to cool down, but it's so tart that my eye twitches. Gabe coughs out a laugh.

"Walton...what a name."

I loathe the sound of my father's name. Maman used the patronym to spite him.

A deep furrow forms between her brows. "Makes sense why you shortened it. *'Oh, Walton!'*" she teases with a soft moan. "Doesn't have any sort of sex appeal."

She's asking for it.

"Careful, Freckles." My leg extends underneath the table to stroke the bare space between her sneakers and ankle with the tip of my shoe as a shit-eating grin splits my face. "I get hard when you make fun of me."

She glowers and kicks me away before taking a large bite of greens, then chews until she can tuck it into one cheek. "Shocker. What *doesn't* get you hard?" Her swallow is audible. "You should give your little guy a breather sometime. You know, get some fresh air, touch grass."

I try to resist. I do.

"Sounds like you want a reminder of my size. I did enjoy how loud you got last time."

Gabe struggles as air goes down the wrong pipe. In slow motion, I mouth my first forkful of salad, content with her reaction.

Fist thumping her chest, she dislodges whatever was stuck in her throat with a hushed gagging sound.

"What a noise," I coo through a sigh. "Brings back fond memories."

Her cutlery clangs against the plate. "I wanna choke you."

"Feeling's mutual. But not in front of everyone, *sweetheart*. Unless you're into exhibitionism?"

"Yeah, no," she backpedals, her low tone turning into a whisper-yell. "I could kill you."

"I don't think I can get into blood play. But it's okay if you are. No judgment."

By the way she silently stabs her fork into the pears and walnuts on her dish, she might be. My fake girlfriend has anger issues. I'll have to sleep with one eye open.

"My turn," I announce, wiping some vinaigrette from my chin.

Gabe *hmphs* in reply.

"Gabe Finch: thirty-one years old—*turns thirty-two Oct 7th, birthday party surprise forthcoming*—works for Canadian Sporting News, used to cover golf before the NHL, played basketball for the University of Waterloo on scholarship. Six feet—"

"Don't you dare guess my weight."

I would never, but I have no idea what she's worried about. She looks fucking *good*. Toned arms, strong legs, and an ass as round as the day is long. I keep going, "Couldn't find any info on your parents."

"That's on purpose. It's called privacy." Gabe's gaze stays on her food. "Dad owns a plant nursery in Kitchener."

"And your mom?"

Her chewing stops, eyes going blank as she echoes my words. "She's not around."

The statement is vague but somehow clear. A heavy cloud—*an unexpected commonality*—tethers us in the long pause that follows.

There's that twinge in my chest again. I wanna take away the pain in her eyes. Maybe she'd take away mine, too.

With one last bite, she shoves her dinner away. "I'm full."

"That makes both of us."

I pay the check, and despite her earlier threats, Gabe lets me lead her by the hand through the cafe again as the restaurant staff and crowd watch us leave.

"Wasn't that fun?" she says dryly.

"And it's not over yet." I motion to the loitering paps in the street. "I'll give you a ride home."

Her glasses slide over her eyes. "No, thanks."

"Will you listen to me for once?" I murmur into her hair, slipping an arm beneath her jacket and around her hips. The onslaught of flashes continues without relent. "I'm trying to do something nice for you."

The small muscle in her jaw ripples. "Fine."

"Oh, God," she laments as I pop up the door of the Lambo. "You *would* bring the most obnoxious car."

I buckle her in. "I told you to be careful about making fun of me once, didn't I? This car's big enough for me to bend you over in."

Another fiery blush. I'll never get enough of it.

The engine rumbles as I rev it before pulling from the curb.

"I hate this car," she says under a breath.

"You hate everything."

"That's not true."

"It's a little bit true."

Her ass shifts uncomfortably in the bucket seat, attempting to shrink herself in the space.

"What do you have against my car?"

She doesn't glance my way. "Kurt has—had the same one."

Fucking Vaughn.

I switch to the left lane.

"This isn't the way to my place."

"You're right. It's the way to mine."

Sudden apprehension strikes like lightning, jolting through me until every nerve crackles, jump-starting my heartbeat and driving it into a rapid cadence.

Gabe Finch is coming over. To my penthouse. Not hotel rooms. My *home*.

Her arms fold as one set of fingers pinch her nose. "And why are we going there?"

My eyes flick to the rearview mirror. "For one, I'm pretty sure we're being followed."

"Really? Shit." Gabe turns to check. "Isn't that what the powers-that-be want? Pictures as evidence?"

"I think they'd rather have us; what did Elliot call it the other day? Controlling the narrative. And also…"

When she turns back, she's met with my nervous smile.

"What?"

I bare my teeth, bracing myself for her wrath. "I *may* have told Skylar that you stay over."

Her eyelashes pat together. Blink, blink, blink, blink. "And why would you do that?"

"She asked how serious we were."

"I don't know how you do it, Boehner, but you give me the biggest headaches." Circle after circle is massaged into her forehead and temples with those slender fingers until she resigns into silence.

Two lights later, we reach my building. The parkade door lifts, and I ease through it. Palpable tension builds as we speed up each subsequent ramp to the top floor before rolling into my spot.

No protest from Freckles when I offer my hand to help her out of the car. No protest when I push my fingers between hers either. She pads behind me down the hallway. My thumb finds the pulse point on her wrist. It's thrumming as fast as mine.

"Where am I gonna sleep?" she asks.

What's this? The infallible Gabe Finch, defeated? There's no satisfaction in the transient victory. I hate the sadness filling her eyes.

I know how to make her mad. I know how to make her come. But I have no idea what would make her smile or laugh. Guess I'll stick to what I know will make that somber expression go away.

"My bed's pretty nice. My arms are also available."

The lock clacks open as I push the key code buttons.

She groans and grimaces, but our hands are still entwined. "It's like you *want* to die."

There she is.

The door shuts, and my restraint snaps. I back her into the wall, hovering so our lips are only a few centimeters apart.

"At your hands? Maybe." My palm sprawls across her stomach and one arch of her hips, pinning her in place.

"Do you ever shut up?"

"Do *you*?"

What the fuck am I doing, and why is it not kissing the sass out of her?

One of her hands moves up my chest to bunch the leather collar. I can't tell whether she's pushing me away or begging for more.

"How can someone this pretty be so mouthy and annoying?"

"Look in the mirror, and you'll find out," she retorts, tipping her mouth up. A tempting offer. The same hand winds around the column of my neck, its light pressure sending all blood southward. Gabe writhes, creating a hungry friction between us.

We simultaneously gasp.

"You think I'm pretty?"

Another hot breath gushes from her when I sidle my nose beside hers. "That's the part you understood?"

"I have selective hearing."

"Clearly."

The tip of my cock throbs against her inner thigh as she hooks a knee around my hip, notching herself to me. Desperate for relief, I lift her by one handful of ass and grind between her legs with a groan.

"So, what'll it be, Freckles?" Our breaths mix, eyes locked in rebellion. Waiting for one of us to cave. "You gonna kiss me now, or you want me to shut you up however I want?"

GABE

"WADE," I SAY THROUGH A LEADEN BREATH, MOVING my hand away from his neck and down his chest.

"Yeah?"

"Let go."

His hold loosens at my command. No battle, no snark, no visible signs of disappointment. Not even Wade's cock deflates. It remains at a 90-degree angle. Pointing at me. Blaming me for its current state.

My legs attempt confidence, and I'm glad for the wall support from behind. The tense air between us is so thick I can taste it. From the way he licks his bottom lip, maybe he can, too.

It'd be too easy to succumb. He's young. I don't have to think too much. And it won't mean anything to him. He's not even the worst option I have. At least this one can get me to the finish line. But no.

"We can't—"

"Okay." He withdraws and backpedals, taking his warmth and leaving behind goosebumps.

A ragged breath escapes from me. "Wade." I don't want him to think I'm doing this on purpose. It's not like I set out to blue-ball him. I'm a horny, weak woman lacking self-restraint. He knows that, though. He was on the receiving end of that lingerie pic from earlier.

Head shaking out a chuckle, he rubs a palm through the back of his hair and nape.

"I know." A smile returns. It's soft and understanding. Probably the most sincere I've seen him since last summer. "You hate me."

He says it like he doesn't want to believe it. I'm not sure I do, either.

"You can still stay." Wade slides off his shoes by the door.

I really shouldn't.

"For a few minutes." I leave my sneakers next to his. "Only to avoid the cameras."

He nods. "Only to avoid the cameras."

We loiter in the foyer. His fist knocks into his thigh, awkward and unsure.

"Are you gonna show me around, or...?

"Right!" His palm meets his temple with a slap. "Come on in. Might as well get familiar." Wade's ruinous smirk reappears. "My girlfriend would spend *a lot* of time here."

"Is that so?"

Lights switch on as we move through the spaces. Motion-sensing, I'm guessing. One space flows seamlessly into the next. Dining, kitchen, living.

I don't know what I expected, but it wasn't...*this.*

Okay, that's a lie.

I expected a bachelor pad. I expected black leather couches, minimalist furniture, a neon Labatt Blue sign, bar stools instead of dining chairs, maybe a bright red rug, and animal heads on the wall. Or something.

Not *this.*

This is cozy.

The kitchen is immaculate. State-of-the-art. There's a sage green subway tile backsplash paired with gray cabinetry and a cooktop with, like, ten ranges. Fridge doors span an entire wall. Copper pots and pans hang from a rack above the massive island.

"Go stand by the island so I can take a picture."

"You're not the boss of me."

"I'm gonna post it on Instagram, smartass. Elliott sent me another text saying we haven't been keeping up. Now, do it. And be casual. And less mad-looking."

I roll my eyes. "What can I say? You bring out the best in me." With an exhale, I lean against the counter edge, curling my hands around it and giving him a fake smile while looking off-camera.

The tip of his tongue pokes from the seam of his lips as he concentrates on snapping a few photos. He shows me the screen.

"Not bad."

He types the words *mine* in the caption, and my stomach flips.

It's fake. It's fake.

"Jeez, I sound like Radek," he says with a scoff. "What a sap."

"The world's a stage, and we're just players."

Wade frowns. "That's not the quote."

"As if you'd know," I snipe back, wandering through the kitchen. "Who cooks here?"

"Me, sometimes." Wade shrugs. "Usually, Mathieu does." Before I follow up with another question, he continues. "My personal chef."

"How fancy."

Long benches flank a farmhouse-style table. A spacious c-shaped sectional and its modular ottomans fill the living area across from the TV. He reads my curious look.

"The guys from the team come over a lot."

Most surprising of all are the floor-to-ceiling bookshelves lining several walls. I tilt one out by the spine. *The Importance of Being Earnest* by Oscar Wilde.

"That's the first edition. From 1895."

I gape.

"What?"

"You *read* this?"

Pretty Boy's eyes narrow. "I *am* literate, y'know. Judging from the way you misquote Shakespeare, I'm not sure about you, though."

"I know how to read, jerk. I thought these were decorative."

He responds with a disgusted face. "People do that?"

"Supposedly."

"What a weird thing to do. Books are for reading. Or at least collecting in hopes of reading."

"Who are you?" I say under my breath.

Maybe he's not a chauvinistic, dumb jock. The last glimpse of that side of him was through a post-orgasm haze.

We stared at the ceiling, every breath heavier than the last. Sweaty. Spent. Naked. Wade's dazed expression held irrefutable proof of what we'd just done. Three times. If this hotel bed could talk, it'd need a cigarette and a strong drink.

Oh, Gabe, you big dummy. Why did you kiss him again? Kissing

Wade—bad. But he's so good at it. Too good, if I'm honest.

Unlike the quickie in the closet, he'd taken his time. Kissed, touched, worshiped. Slow, patient. Swallowed each of my moans and fed me groan after groan, whispering filthy praises while filling me up in a way that I hadn't been in many years. Maybe ever.

"You sucked my cock so good, Gabe. Your tight cunt's gonna take all of it, too."

Between Vaughn and I, sex was about pride. A competitive sort of race for who could get the other to the finish first and the most times. I usually won, because men are easy. A blowjob here, a finger in the ass there, and kapow! Cum shot everywhere.

Wade fucked like what I wanted mattered. Like I mattered.

If only outside of that night, outside of that hotel room, he wasn't obnoxious.

I hid my face and aggressively sighed as he snuck off to the ensuite for a piss before returning to the mattress.

At least he had the decency to throw on a pair of pajama pants. Its matching striped top got lobbed my way. Shifting to his stomach, he tucked a hand under his pillow. His hair fell in a voluminous wave against its surface, eyes drooping closed with the next exhale. Lush lashes darkened the crest of his angled cheekbones with their shadows. Pretty Boy was almost angelic.

"I should...go."

He hummed through a soft yawn. Good, he agrees. *My gaze lingered too long.*

"You sure you don't wanna keep staring?" Wade mumbled, not moving from his comfortable position.

I cringed and scooched down to yank the sheet over my head.

"Don't go shy on me now, Freckles." He joined me under the white bedsheet, those sleepy eyes narrowing. I pulled both lips into my mouth and shook out a denial. "I've already been inside you."

"I should definitely go."

When I tried to escape, Wade curled an arm around my hips and tugged me close. "No." He wrapped me in his shirt and buttoned it over my chest. "You can't."

"Sure, I can."

"You're not some fling that can sneak away in the middle of the night."

"Aren't I?"

"Stop arguing," he admonished quietly while his hand squeezed my waist, repositioning us so we were face-to-face. "Just stay." Calluses on his fingertips stroked a sensitive stretch of skin at my midsection, his swollen, red lips brushing my cheek. Knots in my sex hair caught in his grip, but he detangled and tried again with aimless, winding lines across my scalp until I responded with an unintentional hum. "Doesn't that feel nice?"

"You treat all your one-night stands like this?"

"Would you believe me if I said yes?"

"Good to know I'm not special." What was meant to be sarcasm sounded like spite.

"All women are special, Freckles. Don't be jealous." His forehead puckered with concern. "Haven't you heard of aftercare?"

"Uh, sure, but..."

He snorted. "Did that motherfucker Vaughn never hold you after?"

I peered to the right, recalling bitter memories. "He wasn't into it."

"Ugh. What a prick." Wade's eyelashes stuttered closed, brows lifting with an entitled expression. "Too bad. I need cuddles." He buried his nose into the crook of my neck and inhaled, tightening his grasp and forking our legs together.

Okay, fine. The idea of a beefy professional hockey player with the athletic prowess of a cheetah wanting to be snuggled is precious.

"Don't you ever get attached?"

"Attachments stem from unfulfilled desire. Suffering follows. My desires are fulfilled. No attachments. No suffering."

I scoffed. "Unbelievable. Did you just quote Buddha?"

"Please." He let out a drowsy giggle. "It's from the Bhagavad Gita."

"Wade Boehner" —a yawn interrupted my wry introduction— "the philosopher."

"Hardly." A shush wafted past my ear, the firm caresses on the back of my neck lulling me into a groggy, relaxed state.

It felt too intimate to end after one night. But I did it anyway.

I blink twice to drive the memory away.

Wade stands with his arms folded across himself. The index finger of one hand rests on his Cupid's bow. Studying. Scanning me up and down. A lump moves down my throat.

"So...?"

"So?" I parrot.

He glances at his watch. "I go to sleep early, but not *this* early. It's only seven."

"What are you suggesting?"

"Since you're staying—"

"*—Only to avoid the cameras—*"

"Right." He nods to the left. "We could...see what's on TV."

"You wanna watch TV?" My finger points to my chest. "With *me*?"

Wade rounds the sectional, never breaking our eye contact. "Isn't that what real couples do?"

"But we're not." I clarify, "A real couple."

"We can pretend." He drops to the couch and gets comfortable, then calls over his shoulder. "Come pretend with me, Freckles."

I huff but step forward, shimmying out of my coat and leaving it on one side of the sectional. "You think you're so cute with that nickname."

"You think you're so cute with those freckles."

"What?"

Was that a compliment?

"Nothing." Wade hands me the remote.

I click through the cable guide: news, boxing, Gordon Ramsay, poker, *Fresh Prince of Bel-Air*. Nothing elicits a response. I linger on an episode of *Gilmore Girls* before skipping past.

"Go back."

"Sorry?"

He shushes me.

Dean and Tristan face off at Rory's dance, and Dean goes deliciously protective when Tristan attacks her.

Like Wade with Kurt.

Wade rests his elbows on his knees. Eyes shiny with attention, lips moving as if reciting the lines.

The scene fades out as they leave and cuts to a commercial.

He reclines with a sigh, stretching an arm across the top of the couch. Suspiciously close to my shoulders. I tilt my head toward him.

"You *don't* watch *Gilmore Girls*."

"Sure, I do. Donovan and I have watched it in nearly every hotel lobby on the road."

"Why the lobby?"

"Before the management stopped it, I used to share a room with Jaeger the Snorlax. And Fletch roomed with Landy."

"Radek doesn't like *Gilmore Girls*? I feel like he would."

"Only serial killers don't like this show. *Nah*, Landy loves it. But he loves having phone sex with Indi more."

I groan. "*Aw*, come on. That was uncalled for. I already know way too many gory details about their sex lives."

"Hey, if we have to know about it, so do you. Now, *shh*, I love this part."

Dean and Rory return to the screen, coffees in hand, sneaking into Miss Patty's after the winter formal. When Dean asks why it's so heavy, Rory reveals she has a book in her purse. I sink further into the couch, mirroring how they settle into a bean bag as Dean starts reading Dorothy Parker to her.

The combination of the acoustic guitar in the show's score, the sweet idea of being cared for and read to, and the warmth of being so close to Wade—it's soothing.

My breathing relaxes. So does he.

Maybe Wade Boehner's not as greasy as he makes himself out to be. He treats his one-night stands gently, knows how to accept the word 'no'— *when it matters, anyway*—cooks frequently, reads classic literature, and watches *Gilmore Girls*.

A weighty slumber settles over me, along with Wade's rounded bicep, and I don't fight either.

CHAPTER 9:
THE MOST FRUSTRATING WOMAN I'VE EVER MET

WADE

ME AND MY BIG MOUTH.

Now, she knows too much about my extracurriculars. And that I think her freckles are cute. That's too much insider information.

I gotta stop before it's all out there. Some things are better left behind closed doors.

Not that she needed any more ammunition to tease me about. She already has a whole arsenal ready to go.

If I'm lucky, she'll forget about it by morning.

I smoosh my chin to my neck and slide my eyes to the lower right corner to check.

Affirmative. Gabe Finch is dozing on my shoulder. She must've been pooched.

There's a subtle warmth from her body where it touches mine, and she's nothing short of stunning.

The cute slope of her nose, the curve of her strong chin, the way her pretty pink mouth isn't scowling at me. Yeah, she's stunning, alright. Like a napping lioness who could wake up any moment and rip my intestines out.

For a moment, I wonder how different it'd be if she liked me. I already know she doesn't like the fake, superficial parts of me. Other than my mouth. Or cock, but that's beside the point.

What would she think of the person beyond that? Would she think my Harvard degree is impressive? Or my rare book collection is cute? Would she agree that a grilled cheese is the cure to pretty much every problem? Or would she prefer to believe I don't have a singular intellectual thought in my brain, like everyone else does?

How could she? No other woman has. Not even in a fake way. Skylar and Maman don't count.

A text notification buzzes, and I mute it from outside my pocket before removing the phone.

It's another sea otter video, compliments of Donovan. Its paws block sunlight from its eyes so it can nap during the day while floating along.

ME

Okay, that's cute, but I have something cuter

DONOVAN

Doubt it

ME

Wanna bet

DONOVAN

Loser buys winner doughnuts from SuzyQ

ME

Done

I tuck a few hairs hiding her face behind an ear, unintentionally touching the faint freckles peeking through fading makeup.

She hums. My stomach flutters.

Putting the back camera on a wide angle gets a good frame of her against me, and a content half-smile bows her mouth when my lips meet her hairline to click a picture. She wouldn't be smiling if she knew what I was doing. I immediately feel guilty for the stolen kiss.

But not enough to stop me from sending it.

DONOVAN

Ugh fine

DONOVAN

We get it, you adore her

DONOVAN

Makes me want to sleep on the highway

DONOVAN

I'm still coming over to watch Antiques
Roadshow tomorrow

DONOVAN

They're re-airing the episode we missed Monday

ME

K

ME

I don't care about the others, but I require at
least one Cinnamon Toast Crunch, one Salty
Caramel, and one Dirty Chocolate

A dampness on my sleeve cools the skin underneath, and I hold back laughter at the trail of drool connecting the shirt to her mouth.

"Oh, *Freckles*. That's gross."

She responds with a hissing inhale.

"Classy." I push out a sigh. "You're lucky you smell nice."

Like a slobbering mastiff smelling like a field of flowers. A true dichotomy.

"Okay, here we go." One of my arms scoops under her knees while the other squeezes her torso so she doesn't flop around like a fish. "Now, lift."

You're talking to yourself again. A bad habit from being an only child.

I had plans to go toward the guest room, but we end up in mine. She's gonna be upset, but that's too bad. My fake girlfriend will have to sleep in my bed tonight.

I tuck her in, folding back the covers so she's comfortable. She thanks me by rolling away and huffing. Even in her sleep, the woman will do everything to get away from me.

She truly hates my guts.

After switching into a pair of pajama pants, I keep an eye on her from the washroom while brushing my teeth. Peter, my PA, sends over the next week's schedule. It reminds me to ask for a favor.

ME

Sell the Lambo

PETER PETER BO BETER

What? Why?

ME

My girlfriend hates it

PETER PETER BO BETER

Can I have it?

ME

Can you afford it?

PETER PETER BO BETER

If you up my salary, yes.

ME

We can talk about it later

Peter responds with a GIF of Will Ferrell from *Old School* captioned, "You're crazy, man. I like you, but you're crazy."

I shake my head and go to the next bedroom over, but it's not far enough. Knowing Gabe's on the other side of this wall has me restless. I toss and turn. Switch the pillows. Flip them over. Kick the sheets off, then layer them on again.

"Get outta my head, Finch."

Does she revisit that night last summer like I do? Nah, she's probably plotting my demise, the hateful freckled thing.

How lucky is that, though? She dreams of me.

I smile at the thought, and sleep soon follows.

———

Fletch takes a whopper of a bite out of his purple glazed doughnut and points to the screen. It muffles his words.

"I'm telling you, that ring is something."

"Bullshit, Donovan." Landon swats the air. "Looks fake to me."

I keep my hands clasped behind my head and let one knee sway. "It's turquoise. How valuable could it be?"

"You know nothing, Wade Boehner." Since he proposed to Indi, Radek thinks he's some sort of precious gems connoisseur. "It depends on the source and quality of the stone."

Smug asshole.

"Whatever, man. I bet it's not more than five hundred."

Fletcher sputters, spraying doughnut crumbs all over my rug. "Nope, I say ten grand at least."

"You're disgusting, Fletch. Better clean that up."

"Or what?" He takes another purposefully messy bite, showering the rug with more crumbs.

My first finger and thumb hone in to twist his nipple. He yowls and accidentally kicks Landon, who jabs an elbow to both of our guts.

"Seven grand for me, now shut up. Geoffrey Munn is talking."

"*...There's good news, and there's bad news. We were talking at the table over there, and you were incorrectly told that this was created in 1960...*"

"See?" My hand motions to the TV.

Fletch pokes a sticky finger in my ear. I palm his face to push it away.

"Ay! Why are you so nasty?"

"*...But that's not true. It's actually from before the turn of the century, and the center gem is high-quality Persian turquoise. Paired with the twenty-two-carat gold band and three-diamond clusters on each side, this piece is worth twelve-thousand dollars...*"

Fletcher flies to his feet, whooping and clapping like an overstimulated cymbal-banging monkey.

"Gah!" Landon slaps a loud thud into the couch cushions.

Another loud thud comes from my bedroom.

Uh oh.

The door bursts open, and a disheveled Gabe Finch appears. Like a newborn fawn, all wobbly knees and doe-eyed confusion about how she got thrown into this world. She hugs her sneakers to her chest.

The boys freeze.

"Uh..."

Landon's mouth curves into a shit-eating grin as he picks his phone up from the coffee table. "Hey, Gabe."

Fletcher says nothing. His beet-red face says enough.

I stand and meet her at the door, hiding her from these dirtbags. "Morning, *sweetheart*."

Don't think I missed where her eyes fall on my gray sweats. I will my dick to stay down.

Don't you fucking move.

It twitches in rebellion.

Gabe peers up as I close in, mouth gaping.

"Take a picture, Freckles," I whisper. "It'll last longer."

Her mouth snaps shut.

Lips pursing as my eyes motion to the top of her head, then torso, I silently ask for her permission. She understands and agrees with a subtle nod.

The dip of her waist slots against my hand as I drop a kiss on her forehead. The contact is short but addictive. Enough to bring my stomach to my heart and my heart to my throat.

Not good. Not good. Bad, very bad.

"Sleep well?"

Gabe squeaks in response.

Stifled snickering echoes behind me. I throw them a glare.

"Let's talk inside."

As I shut the door behind me, Gabe storms around, furiously wiping the spot where I kissed her away with the back of her hand.

"Was that necessary?"

"*Shhh!*" I stiff-arm her and push, shuffling to the back of the room until we make it to the furthest corner. Can't risk eavesdroppers.

I whisper-yell, "You're my girlfriend, remember? I'd kiss my girlfriend good morning. You're lucky it wasn't on the mouth."

Her voice lowers as a finger pokes into my pec. "Fake." Poke. "Girlfriend." Poke.

Fake. Every time she says that my chest burns.

My hand wraps around hers to remove it. "Your morning breath stinks."

"Good!" She sends a sour puff of air right at me.

I kiai with stiff karate hands, but it's ineffective.

"Oh, my *God*," she adds, tossing her head back. "I can't believe I fell asleep here."

"What was that?" I ask, hand cupping an ear in her direction. "I didn't hear a 'thank you.'"

She curls her lip and then mutters, "Thanks."

"Wow! Now that's what I call character development."

Her eyes roll as her arms cross, drawing her attention to her watch.

"Shit." She facepalms. "I'm supposed to meet with my producer in forty minutes. I can't show up to work in-in..." Those honey-colored eyes dart about in panic. "...in the same clothes as yesterday!"

"Or you could and proudly do the walk of shame—"

"*No way.*"

"Alternatively, I have some things—"

Disgust replaces her panic. "*Ew*, I don't wanna wear something some other girl left here!"

"Keep your voice down." My tone rises to an exaggerated volume. "*Babe*, don't you remember? You left some stuff here *last time*." It returns to an angry murmur. "They're new, okay? Have a look."

The light in the walk-in switches on when I enter and present a small section of clothing.

"Why would you buy—"

"I told Skylar you sleep over here. You don't know her. She'll go into my closet and poke around. I couldn't risk it."

Her arms uncross to flip through the hangers. "How did you know my size?"

My shoulders rise and fall. "Lucky guess."

"But the style?" Her hand moves between the fabric of a white sweater sleeve, testing its texture.

"Freckles, you've been covering the league for four years. Jeans, sweater, wool coat. It's basically your uniform."

"You notice what I wear?" The expression quickly morphs into surprise.

"Don't get carried away. I happen to be very observant."

Her lifted eyebrow suspects otherwise. And it'd be right, but she doesn't need to know that.

She reluctantly returns to studying the clothing, rapidly turning the tags still attached to them with a lilting whistle. "Holy shit. These sweaters are three grand apiece. I don't know if I…"

This is the most frustrating woman I've ever met. Who refuses free clothes?

I groan through clenched teeth, my fingers spreading and tensing in mid-air as if about to shake the stubborn out of her. "What do you care? It's my money, and I have heaps of it. Just choose something!"

"Fine." She wags a finger at me. "But I won't like it!"

"Of course, you won't. You don't like anything other than driving me up the wall!"

"Me? *You're* the annoying one. I was trying to sneak out of here, but *nooooo*. You had to invite an audience!"

Now I feel bad. My tone softens.

"That wasn't on purpose, okay?" My hands tap their respective thighs in an alternating rhythm. "I forgot we had plans. I'll give you a heads-up next time."

"*Next time*?" Gabe's brows jump.

"Be for real, Freckles. You think this is the last time you'll be staying over here in the next few months?"

Eyes closing with frustration, she sighs through her nose. "But not in your bedroom."

"I have seven others. Take your pick."

"Show-off."

"Hardhead."

Gabe glares. "Don't you have a morning skate or something?"

"We got rid of it this season. With how much we're on the road, constantly crossing time zones, and sleeping on a different mattress every other night, rest is more beneficial. Olsen and Szeczin are probably still in bed."

Outside of interviews, this might be the most civil conversation we've had.

Gabe selects a pair of dark jeans and a tan sweater. "Tell me you didn't buy underwear."

Never mind.

My hands reach for surrender. "You're on your own."

There's a thudding in my chest and some mystery movement in my pants at the idea of her walking around wearing day-old panties. Snap out of it, you filthy fuck.

"Closet in the washroom has fresh towels."

"Got it."

I exit the bedroom, fully aware of the absolute crap awaiting me in the living room, and call through the door, "Enjoy your shower, *sweetheart*. I'll make you some breakfast. You can take it to-go."

Landon paces on the phone with Indi, the tattletale. "Right? I couldn't hear what they were talking about, but she went to shower now."

I get to work in the kitchen. The egg whites fold perfectly around a slice of Havarti, and I lift a fist in victory. For a level placement, I lower to counter height, sliding it off to the center of a lightly toasted English muffin, like a kitchen scientist. I wrap it up in foil and put it in a brown paper bag, rolling over the top for easy carrying.

Easy carrying? Since when have I wanted to make Gabe's life easy?

I unravel it but can't get myself to crumple it. That'd be rude. I neaten it just as she gets to the island.

Fletch has resumed the form of a seated couch statue, cheek bulging with more doughnut. Landon cups a hand over his phone and walks toward the outdoor area.

I shake the bag. "Your breakfast sandwich, mademoiselle."

"*Er...*"

"A simple egg and cheese. Woulda been a Benny if I had more time."

Shut it, you dolt. No one cares that you can cook. Least of all, Gabe Finch.

When she reaches to take it from me, I pull it back, and the proximity has the mahogany and teak scent of my soap wafting up from her skin. As if her usual flowery perfume wasn't intoxicating enough, this is pushing me to the brink.

I must've inhaled too audibly because she smirks. "Did you just sniff me? Are you a hair sniffer, Pretty Boy?"

My smug smile matches hers. "What's up with you using my soap, Freckles? You like smelling like mine?"

Her face blooms with a blush.

Mwahahahahahaha. *Yes.*

Gabe snatches the bag.

"Too easy," I add.

"*You're* easy."

"And?"

Someone clears their throat.

This time, *we* freeze, slow-motion, turning our faces to find Fletch and Landon staring at our exchange.

I crack a cheesy smile, ignoring the beads of sweat forming at my hairline, then tap my cheek and offer it to her. "Need my goodbye kiss."

From my vision's periphery, her gaze sparks with a vengeance, but she plays along.

Her lips—*God, her lips*—are pillowy soft against my morning stubble and leave me wanting more. I hate that I can never have enough of her.

"That's it? You two are *super* lame."

I glare at Landon. "We were *trying* to spare you. Maybe next time we won't be so considerate."

"Heh-heh." Gabe nervously lifts her breakfast. "Gotta go."

"Oh, yeah, sure. '*Next time,*'" he mocks me. "And when will that be?"

Look sharp, Boehner.

"Gabe's birthday party, of course."

Nice save.

"Does Indi know about this?"

"Not yet, but invites are on their way. I was gonna keep the plans under wraps, but since you're all so *nosy*—"

"Looking forward to it!" Landon waves a politely smiling Gabe off as she escapes. "Bye, Gabe! Have a good day at work!" He re-focuses on his phone as a string of text notifications ring out. "*Ooohh.* Husband duty calls."

"Yuck. No need to rub it in how much sex you're having." Fletcher's mouth turns down. "Guess I'm off to the bookstore."

Poor guy needs to get laid so badly. Hell, I need to get laid. I don't know how Fletcher lives without sex, but I am not strong enough to stay celibate with Gabe Finch around.

On my mind, in my house, at the games. Fuck, she's everywhere. And it's not at all where I want her to be. In my arms, against my mouth, on my cock.

It's too bad she doesn't want any of that from me. Or does she?

FRECKLES

Fuck off, you're not throwing me a birthday party.

ME

It was supposed to be a surprise, but a certain Indira Davé-Radek ruined it, remember??

FRECKLES

You're literally the worst.

ME

I'm the best at making you breakfast

ME

And making you come

FRECKLES

Have I mentioned I hate you?

The dopiest smile splits my face. The more she says she hates me, the less I believe it.

As soon as the penthouse empties, I call my chef.

"Allô."

"Allô, Mathieu. Any chance you could cater a party for me two weekends from now? It's my girlfriend's birthday."

CHAPTER 10:
A HARDENED THIRD LEG

GABE

"KEEPING BUSY, HUH?" INDI INHALES THROUGH HER nose as the treadmill speed picks up.

Wiggly eyebrows suggest something I can't decipher. I take a stab at a response.

"Yeah, you know me: all work, work, work."

She side-eyes me. "Nice try. Spill."

The corner of my mouth twists. "Sorry?"

"You've been officially dating Wade for three weeks, and I feel like I know more about it from the internet than you two."

Kinda like we're making public appearances on purpose.

"Hitting up all the usual haunts: Cafe Jardín, Avec, Au Lait. Holding hands, he's posting cutesy pictures of you on Instagram..."

Warmth radiates through my palm with a memory of his clasp. I stretch my fingers, then clamp them into a fist before refocusing on running. Even out of my sight, Wade Boehner won't leave me alone.

"I used to get all the dirty details."

Don't think she wants to hear about me frustratedly rubbing myself to sleep.

"No worries," she says through a pant. "Landon, as it turns out, *loves* to gossip. My guy gives me all the piping hot tea, sometimes in real-time."

Doesn't surprise me. Those two share everything. The man would crawl into her brain and stay there, given the chance. It's disgusting. And also induces envy.

What is that like? To have someone to share with other than a bed or a body? Having a conversation with Kurt at any sort of emotional depth was like pulling teeth. Everything I gave, he returned in a fraction, and I accepted the bare minimum while he doted on every other woman instead.

Being in love makes you so stupid.

"I bet."

"Yep, and all I've" —she struggles to speak— "heard about" —*huff*— "for the past two weeks" —*huff*— "is how you've broken every bed in the place."

"*What*!" I whip my head to her.

"Good for you, girl. Get it."

"You know how it goes" —I shrug and scoff with an uneasy smile, wanting to tell her it's not what she thinks— "we're optimizing our time together before going on the road."

What's one more lie to top off this Jenga tower?

In reality, Wade's place has been nothing short of a shipwreck.

We agreed to three nights a week where we make a quick public appearance, post a picture or short clip on social media, and I stay over. Despite promising me the choice of any guest room in the penthouse, disaster has struck one by one.

The first bedroom, furthest away from him, had an uneven bed frame. Like a shady bar's table where one leg is shorter than the rest. Semiconscious me thought we were hit by an earthquake every time I rolled over.

My drowsy form swayed in the doorway of his bedroom, pillow raised above me, ready to attack the sleeping bastard. I knew it wasn't technically his fault, but at 1 a.m., I didn't give a shit.

I shrieked like a banshee and smacked Wade several times. He protected his head with both arms. "What the fuck, Gabe?"

One more slap with the pillow to his stupidly hot face is for good measure. "I thought I was dying!"

"From what? Snoring?"

"Shut up! I don't snore. The bed is broken." My feet stomped back to the room and climbed carefully back onto the mattress, hoping fear wouldn't off me in my sleep.

Plans to have a quiet night in watching The Great British Bake Off alone was a failure. It's supposed to be a family show, but they're no better than the hockey team with the constant innuendos. And if that didn't get me overheated, faulty wiring in the next bed's mattress pad almost burned the skin off my back.

"Why can't you replace it?" I chided. "This is the kind of problem easily solved by throwing money at it. Not like you don't have enough."

"I would if I could, but my PA tells me these things are on back-order." Wade groaned and pulled his cover up. "Are you always this difficult, Finch? Just choose another room."

I almost fell into a black hole in the third bedroom. Some of the bed slats were hanging by a thread, and my ass got sucked in the second I laid down, shooting my limbs up directly into the air like a folded-over Barbie.

"Hold on."

I couldn't believe this was happening.

"Got it? I'm gonna pull!"

My fist gripped the thick nylon rope attached to the lifesaver, a leftover prop from one of Wade's infamous theme parties.

The harsh tug launched me right into his arms, and I recovered by shoving him back through the doorway from where he entered.

The fourth bedroom sprung a leak in the washroom and ruined the hardwood. It's a construction zone now. The planks, padding, and plywood have been ripped out, baring the cement foundation.

"You're not here that much." I paced his bedroom length. "And have only owned the place for five years. How is it possible your penthouse is falling apart?"

"Go to sleep, Nancy Drew. You can solve this mystery in the morning."

I didn't dare to sleep in the one that stored previously used hockey equipment. It was somehow worse than the locker room and smelled like someone hoarded piles of steaming raccoon shit for no less than a decade. You couldn't bribe me with a hazmat suit to go in there.

The door immediately snapped shut after a single sniff. My gagging echoed down the hallway.

"Yo!" Wade yelled from his bedroom. "Cut out the gagging, will ya? Unless you want to be gagged."

I mocked him, warping my face.

"And in case it wasn't clear," he continued. "I meant with my cock!"

After he booked out a movie theater—*not one theater, the entire Cineplex*—to watch Mean Girls on October third, I was convinced his place was haunted. All four of the bedframe's legs gave out at once in the sixth bedroom.

"Hey, Pretty Boy, maybe if you spent less time on making your hair wispy and more time selecting quality furniture, I wouldn't be at Death's door every time I stay over. With your eight figures, one would think you'd be able to afford nicer stuff."

Our arguments became a regular occurrence, and I swear he got some sick pleasure from it.

"Me? You keep breaking all my shit! It's not like I want you closer to me or something."

"I'm so sure! I bet you'd love to torture me by sharing a bed."

"Sounds to me like you wanna, Freckles."

"Please get over yourself."

"You first."

We separated in a huff, and I promised myself a long stay at Miraval in the off-season to recuperate from the aggression this man awoke in me.

Now, the only option is the room directly next to his master suite.

Indi's wheezy complaining snaps me back into the present. "Oh, God. I can't do this anymore."

My best girlfriend props her feet up on either side of the moving belt and hits the emergency stop button. When the machine powers down, she dismounts and doubles over, gasping through every breath. "This trip to Italy ruined me," she says through a pant, shaking her head. "Nothing...

in these veins...except arrabbiata. No strength...left, muscles...replaced with...spaghetti cacio e pepe."

I lower the speed, but she holds up a hand.

"Go on without me."

"Are you sure?"

"I'm fine."

"Thanks, I have a lot on my mind and—"

She interrupts before I finish. "*Awww*, you miss Wade. I knew you two would be good together."

"*Uh-huh*." My nostrils flare in disbelief. "Sorry, are you the same Indi who insulted my boyfriend when we announced we were dating?"

My boyfriend?

Oh, no.

"I was shocked, okay? It's weird thinking about Wade in that way. He's like" —she waves a hand around seeking the words— "that dog on Instagram who's called 'a humper', but he's not ashamed about it. I know he's a good guy, but you're my best friend. I wasn't gonna stand by and watch you get hurt again."

He can't hurt me. We'd have to like each other first.

Water lines Indi's lower lids with the threat of falling. A lump swells in my throat. She better quit. We can't be crying at the gym.

"And then I saw this." She pulls up a screenshot on her phone and zooms in on an image from our short interview-date-thing at Cafe Jardín. Chin rested in his palm; Wade's dreamy gaze is fixed on my side profile as I speak to the waitstaff. "He's crazy in love with you."

Pinpricks sprawl across every inch of my exposed skin. She couldn't be more wrong.

"Gabe?" Indi halts my incoming dissociation, using the safety rail to straighten and bore into my soul with her giant, round eyes. "Are you in love with him?"

Absolutely *not*. But I can't say that. And I can't say yes, either. What if it comes true?

I play it cool. "*Pfft*. Please. It's not that serious. We're having fun getting to know each other better."

At least the latter half of the statement is true. Wade Boehner is not at all who I thought he'd be.

"*Sure.* You can deny it all you want, but I have all the evidence I need, my little lovesick friend."

I lose my pace when I fake-gag, sending me flying off my machine.

She turns green and grasps her stomach. "*Ugh*, don't do that. I'm gonna be sick."

"Sorry." I offer a swig from my water bottle and rub her back as she accepts and takes a few pulls. "What's going on with you? Your stomach has been extra messed up lately."

Indi shakes her head. "It's all the rich European food I ate on vacation. And between summer training camps and the start of the girls' season, I haven't been able to go home and eat mom's home-cooked food. I'm desperate for some of those desi spices to clean the system out."

"*Oof.* That's rough."

She groans. "I think I hear a bench by the lockers calling my name."

"Are you gonna be okay on your own? I was gonna hit up the basketball courts before my training session." I mime a fadeaway. "But I can come with you and then go back—"

"Don't be ridiculous. I'll be fine, go."

"Text me if you're dying?"

"My hero," she croons, clasping her hands to her shoulder and lifting her pitch, swooning like Olive Oyl, then beelines to the changing room, still rubbing her belly.

Every court except one is occupied by groups playing three-on-three. I grab a ball and dribble it back, the squeaking of sneakers and noisy trash talk fading away to nothing except my breath. Basketball never fails to empty my mind.

A couple of bank shots follow easy layups before I get into a rhythm and make a clean shot through the net. "Swish, swish, baby," I whisper into my victory fist before taking the ball beyond the point. The success is short-lived because when I put up a three-pointer, a voice breaks my focus.

"Bro, look, it's Stephanie Curry."

Four men approach as the ball bounces off the rim and into one moron's hands. Discomfort knots my stomach.

"Funny." I roll my eyes and ready my hands, waiting to receive the stolen basketball. "Pass it back."

"Sorry." He tosses it to a taller friend, who passes it over my head to another. "We've got this court booked." Face leaning into mine, he gives me a grimy smile. "But you can cheer us on if you'd like."

I could hustle these fools if I wanted, but I have better things to do.

"No, thanks." I give them a facetious thumbs up. "Enjoy."

It's not worth it to argue with douches like them. At least with Wade, it's a fair fight.

Turning to hide my clenched-shut eyes, I grimace.

Why am I thinking about him again?

"Hey, wait. Don't I know you from somewhere?" Their fourth man calls after me.

"Doubt it!" I throw over my shoulder.

"*Yoooo*, that's Gabe Finch!" The tallest one punches Moron Number Two in the arm as the door clunks open underneath my push. "She's that CSN chick who covers hockey games. You know, the one dating the Regents' tendy."

"*Aw*, man!" Their groans echo behind me. "We could've gotten a signed jersey or tickets or something."

"Too bad, so sad. Shoulda thought of that before you were dicks to me," I say to my watch, where a message from my boss pops up.

MEL

Boehner's Instagram posts are so cute!!

Great. Another Pretty Boy fan. Just what the world needs.

MEL

He's such a charmer

I huff.

ME

You like him so much, why don't you date him?

MEL

Hilarious. You're hilarious.

> MEL
>
> And I would, but he's taken ;)

Barf.

I stop myself from typing anything else.

As if the Devil knew he was summoned, Wade's text appears.

> PRETTY BOY
>
> Heyyyyy girlfriend, wyd??

> ME
>
> None of your business.

> PRETTY BOY
>
> Tell me anyway, Freckles

> ME
>
> I'm at the gym, if you must know. Do you need something?

> PRETTY BOY
>
> Running!!

> ME
>
> That was earlier. I'm about to lift.

When there's no reply, I give myself a smug nod. Good riddance.

My trainer, Justin, touches his toes in a corner of free space on the right side from the free weights area and waves me over. I put my phone on Do Not Disturb mode and slip it into the deep leggings pocket on my thigh.

"Morning!" He pulls me into a hug.

I'm always skeptical of people who are chipper before having coffee and a workout. Like, how? Have they taken some sort of supplement that alters their brain chemistry? I've been waking up before dawn since high school, but the serotonin never hits until after I break into a sweat.

"We'll start with calisthenics, then head to the floor and do deadlifts."

"Sounds good."

I get on my hands and knees to stretch out my wrists, then hop to my feet, rotating my shoulders while Justin finds an open rack.

"You think you can do sets of ten today?"

I shake my arms and eye the pull-up bar above me, adjusting the strap of my sports bra. These itty bitties won't escape anyway, but it's a habit. "I did eight last week..."

Two thumbs go up in reply. "You got this."

Yeah, I got this. I'm fake dating Wade Boehner. I can do anything.

The first five are cake. The following three are increasingly difficult, and I'm almost ready to drop.

I wasn't raised to be a quitter, though.

Sweat trickles down my arms, and into the bra fabric as I hang at rest, ankles crossed behind my bent knees mid-air. Every breath strains exiting my lungs. My head drops back until the ends of my ponytail tickle the spine on my lower back. I lift it again to shake out a no to my trainer's reflection in the floor-to-ceiling wall mirror.

"Not happening." I heave.

Justin straightens from his squat to spot me.

"Push through it," he encourages from behind. "C'mon. Up."

Each muscle in my arms tense and tremble. The veins in my neck bulge, all the tendons terrifyingly taut as I get stuck halfway, too stubborn to give up and too tired to move. Justin's hands hover over my hips, not quite touching me.

"A little more, keep going—*oof*!"

Out of nowhere, Justin stumbles to the side, replaced by an un-amused-looking Wade Boehner. Before I can scream at him, his hands flank mine around the bar. He positions under me, thighs pressed into the backs of mine. They're firm. Warm. And there's a hardened third leg at the ass-seam of my leggings.

Don't get distracted. It's a penis. Not like you remember how big it is or how it felt inside of you.

At the top of the pull-up, I face where his chin rests in the crook of my shoulder.

"What the fuck are you doing?" I yell through a hush.

He replies at the same volume. "Helping you through your last reps."

"Why are you here?"

"Kept thinking about your ass in leggings. Had to run here and see if it lived up to my imagination."

He's not wrong. What I lack in boobs, I make up for in butt. It's the only curve I have. I lower slowly, the scorching burn in my lats traveling down their attached triceps. "What's the verdict?"

His lips meet the shell of my ear, searing the skin and spreading the burn southward. "If you want a compliment, Freckles, just ask."

A grumble vibrates in my throat. "You're a jerk for pushing Justin."

"*Justin* was about to touch you."

"This will be number ten," Justin calls out, confusion circling his tone.

"He's my trainer," I grit through my teeth, pouring whatever strength is left into the last lift. Calluses threaten my palms.

"Ask me if I care, Freckles." The man is thoroughly unfazed by doing pull-ups. He hasn't missed a beat or lost track of his breath. I, on the other hand, am huffing so hard you'd think we were doing something else. "New rule: while we're together, no one gets to touch you like this but me. *No one*," he breathes past my ear.

The descent is nothing short of agonizing. Physically, I'm spent. Sexually, I'm so frustrated I could cry. Emotionally, I'm angry at myself for allowing this level of desperation.

A silent, wide-eyed Justin stands frozen to one side as my stupid fake boyfriend keeps me stable. Wade spreads a palm across my bare stomach as the tips of my toes meet the floor, and I remove my grip from the bar.

"Nice work, *babe*," he announces, wrapping his other arm around me, too.

I want to escape his hold and run, but we've garnered too much attention. Too many eyes follow us.

My arms layer naturally over his, shoulders rising against the bristling stubble of Wade's chin. "*Thaaaaaanks.*" I'm not sure the attempt at masking my disdain with singsong is working. "I didn't expect you here."

"Had a couple hours before practice and was missing you." He releases me, but only to curl an arm around my neck, trapping my ponytail under his elbow.

"Wade Boehner." He extends a hand.

Justin accepts with a firm shake. "Justin Liu."

"Do you mind if I steal her away for a second?"

"Be my guest."

Wade tugs me by the neck. "Let's go."

There's no time to argue before he's marching us toward the changing rooms. "I like your ponytail. It's so pretty." His fingers twirl the ends.

I glare and tip my chin up. "I bet. You have a thing for pulling them?"

"Maybe." An unusual, soft smile replaces his smirk. "Wanna braid it, too."

There's that sinking guilt again. The one that roils in my belly every time Wade dissipates whatever assumption I have of him.

"Are you thinking what I'm thinking, Freckles?" He backs me into the wall next to the water bottle filling station, sweeping his tongue across his lower lip. "Say it on three. One, two, three."

We blurt in chorus.

"You braiding my hair—"

"—Kissing you."

Uh oh.

CHAPTER 11:
PRETTY SURE GABE FINCH LIKES ME NOW

WADE

IT'S SATURDAY NIGHT, AND MY ONLY COMPANY IS A DOG.

I pout.

"I don't know why she doesn't like me, Dougie."

He whines in response.

"I'm very likable."

This golden retriever has the nerve to sass me by moving those puppy dog eyes upward from where his head rests on my lap.

"What? I coulda sworn she wanted me to kiss her." I stare at the ceiling and slide his velvety ear through my hand. It's so floppy, the dark golden fur so shiny. "I'm so good at kissing her."

It might be the best thing I've ever done.

Doug licks the air.

"You're sweet, but no. I won't be kissing you. Best save the slobber for your parents."

Skylar and Jaeg had dropped the poor pup off this morning, desperate for some alone time. I wish I didn't know what their *alone time* entails, but Sky is an oversharer.

Apparently, Doug likes to watch them make out and they think it'll be traumatic if he sees anything else. Hell, I'm traumatized just thinking about it.

"Good boys don't need to be seeing all that, do they?"

He agrees with a woof.

"I know. I like being called a good boy, too."

Though I haven't been a very good boy lately, I've all but wrecked the penthouse with the sole purpose of leaving Gabe no choice but to stay with me.

The night I slept in my bed after she did was the best sleep I had in months. Every trace of her presence on the sheets was washed away in the laundry too soon. But I was a determined man.

What else was I supposed to do? We agreed to sleepovers after public appearances, and she went and chose the bedrooms on the other side of the place. I wasn't gonna sit back and let that happen.

Gabe Finch might be a thorn in my side, but she's *my* thorn. And fuck, I don't wanna die before I get to kiss her again.

So, I did what I had to.

I shortened a leg of the wooden bedframe by five centimeters. Who cares about the one-of-a-kind Danish design? I'll get another made. In return, I got a pillow to the face at 1 am. Worth it. The way she paused before leaving my bedroom? I could see it. She thought about joining me.

I took a plier to the wiring of the heated mattress pad in the next room she chose, fraying the ends that went into the temperature control dial until it puffed a small cloud of smoke.

The section of foam and spring I cut out from the middle of the mattress lined up with where I split the slats beneath it—*Hulk style*— in Bedroom #3. The wearable Hulk fists don't make a sound anymore, but who cares? Gabe had to be rescued, and I loved every second of scooping her out of that trap.

The pipe leaking in the washroom into the next bedroom over was a happy mistake. I meant to simply remove the shower head so that water sprayed everywhere when she turned it on, but instead, I messed up a pipe so badly that it ruined the room. Oh no, I'll have to get the flooring redone. No matter. We forge ahead!

I couldn't have planned the situation with Top Beer Cheese if I'd come up with it myself. In the past, we've played against one another in friendly charity games, so when their GM mentioned the state of their equipment to Jules, I leaped at the chance. In return, I asked for their old gear, which I conveniently consolidated in Gabe's newest selection. Once I turned the heat in there up to thirty-two degrees and let the stench soak into the space, she wasn't able to handle it.

And last but not least, I skipped an arm day to saw each of the last bedroom's legs—*not all the way*—enough that the slightest movement would have it collapsing on top of itself.

The evilly genius plan is working so far, but I have yet to scheme up what accidental atrocity plagues the seventh bedroom.

I look at Doug.

Doug looks back.

My brows raise in suggestion.

"Y'know, every once in a while, dogs get curious and eat things they're not supposed to."

Doug snorts.

"And sometimes, if they eat something like, I don't know, *chocolate*" — the dog snaps his open mouth shut and drops his usually goofy smile— "it makes them sick. Sick enough to...leave a mess behind."

He places a paw across his snout as if to hide his eyes.

"A very stinky diarrhea mess."

He huffs at me, straightening his front paws at the *ding* of my phone notifications.

FRECKLES

Why did my PA send me a schedule for next weekend with time blocked off for a birthday party?

ME

Because there's a birthday party

FRECKLES

I told you to cancel it!

ME

No can do

ME

It's your birthday! We HAVE to celebrate!!

FRECKLES

We absolutely do not.

ME

Mostly because we already told everyone
weeks ago that I planned to

FRECKLES

How is that my fault? You didn't even ask
me if I had plans.

ME

Do you have plans??

FRECKLES

No.

FRECKLES

But I could have!

ME

Now you do

FRECKLES

...

FRECKLES

Fine. Whatever.

ME

I like it when you're nice

FRECKLES

Guess I'm gonna have to be meaner.

ME

I've told you this before but

I snicker to myself while searching for and selecting the meme GIF of Skeletor pointing and moving his jaw captioned with, "joke's on you I'm into that shit."

Just when I think I've rendered her speechless, she returns a GIF of an Elmo muppet with his arms raised, flames flickering in the background. The text reads, "I'M IN HELL." I choke on my spit and hack out a horrendous, cartoonish laugh akin to Goofy.

Thank God no one was around to witness that.

Doug's judgment comes down with a heavy side-eye, his worried expression making me chortle again.

"Judge me all you want, buddy. But I'm pretty sure Gabe Finch likes me now."

———

I take it back.

And kinda regret giving her access to the penthouse.

No, no, that's too far, but by the way, my kitchen has been turned into some sort of wholesale bakery at 4 a.m. two days before Gabe's birthday party; she absolutely must hate me.

A KitchenAid whirs loudly on the back counter. Hair tied into a ratty top knot, haphazard swipes of flour marking her face and arms like war paint and donning a black apron that reads, "Don't Test Me, I'll Poison You," Gabe moves through clouds of flour and icing sugar, which have appeared on every surface.

She frantically mixes the contents of one bowl, then turns to stir a pot on the stove before catching a few lemons escaping from the chaos by rolling off the marble. Raspberry-colored goo hisses and pops, splattering on the backsplash. She wipes her hands on the towel tucked into her apron string and lowers the heat before moving on.

It smells as delicious as she looks, but all the racket this early in the morning is enough to send anyone running away screaming. Good thing I'm not anyone.

Gabe doesn't notice me nearing.

"What the fuck are you doing?"

She jolts and nearly drops the bowl of batter and whisk. When she regains composure and balance, she rubs the back of her hand against her forehead and sighs. "Eating ass. What does it look like I'm doing?"

My heart stops. "You do that?"

"I'm. Baking," she grits through her teeth.

Okay, maybe now's not the right time to ask, but we'll be discussing this ass-eating situation later. Would I eat her ass? Absolutely. Would I let her eat my ass? Not sure if it's a yes, but it's not a no.

Oh, God. This morning wood has taken over my brain. She won't even let you kiss her. Forget about anything else.

"*Why* are you baking?" Sphincter clenched, I make it to the island and attempt to lean on it, but there's not an inch of space. Dozens of already poured lemony cupcakes in trays sprawl the counter. "And here? It's four in the fucking morning." The heels of my hands dig into my eye sockets before dragging down my face.

"Your kitchen is bigger, and I thought you would've already left for the gym." Her hand uses a scoop to drop batter into empty cupcake liners. "I bake when I'm stressed, and you throwing this stupid birthday party has me *stressed*."

"Jesus. Who's gonna eat all these?"

She returns a sarcastic laugh and keeps scooping. "That's a problem for future-Gabe. Present-Gabe needs to finish this last batch before moving onto the icing."

"If they're any good, we could use them for the party. I'll talk to Mathieu—"

"What do you mean, *if*?" Gabe's face returns to her signature glare and scowl. "I've been baking since I was thirteen years—"

The red goo bursts again. We both yelp.

"It shows."

She rolls her eyes, and my hard-on is not going away. I wanna push every button this woman has.

"How dare you? They're delicious. And having them at the party is the first good idea you've ever had."

Seriously, why do I like it when she insults me?

When she backpedals to turn off the stove, I hustle over to trap her between me and the edge of the counter, socks slipping in the white powder speckling the floor. My arms post themselves on either side of her hips. She shrinks away like the distance between us. I drop my head slightly to meet her at eye level.

The proximity sends my heart racing faster than it did at her sass, the flowery smell of her skin mixed with the sweet lemon in the air.

"Oh, Freckles. I have a lot of good ideas."

Her breath hitches as her gaze flicks down to where my clothed cock remains upright. A muscle in her jaw tightens.

"Get that thing away from me, Pretty Boy."

"I love that you think I'm pretty."

She scoffs. I stop the noisy exhale by pressing the tip of my nose to hers and speak into her parted mouth, keeping my hips angled away.

"And by the way, I don't plan on giving it to you until you're begging for it."

Her chest heaves as I draw space between us once more, reaching into the next drawer over to retrieve my car keys.

"You're lucky I have to go work out." I flick her apron with my index finger before sauntering to the door to put on some sneakers. "Or else I'd have to pin you down and make you call me pretty again."

Gabe clears her throat and calls after me. "Those lines don't work on me!"

"You're a terrible liar." My keys jingle in hand as I wave her off. "And don't forget to wear something nice on Friday. It's a party, after all."

"Can't look too nice, or *your little problem* will never go away."

I stop in the foyer and adjust my boxer briefs. "*Little problem?* Is this you begging for a reminder?"

Freckles groans. "*No.*"

I give it a rest. The door creaks under the weight of my shoulder. "Will you be here when I get back?"

She shakes her head. "I'm working."

A hint of solemnity replaces the usual fiery spark in Gabe's eyes. I rub the dip of my sternum, where a heartburn-like sensation grows. I really need to figure out how to make this woman smile. Annoyance will do for now. Anything except sadness.

"See you Friday, Freckles."

I don't wait for a snarky response, but as her profile disappears from view, her eyelashes flutter over her exasperated face.

Relief sighs out, and a satisfied smirk paints my face for the rest of the day.

CHAPTER 12:
TELL ME IT'S OKAY

GABE

NO MATTER HOW MANY TIMES I REFRESH IT, WADE'S comment on my Instagram post won't go away.

Maybe it wasn't the best decision to take a selfie biting into one of the cupcakes I'd made and captioning it "me vs. dessert: who's sweeter?" but I'd gotten social media manager approval, and for what?

Twelve hundred fifty-one likes for wadeboehner31 commenting, "No competition, not even close"? And don't get me started on all the replies gushing over how cute Wade is, how we're relationship goals, how lucky I am to have a boyfriend like him. Good thing they don't know about the filthy follow-up texts.

PRETTY BOY

> No offense to the cupcake, but you taste way better, Freckles

ME

> Gag me.

PRETTY BOY

> I'd be happy to

ME

> In your dreams.

PRETTY BOY

Every single night

ME

I can't stand you.

PRETTY BOY

You wouldn't even have to stand

PRETTY BOY

Just tie me up, take a seat right here on
my face and ride til dawn

It's not normal to get turned on by this.

End me now.

That way I have an excuse not to show up to this ridiculous birthday party.

Why is it such a big deal anyway? We're all born, and we all die. And for my family, both events happened in October. My birth and Mom's death. Grief and joy were forever and inextricably intertwined.

I tilt my head at the reflection, studying how the black dress fits. The material is gorgeous, chiffon or something, and the lace-up back plumps my chest against the scoop neck and creates a waist where there otherwise is none. My thigh peeks from the high slit, and I sway my knee to and fro with a pointed toe, accentuating the length of my legs. Okay, that's sexy.

My eyes wander up, and a frown appears.

When I mentioned having to dress nice, Indi's friend, Sheena, had it mailed over. I don't want to sound ungrateful, and having fashion influencer contacts who can hook you up is nice, but it'd probably look better on either of them. Or even Bea. Their boobs would actually fill it, and as a long-standing chair of the Itty Bitty Titty Committee, I simply am not capable.

"It's fake," I say to the mirror, splaying my palms over the bust. "It doesn't matter if my boobs look good or not."

I dread having to put on a full face. I should be used to it, but it's different when it's for work. Jas and her makeup crew are magicians. I nearly take my left eye out when applying a set of lashes and curse myself for not asking her to help me get ready tonight. Once it's on and I've fixed the teary smear of foundation, it's not so bad.

Hair free from their roller prisons, I do a quick floof and let the long curls bounce past my shoulders. Choosing between sensible sandals and uncomfortable stilettos just to surpass Wade's height wastes some time, but I finally opt for a pair of open-toed block heels.

I can never manage to get these on without looking like a tangled grass-hopper, but after a lot of huffing and puffing, they're secure. I'll sleep in them before having to go through that again.

Unless someone takes them off for me.

Shut up, brain. It's not happening.

He's not even here, but somehow, he can still get me worked up.

How annoying.

Off to this celebration, I go.

Goosebumps and nerves prickle across my skin as I exit the Uber. The doorman to Wade's building stiff-arms the crowd and ushers me through the incessant flashing of paparazzi cameras, but despite the warmer tem-perature inside, the goosebumps remain.

It's a party. Could be fun, right? Or it could be unbearable to have Wade at my side, callused hands touching me in surprisingly gentle ways and making me feel things for him I have no business feeling.

Bappa, give me strength.

Oh, my God. This man has me praying.

The elevator beeps as I get to the penthouse, and they slide open to equally wide-open doors. An instrumental indie folk tune softly plays from within, like Bon Iver and Hozier had a baby. I don't hate it.

But the real kicker is walking in.

I should've known better than to make assumptions.

This isn't his penthouse. It's a private venue.

String lights hang from the high ceilings, softening the usually bright light fixtures. His cozy sectional has been repositioned, with classic white-cloth-covered cocktail tables surrounding it.

A few uniformed servers delicately place hors d'oeuvres on trays at the kitchen counter and pour champagne into glass flutes. The cupcakes I'd made are on display on several tiered cake stands on a dessert table off to the right and lead to two large dining tables.

Boughs of gardenia flow from tall vases between shorter candles and heavy tableware on charger plates.

The flowers are my favorite. My fingers reach for a bloom and I lower to take them in.

They smell like me.

Like I'm home.

Tears of rage blur my vision. Someone who doesn't even care about me put so much thought into something as insignificant as a birthday party, while the man I was in love with for years, who I almost married, never did it once. A fake boyfriend did more than my real ex-fiancé. The anger and rue bubble up from my gut, heated and sour.

I swallow it down.

"You like it?"

Wade's question echoes, his cognac Oxfords clopping against the floor where my gaze lingers. It wanders up the faint weave of his gray slacks, then follows the veins snaking over his forearms, where he rolls back a black sleeve.

His fingers clasp my chin and lift.

Those melted chocolate eyes of his deepen with concern. "Don't look at me like that, Gabe. You don't like it?"

"I—"

Hate it. Am overwhelmed by it. How did he know about the gardenias?

"*Whoooaa.*" Landon booms from the entryway.

Wade's hand drops, taking whatever blood is left in my face with it.

"Holy shit, man. This place looks great."

Indi's dimpled smile shines across the room with a gasp. "Gabe!"

"Tell me the truth later, Freckles." Wade wraps the same hand around the cinch of my created waist. His whisper against my neck has my heart climbing out of my chest through my throat. "For now, pretend like you're happy being here with me."

I'm not gonna survive the night if I have to be pressed against his firm torso the entire time, with layer upon layer of pretending to like him over not liking him over something in between, and all while he smells like a fresh morning in Heaven and holds me like I'm *his*.

My friend rescues me by pushing him aside when the four of us meet. "Unhand her, goon!" Our hands clasp before she draws me into a tight hug, then checks me out. "God, you're so freaking *hot*."

"What about me?" Landon pouts and moves his hands up and down his body.

"Christ, Radek." Wade's palm slaps against his forehead.

"It's Davé-Radek," Landon corrects.

Wade coughs out, "Pussy whipped."

I thought Indi would've rolled her eyes, but she doesn't. Pretty Boy gets a pitying, disappointed look thrown at him before she turns to her husband.

"*Aww*," she coos and steps away to leave a kiss on his bearded cheek. "You're the *hottest*."

Pride beams through the well-loved bastard. Obviously, the two are disgustingly obsessed with each other, but Indi always kept her sharp edge. Suddenly, it's a plastic, collapsible knife, like the ones used in stage plays.

I seek Wade's attention to exchange a confirming "did-you-see-what-I-saw?" regarding her softened behavior, but it's already on me. He blinks and recomposes a welcoming smile toward his teammate.

"Alright, Landy. Let's grab a beer."

More guests come in. Most of the team arrives, led by Fletcher Donovan, Theron Olsen, and Blake Szeczin, before people from the network, Mel, Jordan, my camerawoman Denise, and her partner, Jen, enter.

Mel and Jordan simultaneously widen their eyes and mouth *wow* in greeting. I play it cool and direct them to the bar with a polite smile. They reply with a thumbs up and an exaggerated wink. I quietly groan.

Subtle. Real subtle.

It's not long before realizing Indi is my only real friend there. I need a drink. Luckily, there's champagne being served with appetizers.

"Bea couldn't make it?" I ask her.

"Sorry," Indi says through a bite of a mini bruschetta at one of the high tables, then rests her head against my shoulder. "She was so sad to miss it. The articling program in Toronto is super demanding. I blocked those grueling eight months from memory."

My lips envelop the circumference of a champagne flute, and I throw back the drink in one gulp.

"That's a handy trick."

"Mmm." I keep down a cough when Wade's eyes reach mine from the bar. I grab two more from a passing server's tray and offer it to her.

"No, thanks." She snags a few skewered caprese bites. "I'm so hungry."

"I think there's red wine somewhere here, too."

There's that green look on Indi's face again.

"Please, *no*."

"No red wine? Who are you, and what have you done to my friend?"

She hushes me and swats my hand away. "I'm serious. I'm all 'wined out' from Italy."

Skylar and Derrick Jaeger's arrival cuts our conversation short.

Wade hugs them first; then, she extends her arms my way. The tiny thing only comes up to my shoulder, even in heels.

"Happy birthday, Gabe!"

"Thanks for coming."

Her hand squeezes my shoulder. "We wouldn't skip it for the world."

I don't miss the approving glance she sends to her best friend, whose smirk has returned. "He did good, don't you think?"

"*Uh*, y-yeah," I stammer. "It's beautiful."

"He's kinda known for throwing the most insane parties, but they're usually not this classy." She inhales deeply and reaches for her husband's hand. "It smells incredible in here. Glad you cleaned up, Wade."

"Hey, it's always clean."

"Only because of the cleaners. And even then, there's always the threatening odor of your musty socks in the air."

Wade's face stills. "Skylar," he chides through his teeth.

Derrick Jaeger chokes back a laugh. I think it's the first time I've seen him smile.

She raises her hands like a white flag. "Okay, fine. I'll be nice to you for the next couple of hours in front of your perfect girlfriend."

Me? Perfect?

My acting must be a bit *too* well done.

"She is, isn't she?" He steps beside me, and I lose track of my pulse.

"You don't believe that, do you?" I ask under my breath, not meaning for him to hear.

But he does.

He announces dinner to redirect the group and leads us toward the dining tables. Despite the music, muted noise in the kitchen, and low chatter, I hear him, too.

"Sure, I do."

My heart. He's melted it.

Why can't he go back to being the intolerable jock?

Too occupied with irritation, I only reorient after I've sat down and the server places a bowl in front of me.

"Roasted butternut squash soup with a slice of baguette, toasted."

I stare at it a moment too long. It's my comfort soup. My dad used to make it for us.

Wade drapes an arm over the back of my chair. "You gonna try it, or you want me to feed you?"

He watches me take a sip, pupils blowing wide when the spoon leaves my mouth. And he's definitely torturing me on purpose by using his tongue as a landing strip while trying the entree himself. As if he knows I'm wondering what he's capable of doing with it.

Even more torturous is how our pinkies brush when our hands settle on the table. He doesn't retreat as his conversation with Donovan and Jaeger continues, instead covering my hand and stroking an apology across the knuckles with his thumb. S-o-r-r-y. But he has nothing to be sorry about.

So I pull away.

Pretty Boy's got his signals crossed because he takes the motion as permission to palm my bare thigh.

Indi whips her head to me and sucks her lips in, eyebrow raised at his hand's position. "*Ooooh*. What's going on there?"

I scoff out a tepid, breathy laugh. "You know these hockey boys. They get possessive over the silliest things."

Wade's fingers dig into my flesh, muscles tightening at the rough contact.

"Don't I know it!" she agrees, looping her arm through Landon's.

Her man is clueless and returns a dopey smile, his mouth full of bread.

The touch releases, but not entirely. His fingertips graze the surface in growing, concentric circles, which is somehow worse. I distract myself by quickly finishing my soup.

"I'm done!" I say to get the server's attention, but everyone else's comes along with it.

Way to play it cool, Finch.

They take away the bowls and replace them. I study the garnished slice. "Quiche?"

"It's a tomato and gruyere tart," Wade answers.

Indi taps my elbow, and when I turn to see what she wants, she glows with the toothiest grin.

"What?"

"He's so sweet, Gabe." Girl is practically swooning.

"Sure."

"I mean it," she repeats. "Everything's vegetarian."

"Okay?" I shrug.

"Because *you're* vegetarian." Hearts form in her eyes.

What has gotten into my friend? Oh, yeah. Landon Radek. He's brainwashed her with his cinnamon roll ways.

"Mmhmm." My head turns back to the enigma clutching my leg like a lifeline. "Everything's vegetarian?" I murmur towards his ear. He nods. "Why?"

"'Cause you're vegetarian."

"I didn't tell you that."

His grin goes lopsided, and his eyes wrinkle in the corners. "I'm not as stupid as I look. We've eaten together half a dozen times. You don't think I noticed?"

Heart in throat, meet stomach.

Deva re Deva, you were supposed to get rid of the obstacles, not create new ones.

"You okay, Gabe?" Indi asks. "I know it's a lot, but—"

"I'm good," I lie.

She knows birthdays are tough, but she doesn't need to know how tough this one is. How frayed my restraint is. And how Wade has scattered my emotions around this penthouse.

I join Mel and Jordan's conversation about the upcoming season's schedule, but I can't get out of my head. And I'm wholly terrified that I'll spontaneously combust if he doesn't stop touching me.

Someone mentions dessert, and Indi gasps and squeals, clutching the crook of my arm as the cake is brought out. "It's lemon raspberry."

Engaged in a sort of auto-pilot mode, I allow myself to be whisked behind the beautiful display. Coated in a simple white buttercream, it's topped with lemon curls and fresh raspberries. Judging from its height, it's probably three layers.

"Where's Gabe's cake? I could eat this on my own."

My fake boyfriend jabs Olsen in the chest.

"Cut it out," Jaeger scolds.

Lucky Skylar. She got the most mature one.

"Yeah, cut it out," Donovan parrots. He and Olsen slap each other around.

Our whispers hide under everyone else's comments.

Wade pumps my side in his grip. "You don't have to pretend not to like it. I know you do."

"How did you know it was my favorite? I only made the cupcakes two days ago."

A server lights a lone sparkler in the middle.

"Are we gonna sing Happy Birthday?" Landon asks. "We have to, right?"

"Your friends are blabbermouths." His lips trace the shell of my ear. "Especially Dimples over there."

"Good to know you give everyone annoying nicknames."

"Don't kid yourself," he says through the smirk that sits against my jaw. "Freckles is special to you and only you. Now, smile. We're about to sing."

Embarrassment fills my cheeks when they start off-key, the men unabashedly cracking their voices and the women sticking their fingers in their ears. I can't stop smiling. Laugh after laugh escapes from me. It's a genuine and much-needed catharsis from the tangle of everything I've felt all night. Finally, they quit goofing around and sing in a crescendoing chorus at the end.

When I lean over to blow out the candle, Indi elbows me.

"You gotta make a wish first!"

Someone sedate this woman, seriously. She's far too cheery. Though I'm one to talk. I look like I'm off my rocker with the wide smile tugging at my mouth.

I wish Wade Boehner would kiss me again.

I steal a quick glance at him and extinguish the flame before I have time to change my mind.

You're so stupid, Gabe. Wishes don't come true.

He cuts me a piece. It's super attractive for some reason.

"Feed her!" Indi instructs. "It's a desi tradition! With your hands!"

Woman is wilding.

"Don't you dare smear it on my face," I warn Wade with a pointed finger.

"That's what she said," he mumbles.

Okay, I'm slightly less attracted to him. But I won't say no to cake, and not while everyone's watching us.

His Adam's apple drops as I take a large bite of the slice. Those smug brown eyes of his grow dark. I'm about to step away as he wipes his hand on a napkin, but he pulls me back.

"My turn."

"See? He knows!" I don't think I've ever seen Indi this overexcited. Landon Radek has done a number on her. "Feed him, too!"

I reach for a fork. He stops me again.

"That's not what I meant." One strong arm rounds my waist, drawing me closer until our torsos are flush.

My jaw relaxes into his grasp, lips parting by reflex.

"Finally!" Skylar claps quickly. "You two have barely held hands tonight."

"Gabe?" Wade asks.

"Do it!" Indi eggs on. "Kiss!"

"*Kiss! Kiss! Kiss!*" They chant.

"Happy birthday, Freckles."

His breath fans across my nose.

My lashes flutter, incapable of focusing on anything but his perfect, bow-shaped mouth.

"You don't have to do this."

"Yes, I do." He releases another ragged breath. I don't. I'm not breathing at all. "Tell me it's okay."

"Okay," says my last working brain cell.

And that was the end of Gabe Finch.

Cause of death: crushed by Wade Boehner's velvety pillow lips.

Our friends' hollers mute to nothing, my ears ringing with silence except for the dull groan vibrating between us.

Wade kisses me like he's dying of thirst, and I'm water, his tongue lapping and lapping. It's desperate. Needy. Like nothing else can give him what he wants. Nothing and no one but me.

I catch a runaway breath. Shrill whistles and raucous cheering crescendo as he pulls away, his lazy smile pressed to my lips.

"Atta girl."

Thank God for his arm supporting me because my knees have buckled. I'm a human puddle. A very, *very* wet one. He shouldn't be allowed to have that effect on me with only a kiss.

I expect Wade to let go and enjoy the rest of the night with his boys. He does no such thing.

He doesn't even move. Eyes locked on mine.

A noiseless lull passes.

"Everyone good with taking their cake to-go?"

Sounds of agreement reply back.

"Yep!"

Skylar herds the group toward the door.

Probably wise. My brain is in the gutter with no logic. Only filth remains.

They're gone within two minutes, and we've scrambled toward the bedroom door, limbs ensnared in a backward tango.

My composure snaps and clasps his throat, slamming him against the door. Every ounce of rage and horniness boils over.

"You're *infuriating*," I grit out. "It's making me feel really out of control."

Wade freezes, stunned. I'm stunned at what comes next, too.

"New rule, Pretty Boy. We're gonna fuck."

CHAPTER 13:
YOU WANT TO USE ME?

WADE

GABE HAS NO RIGHT FEELING THIS GOOD.

The cake mixture we exchanged is tasteless compared to her. She's a sweet, sweet torture in my arms and against my mouth.

She drinks everything I pour into her, and somehow, I'm the one drowning, drowning, drowning. And right when it's my last breath, she pulls me back to the surface.

I thought I'd get used to it. That the novelty would run out. I was wrong. So horribly, terribly wrong. And hard. Painfully, woefully hard.

Her moan travels straight down my dick. Twitchy bastard is gonna embarrass me. So, I keep her close, using her body to cover the boner. Gabe sends a silent, unspeakable rage my way.

God, I'm a douche.

I need everyone to leave right now so I can apologize. She can hate me later.

"Everyone good with taking their cake to-go?"

Skylar confirms, and the catering staff shove gift bags of cupcakes into their hands as they exit.

Which means Gabe Finch and I are finally alone.

In a fumbling blur, before the sorry can form, her hand traps my throat with the same exciting pleasure as the first time that one New Year's Eve.

I was overconfident—no, downright cocky—in thinking that my usual charms could wipe Gabe Finch's frown away. Landon and Indi warned me to stay away. But what did they know? I'd been trying to give her my condolences all season, but she wouldn't even look at me unless there was a mic in my face.

Ready to bury the ax once and for all, I approached her at the packed club with a drink.

"How's it going?"

She stared into the bottom of her nearly empty glass. "Fan-tastic."

"Listen, I didn't mean—"

"Respectfully," Gabe said flatly, cocking her head. "Fuck off."

"Wait, what'd I do?"

Her head shook. "Just go away."

The vodka tonic I'd downed set itself in motion. "Ohhhhhhh, I get it. You're still mad because I caught your shitty ex cheating."

Those hazel eyes ignited with pure hatred. "Get. Fucked."

At least her angst had disappeared. Mission accomplished. I couldn't help myself.

"Is that what you want from me? I'm all too willing—"

The next words are strangled. She'd gotten to her feet and grabbed me by the neck. In two strong strides, the back of my head hit the nearest wall.

"You couldn't pay me enough to sleep with you."

"We—wouldn't be—sleeping very much. At least—not 'til after..."

Her grip tightened, crushing my windpipe. I ducked with a choke, and the loss of air doubled my dick.

She'd unlocked something feral, something that made me follow her to the rooftop that night like a madman. It seemed I'd done the same for her because when I got up there, she fucking kissed me. She. Kissed. Me.

How am I supposed to free myself of her now? She can do whatever she wants to me. If she says, "Jump," I'll ask, "How high?" If she says, "Down," I'll kiss her feet, then lie back to let her ride my face into the floorboards. I can follow directions. Maybe she'll call me a good boy again.

"You're *infuriating*," she says through her teeth. "It's making me feel really out of control. New rule, Pretty Boy." Intense demand bores from her eyes. "We're gonna fuck."

Oh.

Beyond broken, my brain short-circuits and crackles with confusion.

Probably from the lack of oxygen. I wrap a hand around her wrist and push, garnering some relief. "I knew you liked me."

The hold goes lax, her jaw skewing to the right. "We don't have to like each other to fuck."

"Who said I don't like you?"

Rings of hazel diminish from her widened pupils as my grip glides up her arm. "You don't."

I softly karate chop the pit of her elbow to unlock the limb and step in her direction, regaining control. Or the facade of it.

"Don't I?" The next stride takes us closer to the perimeter of floor-to-ceiling windows encasing Ottawa's skyline. "You think I'd throw a party for a girlfriend I *don't* like?"

"You had to—" A short gasp sounds from her pretty mouth when her ass meets the glass. "And it's *fake* girlfriend."

My hands drop to reach for the arches of her hips. Our relationship is fake, but I need to know she's real. That this isn't a moment in another wet dream I'll be disappointed to wake from.

She allows the touch.

I stupidly move her hand from my neck to my chest, over the roiling beat of my equally stupid heart, tempted to ask if it *feels* fake to her. But I don't.

"I won't fuck you when you're sad."

"Get a grip, Boehner. You won't fuck me when I'm drunk, you won't fuck me when I'm sad. I'm starting to think maybe you don't want to fuck after all."

Tell that to my dick.

"And I'm not sad."

Fear flashes between us, and she moves her hand further south, relinquishing one tension but fueling another. The lightest contact on my groin has my cock leaking. I raise an eyebrow and hiss.

Gabe scoffs. "It's just sex. I thought you, king of all fuckboys, would understand."

"You know me so well, huh?" A facetious question, considering she's seen more of me than most. She continues to smirk.

"I know your hand must be tired from overuse."

A *ha* coughs from my throat. "No need to worry about my dexterity, Freckles. These bad boys are the money makers."

"Prove—"

I cut her off with a rough kiss, restraint slipping through my fingers like her lush curls and the deep cut of her dress. It leaves nothing to the imagination, her nipples already hard against the thin, soft material. I trace the neckline, teasing over one peak, then the other. Relishing how they tighten further under my touch.

"I'm dying to lick these tits." The admission is breathy and swallowed by another tongue-filled, angry kiss.

She bites my lip upon release and swats my hand away, placing it on her bare thigh. "Maybe later." A harsh yank against my nape forces our eye contact. "Get to work. I'm dry as a desert."

Our joined hands climb up the slit of her dress, soft, delicate skin against my fingertips, getting softer and softer the higher I go. They land on the edge of equally delicate fabric, then move lower. I gasp at what I find. She's warm. And so, so wet.

"You're such a little liar." Our noses slot together. "You've soaked through the lace. Have you been sitting on this all night or was it my kisses?"

"Mostly it was counting Donovan's abs through his shirt."

I stroke over the panties, spreading the wetness through the split of her pussy, eliciting a shaky exhale from her. "Lying through your fucking teeth." One finger pushes the fabric into the glazed slit, swirling around and homing in on her swollen clit. It pulses in response. The same finger swipes her panties aside and enters her pussy. She gasps again.

"Shit." Gabe sighs when my middle finger joins, the slow spearing making her squirm and angle her hips.

My hand stills. "Should I keep going?"

"Goddamn it," she laments into my shoulder. "Do I have to spell it out for you? Make me come already."

I tsk. "You gonna beg me for it?" A frustrated grumble mutes between our lips. I want to smear her lipstick, ruin it by having it all over me. It doesn't budge.

Still knuckles-deep inside her warm cunt, I spin her so she faces the glass and pull aside her dress. My hand disappears at the split of her legs. "Look at yourself—how perfect that pussy looks stuffed with my fingers." Another soft, desperate moan escapes. "Is that what you wanted? Getting finger-fucked at the window for everyone to see? You want everyone to know how you wish it was my cock?"

My dick shifts at being named. The fucking audacity. As if it isn't hard enough.

"Go ahead and finish all over them. So the whole city knows who makes this pussy come. Knows how mine you are."

"I'm not yours." She braces against the window, rebellious hazel eyes peering back. "And aren't these tinted?"

"Yeah, but the thought of everyone watching is getting you off, right?"

A disapproving groan and eye roll join her reply. "Not yet."

Her sass ends when the pads of my fingers push circles into the heated wall of her cunt.

"*Wade.*"

"You're such a terrible fucking liar. Literally soaking my hand while moaning my name and can't admit you like me."

"I don't."

"Then show me how much you hate me, Freckles." Circles of fog form where her open mouth sidles the glass. I scissor and stretch my fingers before quickening the speed of their thrusts. "Treat 'em like my cock and squeeze."

She obeys with a tighten.

"Go on. Come on my fingers."

Wetness coats my hand, every impatient movement drawing simpers. Her clammy palms and clawing fingers squeak against the smooth glass as a shudder wracks her body, vibrating against where my lips graze the curve of her ear.

"Stop."

I do.

Gabe sighs when I remove my hand. I'm tempted to lick my fingers clean like a hungry dog, but I don't. Not without her permission.

"What do you want?"

She doesn't respond, but her eyes reflect a mania. "*You're infuriating. It's making me feel really out of control.*"

"You want control?"

Hesitation preempts her slow nod.

There's no going back. Not for me.

"Tell me what to do." My hold loosens, and I backpedal. "You want to use me?"

Nothing new for Wade Boehner. I swear I was fated to have a big dick, enough talent to secure an eight-figure salary, and long bouts of loneliness: a perfect trifecta to be used for sex.

Her surprised glance follows the unsure gulp traveling down my throat.

"It's just sex," she repeats in a whisper. "Okay?"

Is it okay? Fuck no. But 'just sex' with her is better than nothing.

What's another lie?

"Okay."

With a pivot, her tentative steps click against the flooring until she's behind me. "And you'd do whatever I want?"

"Yes."

Her gaze flashes up from her feet when I also turn and halve the already short distance. Attention now fully on me, the uncertainty of her expression changes to determination.

"You can't do this with anyone else," she adds. "Only me."

As if I'd want anyone else.

"Only you," I promise.

Face brimming with victory and mischief, she scans left and right. "If you turn the lights all the way up, can people see in?"

"Yes."

For fuck's sake, say another word.

"Do it."

I don't question the command and simply pull my phone from my pocket to bring the space to its full brightness.

"Kneel."

Fuck, yes.

My fingertips reach upward, preparing to wrench the slit of her dress apart and gorge on her. "Fuck, Gabe. I've been dreaming about—"

She leans over to push her first finger against my parted lips. "Shut up."

Her clenched jaw relaxes while backing into the nearest sofa cushion, never breaking our eye contact. One slow tilt forward has her elbows resting on her spread knees, exposing her insanely long legs.

I'm a little surprised, a little scared, and really, really fucking turned on.

"Anything?"

"Anything," I answer. The next moment goes on forever before she breaks the silence.

"Crawl to me."

Crawl? I'm about to bark.

My fingers stick to the floor with remnants of her arousal every time my hands meet the hardwood, knees clopping with every tread.

She doesn't stop me until I'm nose deep in her damp, lace-covered pussy, then fists my hair, yanking and tilting my head back and replacing my nose with my mouth.

I groan out of pain and need.

"Now eat."

CHAPTER 14:
I STILL HATE YOU

GABE

I'M DRUNK WITH POWER.

And about to make a mess on Wade Boehner's couch from the way he stalks toward me. On all fours. Like an animal. Sinewy muscles flex and strain through his clothes with every stride. My confidence surges, soaring at the renewed sense of control. He's gonna pay.

How dare he put together a thoughtful party and make me feel like a fool?

I straighten when he nears, letting his nose brush against my soaked panties, then grab a handful of the messy waves atop his head to force him to look up.

"Now eat."

His eyes, those annoyingly pretty browns, gleam as he groans. He's enjoying this. I know I am.

I shove his face harder, grinding against his mouth. The combination of his moans and the friction of lace on my clit sparks jolts of pleasure.

"Is this your way of punishing me for ruining your birthday?"

I glower at his interruption.

"Because it's not much of a punish—"

"Goddamn it, Wade. Can you still breathe?"

"Yes."

"Then you're not trying hard enough. I'll accept whatever apology you come up with if you can make me come."

A determined wrinkle in his brow forms as he laps at the fabric, matching the speed of my rocking hips and shallow exhales.

"Take them off."

One of his large hands lifts to grab it, but I nudge him away with my knees.

"With your teeth."

The black mesh bunches in his mouth, his head shifting side to side to slip them off, scratching my thighs along the way. Buttons loosen on his shirt, the shine of sweat glinting across his chest and up his neck. My eyes stretch to take it in.

This might be better than having a puppy.

He adorns each ankle with a tender kiss when I lift my heels out of the thong, and I almost feel guilty. But there's no time for guilt because his lips—*how are they so soft?*—course up my calf and inner thigh, tightening my skin with goosebumps.

"Should I keep going?" he murmurs, closing into where I desperately want him again, fingering through those thick brown wisps and tugging him closer.

"Until I finish."

Swipe after swipe, he sucks and licks and sucks and licks. He eats like he kisses. It's greedy, thirsty.

My pussy throbs, aching for release. I reach for my shoulder and drop a strap, baring a hard and needy nipple.

Wade groans, eyes sagging with lust while watching me tweak and play with it, but his tongue doesn't stop. I half expect one of his hands to join. Instead, he strokes himself over his slacks with a grumble, then unbuttons them to reach inside.

The knot of pleasure deep within my core threatens to unravel.

"Did I say you could touch yourself?"

His hand returns to the floor with a whimper, mouth still at the soaked cleft of my legs. "Gabe, please. I need to come."

"Me first."

He goes back to noisily eating me out, the attention to my clit sending me in a spiral, barreling toward a blinding orgasm. My head tosses back with a whine, legs clenching around him as I reach the peak. The orgasm bursts, and I let go of everything.

My vision, my hearing. His hair. My control.

My balance, too, because I fall back.

Wade catches me by the nape, drawing me into a swarmy kiss. Aftershocks shiver through me as I taste my cum on him.

The high keeps me in a haze, relishing his wandering hands on my torso and warm mouth down my neck. I almost don't realize he's lifted me around him and walked us to his room.

He cradles me with the gentlest placement on his bed.

"Can I lick your tits now? Please?" He waits for my agreement before lashing at a peak. "Tell me you want me to."

My sigh comes out frustrated and impatient. "I want you to."

A satisfied sound follows, his eyes rolling back with pleasure as he tongues one nipple. The light graze of his teeth makes me shudder and arch from the mattress. "They're so fucking sensitive." He suckles the other side, caressing the exposed skin on my hips. "God, I wanna be inside you."

I moan at how his hard length brushes against my thigh and seethe at how good his hands feel.

The need to punish him returns with a vengeance.

"Do you think you deserve that?"

He answers with a whine. "Please, Gabe? Need to feel you."

Need? He *needs* me?

"*Yes*," I rasp.

I'm a weak woman with an even weaker resolve.

He mutters a *fuck* before pulling a condom from his back pocket and tearing it open, then undoes his pants entirely to sheath himself with a sigh.

"This doesn't mean anything," I remind him, propping up on my elbows.

He freezes. "What?"

"It changes nothing," I add. "I still hate you."

Wade chuckles. "You know, I didn't believe you before, but from the way you're fucking teasing me, I'm starting to."

"Good. Now you know where we stand." My foot docks at the hard plane of his torso, maintaining distance and dominance.

He submits, gently holding it, kissing the inner ankle, and toys with the heel strap. Something softens in my chest, and I hate that, too.

I push myself away. "Shirt. Off."

His compliance is eager and swift, and we keep our eyes locked.

"On your back."

"Oh, fuck *yes*—" He practically dives onto the top of the bed, pants catching at his knees as he gets in position. Large, grabby hands summon me.

I smirk. "Nope."

His excitement wanes, and those warm brown eyes round out like a sad puppy. "No?"

The bowtie on my laced-up bodice unravels with a deft tug, naked breasts and stomach on display, leaving the dress pooling around my hips.

"Hands on the headboard."

"Shit," Wade laments, baring his frustration by pulling on his hair but ultimately lifts his arms.

It's a necessary distancing. Because if Wade touches me, I'll feel...everything. And I'd rather be numb.

My knees climb over to straddle him, the toes of my shoes catching against the sheets. As I roll the dress fabric over itself, the heavy head of his cock sweeps through the seam of my pussy, and a hum escapes me.

Wade intakes a sharp breath when I reach between my thighs to fist his length. Veins in his neck bulge as I spread my legs further to line him up at my entrance.

He makes a tortured noise when my body resists his size, fingertips paling in the grip on the headboard. "Please, Gabe," he repeats. "Please."

I relax my walls with a sigh and push him through the wet flesh in a shallow thrust. We both gasp at the delicious stretch.

My hips find a slow rhythm, taking more and more of him with each stroke, hands seeking contact with my hardened nipples, switching between palming them in a rough squeeze and light pinches to their small peaks.

"*Yes*," Wade encourages. "*Fuck*."

I pick up the pace, wanting more praise, and relish what's before me.

He's glorious to watch, twisting with need and want. His defined arms bunch and tense, and his head tips back, panting moan after moan through those pink, bowed lips. Wade writhes as I ride, the speed of his cock hitting my G-spot and the friction on my clit driving the orgasm closer.

Eyes fighting to stay open, he flashes them to me with a warning. "If you keep going...I'm gonna come."

I stop touching myself to lean forward and cup his chin. "No. You'll come when I say you can" —my hips rise before sinking onto him again— "Be a good boy and wait for me."

"Make yourself come." He groans. "Use me to make yourself come."

A simple brush of a finger across my clit has the sensitive bundle throbbing. I moan out.

"Fuck, you take me so well." Wade squirms, the lowest part of his belly coiling as his knuckles go white and the sinews of his thighs shake under mine. "Fuck, fuck, fuck," he chants.

I teeter at the edge, tightening and tremoring around how full I feel. One more intense plunge bubbles my orgasm over, and I bolster myself on his thighs, back arched to its furthest ability.

It sends him bottoming out with a jolt, screaming my name so loudly, his grasp on the headboard so strained he tears it from the wall.

Sweaty, half-clothed, and spent, we crash together in a cloud of dust from the drywall, our hearts racing and chests heaving in the aftermath.

Wade catches my limp body again and rolls us over; his dazed chuckles muted through feathery kisses on my collarbone as my vision returns.

"We broke it." His smile presses into my skin. "Are you okay?"

Panic settles in. Sex with Playboy wasn't supposed to be intimate. It wasn't supposed to be caring or sweet. We're gonna have to stop all that.

"Of all the professional athletes," I say through a puffed breath, "I get into bed with one that has no stamina. What shit luck."

Wade scoffs and stretches my arms in a single hand above my head, pinning my wrists in his grasp.

"Just for that, I'm going to sit in this pretty cunt for a while longer." He rolls his hips in a sharp drive.

I hiss, still tender. "It's not my fault you can't last more than two minutes."

It was definitely more than two minutes.

"Some women would be flattered."

"*Ah*, yes. I'm beside myself at being another notch in your metaphorical bedpost."

The dazed, playful smile on Pretty Boy drops. "Don't ever say anything as stupid as that again."

My eyes slide to the left. "You expect me to be proud of being one of many?"

"One of many what, Freckles? You think I bring every girl to my bed?"

Doesn't he?

Wade sputters and shakes his head, releasing me and climbing off the bed to tie off the filled condom.

I cover my face with both hands.

Only you, Gabe Finch, would be insecure after putting a guy like Wade Boehner in his place. Get it together.

When I join him in the washroom, he's changed into black lounge pants and nothing else.

I shake the distraction away, then pee and clean myself up as he washes his hands.

He studies the sink. "I don't bring anyone to my home. Only hotels," he admits. "And they leave once they get what they want."

There's an unfamiliar longing in the darks of his eyes. My heart clenches.

"Girls don't stay here," he adds.

"I stay here, and I'm a girl."

Wade denies it, crossing his arms across that broad, chiseled chest and leaning against the doorframe. "Not some girl."

The edge of my mouth curls into a sneer as cool water rushes over my palms. "Right."

He doesn't blink. "Gabe."

I push past him back to the bedroom and unsuccessfully try to free myself of the lacing on the back of my dress.

"Are you always this defiant?" Wade lightly taps away my hands and loosens the ties. The chiffon falls away. He pulls a soft white shirt out of God-knows-where and fits it over my head, guiding my limbs and covering my sudden nakedness.

"And if I am?"

"That's too bad," he murmurs. "No worries, I'll find new ways to make you succumb."

"You're so full of yourself." It's aggravating, and somehow, *I'm* the one climbing into his bed and tucking myself in. What the fuck am I doing?

It's too late, and I'm too stubborn to back down. I have pride!

Or something.

"Try me." Wade shimmies below the covers and notches himself into the crook of my neck. He positions me around him, placing my arm over his shoulder and hooking my leg around his. "And don't lie and say that doesn't feel good."

I don't argue. I don't fight him. He's warm and firm. His heartbeat is steady against mine. Those strong fingers thread through my hair and massage hypnotic circles into my scalp.

Good? Yes.

What's worse is that it feels *right*.

Stop it. It's only sex, Gabe. Sex with aftercare.

"I still hate you."

"Hate me all you want, but don't move," he warns. "You accept my apology?"

Our breaths grow long and slow.

"Yeah," I say selfishly. He has nothing to be sorry for. I should be apologizing for being a dick the whole evening.

Wade hums into my skin. "You're the only woman who's ever stayed the night, Gabe Finch."

I am in the deepest of shit.

———

Pretending like I didn't sleep with Wade Boehner again is proving difficult. Pretending I didn't feel something this time, too? Even more difficult.

Mostly because he wouldn't stop texting me while we were separated this week, but partially because I just let him eat me out in the backseat of his new SUV.

"You didn't have to pick me up."

"What kind of boyfriend would I be if I didn't?"

Wade didn't need to know I was relieved by not having to drive the hour-and-half from Toronto to Kitchener alone after a long flight from Florida. Or that I kinda felt bad that he came down from Ottawa simply to get me.

"A fake one," I sniped back, chewing on a hangnail.

"You keep saying that, but the way you took my cock last week was very real."

I slapped his arm. "Shut up!"

"Make me."

My hand lifted to smother his pretty mouth, but he swerved the car, turning onto the exit ramp and parking at the far end of the visitor center.

"What the hell are you doing?"

He grabbed my throat with a firm but tender hold. "It's been a week since I've tasted you. Now make me shut up."

First, I shut him up with a kiss.

Then, with my crotch.

Wade firecrackers into a smile when he catches me staring. I roll my eyes.

"Trying to make a good first impression with my dad, are ya?"

"What do you mean?"

"You're wearing a cable knit." It makes me want to wrap myself in him, and I'm not sure which I hate more: myself, him, or the fact that I don't own that cute sweater. "And driving a Range Rover."

"So?"

"What happened to the Lambo?"

"Got rid of it."

"What! Why?"

He shrugs. "Saw Radek's and felt inspired. And I'll have you know, Jaeg made this for me."

"Jaeg? As in Derrick Jaeger?"

"Yep." A proud grin brightens his face.

"Huh."

"He's crocheted for years but took up knitting over the summer. Really bearing down on the whole ancient veteran player."

My nose wrinkles. "He's only a couple of years older than me. You calling me ancient, too?"

"No. You're perfect."

I fake-vomit and shove his shoulder, breaking his doe-eyed look. He giggles with his tongue caught between his teeth.

"*Ew.* Stop trying to be cute. It's nasty."

"Going down on you once wasn't enough, huh? I can get nasty again, really quick—"

"Shut up."

We reach the outskirts of Kitchener and pass the nursery sign on the road.

"Terra Bella," Wade reads.

The shared gravel driveway leads to the house I grew up in, now a faded purple. The paint on the white shutters is cracked and peeling from the weather.

Porch creaky, yard lawn overgrown, I frown at the state of the small farmhouse. Maybe it's because I'm not alone this time, but I'm embarrassed.

Kurt had only visited once during university and only dropped in for a short while before heading to his parents for Christmas. He didn't seem to care, but I doubt he even noticed.

A tall planter sits beside the door, a lone bamboo cane sticking out from its soil. Left behind, months after Gudi Padwa. At least he remembered to take in the gudi and kalash this time.

"What's that?" Wade asks.

I shush him, then knock and twist the door open.

"Dad?"

Sandalwood incense pours out, sweet and woody, the background recording of "Sukh Karta Dukh Harta" and the ringing ganthi signals his evening routine is well underway.

A tinge of anger sparks within me. Dad loved my mother—*loves her so much*—that years after she's gone, he's still upholding her faith, her traditions, her culture.

And she couldn't bear to stay.

When I was young, he did it for me so that I would know who I was. Who she was. But the grief was too great, and I rebelled. Accepting the part of my identity that was hers had been a lifelong battle. It was easier to ignore it and fit in.

Only after rooming with Indi at university did I even admit to anyone that my mom was Maharashtrian.

Poor Dad hasn't given up. He shares a soft smile and brings the thali to us, welcoming us by drawing three circles around us. "Go on. Take the Aarti."

My hands hover over the lit diya and pull its warmth to my eyes and over the crown of my head.

Dad offers it to Wade as well, who imitates me to near perfection. He returns it to the platform in front of Bappa's murti and bows with joined hands.

"Bala." His eyes brighten as long, open arms extend for an embrace. I step into it, absorbing his loving kisses on my forehead and cheek. "I've missed you. It's already been two months since Ganeshotsav."

"I missed you, too."

Wade clears his throat.

"Sorry," Dad says through a nervous laugh, letting me go. "Come on, bala. Introduce us."

"Oh, right." I usher Boehner forward. "This is Wade Boehner, my—"

Fake boyfriend. Who ate me out for thirty minutes roadside.

"Boyfriend," Wade fills in the blank for me, holding his hand out to shake.

"And this is my dad, Terry."

"Terry Fink," Dad adds.

"Nice meeting you, sir."

Wade's reply is curt, sparkle suddenly muted, all charisma, dimpled smiles, and social butterfly tendencies nowhere to be found. His free hand quickly clasps my hand and squeezes.

What is up with him?

"Please. Everyone calls me Tez. Good to finally meet you," he says with a toothy grin. "Wow. You athletes are always bigger in person than on TV." He waves us in, pointing where to take off our shoes and detouring through the kitchen to turn off the oven. "Sorry, didn't want to burn the butternut squash."

Dad leads the way to the back of the house, passing a wall of framed family pictures from over the years.

Baby pictures, various basketball rosters, graduation pictures. Every important milestone. The absence of Aai glares back.

My father stalls at the garlanded headshot of his late wife, plastic pink and white flowers circling her face. His fingers rest on his lips before pressing them against her encased cheek. He exhales.

I seek Wade's attention, but he's busy, silently studying the various trophies and medals on display in a glass case.

"I'll leave you two to get situated," Dad says, moving his eyes between me and Wade. "Meanwhile, I'll get dinner ready."

Without another glance, Wade leaves to get our overnight bags and my hand goes cold from the loss of his grasp.

I enter the kitchen and hug Dad from behind. He pats my hand on his chest.

"Soup okay, kiddo?"

"Always."

Not much of a cook, he made various soups and stews when I was younger, experimenting with various veggies and lentils. Now, it's become a Thanksgiving tradition.

"Things going well between you and Mr. Hotshot Goalie?"

You mean how they're not going at all as planned?

I don't intend to, but I flush. "Yeah." Instinct has me scratching my nose as if checking it didn't grow from the lie.

"He's quiet."

"I'm not sure why; he's usually not."

"Maybe he's nervous," Dad suggests, lifting a shoulder. "I don't want to get ahead of myself, but there's something special about him."

There is, isn't there? A small voice inside my head agrees.

The front door opens and closes with a whine. I motion with my thumb and Dad nods in understanding.

"I got it." Wade denies me my suitcase. "Where do you want me to put it?"

I may not like him, but I don't like him subdued, either.

"Upstairs, second door to the right."

"Mine, too?"

"Unless you want to share a bed with my dad."

Wade's lips stifle a smirk, and I'm almost disappointed at the lack of retort.

In the time I set the table and Dad brings out soup, salad, and a basket of bread, our guest approaches the dining area.

He politely answers Dad's questions about the upcoming season and makes small talk over dinner.

Totally natural, normal for most, but not Wade. It's unnerving.

Pretty Boy even washes up, thanking my Dad for dinner and banning us from the kitchen.

I recline on the couch, doom-scrolling on my phone until they both simultaneously reappear. Dad has an album under his arm.

Oh, no.

"It's that time again."

"*Dad*," I complain.

"Don't 'Dad' me. It's tradition."

"We don't have to."

"Don't have to what?" Wade asks, settling down next to me.

Dad mirrors him on my other side and plops open the photo album in my lap. "A trip down memory lane."

My heart seizes within its cage.

"That's Bela," he taps. "Love of my life." Light brown eyes peek from their corners at the camera, the young image of my mom donning a nauvari sari and embellished with traditional Maharashtrian jewelry: a bejeweled brahmani nath, thushi necklace, heavy jhumka and gold bangles, a giant dhol strapped to her torso. "Gabe's mother."

Wade's eyes narrow in question. "You're Indian?"

"Half."

"You look like her," he deadpans.

"Doesn't she?" Dad nudges his knee into mine.

"The freckles," Wade whispers.

Goosebumps rise across my arms.

"She led dhol tasha every chance she got." Dad's smile wanes. "Her parents cut contact when she immigrated here to pursue a Master's against their will. We met at an ISKCON event on campus. She was vibrant, a burst of light in the darkness I was escaping." His hand sweeps over a series of their wedding pictures. "My relationship with my family was already strained from leaving the church. Swedish Lutherans. They were so tightly wound, and there was so much life I wanted to experience. They completely severed ties when I told them I was going to marry her."

He pauses over a photo of their joint hands. "We only had each other, but it was enough." Images of her gardening with others appear. "Our community understood our search for love and acceptance. To belong."

A few faded snaps of the original greenhouse and farm come up. Rows of potted hibiscus, gardenia bushes, frangipani trees, jasmine, tiger lilies. None of them beam as Aai does.

"She was so naturally nurturing, spent hours caring for her plants. Friends and community, too. Always dropping off meals and herbal remedies to anyone who got sick or needed a little help. Never put herself first." He turns to another page. "And then..."

Welcome to the world, Gargi Bela Fink announces my birth on a banner at the top. Scrapbook style, there's a card with my height and weight next to a pink, swaddled newborn in her arms. Aai's face glows despite the weariness in her eyes.

Wade lowers his head and squints. "Who's...Gar-gi Be-la?" The enunciation cracks a smile.

"That's me."

"We named her after the great intellectual Sage Gargi and kept her middle name Bela after her mother, but she wanted to change it in high school, right before the prospects of playing university basketball came around."

I'd had enough of being called Gaggy and Gargle Fink Rat. The name change ultimately worked in my favor professionally and severed cultural roots in one fell swoop.

"Where did Finch come from?"

My father points to himself. "My last name, Fink. It's the Swedish word for finch." Dad sighs, melancholy and nostalgic, showing off photos of some of my milestones. First steps, first tricycle, first day of preschool. Aai blows out candles on a cake with me on my fourth birthday.

"We lost her shortly after." There's a guilty tremor in his voice as he keeps flipping pages, revealing more and more pictures without her. "She wasn't taking care of herself. And maybe I didn't take good enough care of her. It was a tough year."

Tears trickle down his face, slow and steady. He sniffles and wipes them away with the collar of his shirt.

My heart rate drops, blood retreats from my face, sending a shiver up my spine.

We do it every year, but I don't want to. Not today, not in front of Wade.

"Dad," I warn. "Please."

"It's okay, bala," he murmurs. "You never let yourself...it's okay to miss her. I miss her every day."

I hate the irrational feeling of missing her. I didn't even know her. I don't remember her. How can I miss someone I don't remember?

Any memories have been fed by these pictures.

Stymied grief regrows like a lizard's severed tail. It's heavy, threatening to suffocate and crush me under its weight.

Wade reaches across my back to palm my shoulder and pulls me to his chest, a silent invite to curl into him and let out every pent-up emotion. I shoot off a pleading look, but it's no use. His Adam's apple wobbles. Water clouds his eyes, too.

If I don't stand in the next three seconds, I'm going to come apart, and not in the way he's seen before. I fight the collapse.

A shallow sob exits my mouth, and I leap upright, excusing myself to the washroom.

I fumble to turn the venting fan on before slamming the toilet cover shut and plopping down. My head finds its place between my knees in an attempt to steady the sharp, gasping breaths.

A soft rap on the door cuts through.

Even softer is his tone. "Gabe, let me in."

I know Wade means the washroom, but I'm not ready to show him the worst part of me. The part I've sliced away, wanting to forget. Like an untreated wound, it festers, the infection too deep for the covering bandage to aid in its healing.

Feet shuffling to the door, I press my cheek to the wood and speak through it. "Just gimme a minute, okay?"

He sighs, vibrating the door. "Okay."

Tears dabbed away and fake toilet flush complete, I emerge to Wade's weak, concerned smile.

"Your dad wants to go to the greenhouse."

CHAPTER 15:
MR. CHARMING, MR. FEEL-GOOD, MR. CENTER-OF-ATTENTION

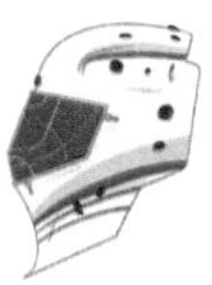

WADE

IT'S KILLING ME TO SEE GABE LIKE THIS.

I have no words of solace to offer her raw, reddened eyes or blotchy complexion from hiding her tears. I wish I could tell her I understand better than anyone what it's like to be left behind and never heal from those scars.

I don't let her ignore me, slipping my fingers between hers on our short walk back to Terry.

He claps his hands together before standing. "Let's visit the plant babies." His focus moves from his daughter to me. "I have an extra pair of boots for you." Terry peeks over his shoulder while walking to the door. "You can show Wade around and do your quarterly inspection."

Our hands remain clasped through the wet grass, rubber boots squeaking on the moss-covered pavers leading to the nursery.

Steel framing and the curved top of the opaque structure make up the classic hoop house.

Each of us ducks as we enter, the six-foot door slightly too low for our height. Hot, humid air greets us with a hiss.

"Welcome!" Terry beams.

Tropical plants and trees in crooked rows and irregular-shaped groups line the inside. Hoses attached to water barrels stretch across the length.

"We've got the palms over here, ferns and philodendrons over here, then the broad leaves like these giant elephant ears next to them. But monstera are more popular these days." His hand grazes over strawberry-shaped leaves that look clipped. "Hibiscus, plumeria, gardenia over there..."

It's so beautiful, the fragrance so sweet I almost can't breathe.

Like Gabe.

I turn to her, the growing ache in my chest needing relief, but she lets go of my hand, knocking the air out of my lungs.

Her steps take her to the furthest white flowering bushes, leaning down every so often to inhale.

Gardenia. Her favorite, like Indi said.

Terry sets his hands on his hips. "She's a tough one. My daughter will never admit it, but she loves this place as much as her mother did."

"You don't?"

"Nah. Until I met her, I did lawns, hedging, some basic maintenance. She was the one who loved flowers and tropical foliage. Said they reminded her of home. She taught me everything I know about them."

The name, Terra Bella, finally clicks. It's their names together.

He tilts his head to the left, motioning for me to follow him.

"And you kept it up?"

He blows a breath through his nose.

"Whenever I want to feel close to my wife, I come here and do what she loved. It's like having another day with her."

The man is hopelessly devoted. Gabe deserves that, too. What I lack in qualifications and experience, I can make up for in determination. I'm getting really good at faking the relationship. Maybe she'll accept the real thing.

"Watch this." Terry crouches next to a potted fern and sweeps a finger across its fronds. They close at the contact. "Sensitive plants. Bela called them 'touch-me-nots.'"

"Do they ever re-open?"

"Yes, but it takes time." He glances across the space toward Gabe.

"I can be patient," I say softly.

For her, I could be anything.

"Good," he adds with a chuckle as he straightens. "You're gonna have to be."

He shows me around some more, and I help Terry move some larger trees, straighten askew pots, and set up a misting hose. An hour passes.

Gabe clips yellowing and browned leaves from a palm. A serene smile graces her face. She's too lost in the practice to notice our approach.

"Bala?" Her dad interrupts. "It'll be dark soon. Wanna go in?"

"In a minute."

"I'm gonna make tea. Will you have some?"

Gabe hums mindlessly. "What kind?"

"Ginger with honey."

"Sounds good."

"What about you, Wade?"

"Sure, thank you."

He claps a hand to my shoulder and winks as he leaves. The door snaps shut behind him.

"He's gone," she says, still collecting wilted and dead leaves. "You can stop looking at me like that now."

"How am I looking at you, Freckles?"

"Like you feel sorry for me."

"I don't—"

"Save it."

My tongue clicks as I look skyward.

Time. Patience.

I give her space, too, trailing behind as we make our way back to the house. He puts on a kettle, and I excuse myself to the porch, citing a need to take in the twilight sky from the front steps.

Speckles of stars appear alongside a crescendo of chirping crickets.

I don't mean to overhear.

"You sent the poor guy out?" Terry lowers his voice to an audible whisper. "Are you two fighting?"

"He went on his own," she answers. "And we're fine."

My next sip hides my smile.

An unsure groan sounds out.

"I'm serious, Dad. He knows how important it is for me to have time with you. Alone."

"And I appreciate that, but..." There's a dull thud of a mug against wood. "I wanna get to know him, too."

Me?

"Yeah?"

"Mhm. Wanna know who's keeping my girl happy. He is keeping you happy, isn't he?"

I watch Gabe's cheeks pink through the screen door. She doesn't say anything. She doesn't have to.

I wouldn't say happy, but I'm doing something, and if the thought of whatever I am makes her blush? I can live with that. A knowing smile splits my face, and I set the mug down on the porch before jogging to the greenhouse to haul hay bales to fill the gaps in its outer perimeter.

An hour later—and after a cold shower—a rustle beyond the washroom door piques my curiosity, and I open it, gripping my toothbrush in my cheek.

Big mistake. Gabe's perfect ass appears above her jeans as she pulls them down.

My jaw loses its hold. The brush sags, sliding quickly.

She snaps, jolting me from the hypnotic trance. *You're staring*, she mouths.

How can I not?

Through tight, pursed lips, she silently motions for me to get back to the sink. Meanwhile, she steps into pajamas, her endlessly long, toned legs and aforementioned perfect ass now hidden.

I whine and gargle before switching spots with her, then go lie on the mattress, searching for answers on the closed washroom door.

Physical confrontation on the ice? Got it.

Emotional confrontation, anywhere? I clearly have no idea what I'm doing.

She faces away when joining me on the bed. Expected. I wait a moment for her to get comfortable. While I could admire the angles of her shoulder blades forever, I need to do this.

"Gabe?"

She sighs. "What?"

I lower my voice. "Why didn't you tell me?"

"You'll have to be more specific."

"About your mom."

"Because I didn't want to have this conversation with you."

My eyes go cartoonishly cross-eyed as the heel of my hand bounces off my forehead.

Of course, why didn't I think of that?

She really thinks I'm stupid. Can't blame her, though. I am a total idiot for this woman.

"Makes sense," I surrender. "Am I allowed to spoon you?"

A long pause follows.

She answers without looking back. "Only if you keep your dick away from my ass."

"You'd like that too much," I mutter.

"What'd you say?"

"Nothing."

Loose waves move aside at my hand, and I nestle up until our torsos and legs line up. Gabe's cool, exposed skin gives me goosebumps. I wiggle my hips.

"Will you cut it out?"

"It exists, okay?" My arm tightens around her waist. "Can we sleep?"

"Fine."

Her breaths grow deep and slow in the next few minutes, but I can't sleep a wink.

All I can think about is how Gabe's wearing a mask, too. Hers is the opposite of mine: poised, perfect, held together for her dad. Protecting herself from any more hurt. I'm dying to know what's underneath the athletic accolades and career wins, and imagine what I'd do if she ever let me see it.

———

Teary goodbyes in the morning have the pit of my stomach growing.

I stand by the Rover, literally kicking rocks. Watching them feels like an invasion of privacy. I curse to myself while averting my eyes, drawing my attention to the unkempt lawn and land surrounding the greenhouse. In the daylight, it looks worse than the night before, despite my best efforts to tidy the line of hay bales.

The initial leg of the drive back to Toronto is eerily quiet, except for Gabe's typing. She switches between checking the connection on her phone and drafting emails on her laptop. The GPS breaks the monotony by announcing there's traffic ahead on the 401.

"Ouch." I move the screen to view our route: a crimson line nearly the rest of the way. "Since we're trapped together for an extra hour, wanna try to have a decent conversation?"

"That probably requires decent company."

I give her a suggestive smirk. "Oh, I see. You *wanna* be indecent—"

"Shut up, Wade."

"No can do. You gonna tell me what happened with your mom?"

She snaps her laptop closed, shooting poison darts through an angry glance. "You don't know anything about me, Boehner! Quit acting like you do."

My heart clenches. She's not wrong. I gulp.

"And what's *your* deal? You went sullen and distant the minute we got there."

Not wrong at all.

Nothing like seeing a loving relationship with her dad to serve as a painful reminder of the father who wanted nothing to do with me.

Gabe continues her rant. "You're always Mr. Charming, Mr. Feel-Good, Mr. Center-of-Attention otherwise. You couldn't keep things light instead of the annual sobfest my dad tries to make it?"

I don't reply.

"So much for decent conversation." It's her final jab before we spend the remainder of the drive in total silence.

She works through her phone. My jaw ticks every few minutes, holding back everything I want to say. How amazing it is that she has a dad who gives a shit. That I know better than anyone how deeply rooted her anger and grief are because I go through it, too. That I'm fucking trying my best to get through to her, but I've never done that for anyone, and I'm failing miserably.

"I'm flying Air Canada." Her mindless statement comes without eye contact.

The line of cars backed up at every terminal due to holiday travel doesn't stop the paparazzi. There are cameras already waiting for us at the curb.

I know we signed up for publicity, but if it didn't give me all of these chances to get close to Gabe, it'd be so fucking annoying.

My tongue wets my lower lip as I turn to her. "Kiss me goodbye, Freckles."

Her mouth hangs open, eyes pulling into a furious glare. "*Excuse* me?"

Insolent brat. My impatience gets the better of me.

I notch my hand around her throat, drawing her to my mouth. "They're watching. Now kiss me."

I might die if you don't.

She responds by mirroring my position, her palm squeezing my neck more firmly than my grip. Our lips crush together, heated and hateful, groaning and moaning every emotion between us. It's as if she's simultaneously trying to drain the life out of me with her hand and bring me back with the ferocity of this kiss. We battle in tongues and teeth and Gabe wins, releasing me with a rough bite to the lip.

And I live on.

————

Three days. I'm out of fucking sorts after three days of no contact with Gabe.

She didn't cover yesterday's game here at home and only reacted with a thumbs-up when I asked her if she made it to Dallas.

Did I watch her coverage of that game alone at home later? Yes. Do I care if that's pathetic? Hell no.

Thank God, Calgary played like shit, and our d-men handled anything that got past center ice because my head was not attached to my body. It was up in the clouds dreaming of Gabe Finch's perfect body riding my cock until I tore the headboard off.

My focus is so poor that Landy got a puck past me at scrimmage.

He taps my helmet with the blade of his stick when we get to the lockers. "What's up with you, Boner?"

I huff while escaping the cage of my mask. "I'm in a mood."

His eyebrows rise, and his eyes widen as he sputters. "I heard. The girls are best friends, they talk. What do you expect?"

Sweat-soaked strands stick to my forehead. I slough the hairs away by ruffling my hand through it. "Did you know Gabe's mom died?"

"Don't pull me into this, man. Indi already gave *me* shit *for you* being an ass to Terry. Like, how is this my fault?"

"I wasn't an ass. I was trying not to get in the way."

"Doesn't matter, 'cause that's not how it came off, apparently."

"She's lucky she has a dad."

"Whoa." He holds up a reeking glove before throwing it off. "That's a fucked up thing to say."

"Yeah, well...Some of us *are* fucked up."

Landon tuts while I unlace my skates. "We're all fucked up. We're all traumatized. Still not an excuse to be a jerk."

The ceiling comes into view as my head hangs back. "She won't talk to me."

"You could go apologize in person. She's back in town."

"She is?"

She's been ignoring me? She's been ignoring me!

"Jesus, do you two talk or what?"

Knife. Twist.

"Last night," he confirms with a confused nod. "If she's as pissed off as I think, don't tell her I told you. I like my balls attached to my dick, thank you very much. I overheard Indi canceling their barre class plans, which will start" —he squints at the analog clock on the wall— "in an hour. I'll text you the address."

A map link to Barre None appears in my messages.

"Hey, I know that place. We went there during dry land."

I haul ass in the Rover to the studio, giving absolutely zero shits that I'll probably be the sacrificial lamb in Gabe's forthcoming murderous rampage.

After buttering up the desk staff with a few selfies and autographed jerseys, they let me into the studio.

Gabe extends her endless leg on the handrail at the teacher's instruction, and my mind goes right down the gutter. As if it could be anywhere else when her leggings and cropped top show off every curve and line of her incredible body.

I'm a lost cause, already imagining all the filthy ways I could have her, here, like this. Me on my knees, her ankle high up on the barre, or knee hooked over my shoulder, wet cunt on my mouth, then pulsing around my fingers and cock.

Her eyes enlarge with surprise and narrow in rage.

The size of my grin at winning her attention makes my cheeks hurt. I stride towards her.

"What the fuck are you doing here?" she says under her breath.

My hand reaches for hers, mouth hungry to kiss her knuckles, only leaving a sliver of space between our bodies before my lips brush over the hard ridges. Hushed sighs and *aww*'s fill the background.

"Surprising my girlfriend," I whisper back.

She rolls her eyes closed before the glower returns.

"And it doesn't have anything to do with how much you're enjoying all these women fawning over you?"

"Which women?"

All I see is you.

"The ones who are tittering and falling over themselves."

I shift, molding my free arm around her hips. "Who cares about them?" The shell of her ear wafts my hot breath back at me. "I'm only interested in you falling apart for me."

She wears a fake smile and dryly laughs with her shoulders. "Whatever."

I dig my chin into the crook of her neck.

"Hey, Miss Diana," I greet the older instructor. Gabe shoots over a look of disbelief as she lets go of our embrace. "What?" I shrug. "The goalies train here sometimes."

"Here? At the barre?"

"Gotta stay limber during the off-season. Mind if I join the class?"

Miss Diana frowns, pulling her wrinkles downward. "I'll allow it."

I wink in thanks before facing Gabe's back.

The instructor continues with her directions.

I use the handrail to maintain balance while stretching my leg up and keeping it there. "Miss Diana is a hardass."

"*Shh*!"

After the series of battements ends, I try again.

"Why didn't you tell me you were back in town, Freckles?"

"Onto the wide leg bends!"

She groans through her teeth. "Why do you insist on annoying me?"

"Plié!"

"Why won't you answer my question?"

"Plié!"

"Why do you keep answering questions with other questions?"

The volley of whisper-yells gets us in trouble.

"Out." Miss Diana points to the door, her body straight as a pole. "Both of you."

Gabe goes red. I'm jealous it's not for the reasons I want it to be.

We gather our things without another exchange, and she lets me walk her to the car, smiling politely behind her sunglasses. This time, she pulls me in for a short, chaste kiss. She keeps me close, nails digging into my nape, donning a sinister, saccharine grin.

"Leave me alone. And for fuck's sake, don't follow me."

The feathery stroke of her fingers against my cheek has my cock aching as she gets into her car and drives off.

I'm going to have to send her my therapy bill.

I stop by Au Lait and treat myself to a double espresso, a far cry from the Timmies double-double's I'll have to endure over the next couple of weeks. Driving through Ottawa has become so routine that I don't even realize I'm already in my building's parkade when my phone beeps with an unknown alert sound. It's the security cameras at the penthouse.

Suspicious activity?

Instinctively, I grab a paddle from my gear bag in the trunk, ready to beat the living hell out of whoever or whatever is in there.

Sneaking into my own place was not on my bingo card for the day, but here we are. The notifications keep beeping, and I tsk, silencing the phone so as not to alert the intruder.

A gust from the ventilation system slams a door shut behind me. I jolt.

The living room is untouched, and no one's in the kitchen, but a strange noise sounds from my closed bedroom.

The fuck?

"*Oh, God,*" the voice moans.

I press my ear to the door.

Gasps. Whimpers. Buzzing.

Oh, my fucking God.

I fumble to unlock my phone to open the security app.

Lo, and behold. I can hardly believe it, but the camera doesn't lie.

Gabe Finch is playing with herself on my fucking bed. And she isn't alone.

CHAPTER 16:
LOOK AT THE MESS YOU'VE MADE

GABE

SLEEPING WITH WADE BOEHNER ONCE WAS FINE.

Twice? Huge mistake.

Between those two times and the way he eats me out like it's his job, it's all I can think about.

Him strutting in, in a stupid Ottawa Regents tee seemingly custom fit to his stupid muscular build and stupid hoochie shorts showing off his toned quads, doing stupid pliés in Barre class? No help at all. The whole hand-kissing, waist-gripping, and longing whispers had me so riled up that I wondered if I should be committed.

Instead, I work on getting myself off with Mr. Darcy in Pretty Boy's bed, hoping he shows up in time to see me finish.

I sink the firm, bubblegum pink silicone toy into myself over and over but can't seem to find a satisfying rhythm.

My mind wanders to his control at the barre. Of course, he's strong and flexible. He's a professional athlete. Those hip and groin stretches hockey players do on the ice? Goalies are a different breed. The man can do the splits with fifty pounds of gear on, no sweat.

Which means fucking me deep would be a piece of cake.

"Oh, God," I groan as the dildo vibrates past my G-spot, searching for the spot higher up.

The fantasy replaces the memory of riding him until he tore the previous headboard off.

That does the trick. I speed up the vibration and press the fake dick's tip into my clit. I moan.

My head whips back to the new headboard, the coil of pleasure tightening low in my core.

"Wade..."

Thud-thud-thud!

I whip forward and nearly lose control of the vibrator at the banging.

"Gabe!" an angry Wade yells behind the door.

All hope for an orgasm is gone. I plot vengeance through a growl.

"Who is it?" I call back in my sweetest tone, knowing fully well who it is. "I'm kinda busy right now." My haste omitted panty removal. The flimsy, tangled lace looks fucking ridiculous shrouding the pink cock.

"No shit! I can see you fucking yourself on the security camera." A black lens in the corner shifts and zooms with a buzz. "Open the goddamn door!"

"*Ugh*, you're a creep." I drive the toy in and out of my pussy rapidly and fake moan, eyes rolling for good measure. Men can't tell if it's the real thing anyway. "If you—can see me," I say through exaggerated, high-pitched *oh*s, "then you know—I can't open it."

"I swear to God, I'll fucking break it down," he shouts. The door and its frame shudder, and I'm wetter.

"I'm so close," I whine. "So, so cl—"

The lock gives, flinging the door open. A sweat-covered Wade stands within the warped frame, keeping the door wide. I part my legs further, giving him a better view, the stretched nude lace now limp across the back of my hands. His eyes grow, mouth agape.

"Go away," I complain with a whine. "You're ruining my orgasm."

You big lying liar.

He looks to the ceiling with a shake of his head. "Fucking fuck. That's not what it looks like." His tongue swoops forward to his full lower lip as if he can taste me from across the room. "Is this payback for getting us kicked out of class?" he says, breathless. "Because I promise you, it's more like a reward—"

I don't want to think about why Wade Boehner cares or why it matters to him what happened to my mom. Definitely don't wanna be thinking about her right now. There are feelings to be avoided. Orgasms to be had. Or *an* orgasm, at least.

So I knock the head of the toy against the front wall of my pussy, hitting two spots at once, and cry out a whimper, flushing all other thoughts from my brain.

One of his hands squeezes his cock through tented shorts. "You're fucking killing me, Freckles."

"Yeah?" I pant. "Show me how much." My gaze drops to his grip. "Pull it out."

His waistband snaps below his balls, upright dick fully engorged.

"Touch yourself," I demand.

Wade responds with a firm stroke, then thumbs over the ripe cherry red crown with a hiss.

"Faster."

"You too." He whines. "I wanna watch you come all over my bed again."

"Good boys ask nicely." A shiver runs through him. "You like that? Being called a good boy?"

"*Fuck*, yes. Call me whatever you want. Just don't stop." His jaw ticks as his grasp tightens, pumps matching my pace. "Please?"

Something about the raw, vulnerable need in his tone and pants-down, cock-out stance stokes the fire of pleasure. It sears through me. "Please, what?"

"Please let me watch you come on my bed." He can barely get the words out. "Keep playing with that pussy."

I yelp and hold the vibrator at a delicious angle, continuing to slide it through me.

"Fuck," Wade groans, his hand moving frantically.

This idiot makes me lose any semblance of sense.

"Tell me how much you hate me again, Freckles."

A garbled noise escapes my throat as pleasure waves through, ready to drown me.

"And don't lie. I can hear how wet you are."

"I'm gonna come," I say through gasps. "But you don't get to."

His hand drops, but his cock doesn't. It bobs mid-air as Wade scrubs the torture on his face and yanks at his hair.

My walls tighten around the silicone shaft, eyes screwed shut. The pleasure peaks as I arch through the high with a scream. I tremble through the steady vibrations of the toy, then relax into the gray cushioned headboard, sighing in content when I pull it out.

Pretty Boy sobs out a laugh. "Maybe you're right. Maybe I do hate you."

Through the daze, a surprisingly sinister idea forms. "You're about to hate me even more."

I abandon the dildo on the mattress and walk the line to Wade, peeling away my sports bra from its sweaty skin. My nipples relish the attention of his gaze.

His throat clenches, like the hands at his sides.

I kneel.

Pre-cum leaks from his tip.

"Better not let that go to waste." I offer my hand. "Can I?"

He rapidly nods.

I fist the base of his cock. "You want my mouth, Pretty Boy?"

"Your tongue, too." The rushed-out ask gulps down the stiff column of his neck.

"*Tsk*. So greedy." I lick the drop away. Wade's eyes flicker shut, his stable posture teetering the short stride to the wall behind him. "Maybe I'll stop."

The lie tastes as salty as he does.

"Please—don't."

Heat and warmth flood the space between my legs, panties doing nothing to contain it. My lips wrap over the swollen head, suckling before leaving it with another lick of his dripping slit. "More?"

"More," he begs. His hands grip the wall.

I study his cock's thickness and weight in my hold with a twist. Wade hisses and whimpers.

One of my hands rises to his bare hip, the other guiding his to my nape, pushing his fingers through the tied hair there.

I take in an inch, then another, letting him glide deeper and deeper. Ridged veins spread his pre-cum over my tongue. It drips down my throat, and I swallow.

"Fu—*fuck*—" Wade stills, gushing the most delicate gasp out when he's slotted all the way in, my nose buried in the wispy trail of hair above his throbbing cock. I put his free hand against my pulse so he can feel himself there. "Your mouth..."

When I shift off, he thrusts in, and I allow it, allow him to wrap my ponytail around his wrist and fuck my mouth as he likes. I suck and gag as he speeds up, moan after unsettled moan flowing out of him.

"Your mouth was made for me to fuck."

I thrill at the filth. My hand slips under the sagging waistband of my destroyed panties and plunge two fingers in without resistance.

Eyelids heavy, Wade peers down at me. "Hell, yes. Get yourself off."

I'm so close it hurts, and I manically rub my clit, struggling to breathe through my nose.

"You're fucking gorgeous with your mouth full."

The orgasm explodes unexpectedly as I choke on him. Muttered curses grate through his teeth, sloppy movements signaling me to finish what I started.

I don't, though. The alarm on my phone telling me to get ready for work rings.

I retract with a pop.

Wade gargles a *no*, jaw locked open at the lost orgasm.

My knees push from the floor to stand, satisfied with the state he's in.

Good. Let him get a taste of the frustration.

"Gotta go. Procrasturbating is no excuse to be late for work."

I step out of the ruined panties and *tsk*. "Look at the mess you've made." The arousal-doused lace sticks where I crumple it in my palm. "I have a right mind to make you clean it up."

His mouth practically waters at the suggestion. I cup his chin and deny him. "Maybe next time you can taste me. Right now, you'll have to settle for tasting yourself."

He quivers when I give him a tongue-filled kiss but doesn't come.

A double pat to his cheek doles out my approval.

"Good boy."

Wade crumbles, shuffling forward while pulling up his shorts and face-plants into bed. His flattened palm slaps the sheeted surface as if tapping out of a wrestling ring.

I gloat.

I won.

"That was fun, Pretty Boy. We'll have to do this again."

He puts up two fingers in a weak salute, still face down.

This entire exchange puts me in such a good mood, I sing in the shower and get dressed while whistling an upbeat refrain. Wade remains in his face-down position as I zip up my gym bag.

"You alive?" I poke one meaty buttcheek from the side.

His words muffle from within the mattress. "Barely, no thanks to you."

"You regret telling me to use you now, don't ya?"

Wade's chest rises and falls through an extended breath. I brace for him to tell me to fuck off and never come back. That he's done dealing with me.

But clear as day, he says, "Not even a little bit."

Pride floats me right to my car.

Almost to the parkade exit, I reach for my phone to text Mel, letting her know I'm on my way but running a few minutes late, screeching to a halt when I realize it isn't there.

Damn. I must've left it on the nightstand.

Mumbling a string of *fucks* to no one but myself, I re-park and rush back into the building, snickering at the memory of denying Wade a proper finish.

I punch in the key code and jog to the bedroom, hoping to make a quick exit. But I am horribly unprepared for what I find instead of my phone.

Wade Boehner. Stark naked. Leaning against the same spot on the headboard as I'd been. Massive, hard cock in hand, a familiar nude lace bunched around the erect length. Moaning with every stroke. His mouth envelopes something pink.

My car keys fall to the floor in a sharp clang. My mouth joins them.

"Back to torment me some more?" He spits the toy out and motions to its lifeless form next to him. "I cleaned up your mess."

A knot lodges itself in my throat. His desperation—*holy fuck*. My fresh panties are in danger.

His eyes sparkle, lips tilting up in one corner, continuing to pump my used, cum-soaked panties down his length.

It's aggravatingly hot.

"Well? What'll it be, Freckles? You gonna stand there and stare, or you gonna sit on this cock and ride me until you're spent?"

CHAPTER 17:
WANNA SEE SOMETHING COOL?

WADE

GABE DOESN'T CHOOSE EITHER OPTION.

"Finish," she whispers, folding a knee to sit at the edge of my bed, her other leg rooted to the floor. "Go on." Short trim nails encourage me with a scrape against the skin of my inner ankle. Goosebumps spread like wildfire up my legs. My balls recoil, hand moving rough, frenzied, relentless, chasing the much-needed high Gabe finally permits. The friction of the fabric, her heated gaze on me—it's too much.

I explode into the lace with a spine-curling jolt, hurling an open-mouthed grunt. My vision pinholes to black. The ringing in my ears wanes as I scramble to regain control of my galloping heart rate and runaway breaths.

She fixes her eyes on my groin while I use her panties to clean myself off.

"You were...sucking on my dildo."

And I'd do it again.

Fear of judgment flashes through my brain for a moment, but there's not an ounce of it in her tone or expression. Only awe.

"How else was I supposed to taste you?"

Pink deepens to scarlet across her face, hiding her freckles. Those swollen, pretty lips hang open.

"Here." I lean forward to push the soiled, balled panties into her gaping mouth, covering myself with a corner of the bedsheet. "Taste us for yourself."

Eyes fluttering shut, a loud groan accompanies her surprised quiver. I scoop her into my lap. "Shhhh," I say into her ear. "Those soft, perfect noises are for me, and me only."

Watery hazel hues stare back as she grazes her lips over mine. The quickest thrust of her tongue forces the lacy pair into my mouth. I echo her groan and lick the panties clean while pulling them out, the salty and sweet combination eliciting another spark of pleasure low in my gut.

Gabe slinks from the bed to let me up. My thumb swipes a streak of cum from her bottom lip into her mouth before I go to the washroom.

I check in on her before showering, but she's gone.

ME

You left??

FRECKLES

I was running super late.

FRECKLES

But that was…something.

ME

Can we talk about it?

FRECKLES

When?

ME

How's tonight sound? Over dinner?

FRECKLES

Isn't there a post-game team dinner?

ME

They won't miss me this once

ME

I'll eat with them before

Three dots bounce on the screen.

FRECKLES

Fine. Where?

ME

My place

FRECKLES

Hmmm. Depends on what you're ordering.

ME

No takeout

ME

I'll make you dinner

The dots flicker faster this time.

FRECKLES

Are you gonna poison me?

ME

And kill off the best pussy I've ever had? Not a chance

FRECKLES

Flattery will get you nowhere.

ME

It got you into bed with me

ME

I'll take my chances

ME

Just say yes

The next moment feels like forever.

FRECKLES

Yes.

I hurl myself into the air, dropping the phone onto the bed and raising my arms overhead in victory. "Yes!" One hand clasps the tuck of my towel while I do a little jig, then collapse back-first onto the mattress, checking my phone once more. I sigh and clutch the phone to my heart. "She said yes."

ME

See you soon

FRECKLES

In hell.

ME

This sounds like a date

ME

I accept

My giant smile won't subside as I dial up my favorite insider. The line rings twice.

"Hey, Wade!"

She's more chipper than usual. I'm not complaining. This bodes well for me.

"Hey, Indi. I have a favor to ask."

"What's up?"

"*Um*," I scratch a spot along my hairline under my ear. "So, I'm making dinner for Gabe tonight."

"*Aww*. That's really sweet."

"Yeah, well..." My laughs stutter out. "I was wondering if you'd help me make her favorite Indian food."

And also, I'm hoping you tell me what that is.

"Oh, boy. You're asking the wrong person."

Shit.

"Radek says you've gotten better at cooking."

"That's true, but…"

"Please?"

She hums. "You're making shahi paneer?"

Score!

"*Uh*, yes."

"Okay, bud. I have a secret for you."

"Yeah?"

"That's not her favorite."

"It's not?"

"No. It's mine. When we roomed together at university, I'd order take-out from this restaurant called the Taj. She'd always let me order shahi paneer for us to share because she knew that at home, my younger sisters got to choose."

My heart melts.

"She acts like it doesn't matter, but it mattered to me. Gabe loves matar paneer—*it's the same dish, but with peas*—but I *hate* peas. She wouldn't let me eat something I hated because she knew I didn't have the option with my siblings. We're the same age, but she's the big sister I never had."

"Why is she the best?" I intone through a sigh. "So how do I make it?"

"I only know of one person who can help you."

———

I side-eye Maddie and give her and her phone camera a nice stinky face wash on the way onto the ice for warmups. I'm the last one out, but I scan the already-buzzing crowd to find the only person that matters to me right now.

And there she is.

On the far side of the rink, Gabe is surrounded, one girl primping her hair while another does her makeup. I skate up and glide to a stop, spraying ice onto the glass and scaring her unsuspecting camerawoman.

Time to turn up the charm.

I clear my throat.

She stops adjusting the large lens.

Mask tipped up to the top of my head, I wink at her. "How's it going, Denise?"

She tightens her top knot and smooths down her undercut. "Sup, Boehner?"

"Could you get my girl for me?"

"What's in it for me?"

"The delight in knowing your friend is happy?"

"Emotional blackmail. I like your style." She shakes a silent finger gun in my direction. "*Psst*. Finch. Your boyfriend's here."

Gabe's eyes stay shut as the cloud of powder and hairspray evaporates. She signals for her staff to stop working with a held-up finger and glances my way.

I wave excitedly, wearing a lopsided smile.

Her eyebrow perks. "Yes?"

"Wanna see something cool?" My tongue stretches to grab the collar of my jersey below the league's logo. I catch it between my teeth, and I tug upward, then side to side, letting out a short growl.

Denise's cheeks puff before she splits into laughter.

Gabe's irritation seeps through an unnatural grin. My balls retreat into my gut when she leans forward. Her mouth is unbearably close to my jaw, breath tickling the stubble lining it.

And I'm hard.

"You're a dog, you know that?"

I startle her with a bark. "I'll be whatever you want."

The girls holding hairspray and makeup brushes giggle and snort behind her.

That gorgeous red tinges her cheeks and fills her eyes with a fire. "Did you need something?"

I wet my lips to loudly proclaim, "One pre-game good luck kiss, please!"

She *hmph*s. "Never needed one before."

"Radek gets one every time."

"It's Davé-Radek," she corrects.

"Right, right. You sayin' you wanna share a last name?"

"I didn't—"

"'Cause I'll propose right now—"

Her teeth gnash behind those pink-painted lips. "Shut up."

"I didn't hear a 'no.'"

"You're. Crazy."

"Still not a 'no,'" I sing.

Every word is hissed through her teeth. "One. Kiss."

The crowd's cheers crescendo. Denise snickers, pointing her camera at us. The Jumbotron displays our exchange. A series of LED hearts throb and dance on screen around us.

Pew pew pew pewwww, an air horn blares in a staccato.

"Try not to roll your eyes," I warn. "You have to pretend you like this."

She's a fantastic actress. Or maybe she actually likes it.

Pulling back and switching the placement of her mouth with her hand, she cups my cheek and presses her lips to mine.

The surrounding cacophony deadens. Air struggles to enter and exit my lungs, but I deepen the connection, attempting a quick taste by dipping my tongue into her mouth. A single, slow, teasing slash from her isn't enough. She breaks the kiss, and my eyes remain shut, an unintentional quiver traveling down my chin.

No matter how hard she stifles it, there's a joy tugging at her lips. She balls my jersey in her tight fist to whisper into my ear.

"You're gonna pay for this."

A chuckle escapes. "Oh, Freckles. I'm banking on it." I give her cheek a loud cartoon smooch. "*MUAH!*"

The sound system plays the intro beats of "*Billie Jean*" by Michael Jackson, and I knock my helmet over my face as if it's the King of Pop's fedora, then moonwalk back toward the rest of the team, gaze steadfast on her. Landon whoops when I pass by but skates alongside.

"You're a goner."

"I know. My girl loves it." I give her another goofy smile and wave across the ice. Everyone else thinks she's ignoring me, but I don't miss her downward pointing middle finger from her jacket sleeve while chatting with another reporter.

"Thank God, they tolerate us." He looks longingly at Indi. "I don't know how I ever lived without my wife."

Colorado plays like ass, giving many opportunities to show off for Gabe. Their center, a little shithead named McKay, rounds the net to drop in a Michigan, but I extend a leg up to the T-bar and block it. Jaeg shoves

McKay from the crease, and Fletch takes off with the puck. I jump to do a split and point my paddle at Gabe. "Whoo!"

By the end of the second period, we're up 5-0, and Coach finally benches me to give Unger some playing time now that he's cleared from that pesky knee injury. Fletcher's taking a breather, too.

"I still can't get over how puffins mate for life."

"Christ, Donovan." I elbow him. "Chill with the animal videos."

A rogue puck makes it over the boards, and I interrupt him by catching it. I pump my eyebrows and hold it up like a trophy, winking at a gawking Gabe Finch. My lips purse, and I blow her a kiss before tossing the puck back to the ref.

The fans lap it up. My girlfriend looks like she's going to burst into flames at any second.

It's a shutout, and we win by six.

Gabe skips over me to interview Fletcher about his goals tonight, and I have to pretend not to be disappointed. Whatever. She's gonna be eating my food, sucking my dick and sleeping in my bed tonight, so Fletcher can wheeze out his rehearsed replies all he wants.

I head home after cooldowns and don't have to face Gabe ignoring me in the press room.

"Tomato-onion gravy, diced paneer." Mentally checking off the recipe step, I add the latter to the former in a wide-mouthed pot.

The round of paratha dough taunts me from its mixing bowl. I rub my hands together and split it into ten even balls and glare when one goes oval between my pressed palms.

From oval to square in five seconds flat.

"Flatbread, not square bread, knucklehead."

It rumples when I ball the dough up again.

Indi's mom made it look so easy. *A western rolling pin is fine*, she said. *It doesn't have to be a perfect circle*, she said.

"Yes, it does, Mrs. Davè," I say to myself. "It has to be perfect for her."

I repeat the exercise no less than a dozen times until a circle forms. "Fucking *finally*."

The pan sizzles when the paratha slaps onto its hot surface.

First paratha? Raw.

Second paratha? Burnt to a crisp.

The third and fourth have spots that also weigh on a darker shade of brown, but the fifth, my God! The fifth is okay; it even puffs in certain parts. The sixth and seventh are almost identical to each other and resemble the ones Indi's mom showed me.

It's just in time, too.

With a beep and a whir, the door unlocks. An excited smile stretches my face so wide, my eyes shrink to slits.

I keep my back to her—*showing off my best assets, obviously*—and continuing a diligent effort in making more paratha, waiting for the chance to pamper my freckled girl.

GABE

I NEED TO HAVE MY BRAIN SCRUBBED OUT.

The cut, toned muscles covering the back of Wade's naked torso tense and relax as he uses a spatula to flip something. Saliva pooling, my eyes draw lower, broad shoulders to narrow hips, two tempting divots above the waistband of a pair of heather gray sweatpants hugging the rounds of his hockey ass.

The black duffle in hand slips from my grip onto the foyer floor.

He turns at the sound, wearing a signature shit-eating smirk and showing off his square pecs and abs. The defined v of his hips is like an arrow pointing downward to the main attraction. His cock bulges against his thigh in a slight curve, the fabric clinging to its length so tautly I can nearly see veins.

"Up here, Freckles."

My cheeks flame.

"*Oooh*, are we having a sleepover?" His eyes flick to my fallen bag and back to me. "Those are my favorite."

The throbbing between my legs transfers to my brain. I groan and rub my temples. "Should have left it in the car."

"And what fun would that have been?" Wade pivots back and picks up a wooden rolling pin from the counter, sprinkling flour onto the marble. His triceps flex as he works.

"Too bad I'm not here to have fun; I'm here to eat—" A very specific scent of wheat cooked in heated oil follows the hiss at the stovetop. I peer over him. Whatever anger and annoyance I held from his obnoxious shenanigans at the game softens. "You're making...paratha?"

I haven't eaten homemade desi food in ages. Language, traditions, food. They'd been discarded to lessen the ache.

"You got it."

"*You*? You know how to?" I stare in awe at its circular shape and the pile of similarly sized rounds on a cooling rack.

"What, like it's hard? I told you I can cook." He transfers one rolled paratha between his hands before smacking it onto the cast iron skillet. "There's matar paneer in that pot, too."

"It's 11:30 p.m., there's no way—" In a haughty motion, I lift the lid, and sure enough, bright green peas and cream-colored cubes of paneer swim in a sea of red-orange gravy. The rising aroma of garam masala tickles, and I hide a sneeze in my elbow.

"Boop." He taps my nose with his pinky. "You're cute."

"*Ew*. Quit being gross."

"Gross?" He halts the rolling, front teeth catching on his bottom lip. "We can skip dinner and get *filthy* instead."

A wretched lament growls from my stomach.

Wade makes an admonishing *click* with his mouth. "Never mind. Gotta get you fed before anything else."

I fold my arms across my chest. "I'm fine."

"You're hungry. Sit down." He uses the spatula to motion to the chairs.

The dominance in his tone almost turns me into a puddle, but I regain composure enough to loiter over to the bar stools on the other side of the island. "You're not the boss of me," I grumble.

"You keep saying that, but it doesn't mean anything. Now, sit. Or else I'll have to use *this*"—he throws a menacing smack mid-air with the kitchen utensil— "until your ass is so red you won't be able to."

"You wanna spank me?" My brows wrinkle together.

"Another invitation? Again, I accept." He slides into the stool next to me, a plate in each hand.

I study the served portion with a squint. My hands search the counter but return empty. "Where's the spoon?"

"Spoon?"

His innocuous, quizzical expression meets my unattractive snort. What a pair we make.

"S-p-o-o-n," I enunciate every letter, "the thing you shove food into your piehole with."

Wade ignores the insult. "I know what a spoon is, silly. But why do you need one?"

"To—"

"You're supposed to eat with your hands."

"Really?" I feign incredulity, then deadpan. "I don't need a white boy mansplaining my own cul...ture."

I trail into silence as he tears a piece of my paratha and uses it to gather the gravy and its contents. "Open."

My lips obey and part.

"Wider."

Fingers pushing past the seam, he strokes the bite of food onto my tongue. Jaw slack, his mouth reflects mine, tongue drawing forward in encouragement.

It's delicious. Rich. Warmly spiced.

I hum through a content inhale, eyes falling shut by instinct. I haven't had anyone feed me dinner like this since...Aai.

A wave of sadness surges in my belly with the faintest memory of her creating tiny mountains of puran poli. Her enthusiastic, exaggerated expression attempts motivation for the next bite. Her mouth forms words but there's no noise, unable to recall what she sounded like.

I know he's mostly innocent and doesn't deserve it, but I can't help lashing out.

Because I'm a dick.

"Why do you enjoy tormenting me? Acting like a whole-ass child while we're working and then cooking me this...this..."

Amazing meal.

He stuffs another bite into my mouth mid-sentence.

"I think you mean, 'Thank you for putting on a good show at the game and making one of my favorite meals from scratch, you handsome devil.' And what about you?" Wade angrily eats his own bite and stores it in his cheek. "You think I fucking enjoy sporting a hard-on while playing? You think that shit's comfortable?"

"*Mmf.*"

"Or maybe you think I don't care that you joke around with Donovan,

Landy and Jaeg, or any other numbnut when you don't for me? I know how you taste, how your pussy squeezes my cock..." Unfazed, he rattles them off like a grocery list, then swallows three or four bites in one go.

Meanwhile, I chew faster so as not to choke. Sweat beads on my upper lip. The man is so unserious that it's hard to stay mad.

"...But I have no idea how to be the reason you genuinely smile."

I gulp.

"Or laugh. Like really, heartily laugh from your gut. I wanna make you laugh so hard you pee your pants—"

"Jesus, Boehner." My fingers snap toward him to pass the paper napkins while finishing my food, needing to wipe a drip of gravy from the corner of my mouth. A slap lands on his naked shoulder, leaving behind a pink handprint.

"I'll happily play the fool for your attention."

"Oh, is that why you sucked on my dildo? To get my attention?"

"That...wasn't planned. I did that because..." He glances up from his plate, dark lashes shadowing his darkened eyes, and replies in a husky murmur. "I like the way you taste."

My heartbeat skips. Something deep in my core pulses.

Wade scratches his full lower lip with his thumb and lifts a shoulder, and the unbothered tone of his voice returns. "I mean, you left me unsupervised with your used dildo and wet panties. What did you expect?"

"Definitely not *that*."

"I..." Pretty Boy pushes a cube of paneer around the curve of his plate before his words and hands halt, but his eyes flick up to me. Begging. "Did you like it?"

Logic doesn't register when he begs like that. My admission comes out breathy. "Yes."

"So, what does that mean?"

The sigh that follows is equally breathy. "That we have inexplicable kinks."

Our gazes avert to our respective plates. I interrupt the brief silence.

"How...did you know?" There are very few people who know I like matar paneer. My eyes blink back at Wade, in silent questioning.

"I have my sources."

I guess. "Indi?"

"Bingo. She was a huge help."

"Indi helped you make this?"

She's supposed to be *my* best friend. I don't need her spilling all my secrets to Lover Boy over here. But I can't tell her to stop without blowing this fake dating ruse to pieces.

"Nah. Her mom taught me a recipe over FaceTime before the game."

My mind sighs with the thought of the closest thing I have to a mother. She's the freaking best. A queen in her own right. Pharmacist by day, supermom by other day.

"You know Anju Aunty?"

"We've only met a few times: at the proposal, their engagement, and the wedding events. But she's very sweet."

"Tell that to Indi. She'd never admit how alike they are. Her dad's amazing, too."

Mentioning Rahul Uncle sombers the conversation.

"I wouldn't know," Wade replies. "Haven't talked to him much."

"*Ahhhh*," I drag out the sound. "Gotcha. Being weird around dads is your MO. Why is that?"

"Probably better to unpack with a therapist."

"Probably. Is it because your dad isn't around?"

His jaw ticks. "Don't."

I back off this time. We finish our meals wordlessly.

I ruined it.

The man is unrelenting. He asked people I love how to make me a homemade dinner, fed it to me with his hands, and I ruined it by bringing up his obvious issues around fatherly figures.

Gabe Finch, if you ever want your pussy eaten by him again, you make up for it right now. Yeah, that's why I'm doing it. Not because I'm sorry for hurting his feelings or anything.

Wade loads the dishwasher as I soap up my hands.

"*So*," I start. "Can I stay the night?"

His eyes brighten at the prospect, dispersing their anguish. "Same bed?"

"Sure. No sex."

"Just sleep?" There's not a trace of disappointment in his tone. "Do I get to cuddle you?"

"Yes." It's a mindless reply, but my insides go molten at the victorious smile he returns.

"Deal."

———

Waking up without him spread over me like a weighted blanket feels strangely...hollow. The gentle fingers swirling through my hair, his hot breath skimming over my skin, the pleasured hums as I stroked his back, the soft snore on my chest when he fell asleep. It's all too addicting to be healthy.

Oh, no.

What is this? Attachment? Feelings?

Psht. *No.* I don't like *him*. I like...how he feels. How he makes me feel. It's not the same thing.

Both palms cover my eyes but do nothing to ease the frustration. "Get a hold of yourself, Gabe. What are you doing?"

I thrash my legs against the mattress before swinging them over one side. My temples pulse harder at the two rings notifying me of new messages.

MEL

Adrienne's sick as hell.

MEL

You cool flying to San Diego instead of Edmonton today?

ME

Do I have a choice?

MEL

No.

MEL

Sending the details now.

ME

Cool, I'll see you at the airport.

I have a couple of hours to head home, shower in peace, and grab my suit-case, but instead, I find myself lackadaisically using all the fancy settings on Wade's bidet, strolling over to the kitchen to make myself some Balinese coffee and then going down a rabbit hole on Wikipedia on why it's the most expensive coffee on the planet.

The coffee cherries of kopi luwak, I learn, are pooped out by what looks like the Indonesian version of a possum, but it's totally sanitary to ingest because of its cleaning and roasting process.

Interesting.

I'm clearly lollygagging.

I wish I was actually gagging on Wade Boehner's magnificent cock.

Pathetic.

The door of one guest room I pass—*the one with the plumbing issue and ruined floor, I think*—is ajar. Curiosity gets the best of me, and I peek in, expecting another of his abandoned home renovation projects.

I gawp at the brand-new, shiny half-court, clear backboard and the un-used net hanging from the orange rim. A rack holding basketballs lines the wall closest to me.

My bare feet test the sealed hardwood with a run and a jump, landing with a thud. Solid. Likely high-performance. Pricey for a home court, but he can afford it.

Sauntering over to grab a ball, I drop it to the floor. It returns to my hand after a satisfying *thunk*. The sound echoes as I walk it to the free throw line and get into position.

Four bounces. Bent elbows. I smile and blow out a sharp breath.

"Morning, Freckles."

I fumble the release, and the ball bing-bongs off the rim. My smile vanishes, eyes narrowing at a smug, sweaty Wade, black t-shirt soaked to a darker shade. Those evil four-inch inseam shorts taunt me.

He follows my gaze and grins wider, yanking the shirt off with a single hand over his head, wiping between his pecs and abs before tossing it over the round of his shoulder.

"Better?"

"You made me miss."

Wade catches the stray ball and dribbles. "Am I that *distracting*?"

"No, just cocky."

The ball switches between hands, similar to the paratha last night. They cover a decent portion of its surface with their sheer size.

My arms motion to the space. "Since when are you so into basketball?"

"Since I found out you are."

A sardonic smile lifts one corner of my lips, the pit in my stomach growing at the possibility he isn't lying. "Yeah, right."

"Let's go, Freckles. One-on-one."

Pretty Boy sweeps his sweaty waves to one side with a brush of his fingers between dribbles. "Please? We've played against each other before."

Don't fall for it.

One arm crosses the other over my chest. "That was at a gym when our friends were secretly screwing each other."

The game between Landon, Wade, Indi, and I feels like a lifetime ago because it was. So much has changed.

"Also, I'm barefoot. Take your socks off," I order.

Will he ever stop smirking? How am I supposed to ignore how cute it is if he keeps doing it?

"*Aw*, Freckles," he intones while lifting his feet, then peels away his socks with a single hand. "If you wanted me to strip, you could have asked—"

"Or you could answer my question."

"Hey, I don't have a lot of spare time during the season, and it's fun to play with the guys now and again. Plus, I convinced my financial advisor that it wouldn't affect the resale value because anyone who wants this place in the future would want a court." The ball tucks between his elbow and hip. "So I combined two guest rooms." He draws a line across the middle of the court with a straightened palm and one eye screwed shut. "All for you, Freckles."

Bullshit.

I sashay to him, getting so close I can smell his minty toothpaste, then hit him with my best doe eyes and a sugary tone. "For *me*?"

"Mmhm." His bottom lip glistens with the swipe of his tongue. "Anything." The seam of his mouth splits. "For." Its gap widens as he leans forward, a silent yearning for a kiss. "You."

The lightest touch tips the ball from his grasp. I laugh and take off, leaping up to make a shot. My silk pajama top flutters from me, exposing my chest. The ball swishes through the hoop as gravity pulls me—and my flimsy tank—back down.

Wade runs up to snatch the ball with both hands. "You're playing dirty." He admires my hardly-there breasts before resuming eye contact. "You flashed me."

I fix my top and point to his shirtless torso. "Takes one to know one. I can take off my shirt to even the playing field if you'd like."

His eyebrows lift in challenge. "You can, but then you'd be on your back in the paint while I suck on your tits. Wanna take the chance, Freckles?" He tosses the ball to me.

Yes.

No!

"No thanks." An eye roll occurs by instinct during the short volley, and my forceful throwback knocks some air from his lungs. "If I win, will you stop calling me that?"

He dribbles twice, jukes me out, and charges, but ends in an easy layup. It goes in. Wade walks the ball back.

"If you win, you can do whatever you want to me."

"Tempting, but I have that already."

"Touché."

The ball returns to me, and our conversation continues amidst the consistent dribbling, the erratic squeak of our soles against the wood flooring, and staggering breaths.

I sneak in two points when his gaze goes down my shirt. He groans and whips his hands into a half-clap of disappointment.

"That's what you get for lazy defense."

His response is anything but apologetic. "Sorry, I get hard by thinking about how nice your tits are."

I straighten from my bent position and hold the ball between my hip and wrist. "Why do you like it, Wade?"

"Like what?"

"How I speak to you. How I treat you."

His hands form a T before grabbing the bunched shirt circling his neck. It's used to wipe his chest and abs once more. "You mean how you're bossy" —this time he tucks the tee into the back of his shorts— "snarky, mouthy...?"

My eyes draw another invisible arch as I deadpan. "Please. Don't hold back. Tell me how you really feel."

Wade doesn't break. "Because I know that's not who you are. You didn't talk to that piece of shit Vaughn like this, right?"

"No," I say under my breath. Every mention of my past relationships feels like a failure. Insecurity toys with my nerves, and I react by bouncing the ball.

"How infuriating." I mistake his nostrils flaring as resentment toward me, but he shakes his head and dispels the thought. "Jerk turned you into a doormat."

My dribbling stills. "I was *not* a doormat."

I was a doormat.

The man got whatever, however, whenever he wanted, and I thought giving, giving, giving to him was the best thing I could do. *She's a low-maintenance girlfriend; she's so chill*, he'd say. More like a spineless creature under the guise of being easygoing. Humiliating.

His elbow nudges my arm. "You still with me? That's not you. But the Gabe you're showing me isn't you either."

I hate that he's right. That he knows I'm terrified of showing him any weakness, anything real. And that I haven't been effective in hiding myself.

You cuddle a guy a few times after sex, and he thinks he knows you. Jeez.

Two steps away from him allows my jump shot. It goes in. I get the rebound, but it's not as satisfying as expected.

"But I'd rather have a fake you than nothing."

The earnest longing in his voice triggers a shiver. I can't shake it.

Wade steals the ball while I'm caught off-guard. "Besides, I like seeing how far I can go. What sets you off." Pretty Boy dribbles the basketball across the court. "Don't you ever get tired, Gabe?"

"Of?" My arms shoot up in defense of any attempts he makes, but there's no point. He's bigger.

His shot from the top of the key goes in. I get the rebound.

"The burden of control, how heavy it is to pretend, to bear other people's expectation of you?"

I do get tired. But I don't trust easily enough anymore to let it go. And I'm not sure he's talking about me.

"Sometimes..." One eye scrunches as he corrects himself and catches his breath, palming his side. "People think I'm an idiot, goof-off, whatever. It's not often I get to just...be. To not have to sit there and analyze to death what I should be doing. One place I get to do that is on the ice. I can shut my mind off and chase instinct."

"And another place?" A dangerous question whose answer I'm not entirely prepared for. I keep the ball against my chest. As if it'll protect my heart.

"With you," he replies, certain. "Giving you control has been" —he takes a pause and drops his shoulders, releasing a burden— "fucking *freeing*. It was so unexpected, a fantasy I never knew how to ask for. With you, I didn't have to. It wasn't weird or awkward. With you, it feels right."

Tension clouds my judgment. I'm about to do something really stupid, aren't I?

Wade's shoulders soften as he folds in toward me. "So you can call me a fuckboy or manwhore or a sex idiot, and I'll take it all. I know you could hurt me, but I kinda don't care. You're the first woman who's asked for me to only be with her. I don't think anyone else bothered."

My chin juts up, finding it hard to believe. "You're saying none of the women you've ever been with didn't want to be your girlfriend?"

"Nope. Or if they did, they never said anything." He huffs softly. "They want a free drink, dinner, access. A good time, a good fuck. And no judgment from me; that's their choice."

"I'm sure you were broken up about it."

"Not saying I was, but..." The thick line of his lashes meets my brow. "It's nice to have security, too. You don't need me for any of those things."

Those butterflies in my gut flutter in a frenzy, then start punching each other, furious.

What a tragedy. The man is a professional athlete in peak shape, handsome in an annoying way, stupidly rich, reads, calls my best friend's mom to learn how to make my favorite meal, literally begs for my attention, and eats pussy like a champ. He's basically a man written by a woman. The perfect boyfriend. How could anybody *not* want to be his?

His first finger latches onto my chin. "I meant it when I said use me however you like. You want control? You got it. You want me to take over? I will." The next few words climb into my heart and ensnare it, trapping it in a spinning cage. "You can have all of me."

"Why?"

He doesn't give himself to anyone; if he does, it's in tiny shards.

"Because, Gabe. You deserve something—someone that's entirely yours. I'm yours."

Mine? He's already called me his, and now he's saying *he's* mine?

So much for fake dating. Just sex, we said. Now look at us. Fucking look at us!

"Pineapple," I whisper.

"Pineapple?"

"It's my safe word."

That I decided on two milliseconds ago.

"For emotional boundaries, too."

"Absolutely." Worried eyes dart across my face, seeming to sense my impending emotional shutdown. "Anything else?"

"What's yours?"

His lips pull into his mouth. "Meatloaf."

"Why?"

"Give it a second."

His hum hints at the tune of Meatloaf's "I'd Do Anything for Love (But I Won't Do That.)"

I cover his mouth with my palm. He removes it by gripping my wrist.

"So, if I ask about your mom—"

"Pineapple."

Wade zips his mouth, mimes turning a lock, and throws away the key.

"And if I bring up your daddy issues?"

"Meatloaf."

We share a snort. Mine's closer to a chuckle.

His hand balls his pec, stumbling back a few steps and swooning with a falsetto lilt. "Oh, Freckles. Did I just make you laugh? You're making my dreams come true."

"You're such a drama queen." I swivel and bump him with my ass, keeping him at a distance from the ball. "It's obnoxious."

He hisses. "Quit making me hard with those insults."

"You really need to talk to someone about that."

"Is that a yes, Freckles? Wanna try new things with me?"

I back up with my butt once again, trying to maintain focus on the ball and not on the curve of Wade's rock-hard third leg.

He groans in my ear and grips my hips with both hands. "Rub that ass on my cock again, and I'll have to fuck it." I don't move. "Or is that what you want?"

I don't say anything to deny or confirm, but my elbow drives into his side, giving me enough leeway to run to the wing.

It's lucky, for sure, but my three-pointer taps the rim and goes in.

I whoop and gloat, running backward to the open door. "Gotta go catch a flight. Later, Pretty Boy!"

"You didn't say pineapple!" he yells after me. "Freckles! I need to know! Am I or am I not gonna get to fuck your ass?"

I send him a text before boarding the plane.

ME

Be a good boy while I'm gone, and we'll talk about it.

WADE

ON A SCALE OF ONE TO TEN, HOW PATHETIC IS IT TO miss your fake girlfriend after two days?

Okay, you know what? I don't fucking care. It's ridiculous, yes. But it can't be as ridiculous as I look right now.

I revisit the hot-as-fuck mirror selfie Gabe sent, the black cropped top so tight her nipples poke through and aubergine color lining her upper lip, tempting me to ruin it later tonight. The black gloves on her hands and utility belt hanging from her slender hips give me a very specific, filthy idea. My dick stirs.

Shh, shh. Not now.

"*So* not the drama," I read her caption aloud. "Oh, sweetheart. There's about to be."

With a swipe, I get rid of the notification for Fletch's sneezing seal video and open up my Messages app.

ME

I am displeased

FRECKLES

What now?

ME

This is not what I meant when I said you could get creative with my costume

FRECKLES

You wanted something sluttier?

ME

Yes, actually

ME

Buck teeth, a blond wig, and turtlenecks are the opposite of slutty!!

FRECKLES

Some may think turtlenecks are very slutty.

ME

Wait

ME

Do you think they're slutty??

FRECKLES

No comment.

ME

I'll take that as a yes

Sometimes I like to pretend Gabe enjoys this shit. And if she didn't say the exact opposite, I'd even claim she *liked* me.

I tug the knit fabric around my neck over my face and breathe in, taking in the trace of her flowery smell before shoving my hands into the pair of khaki cargo pants she ordered.

Beyond pathetic.

My knee knocks against a firm object inside one of the large pockets below. The fifteen-minute walk to the Davé-Radek's is spent giggling to myself while thinking about the look on her face when I show her the toy.

Landon and Indi insisted on hosting the team's annual Halloween party this year, and I'm positive it'll be a far cry from the usual ragers. It's probably for the best since more of us are coupled up and less likely for a night of debauchery.

Us?

They.

They have relationships. Marriages.

Gabe and I? God, I don't know anymore. It's somewhere between real and fake, and I can't make up my mind on whether I want her to end my suffering and let me go or keep me forever.

How did I turn into such a needy asshole?

A question for another time because the river comes into view and Scott Street approaches.

I loiter in the lobby after entering.

ME

ETA?

FRECKLES

Already here.

FRECKLES

Got in early to help Indi with food.

ME

Like the blind leading the blind

FRECKLES

middle finger emojis

ME

Have no fear, cooking daddy is here

FRECKLES

Never say that again.

ME

Cooking daddy

FRECKLES

Fuck around and find out.

ME

Cooking

FRECKLES

Don't.

ME

Daddy

FRECKLES

facepalm emoji

Maniacal laughter echoes alongside thunder and ominous strobe lighting as I exit the elevator on the top floor. Classic spiderwebs stretch from floor to ceiling in the hallway, the walls dripping blood-red and decorated with ornate gold crown molding, like an old, haunted movie theater.

"Nice touch," I say to no one, brushing a cottony web from my face.

Pushing open the door reveals more of the same theme. A concession stand replaces their kitchen, and catering staff dressed as zombies offer a variety of drinks, cartoonish sweets, and flavored popcorn.

Fine. They did a good job.

A red-headed Landon in gladiator garb and painted-on eyebrows twirls a strand of Indi's brown ponytail and fiddles with the pleats of her purple Grecian gown. They share a look of adoration as she smiles over a few cheesy kernels.

I tap Landon's bicep with the back of my hand. "Earth to Hercules." He straightens and offers a hand to dap, then pretends to punch me in my fake, oversized front teeth. "Place looks great, Indi."

She flings her arms up and wraps my neck for a hug. "*Aw*, thanks, Wade." Her knuckle digs into my dimple as she pinches my cheek. "You look adorable."

Someone got laid.

I'm mad it wasn't me. But the night is young.

My eyes search for Gabe across the sea of cartoon couples. There's Homer and Marge Simpson, Woody and Bo Peep, and Mr. and Mrs. Incredible. Olsen and Szecze and their dates make up a scantily clad Scooby Doo crew.

Why am I wearing the most clothes out of all these fools?

My hand wipes sweat from the back of my neck. "Where's my girl?"

"*Ugh*," Indi intones. "You two are gonna look so cute together. But, *um*, I did a bad thing."

"A bad thi—?"

Before I can finish, Gabe parkours from behind a couch and pounces me. Her arms cinch over my shoulders, legs wrapping around my hips until the jagged treads of her combat boots dig into my back.

"Hi," she coos.

The citrus on her breath stings my eyes.

"*Uh*, hi." I'm thrown off by her unusual affection.

"I missed you," she adds, nuzzling close with an onslaught of bunny kisses. Her freckles nearly disappear under a pink flush, full lips pulling into a dazed smile.

Not sure what possessed her to say that, but I'll take it.

My grip on her bare midriff tightens, absorbing all her warmth. The ends of her reddened hair tangle with my fingertips. "I missed you, too."

This is what I mean. We're teetering in this blurred twilight zone. Too real to be fake, but too fake to be real.

Both Davé-Radeks muffle squeals. Landon titters. Indi lightly slaps his bare arm with a shush.

I raise an eyebrow. "Is this the bad thing?"

Because I don't mind it one bit.

Indi cringes with a hiss. "She seemed really uptight when she got here. I may or may not have encouraged her to have half a gummy."

"She had an edible?"

Gabe gets to her feet and claps both her hands to my pecs. "It was" — her eyes cross for emphasis— "*yum*! You should try one!"

A nervous chuckle follows. "*Heh*, yeah." Disapproving looks are sent to both culprits, received with innocent smiles and shrugs.

Troublemakers.

I clasp her hands in mine. "Maybe later, sweetheart."

"Your freckles got smudged," Gabe says through a dramatic pout. She pulls a black tube from a leather satchel hooked on her belt and uncaps it. "Don't move."

My hands settle at the base of her spine, letting her chest press into mine, savoring this rare moment. She squints, concentrating on spotting each cheek with a dark liquid. "There."

Olsen boos from a cocktail table. "*Get a room!*"

I flip him off.

"Here, Lover Boy." Landon passes me a dark red Jell-O shot. "You can take one of these with me."

"What about you, Indi?"

"Yuck, *no*. It's Fireball."

Landy and I toss it back together, but it's Jell-O, so it's more like a slow, slimy descent that we have to slurp. The cinnamon burns all the way down, matching the heat in my belly to where Gabe tucks into my side.

I suck in a sharp breath afterward.

"What a wimp." Skylar strolls up in a frilly, yellow Victorian-style dress. Jaeg stands behind her, but their size difference doesn't hide the muscles bulging in every direction from his tiny loincloth. She takes a Jell-O shot without a sound.

"Are you seeing this, Freckles?" I complain, motioning with my hand. The whisky kicks in, loosening all the taut wrinkles in my brain. "I coulda worn that! Look how slutty Jaeg looks."

Gabe hums and kisses my jaw, waking goosebumps and hardening my nipples. She lowers her voice to a whisper.

"Maybe I don't want anyone else to see you like that." Her tongue flicks my ear lobe. "Maybe I'd get jealous."

My dick is more confused than I am. This woman has me so fucked up.

Speaking of jealousy, Fletch winces over a beer. "When I die alone, bury me with my books."

Gabe swivels to him. "What'd you say?"

Fletcher turns the color of a bright, ripened tomato, the same as his oval, painted-on nose. He mumbles. "N-nothing."

"And what's this costume?" I point to his orange and brown-spotted foam get-up and flick a cat ear, then motion to the backward paws on his feet and the dog face attached to his ass. "You're a cat and a dog?"

He rolls his eyes and gets on all fours. "I'm CatDog."

"I don't get it."

"You might be a little young for that one." Landon draws his mouth to one side and hides it behind a hand, tilting to me. "He's his own date."

"It's okay, buddy." Indi soothes Fletch with a gentle pat when he stands again. "Can we sit down? These sandals are killing me."

We migrate to the couch, finding our spots musical-chairs style. Landon unties the straps crisscrossing Indi's ankles and calves, then props her feet across his lap. She sighs out a hum of relief.

Do they have to be so cute?

Skylar and Jaeger claim the other end, and we force Masterson and a couple of rookies to scooch. Fletcher squeezes in next to me. I throw him a glare.

"She's a genius for making you dress as Ron Stoppable."

"Shut up."

"Where's the naked mole rat?"

I refer with my eyes to my crotch.

"*Ew*. You're gross."

Freckles bunches her fists at her hips.

"Where am I supposed to sit?"

"Right here, baby." I smack both thighs, spreading them apart to make room for her. She doesn't hesitate, and I instantly regret the suggestion.

"Fuck me," I mutter inside my own mouth. But she reclines to my front and is within earshot.

"Maybe later," she mutters back, ass shifting up and down, working my cock until it's so hard, it aches. I can't focus on anything but her goddamn perfect ass.

My fingers dig into her hips. "Stop that."

Gabe ignores my warning and flashes me a glare. "What was your question?" she asks Daphne.

Her name's not Daphne, but that's who she's dressed as, and I couldn't care less about any woman other than the one reverse-cowgirling me through my pants.

Fuck, that's what I want. Her riding me so hard I can't see. But not in front of everyone.

"Would you slap your boyfriend, husband, partner, whatever you wanna call him...for a billion dollars?"

Skylar sputters. "Hell no. That's my baby. We don't need a billion dollars. We have more than enough money, don't we, my love?" She dots Jaeger's mouth with two short pecks. His eyes glaze over for a moment before returning to their deadened state.

Fucking goon.

"I'd do it," Indi replies through a yawn.

Landon protests. "*Babyyy.*"

"What? Get real, Radek. It's a lot of money! Don't worry. I'll give you a billion-dollar blowie after."

"Can I get one of those tonight?"

"For free?" She denies with an exaggerated *nah.* "Without the money, you get the regular service."

"Deal!"

"What about you, Gabe?"

My girlfriend turns her head to pore over me. "A billion dollars?" She turns back to the girls. "I'd do it for free."

Jaw askew, the tip of my tongue presses into these horrible buck teeth in disbelief.

Bye-bye, nice, touchy-feely Gabe. Guess the edible wore off.

Each dude on this sectional erupts into laughter. Landon's shoulders shake from where he hides in the crook of Indi's neck as she chides him. Olsen does a Patrick Star dopey chuckle while Szecze slaps a knee. Fletcher tips forward off of the cushion, snorting through short breaths as he holds his stomach, the dog on his ass spasming without relent.

Freckles has some fucking nerve to be a brat right now.

She launches herself up by pushing her hands on her knees. "Sorry to cut the fun short. I have to use the washroom."

When she disappears down a hall, I jump to my feet. "Be right back."

There's only one way to deal with a brat effectively.

I use my thumbnail to turn the lock of the powder room. Gabe's seated on the pot. The color spreading over her questioning face matches her temporary hair color.

"Um, hello?"

"I—" The trickle of pee hitting the toilet water interrupts my original train of thought. I stumble through confused words. "You-how-but... you're still wearing your pants? How are you peeing?"

She wipes and stands before closing the lid and flushing.

"They're for hiking. So women can go in the middle of the woods without having to flash everyone the goods." A zipping sound begins as Gabe closes the zipper back-to-front. "Also, excuse me?" She bumps me with her hip to wash and dry her hands. "Can't even pee without you following me like an attention-starved puppy."

Attention-starved puppy? Okay, she's not wrong, but no need to say it to my face.

I relock the door, switch the venting fan on and turn both the handles of the faucet fully, hoping it'll drown out our bickering, then drop my voice to a yelling whisper.

"Excuse *me*? Excuse *YOU!*" My index finger accuses. "What the hell are you trying to pull out there?"

Gabe glances at me through the mirror, lifting her brows, and gives a slow blink. "I don't know what you're talking about."

"That's bullshit—"

Her gaze sharpens. A salacious grin appears. "What are you gonna do about it?"

Oh.

I swallow, the air suddenly thick and suffocating, my semi from Gabe's mini-riding session growing harder. "So that was your plan all along? Get me so riled up I take you right here in the wash—"

"Maybe." Facing me, her hand balls the hem of my shirt, nails scraping the skin underneath. She tugs my mouth to hers. "Maybe I want you to."

"Fuck."

"And don't make excuses." Our lips brush. "I'm not high."

"How do I know for sure?"

Gabe backs me into the wall by the throat, treating me to a sweltering, tongue-first kiss that has me moaning into her mouth and hungry for more when she stops. It's intentional, calculated.

Clarity and challenge gleam in the hazel streaking her eyes. "How's that?"

"Turn around," I say huskily. "And unzip your pants."

She does.

"Now bend over."

Gabe listens again, bracing her arms against the sink top and giving the most incredible view of her ass, split down the middle with a flimsy thong.

"Are you wet, or do you need more of my kisses?"

"That's for me to know and you to find out."

"Gladly." My hand curls around her to the open split of her pants, moving aside the string to test her wetness. It's damp but not nearly enough. I want her sore, not torn up.

From my right cargo pocket, I retrieve a black satin satchel. Its resident slides from the smooth fabric into my palm. Heavy, ridged with veins. The bright pink silicone dick that she likes to pretend is me.

"I figured out why you love this thing so much. It's me, but portable."

Twisting the dial at the bottom makes the toy buzz softly. I move the tip onto one nipple, watching how it puckers through the black fabric before repeating it on the other side.

I spit on the head and mouth it, coating it with saliva as far as I can without gagging.

Gabe's breath staggers.

My cock swells, eyes unwavering from hers. They blow wide as I prod the slick tip through the cleft of her pussy, gliding it past her clit.

Her fingers crook into arches against the counter, each gasp and sigh shallower than the last.

Another twist increases the speed of vibrations and she winces, then tosses her head, bowing her back when I thrust it inside. In and out, in and out, only stopping briefly over her g-spot.

The vanity shakes as her knees clack against its cupboard doors.

I use my free hand to cover hers, thumbing the vein at her wrist. "This drumming, your pulse. It's for me, right?" I search for it every time we're together, and it's the same. Steadily climbing. "It's because you're mine, Freckles. Every beat, every orgasm, every part of this stunning pussy. All mine. Even when I'm not there. It's me you use to get yourself off. Tell me I'm wrong."

"You're..."

"Go ahead. Lie to me."

The highest setting of the toy cuts her off. "Oh, my God. Fu-*fuck*."

"Go on, Gabe, fuck this fake dick and pretend it's me. Squeeze those tight pussy walls around it until you come."

Tremoring through a whimper, she finishes so hard that the dildo slips out. I toss it into the running sink, afraid if I wait any longer, I'll come on myself.

I tear open a condom from my pocket with my teeth, undoing my pants enough to roll it on. It stretches and stretches around the curve, dulling the red crown to pink.

"Throw this fucking ass back," I demand, positioning her hips to line up to her soaked, freshly fucked cunt from behind. I tap twice against her opening. "This is what you want, Freckles?"

She gasps, then gasps again when I insert the head. "More."

I inch in deeper with each thrust, my grasp on her shoulder wrenching her shirt up and revealing those pebbled nipples. "To be tits out, letting me hit it from the back while the entire Regents roster is out there?"

"*Fuck*." Gabe whimpers when I steady my pace. "Yes," she admits. "Harder."

The next slam has her crying my name. "You want 'em to hear how badly you need my cock?"

Heavy breathing, shameless moaning—no idea whether it's her or both of us, and it doesn't fucking matter. All that matters is how the rough slapping between my hips and her ass is gonna finish us off. I spread her cheeks to stroke my thumb over the pink asshole, and her walls clench around me. "Is this okay?"

"Yes."

I fill her entirely with a groan. "What about degradation?"

"Yes," she repeats.

"Thank fuck." The speed of my thrusts return. "You're fucking made for me, you know that, Freckles? This snug cunt fits so perfectly around my cock. Gets so tight when I play with your ass."

The filth has her making a mess on me, and I drive faster, pleasure coiling into a painful knot at the root of my spine, balls aching for release. But I need her to finish with me.

One hand steadies her hip, and the other reaches for the column of her neck. A gentle compression draws out her pleasured gurgle.

"Eyes on the mirror. Want you to see your pussy being a greedy little whore for me. For this cock and no one else."

When she shatters, I shatter, staying deep inside her until we stop trembling.

Through shallow pants, I lick her throat. Salt from the sweat beading on her skin collects on my tongue.

"Why do you look at me like that?" she asks.

"Like what?"

"Like I'm the best thing you've ever experienced."

I swipe my finger through her wetness and suck it clean. "Aren't you just?"

Running water rinses the toy off, and I tuck it back in its satchel and my pocket. We straighten up.

"What a missed opportunity." Gabe tuts.

"For what?"

"I thought for sure you were gonna fuck my ass."

"Have you ever been fucked like that?"

"No."

"You'd be my first, too. And that's exactly why I wouldn't do it here, in Landy's powder room. And without lube? Not a chance."

"Dang, Pretty Boy. We gotta get you a new hobby other than making me a bunch of your firsts." Gabe finger-combs her hair. "Do you think anyone realized we were messing around?"

"Nah." I unlock the door and turn the knob. "The music's loud, and they're probably all busy chatting—"

A wave of our friends ebbs from the door.

Holy shit. Were they all standing here listening?

Every single one of them fakes distraction. Skylar jumps Derrick and starts making out. Olsen and Szezce take their dates on piggyback rides away from the crime scene. Poor Fletch flips around and sticks his nose in a corner. Landon presses a cheek against the wall with a squint.

"Would you say this paint color is eggshell or pearl?"

Indi studies it with narrowed eyes as well. "I'm no expert, but...I think it's alabaster."

"Yes!" He snaps and wags a finger. "That's the one! Alabaster!"

Gabe covers her eyes with a spread palm.

I play it cool.

"Hey, what's going on out here?"

A chorus of "nothing, oh, nothing" chimes back.

"What's Donovan doin' in the corner?"

"I'm in time-out," he says.

"Why?"

"I put myself there."

Before I embarrass these idiots further, Indi claps her hands together. "Time for a game!"

I mumble into Gabe's shoulder as they garner the attention of the rest of the team. "You're gonna punish me for this, aren't you?"

"Punish you? You made me come twice in ten minutes." Her eyes peer at me from one corner. "You want me to?"

"Only if the punishment includes you in my bed, on your hands and knees."

"*Hmm.*" Her lips purse. "That sounds like a reward for good boys."

"I made you come twice in ten minutes," I parrot. "Doesn't that make me the goodest boy?"

"You're such a dog." Gabe cracks a stifled smile, swathing my torso in a familiar warmth. "And don't you dare fucking bark."

Too lost in the bubble of our own banter, we almost miss Indi's instructions, pointing to me, Skylar, Jaeger, Fletcher, and Gabe. "It's like Telephone and Pictionary and we'll draw at the same time. Line up facing the wall." Landon tapes a piece of paper to each of our backs, handing us all black markers.

"Why am I last?" I whine.

"And don't be a cheat and look back," Indi warns. "I'll start drawing something, one line at a time, until everyone has a picture."

My fake girlfriend pinches my ass while we wait. "Gabe Finch!" I chide in a southern drawl, protecting the assets with both hands. "Have some decorum, young lady."

She returns a giggle.

My heart feels like it's going to explode.

I turn to witness it for myself.

"Alright, that's it, lovebirds!" Indi yells. "Switch spots."

Gabe steps ahead, now in the last position. A piece of paper hangs from the wall for her.

"Stay still," Fletcher directs, his hand on my back, keeping the paper in place.

"It tickles."

He starts with a vertical line. And then another, followed by a v and yet another vertical line. I M?

"The fuck, Donovan? That's not a picture."

"That's what's being drawn, okay? Now let me concentrate."

I recreate the letter shapes onto Gabe's back. I. M. P. R. E. G. N.

Hold on.

My head whips around to the Radeks at the same time as Fletcher's. We stare, gawping at the enthusiastic double thumbs-up they give us.

The crowd collectively *aww*s. Skylar lets out a high-pitched squeak before Landon quiets everyone.

"What, what? Why'd everyone stop?"

"Sorry, sorry. I'll keep going."

I peer over her shoulder. Gabe drew the lines detached from one another.

"*Psst*! Connect the lines, Finch!" Landon calls through cupped hands.

"I'm...preg-nant?" She sputters. "Pregnant? *Pfft*. No, I'm not—"

Realization dawns on her, and she spins, rushing to Indi.

They clasp each other's hands, their welling tears barely held back. "You're pregnant?"

As if my heart hasn't been through the wringer throughout the evening, seeing Gabe get emotional is like getting hit by a bus.

Silence only lasts for a moment before morphing into full-on sobbing. The girls lace their fingers together and let go to hug and weep. Landon wipes his eyes, too.

"Holy crap, *you're* crying?" Fletch outs me.

"They're having a baby, for fuck's sake." I sniffle and rub away the tears, approaching Landon and Indi to join Gabe to share a group embrace. "We're having a baby!"

Teammates, brothers, and friends huddle around us, filling the air with the unbelievable high of love and pride that rivals winning. Hell, it's pretty damn close to sex with Gabe.

Our eyes find one another in the chaos, untangling from the web of arms, the adrenaline crashing our lips and tongues together in a fury.

And the high doesn't end there. It continues in the cab ride home, where Gabe and I make out like horny teenagers.

It continues on the ride up the elevator, where we dry hump against the handrail.

And it continues when we strip each other down, and she seats herself on my bed, legs wide with her fingers strumming across her reddened pussy.

"Fucking hell." I grip the base of my cock and pump, spreading pre-cum up and down the shaft. It's already so slick. Squeezing provides no relief.

"Don't touch yourself," she whines. "Get inside me, already."

I drop it from my hand, but it stays upright, curved, and hard as fuck. "Then flip over and grab a condom from the drawer."

Her obeying has my dick bobbing. I sheath the impatient shit.

"Hands and knees, Freckles. Like you said you would. Wanna see my girlfriend be a needy slut for my cock again."

GABE

"I THINK I'M IN LOVE WITH WADE."

I choke on my mimosa and use the napkin as a face shield. "You're what now?"

"He's uh-maz-ing."

"Landon's gonna lose his shit."

"Seriously, *Gabe.*" A whiny faux sob pairs with Indi's pained expression. She pulls something from her purse. "Your boyfriend got Derrick to crochet this matching beanie and sweater—*look at this freaking tiny sweater!*—for the baby. And the little booties?" Her first two fingers make them march on her side of the table in sync with a series of *boops*. "I cannot. They're too cute."

"Cute? What is happening to you?"

Her hand dismisses the question. "And how precious is this garnet color? Did you tell him it was my favorite?"

"I had nothing to do with this."

"See? This is what I mean. I knew he was sweet, but the man might be perfect. For you, I mean." A waiter interrupts to refill her water glass. She passes a polite smile before continuing. "He worships the ground you stand on, makes you food, does all the things crusty, dusty Vaughn couldn't handle in bed..."

My breath hitches, asshole clenching at the memory of how we kept our promises post-Halloween party.

Wade spent hours between eating me out and using Mr. Darcy on my pussy until I relaxed enough to let him in the back door. Copious amounts of lube helped accept his size. And after? I almost passed out from the tenderness.

Our skin clung at the hips, my ass to his groin. Amidst a deluge of sweat and cum, Wade growled out an orgasm while buried halfway in my ass. It was all I could take.

He didn't pull out right away, simply panting through groans, cock still hard and twitching inside me. Kisses from his swollen lips trailed behind callused fingers over every ridge of my spine until he neared my nape. Pinpricks tightened my skin further from his hot breath in my ear.

"I can't stand how gorgeous you are." The praise and degradation combo was definitely going into regular rotation. "You're a fucking wet dream come true."

Later, I admired him through the steam from the shower. There was no denying Wade was beautiful. Cheeks puffed from swishing mouthwash, he spit neon blue foam into the sink.

While I began to dry off, he pulled me into a relentless, openmouthed kiss, tossing my towel to the floor before lifting me to bed.

I may never get over the way he moans. From deep in his chest. Pure agony and want.

"Wade."

"Do you know how insane you make me feel? I want you" —the noisy, sloppy kisses moved to my neck— "so badly. All the time."

He worked a sensitive spot under my ear, and my pussy cried, raw and sore from earlier.

"For sex?" I asked, knowing any answer would hurt.

Frozen otherwise, his Adam's apple tensed and bobbed while he hovered over me. "Yeah, yeah. For sex."

The longing didn't disappear from his gaze. He fell away from me in a heap.

I shove my fingers into my hairline, baffled at how this-this-this thing snowballed. "How did we get here? We hate each other."

Wade broke the tension with a dry chuckle. "Do we?"

"Ahem."

I blink three times, giving my best impression of a deer in headlights at Indi's interruption.

"Adorable. '*We're just having fun*,' she says while having a dirty fantasy in the middle of Sunday brunch."

A shrug is attempted, but Indi doesn't buy it. "We *are* having fun."

Fun with toys and kinks.

"Ma'am, if you don't put a ring on that boy's finger..." Her voice weakens, tears emerging and streaking down her cheeks.

"Indi? Are you okay?" I switch my seat to the one next to her. She topples over and sobs into my shoulder.

My finger swirling into the air signals the waiter to wrap it up and grab the check. I offer my friend a napkin.

"Sorry, I don't know what came over me." She blows a honk. "I have no control over my emotions these days."

"It's the hormones," I comfort her. "But to be honest, you're generally much softer since—"

Another round of wailing ensues.

"I *know*! You're *so* right." Her hand points to her lower belly, frustration lacing the raised tone. "It's Landon Radek's fault for putting his cinnamon roll baby inside me!"

And we've got an ugly crier.

I cringe and massage her arm. "Oh, honey."

"I used to be a smartass, Gabe! Now I'm all gooey and...*nice. Ugh.* Who am I?"

Using a folded part of the napkin to dab away the clotting mascara at the edges of her eyes, I give another shot at consolation. "I ask myself that every day."

"Please. You're a badass."

"This is true." I accept the compliment with a seated curtsy. "But you know what else is true?"

Indi pushes out a leaden sigh. "What?"

"Soft looks good on you."

———

The Uber drops Indi home first.

PRETTY BOY

Come over

ME

Now?

PRETTY BOY

Please

ME

You're so desperate.

ME

It's hot.

ME

Be there in 10.

I should question my sanity. I don't have feelings for Wade Boehner; my vagina does. Let's not get the two confused.

A lean woman stands in Wade's kitchen in classic black leather boots to her knees and a fitted black dress. An emerald shawl gathers over her shoulders.

She gasps, uttering something French, causing Wade to straighten from the counter.

Of course.

Same brown tone of her hair. Same angle of her nose. Her chocolate-colored eyes light up the same way.

Any unease disappears when Wade rushes over to clasp my hand, weaving our fingers together. His thumb draws into my palm as he leads me to her.

O-K-?

I trace a shaky Y in reply.

"Maman. This is Gabe Finch, my girlfriend."

Every time he says it tastes more and more like the truth.

"Gabe, this is my mother, Naomie."

"Nice to meet you."

"Enchanté."

"Wow," I gush, awestruck. I've seen pictures, but they don't do justice, not even the ones from her competitive rowing or modeling days. "You're beautiful."

Every subtle move she makes—*the way her shoulders lift, hand drawn to her mouth, eyes crinkling and fluttering shut with the praise*—is full of grace and control.

She waves a finger at Wade, and I can't tell if she's scolding him or what.

He returns a sly smile and a shake of his head.

Nerves manifest in titters. She understands the confusion in my smile. "Oh my, pardon us."

Her accent is like a sweet melody.

"Sorry, I barely passed French class."

"No, no. My apologies. I sometimes don't notice when I've switched. Walt, where are your manners? Please, let's sit."

We head over to the sofa. Wade swings our hands, the hold loose and playful but unwilling to part. "Surprise visit?" I whisper.

"Quick stopover."

Naomie motions to the spot across. "Walt talks about you constantly."

"Does he?"

"C'est toi, évidemment!"

I look to Wade for translation. "She said, 'of course, it's you.'"

"Well, that's sweet."

"He's a sweet boy."

He is.

"And he's so proud of you."

"He is?"

"Oui, he sends me clips of your interviews and links to your articles online almost daily."

"I had no idea." I glance over at Wade, and he's blushing. The hand he's not holding reaches for his thigh and squeezes.

"Bin oui! It's the same with hobbies. When Walt finds something he enjoys, it turns to obsession. I took him along for a library story time I attended after the Olympics, and look" —her arm draws a circle toward the bookshelves— "he can't stop reading. Reading led to children's theater, but he was teased a bit, so he took up rollerblading to combat the neighborhood kids. Rollerblading became ice skating, and now he's a professional athlete."

"All because of reading?"

Naomie nods. "At least it's a good habit. It led him to Harvard."

"Wasn't he on an athletic scholarship?"

"That happened after. He had early admission."

I didn't know that.

"*Really*? How interesting." One knee crosses over the other, my chin in my hand as I peek at Wade. "I don't think that's public information."

"You didn't tell her?"

"*Maman*."

Is he actually a genius masquerading as a dopey fuckboy?

"I'd only read he was drafted sophomore year."

"Oh, yes. He did finish his degree—*English literature with a minor in theater*—what do they call it? Ah yes, distance learning."

"Impressive."

"My boy doesn't like to brag, except in the ways it doesn't matter."

"*Maman*!" His embarrassment deepens.

"What? You are! You're cocky about the way you look, but it's simply genetic." She sweeps a delicate wave of hair behind her ear. "It doesn't take any effort."

Wade's hands move up and down over his torso. "*This* takes effort."

"Okay, Monsieur Hotshot. You're a professional athlete who has been honing his skills since you sprouted your first chest hair. I'd be disappointed if you didn't have a decent physique."

"Decent? I'm in top-notch shape—"

Their animated squabble quickly converts from mixed French and English to French and I'm relishing every second. There's palpable love and pride in her criticism.

Reclining into the couch cushion, I cross my arms. "I'm learning so much about you, *Walt*."

"Oof, he loathes the name. But I can't help it." Her hands lift in surrender. "Sorry, mon bébé."

"She called you a baby," I tease, tapping my knee to his. I'm tickled by his wry expression.

"*That*, you understand."

"This is fun. I want more stories about bébé Walt."

"There's so much more. Happy to share over lunch. Will you join us?"

"Oh, no. I couldn't impose."

"You wouldn't be. We have reservations, but I'm sure they can add a chair—"

"No, please. Thank you, but no. I came from brunch. And I should be preparing some things for work."

"*Ah*, that's too bad."

"So, what brings you to town? Wade mentioned you live in Lac St. Anne."

"I travel often, mostly consulting for coach training. This time I'm going to the English countryside. Devon."

"What's there?"

"Mom's been coaching world-class rowers for the past ten years," Wade explains, straightening his shoulders. "I've been trying to get her to slow down after her knee surgery—"

"Ouf, you're not my boss."

"See what I mean?" He looks to me, then the ceiling, as if addressing the universe. "What have I done to deserve being surrounded by stubborn women?"

"*Anyway*." Naomie intones, ignoring his dramatics. "I'm upset you won't be joining us for lunch. I don't know if I'll survive two hours alone with this one."

I hum my agreement. "It's a shame, really. Maybe next time you're in town, we can have dinner without him?"

Wade rolls his eyes.

"Sounds perfect."

When I get home, he texts me.

PRETTY BOY

Can I take you on a date tomorrow?

PRETTY BOY

And do filthy, unspeakable things to you afterward?

The second message unleashes a witchy cackle from deep within me.

ME

Can't wait.

———

Grief is a strange animal.

One day I'm fine, happily distracted by Wade's phenomenal dick, and proud of myself for not being jealous of his relationship with his mother, and the next, the most precious picture of them posted on his Instagram serves as a trigger and sends me swiftly spiraling.

I can't stop crying. Running a hot bath to calm down presents a new problem. Now that I'm in, I can't find the will to get out.

The mentally stable would contact their therapist, but I haven't seen one since I was sixteen. Mel understood and supported the need for a mental health day, luckily, and got Adrienne to cover the game.

I hesitated to text Indi, not wanting to have her shoulder my burden while in anticipation of motherhood. A simple message does the trick.

ME

Feeling super down today.

INDI

I'm sorry, girl. What do you need

ME

Nothing, wanted to say it somewhere.

INDI

Want me to come over? I can bring India House.

ME

No, thanks. I'm taking a bath.

INDI

Well, let me know if you change your mind.
I'm a text away.

Since uni, Indi knew to give me the space to sort out any complicated emotions, but it was much easier to pretend. Pretend that the anger washed away instead of being too tired to harbor it, while internally holding a candle to it, letting it burn and burn within until it got too much.

It's been hours, I think. I've lost all sense of time. The hot water has been refreshed four times. And gone cold since.

I'm not even sure if it's still the same day or sometime past midnight.

The skin on my fingertips separates from the layers underneath.

Cracking wood follows a thud. Uneven stomping traipses through my condo. Door after door is opened and slammed shut.

I'm defenseless against any sort of violent burglar. Maybe if I hide under the surface of the water, they'll take whatever they want and leave.

My nose reaches the water just as Wade throws the washroom door open, nearly tearing it off its hinges. Wearing a dark suit and tie, no less.

"What the fuck, Gabe?"

Where'd he come from?

"You stood me up?" He unbuttons the perspiration-soaked collar and loosens the knot of his tie.

Oops.

I don't respond.

Soft *blubs* from my fingers splashing the surface of the cold bath water fill the silence.

"I've been losing my shit, Gabe."

A vein bulges on his forehead. More of them snake down the sinews of his neck.

"Called you at least thirty times, texted you even more—without answer. I scoured the city—thinking you were dead in a ditch somewhere. And you? You're here—*at home*—leisurely taking a...a..." His hands fly around, searching for the word.

"Bath," I provide.

A sarcastic laugh of disbelief comes out. "Bath. Your friends were practically no help, by the way. Telling me not to fucking disturb *my* fucking girlfriend. Actually, it was only one. I don't even know any of your friends besides Indi. What is she, your only friend?"

"Yep."

Salt, meet wound. But I'm too numb for it to burn. I let him keep ranting. I deserve nothing less.

"What's the point of getting attached?" My knees curl to my chest, seeking warmth but finding none. "People always leave."

Wade rubs an oval into his forehead. "Fucking hell. Did Vaughn do something?"

"Good guess, but not today. Today's depressive episode is compliments of my mother."

"Gabe."

I have nothing to lose.

"I was four. Remember that picture on my birthday? I had just turned four." A resurgence of tears blurs my vision as I gaze past a watery blob-like Wade. "I'm not sure how soon after, but Dad found her cold one morning. She killed herself."

"Holy fuck." He drops to a squat, palming the rim of the tub.

Pent-up resentment boils and blisters, spewing onto the wrong person. "How's that for an *answer*?" I yell, shoving my hand through the water, hurling a mini wave onto him, and dousing his shirt. "Now you know why I'm fucked up. Does that make you happy, Wade?" My voice cracks, dry, hoarse, and itchy from the raised tone. "To know I'm such a piece of shit, my own mother couldn't deal with raising me?"

His mouth downturns before he goes upright and steps into the tub, dress shoes, suit jacket, and all.

"No, *God*. It fucking breaks my heart." He kneels and leans forward, trapping my naked body between his limbs and sloshing water onto the tile. "I can't stand seeing you like this."

My head lolls to one side, unsure if these tears are old or new. "I needed her. I was a baby and needed my mother."

Wade pushes his forehead to mine.

My shoulders shake out sob after sob. "I need her now. I'm thirty-two years old—and I don't have a clue who she was—what parts of me are hers—outside of these fucking *freckles*. I needed her to be there and share herself with me, and she was so—*fucking—selfish*— she couldn't bear to live for me for another day."

He peels away his jacket and shirt, standing to rid all of his clothes while the cold water drains away, and sneaks in behind me as hot water replaces it. "It's not your fault."

"Then why does it feel like it?"

Our legs stretch in parallel, his outlining mine. Lush lips sit against my temple, one of his strong arms curled across me, keeping my back against his warm front. "I see a lot of myself in her. She lost her family too young. But I loved her. Dad was devoted to her. Why wasn't it enough?" Slow breaths steady mine, his soothing heartbeat like a salve to my ache. Almost, anyway.

"She didn't bother to stick around to walk me down the driveway on the first day of school, or watch me develop a passion for basketball or grow six feet tall, graduate uni, or get my dream job. She didn't congratulate me when I fell in love or wipe my tears when I was forced to fall out of it. She'll never watch me grow in my career, and I'll never get to see her grow old...Why did she rob me of that, Wade? Didn't she love me? Is it so hard to love me?"

"It's not," he murmurs.

"No? Then why did Kurt fuck around?"

"Because his tiny prick has bigger issues than you do."

"Funny. You're a jerk, but funny."

"Whatever you say, Freckles, but I'm here. And I'm not leaving."

His promise acts a salve on these hidden scars, too, so I stay in his arms as long as possible.

Eventually, he goads me out of the water with a warmed robe. He finds himself another and doesn't seem to mind how ridiculously short and snug the fuzzy purple robe is on him.

"What?" He catches me staring.

"Nothing." I point to the dryer in the bathroom closet. "Set it to permanent press, or your clothes will be ruined."

He does. The machine whirs.

"Listen, Freckles. This is a nice laundry room, but you gonna show me around? It's my first time here."

My place is nice, but it's no penthouse. We go through the main living spaces, my lackluster office, the small balcony, and the bedroom, where an embarrassingly large amount of laundry piles on one side of the bed.

The last room has my nerves rattling in my gut. "And this" —I push open the door— "is the indoor greenhouse."

Balmy, humid air circulates within the plastic-covered framing, imitating tropical weather. Sun lamps hang over the rows and shelves of my plants.

"It's...incredible. It looks like a mini version of Terra Bella."

"Just about," I confirm, picking one yellowed leaf from a pothos. "Dad gardens because that's where he senses her presence, where he honors her memory, but..."

"But?"

I shake my head, unable to lie to him this time. "I've been trying for years, Wade. *Years.* It doesn't matter how hard I work or how much my plants thrive. I can't seem to connect with her. Every year that passes, it seems less and less likely that I ever will."

A defeated sigh leaves me. He extends a beckoning hand. "Come here."

Reaching back feels right, so I do.

CHAPTER 21:
WHAT A GOOD BOY

WADE

I BREATHE IN AS SHE NUZZLES MY COLLARBONE, LIKE A black cat with claws retracted, the smell of her and the carefully curated white gardenias lulling me to the point of intoxication.

My arms boost her up and around my torso to carry her to bed.

Unkempt sheets pushed aside, I set her down in the middle, then stretch to shift my weight and flank her with my forearms. While I guide her long fingers into my hair, she exhales from her nose.

"We're the same," I confess.

"Are we?"

A set of short nails drags across my scalp, and I lean into it, fighting the urge to close my eyes. But I don't want to miss a moment of her attention.

"My dad didn't want me either."

Her caress on my cheek and jaw cracks me open like the widening of a rift through arid soil.

"Wade."

"You looked me up, but you didn't find him. That's on purpose because he wants nothing to do with me. He makes sure the world never finds his bastard."

The strokes shorten into circles. I clasp over her hands to keep them still.

"Walton Quade. By title a Baron, by character, a flaming pile of garbage."

Sympathy deepens the hazel streaks in her eyes to sable.

"We received a lump sum every year in exchange for our silence. He got to keep up the façade of being a perfect family man and stay in the good graces of the royals."

I tighten my hold on her. I don't want to let go. I don't want her to let go.

"I only met him once. I was twelve and ended up hiding in my room while he and Maman argued over the stipend. She wanted him to take responsibility, to be an actual father, and help raise me. He called her a gold-digging whore. My mother kicked him out and told him to fuck himself with his own money."

"Oof."

"I'm sorry I wasn't myself when meeting your dad. Jealousy took over."

"Seeing you with your mom triggered the same feeling in me."

My eyes fall shut, wishing I could dispel her insecurities. "Sorry I have daddy issues."

"And I'm sorry I have mommy issues."

Her lips brush my knuckles, hands switching position to cup my cheeks. "Guess we're both fucked up."

"Basically."

"Did...did we just become friends?"

My forehead drops to her chin with a snort. "Yep."

"Oh, no. That's the worst thing that could've happened."

That's not the worst thing that could've happened. Je veux te donner mon cœur.

"Whoops."

She brings my attention back to her with a light graze of her thumb over my cheek.

"What do you need, Wade?"

I dock my arms beneath hers, twining my fingers into the lush strands spreading over the pillow.

"I need you to lie here and not make fun of me tonight, okay?"

"Okay."

The room fills with silence, dead except for the tandem rising and falling of our chests.

"Wade?"

"Mm."

"What did your mom say when we met?"

"When?"

"When I complimented her."

"Wade, épouse-la!"

"Je pense qu'elle est la seule femme que j'aimerais épouser." What an admission. *"Peut-être un jour elle me laissera."*

Maman hummed. *"Est-ce qu'elle t'agace?"*

Yeah, she annoyed me more than anyone.

"Même plus que toi."

"Crétin!"

"She told me to marry you."

"I like her. She's funny."

"Bin oui. It's where I get it from."

"You're *not* funny."

I headbutt her collarbone gently. "Yes, I am. You said so earlier."

"I was upset. I got caught up in the moment."

"Too bad. No takesies backsies."

Gabe harrumphs. "Some friend you're turning out to be."

"Watch it. I know your deepest, darkest secrets now. I could misuse that information."

"Well, I know yours, too."

"Not all of them."

"You have more secrets?"

"Wanna find out, Freckles?"

———

If getting Gabe Finch in a sex swing didn't kill me, sharing a bed with her on a regular basis might do it.

Though it *was* downright adorable when she thought it was a set of over-the-door portable TRX straps. I set her straight, fucking that pussy from behind, her legs Velcroed high and wide and in plain view of the giant mirror tilted against my bedroom wall.

Earlier tonight, I snuck into her hotel room. She's covering the game with Vancouver tomorrow and we both need rest, but it's 3 a.m. and I can't sleep. One, she's wearing my fucking jersey, and two, she won't stop squirming in her sleep while we spoon, pert ass grinding against my excited cock. My fingers sink into her hips as a rumbling groan spills out.

Freckles whines. "Get your leg away from my buttcrack. It's hard and uncomfortable."

"That's not my leg." I fiddle with the end of her braid, mindlessly brushing it over my mouth and nose.

She sighs, exasperated, but hums when I roll my hips to seek the same delicious friction.

"Wade, if we fuck right now, will you let me sleep in?"

"Hell, yes."

Gabe wiggles against the mattress before her silk shorts billow onto my face. "Grab a condom."

I scramble for one from atop the nightstand, sliding it over the shaft without removing my boxers.

"And this," she commands, wrapping her braid around my wrist.

A delicate yank twists it until her head tips up. My other hand dives between her legs, splitting them apart to position myself and attempt some sort of prep, but she's already wet.

"Been dreamin' about me, Freckles?"

"You wish. I was in the middle of some truly disgusting stuff with—"

Without hesitation, I tease the tip in from behind and give her clit a light pinch. "Don't you dare say anyone's name but mine..."

She gasps. "Oh, *God*."

"That's more like it." My lips find the shell of her ear, delving in inch-by-inch. "Fucking love when you call me that."

"I hate you."

"Is that so?" The next rough plunge shakes moans from both of us.

"Yes." She pants between every slam. "I hate your arrogant" —I pull out until her pussy can only tighten around the head of my cock— "handsome face. And your" —her hips adjust, angling to swallow me again until I hit a spot so deep she whines through a pause— "stupid dimpled smirks."

I disrupt the languid pace, my heartbeat ragged between punishing thrusts and questions I know the answer to. "You hate me right now, Freckles?" Her walls pulse without rhythm when I stroke her G-spot. "Hate how good you're taking every inch of my cock with my name plastered on your back?" We share a loud, shameless groan when I push in once more. "Hate how your little cunt makes a mess for me?"

"Oh, my—fuck—*Wade*—" Her nails clip into my forearms, shredding the sweat-lined top layer of skin. "I'm gonna—"

My hands abandon her hips, climbing under the thickly knit polyester to pluck at the hardened peaks of her nipples while nibbling a tender stretch of skin along her neck. I throb, fully inside her, twitching for relief but desperate for her to finish first. "Please, Gabe," I beg through a grunt, about to explode into the condom. "I'm so fucking close."

She plays with her clit, cunt clamping down as my thrusts go uneven and sloppy, spitting curses against her open mouth. Tremors take over before launching us over the edge and tearing through parallel orgasms. Our breaths catch, hearts rattling against one another behind their cages.

"*Christ*. That was too fast—"

Gabe replies with a soft snore.

"Oh, good. Now you can't call me needy for staying inside you."

I relish in the cocoon of her freshly fucked pussy until my dick goes limp, then slide out. Once discarding the condom in the washroom, I return with a damp cloth in hand.

A few hours later, I tiptoe from bed and quietly close the washroom door to shower before going back into my hotel room.

The pressure and hot temperature of the water loosens a tight spot in my shoulder. My head dips through the steady stream as Gabe joins, braid bolstered up by a giant claw clip.

She leaves a long, heady kiss on my damp lips. "Good morning."

"I bet it was," I gloat, pushing hair away from my forehead. "I fucked you to sleep."

Gabe pivots in the cascade, trickling water down her tall, lean figure.

My cock has no chill. It swells and sways, practically swooning at the attention.

"Stop looking at it," I scold her.

"But how?" The wicked gleam in her eyes makes me shudder. "Even if I look away, it's so big I can see it in my peripheral vision."

I lament and cup both hands over it, wishing it would soften. "Complimenting is not gonna make it go away."

"Lucky for you, I don't want it to. You're not the only horny person around here." Her hand stretches over the tense muscle rounding my shoulder and squeezes. "Kneel."

Being bossy doesn't help either because I love being told what to do. Only by Gabe, though.

My knees bear my weight against the heated marble, hands lifting to the arches of her hips to pull her closer.

"You were so good last night." Her praise and fingers pushing through my hair slackens my jaw, and I snuggle into her palm. "What a good boy."

"Yes," I confirm with a gasp, desperate for more.

"You deserve a treat."

A black oblong object see-saws between her first finger and thumb. When she presses the button, it buzzes to life, shooting a jolt of pleasure behind the base of my cock.

"That's...my..."

"Fell out of your shorts when I moved them. Had to do a reverse Google Image search to figure out what it was." Her tongue clicks in disappointment. "Were you planning on using it without me?" She angles the shower head to one side, away from us, and holds the vibrator under the water. "If you want me to play with your ass, all you have to do is ask nicely."

"Fuck yes." I clamber to my feet and backward, eager to have yet another fantasy come true. My cock bounces.

Gabe drops to her haunches, scratching across a hip and into the trim hairs below my belly button. She fists my length and brings it to her mouth. Her blown breath is warmer than the surrounding steam. I recline, bracing against the shower wall.

"I'm gonna suck your cock now. Don't come until I say so. Okay?"

I nod.

"Words."

"Yes, please."

"And how will you know when to finish if my mouth's full?"

"You'll...tap my hip twice?"

"Good."

The drop of pre-cum gets licked away, more and more of it leaking from me in sync with the increased vibrations on the underside of my dick. My balls recoil to the point of pain.

Her eyes widen as the thin trail drips down her chin, neck, and sternum. She kisses its source before wrapping those plump lips around the aching head, then swallows more of me, stroking her tongue over the veins and sucking like her life depends on it, inching the toy closer and closer to where I need it.

I spread the stickiness over her nipples. They purse under my touch. "Fucking—obsessed with your tits." My hands clamp around them, hissing with an unintentional thrust into her mouth when she presses the silicone bulge into the sensitive flesh behind my tightened balls. "Right there, yes. Goddamn your mouth. Your hands. Your tiny cunt, your ass. I'd fuck them all at once if I could."

She deepthroats me with a gag while corkscrewing around the shaft and massaging the toy against the sensitive spot, forcing me to use her to prop myself up. "Gabe–Gabe—Gabe," I chant. Her name's a plea for mercy, and each time, it's denied.

"Fuck–*please*. I need to."

Head shaking out a silent no, she bobs at a mind-numbing cadence, the noisy squelching with each thrust testing my restraint beyond limits.

My leaden, shallow breaths alternate with desperate groans. They echo off every wall. I stammer through curses, knocking my head into the marble stone wall behind me, toes curling until they go numb.

"Gabe, please, please, please. I'm gonna—come so hard."

I might black out.

She taps my hip.

Once.

Every muscle writhes and strains. I grunt as my cock fills her throat.

Twice.

The orgasm bursts, violent spurts of my cum pumping into her, the load so big it leaks from her mouth and onto my balls in a hot and sticky web.

Vision lost, the ringing in my ears recedes as I drown in the sensory overload.

When the high subsides, Gabe repositions the shower stream between us, cheeks puffed. She reaches for my jaw and spits my release into my gaping mouth. A judder rolls through me as it lands on my tongue, salty and thick.

Her hand places mine over her throat as she gulps the rest of it.

"See you at the game."

A pang from lost contact settles as she exits the shower.

"No good luck kiss?" I call after her. "No kiss goodbye?"

"Win tonight, and I'll kiss that sweet round ass."

CHAPTER 22:
I WILL NOT ASK TO GET FINGERBANGED ON MY FAKE BOYFRIEND'S BUS

GABE

FINDING YOUR FAKE BOYFRIEND'S SEX TOY AND playing with his taint while sucking the soul out of him: cannot recommend it enough. Ten out of ten. No notes.

His desperation, his neediness, the way he begs. It's delightful.

Mood lifted, I let Candace style my hair as big as she wants and even agree to the purple smokey eye with gold glitter Jas has been wanting to try instead of the standard neutral tones.

During warm-ups, I review notes while Denise checks her battery. She bellows a groan as Wade skates over, beaming with child-like glee. "Here comes trouble."

I ditch my earpiece. Can't risk anyone overhearing our conversation.

My hands clinch the top of the boards to lean in and meet him halfway but fly up to his pads when he drops his goalie mask to the ice. He spits his mouth guard to the side and hides his face between the wall of my hair and jaw. I squeal at the tickle of his breath and scratchy stubble.

Fans behind us gasp and titter.

"You left without my good luck kiss, you wench."

The sincere smile on my face stretches wider and preempts a hearty laugh. "This is a family sport, Boehner. What're you gonna do about it?"

To everyone else, it looks like a sweet hug.

"Steal it from you" —he nips the sensitive spot below my ear— "gonna take what's mine." His tongue swipes and swipes at the column of my neck, flattening to create a deep suction from his dampened lips. I giggle— *freaking giggle*—at the combination. "Remember how that feels."

"Why?"

"'Cause that's how I want you to eat my ass."

"You'll have to wait until we get back to Ottawa. I'm not rimming you in some hotel bed."

"I can be patient."

"Atta boy."

We pull apart, grinning at each other like the two horny fools we are. One last quick peck is met with whistles and whooping from the surrounding sections.

"Have a good game," I sing-song with a flirty wave, wiggling my fingers by my shoulder to complete the spectacle.

Wade collects his mask and chews on his mouthguard, gliding away with a wink.

The Bears play hard but are no match for the previous year's champions. Between the forwards alternating goals and assists, and Jaeger and Olsen's solid wall of defense, Boehner has been sitting pretty in the net, crease almost untouched in the first two periods. He blocks and slaps away the two attempts with ease.

I have to stop myself from cheering for the Regents more than once.

At the end of the game, Mel tells me to nab Landon before he gets off the ice.

"Radek! Over here! Got a second?"

He nods and heads my way, tilting toward me to hear through his helmet and over the raucous in the arena.

John Fairbanks from the press box prompts the switchover. Denise's green light signals I'm on air. I slap on a smile for the camera.

"We've got Gabe Finch down at the rink with the Regents' alternate captain."

"Thanks, John. Here with Landon Radek, who scored two goals and made two assists in this shutout game." My best friend's husband pants out a humble laugh and inhales through his nose. "Just over a month into the regular season, Ottawa has racked up a twelve-game winning streak—sixteen if you count the preseason—are you attempting to break a league record? Is this something the team talked about?"

Landon catches his breath, his dimpled smile oozing charm and charisma. "Y'know, we didn't set out to do it; we're playing to win—and that's what we'll keep trying to do."

"Your next game is in Seattle. The Specters are a newer team, but talented and determined to compete for the Cup this year. How do you think you'll stack up?"

"I think we can handle whatever they throw at us."

He's obviously exhausted, so I let him go.

"Sounds like you have a plan. Thanks, Landon. See you in Seattle."

With that, he coasts away, stopping to sign a puck and toss it over the glass to a young fan, then jumps through the gate and disappears down the hallway at a slow jog.

"Should be an exciting match-up. The Ottawa Regents play the Seattle Specters in Washington tomorrow at 7 p.m. Eastern. Back to John for the post-game analysis."

Off-air, I sigh in relief.

"Nicely done, Finch," Mel says in my earpiece.

"Thanks." I hand the mic over to Troy.

"You still there?"

"Yeah. What's up?"

"I have good news and bad news."

I squint up to the suite where she stands akimbo at the glass. "Bad news first."

"Our flight's canceled. It's pouring, and the runway's too slick to take off."

"And the good news?"

"There's space on the Regents charter."

"We're hitching a ride on their bus?"

"Yep. You good with that?"

"'Course. Why wouldn't I be?"

One of the PAs loads the media equipment and our suitcases. I shake droplets from my umbrella and prep myself as we board.

I will not ask to get fingerbanged on my fake boyfriend's bus. I will not ask to get fingerbanged on my fake boyfriend's bus. I will not ask to get fingerbanged on my fake boyfriend's bus.

Coaching staff, the GM, and the equipment manager acknowledge our presence as we walk down the aisle. I trail behind Denise, Candace, and Jas as Mel and Troy sit on opposite sides of the aisle between rows of some second-line defensemen.

Denise finds the last empty row and hogs it for herself, putting her backpack into the seat.

"Real mature," I deadpan.

"What? I need space."

Someone clears their throat. "That's too bad, Freckles." The silky timbre of his voice traps a breath in my throat. Wade's toothy, wicked smile gleams back. "You'll have to settle for sitting next to me."

Warmth coats the hollow of my chest. What is happening to me? Two months ago, I would have boiled over with annoyance.

Today, I find his wisecracks endearing.

My eyes roll for good measure. Can't give him goo-goo eyes simply because we're friends.

He pats the seat cushion. "Fartless. Only the best for my girl."

"Classy."

"Always. Hey!" Wade interrupts himself, poking a hand between the seats ahead of us. "Eyes forward, Donovan."

"*Ow!*" The redhead pops his fist over, one eye screwed shut from getting jabbed, and smacks the top of Boehner's head. Poor guy gets bopped back.

"Headphones, Fletch. Headphones!"

He pulls on a set of white over-the-ear headphones with a loud grumble.

"So authoritative."

"You like that, huh? Finally, some privacy." With a yawn, his arms stretch above his head and plop over my shoulder. I move my gaze from the hand placement to his dopey expression.

"And smooth, too."

"So...?" His suggestive glance pairs with a goosebump-inducing caress against my thigh.

What was that I said about not getting fingerbanged on the bus?

"So...?"

"You wanna...?"

"Wanna what?" I have an idea, but I wanna hear him say it.

"Wanna watch a Bollywood movie?"

"You watch Bollywood movies?"

He gapes. "You don't?"

"That's all Indi. She made me watch them." She made me join our uni's dance crew, too—a hopeless effort to connect me with my Indian side. Only lasted one year, though. The basketball team's schedule was too demanding for anything else but studying.

"Landon got me hooked. They're so fun!"

I succumb to his puppy eyes. "Fine, I'll watch. Did you have one in mind?"

Wade points to his tablet, where "*Yeh Jawaani Hai Deewani*" finished downloading. "This one? It's a favorite and came back on Netflix finally."

"Sure."

"Can we make out, too?"

The innocent question catches me off-guard. "Make out?"

"Please?" There's a nudge of his nose against my cheek. The brush of his warm lips, his hot breath. Begging and begging.

My shoulder crumples, sandwiching him in the crook. "You wanna kiss me?"

"Only all the fucking time." His words melt into my skin, buzzing with a desperate whimper.

"*Aww*," I coo. "Okay."

"Perfect. It'll get you primed for my fingers later."

"In front of the team? And management?"

"Didn't seem to bother you on Halloween."

"We weren't working. My boss is sitting, like, five rows up."

"Everyone's gonna be passed out in a second. And if they hear, good. They deserve to know my girlfriend is well-fucked."

—

Well-fucked indeed. The fake part of fake girlfriend seems to be withering away day by day.

No, no. Wade and I are friends.

Friends who fuck.

I tighten the belt of my pea coat in the cab.

PRETTY BOY

Flight tracker said you landed

ME

You tracked my flight?

PRETTY BOY

I'm fucking DYING to rail you seven ways to Sunday

PRETTY BOY

What did you expect??

ME

You're so dramatic.

PRETTY BOY

Whatever

PRETTY BOY

My ass is ready

PRETTY BOY

Clean as a whistle

ME

And here I thought I'd surprise you.

PRETTY BOY

Nah I'm too quick

PRETTY BOY

Like a ninja

PRETTY BOY

ETA??

A stiff edge of boot leather bites the back of my knee as I exit onto the curb of his building. The wind on the short walk to the door almost exposes me and my little surprise.

Anticipation has me so wet, my thighs stick together in the elevator.

Wade bounds from the bedroom, meeting my rushed strides. He wins the battle for dominance, and my back meets the nearest wall, pinned under the firm breadth of his chest in a frenzy of crossing limbs and crashing mouths.

My lips burst into a knowing smile between restless, slithery kisses, satisfied with the contact. "Why are you so obsessed with me?"

"You're insufferable," he groans. "Why are you still wearing your coat?" His question is closer to a lament and comes with a feverish attempt at removal.

I undo the top button of the coat. "You'll see in a sec." The towel does nothing to hide the hard curve between his legs. I toy with the tuck on his hips. "You haven't been playing with *my* cock, have you?"

"*Your* cock?" His eyebrows raise halfway up his forehead.

My neckline deepens with two more opened buttons. I confirm with a hum, cupping over the terrycloth. "*Mine.*"

His eyes gasp with a fluttery blink. "Fucking *fuck.*"

"That's not an answer." I tighten my grip around the fat, heavy length.

A hiss follows. "No."

"Good boy."

He gulps, but the corner of his mouth twitches, twinning with his dick in my hand.

"Towel off."

Wade drops it with a cartoonish speed, and his pink, rigid cock slaps his abs.

"Now turn around."

Chocolate brown eyes brightening, he does as he's told. "Should I bend over?"

The little brat thinks he's cute.

Tongue wetting the seam of my lips, I deny him. "On the bed. Hands and knees."

A fiery blush licks up his neck to the top of his ears. "What—?" His question dissolves, mouth agape as he watches me retrieve something from my pocket before the wool coat slips from my bare shoulders. Pupils blown, he gawks at the black harness cupping my pussy, unaware of how soaked I am. I pivot slightly, allowing a view of me adjusting the metal snap that secures the strip of leather lining my ass.

His statement is a barely audible breath. "Fuck me."

"Soon." Recognition of the black satin satchel strikes something wild in his heated gaze. Metal clinks and clangs when I pull the straps on my hips tighter, the fit deliciously nipping into the delicate flesh there. "But not yet."

Brash confidence surges through my explosive smile.

"Face down, Pretty Boy."

CHAPTER 23:
CAN I TELL YOU A SECRET?

WADE

A SINGULAR FEATHER-LIGHT STROKE STARTS AT MY ankle, then traces the arc of my calf and continues the climb up the back of my thigh.

Divots form in the mattress where my knees shift. The cotton sheets cool the flush on my cheek, pinpricks bursting through the dew of sweat as Gabe repeats the motion on the other leg.

The large mirror in the corner confirms our positions. A sheathed dildo, resting lifeless on the bed. Me, ass up. Raw, exposed. Her, anchoring behind me. Shoulders back, chin confident. A pristine picture of submission and dominance.

She traps me with a molten gaze.

Everything tightens.

Her touch lingers on my ankle. When she replaces it with her mouth, I choke on air.

"Good?"

My answer hangs through a breath.

"G-good."

Plush, wet lips travel the same path as her fingers. Kissing, suckling, licking, doting. I wrench my eyes shut, imagination running wild. My cock weeps.

Hands claw into the flesh of my ass. I reactively widen my stance. Begging.

"This is what you want?" She noses the contour line at the peak of my thigh.

"*God*, yes."

"Has anyone ever had you like this?"

"No." I gasp. "Only you."

"Can I be rough with you?"

I wiggle, seeking her touch. "You can be anything you want with me. Take it. Take me."

The kisses reach the crest of the crease, splitting my lower half, and my pulse roars when she pulls me apart.

She hums. "Fuck, I could get used to seeing you like this." A trail of warm saliva coasts down, coating the hole. It pulses with the pass of her finger. Astonishment brightens her husky tone. "You're so...pink, Wade. So wet, so shiny."

I moan at the praise and quiver when the harsh force of her spit lands on the opening and clench with each caress that stops to massage at the sensitive spot below.

A crack sounds as she slaps one cheek.

"*Oh*," comes out. Plaintive. Heady.

"More?"

"More."

Another finger joins in the travel past the slick crevice, this time with a hearty snicker. "Everyone knows you're a slut, Wade" —the same fingers knead my perineum again— "but only I know what a needy slut you are for me."

My face buries in the sheets, unable to control the nonsensical sounds exiting my mouth as she licks and licks, closer and closer to the greased hole. I simultaneously tense and go pliant at her hot breath blowing over the puckered opening.

I keen. Her tonguing my asshole has my head spinning. All I can say is *fuck* and *Gabe,* and both words are mashed together like boiled potatoes. Which is precisely the current state of my brain.

There's a click. For the briefest second, I think maybe my mind is falling apart.

Cold lube glides over every overheated inch of flesh, spread by those perfect fucking fingers.

"Relax," she rasps, the pad of her index finger experimenting with pressure against the opening. "It'll hurt if you don't." She knuckles the space behind my balls, and I loosen with a jerk.

The tip slides in, and I wince, the rigid finger stretching the canal's delicate tissue.

"*Ungh.*"

"You're doing so good," she purrs, pressing in and retreating in languid strokes. Her encouragement has me tilting my hips back to suck her in deeper.

My thighs stutter when Gabe reaches the swollen dome of flesh inside me. I cling to reality with every rubbed circle. Pre-cum leaks from me like a faucet. One of my hands seeks out my anguished cock, wanting to jack myself into a frenzy.

Crack.

The impact of her smack on the other cheek ripples through my body.

"Hands where I can see them."

"Fucking shi—*please.*" They obey, rising above my head, only to bunch the fabric in my fists.

"You'll come like this," she demands. "Without touching yourself."

The slow strokes and circles speed up with the addition of more lube and another finger, changing my muffled sounds of pleasure to those of pure, frantic need.

"How's that feel?"

"Full, so *full*," I drone.

My cock paces the surface of the mattress, tangling itself in a sticky web. I'm already teetering on the edge, and the orgasm whips through a white-hot flash. I topple and cry out for Gabe.

"I'm here," she coos, kissing my hip and shoulder and stroking the sweaty, barbaric strands of my hair. "Can you be a good boy and give me another?"

I groan a *yes* while drooling into the mattress.

Still half-hard, I ball the sheets while a blurry Gabe prepares the toy, notching it through the o-ring of her strap-on and then lathering a generous amount of lube over its length. Her fingers glaze with some of the excess, and she uses it to coat my insides as prep.

No words, only inhuman, primitive noises flow from me.

"Want you to be loud, Wade." She takes a deep breath, tapping the buzzing silicone head of her dildo against my lube-covered hole. "Let everyone know how greedy you are for me, for this dick."

One easy push in, and I'm gone again, lost in the high doled out to me.

"You're taking it so well."

My hips pop back in answer to the rolling motion of hers, soft, happy noises escaping from where I bite the sheets.

"So, so well."

Inch by inch, she takes and takes and takes, every withdrawal blending relief and loss and gluttonous desire together. Each plow, she asks if it's too much, and each time, I deny it, savoring the delicious stretch. Overwhelmed by how the line of pain and ecstasy becomes less and less clear.

The fake cock bounces off my prostate on the way in and digs against it on the way out. This time, pleasure doesn't build brick by brick. It appears suddenly and sneaks up like a phantom, ready to devour. I wrack through it, moaning a scream until my throat goes silent.

"Fuck." Gabe falters. "I'm gonna come."

The constant spearing goes uneven, and I break, coming so hard I can't see. Coming and coming and *fuck*, it can't be possible for me to *still* be coming. Hot, thick cum stripes between my chest and the bed below.

Her thighs judder against mine, nails clipping the skin of my ass. But she stays vibrating inside me, panting in the wake.

A dull rush of blood in my ears mutes her low, dulcet voice.

"Making you come" — she laughs through a huff— "is better than denying you orgasms. I might be addicted."

The sound wraps me like a warm blanket on a chilly day, and I want to live in it. Live inside that laughter.

"You think you can handle another?"

My eyes flip open to her maniacal smile.

"*Can't*," I blubber through a groan.

"I know you can do it." She soothes me with a hush, spread palms skimming over my backside. "Let me make you come again."

Short respite complete, my leaky cock bobs against my abs. Ready for more.

"Okay." I agree. I must be crazy.

"That was only half. Can I fill you up?" she says. "Unless you don't want me to."

"I want you to."

It's true, and I mean it. I might be addicted, too.

Large spurts of lube add to the mix before she delves in. Gabe pores over the tender, overworked p-spot. Sweat pours down my back.

"The way your ass swallows the tip of this dick is *obscene*." The last word gushes from her, erotic and awful. "Like those pretty sounds."

Silky strokes crescendo into ravenous ones, sending me and my cock slobbering into the bedsheets. Every other breath hitches between my gruff, elongated inflections and lazy grunts.

She quakes and curls over me, puffing out a string of bad words while filling me to the hilt, leather and metal sandwiched between her hips and my bare ass. The pitch of her moan skips an octave with the next deep slam.

And just like that, I come, fierce and ruinous, like being set on fire, the load splattering every surface within a short distance.

Gabe whimpers my name, and every thread of my sanity unravels.

I shatter across the bed when she pulls out, wobbly knees no longer able to support me through the aftershocks. I'm numb and blind—no color but Gabe and no sensation except for her touch gathering me up like a pile of laundry before I lose consciousness.

I ebb in and out, experiencing a hazy angel armed with a hot, damp towel. The contact to every crook and cranny of my chest, my abs, my cock, my ass, is lush and needed. I black out when it stops and wake up to the thrumming of her heartbeat. Her naked hips and legs, shed of the harness, shift beneath me.

Weak and groggy, my head lifts from her skin.

Her fingers skate through my hair and down my back. I savor it with an indiscernible noise.

"You okay?"

A dopey chuckle sputters. "I think my mind exploded into bits and spilled out of my cock."

She collects one of my hands and moves her lips over the knuckles, her whine regretful. "I was too rough, huh?"

"Far too rough."

"I'm sorry," she murmurs through a hum, her kisses like salve on open wounds. "Do you hate me?"

"My ass might tomorrow."

We share a dazed giggle.

"But I could never."

"Never? You hated my guts a couple months ago."

"Untrue," I rasp, nuzzling into her once more, the valley of her sternum a stunning fit for my cheek.

Her content sigh follows. "No?"

"No." Air rustles through my nose. "Can I tell you a secret?"

"Yeah."

Slumber threatens me with a sharp knife, but I manage to get the words out.

"I've never hated you." I notch my chin on her chest, needing her to know. Needing her to see me. "I hated how much I wanted you. Hated how I couldn't have you. I hated how much you hated me. But never you."

Tawny eyes gazing back soften, fingertips brushing through the hair on either side of my lax head. "Wanna know my secret?"

"Yes."

"I still kinda hate you." Her lips purse in the corners, sly and joking, before turning serious. "I hate that you hide yourself. Hate that I had no idea how incredible you are. Hate that no one has appreciated your gentle heart and thoughtful mind. I'm so lucky to know all these amazing parts of you, Wade." She pecks my nose. "I promise I'm not taking it for granted."

My heart soars. It flies so fucking high.

This. I wanted this.

Adoration and awe, tenderness, and teasing. The culmination of an intimacy that only vulnerability allows.

It's what I chased every fling, with every other person I'd been with. And now that I have it, I want nothing else, with no one but her.

I wanna tell her—*then the world*—that I was too afraid to show so many sides of myself until she stripped me down. That only she can pull me apart and piece me back together. That she's it for me.

The various parts—the playboy, the submissive, the intellectual, the athlete—stare at one another in a house of mirrors, debating.

It'll be over in the New Year. What's the point? one whispers. *She'll find someone else.*

Instead, my eyes shut, casting away the voices, unready to leave this perfect moment for a spiral of pessimism.

"Sleepy baby boy," Gabe sweetly mutters, pelting short kisses in my hair. "Mine, mine, mine."

Thank God.

I cherish the confirmation and kiss her heart. "Mine," I mutter back. "Yours."

CHAPTER 24:
BORN TO BE A PASSENGER PRINCESS

GABE

GETTING RAILED TO HIGH HEAVEN THREE TO FIVE times a week is like the merriest of holiday seasons.

It makes everything better. Nonexistent sun? No problem. Birds flew south for the winter? Okay by me. Neither No Nut November nor overcast skies are effective. Wade didn't even make it twenty-four hours, and I'm getting more than enough Vitamin D to last me through saddie season.

Sleeping through the alarm this morning gave me an excuse to use a new dry shampoo. The botched batch of cupcakes I was supposed to donate to the Boys and Girls Club's annual bake sale simply meant swinging by Go Ahead, Cake My Day on my way to work. Even the blizzard raging throughout the day doesn't get me down.

I shake my head and smile at the frozen, snowy tundra of the network office parking lot. Someone's started to clean it from one side. I can't tell which of the custodial staff it is, considering they're bundled head to toe, but wave a hand in thanks as I take a sip of coffee and move toward the parked Beemer.

I'm pleasantly surprised there's a shoveled path to the driver's side. "That's nice." Neither of the neighboring cars piled high with the fresh white snow have gotten any attention. I shrug.

Overnight bag thrown in the back, I get into the front with my tumbler, humming the network's new theme song.

The engine turns with the automatic start button, and I set my lidded mug into its holder. While waiting for the car to warm, I lower my hooded scarf. Something white glimmers in the periphery.

I jolt at the silhouette of a person in my passenger seat with a shrill scream. "*Ahhhhhhhhh!*"

My legs push to scramble backward as far as possible from the intruder, fingers searching for the handle.

But it's not a person. A six-foot, plush snowman looking smug in his silk top hat, striped scarf, and corncob pipe stares blankly at the visor, a permanent smile embroidered onto his rotund snowball face.

"What the actual fuck?" I curse to myself. Finally, the car door gives and creaks open.

A head pops between me and the door. "*Heyyyy*, Freckles."

I swing a fist but miss.

"Jesus!" The handsome culprit clasps his toque as he tumbles backward.

"Wade!" I seethe, bounding out of the car. "I'm gonna fucking strangle you!"

He prances in a jog through the snow, bursting with giddy laughter at our slow chase. "And I'll enjoy it!"

"Why are you like this?" I yell. "I thought I was gonna die!"

"*Aww, babycakes*," Wade croons and stops in his tracks and turns to scoop me up, arms tight around my puffy coat. "I'd never let anything happen to you."

The snow crunches under his boots as he toddles us back to the XM.

"*Ewwww*. Ironically, I prefer Freckles."

"Ironic? I'm nuts about these gorgeous things." His nose grazes each cheek before planting audible kisses over them.

"You're such a simp." I attempt to uncouple from him by pushing with both hands, but it's useless. He plops me down by the door.

"For *you*."

"And cheesy, too," I deadpan.

"You love it." That knowing smirk makes me wanna wipe it off by doing punishing things to him, but there's no time to act on my less-than-savory intentions. "Want me to drive?"

"No, I will." My finger draws a circle, motioning for him to round the car.

"*Phew*," he mimes wiping sweat from his brow, "I was born to be a passenger princess."

Duffle and hockey sticks stored in the trunk, Wade buckles the snowman in the seat behind him and hops into the front.

I reverse and pull out of the lot. "I thought we were meeting at your place to drive to Landon's family farm. I was heading your way."

"I know, but the Rover is getting serviced, and I wanted to surprise you."

My eyes fall on the sizeable plush figure in the back row through the rearview mirror. "I have many questions."

He sucks down a gulp of the green contents of his protein shaker. "Ask away."

"What's with Frosty?"

He looks over his shoulder. "Whaddya mean?"

"Why is he here?"

"*Ohhhhh*! That's for Radek's niece and nephew, Sadie and Gunnar." His arrogant smile returns in a flash. "I'm their *favorite*."

"*Riiiiight.*" I'm pretty sure Indi is their favorite, but don't want to be the one to remove him from the delusion. "Where do you buy such a thing?"

Wade shushes me loudly and whisper-yells. "He can hear you. Frosty." He turns over his shoulder to address the silly stuffed toy. "Don't listen to her. She's mean. Santa told me he's putting coal in her stocking."

"You didn't answer the question."

"Where does one buy anything good?"

His hands beckon the answer from me.

"Amazon?"

"Costco."

"Costco? Why do *you* have a Costco membership?"

"Why do *I*" —he cuts himself off with a sputter of disbelief— "The real question is, why don't *you* have a Costco membership?"

"Because I'm only one person."

"That's no excuse." Wade pretends to lick a pen in the air and make a note by drawing squiggles on his palm. "Putting this on my list. Get Freckles a Costco card."

"Oh, good. Now we won't forget." If sarcasm and schtick were a love language, we've got it down pat. "Also, how did you get Frosty into my car?"

"I'm *very* persuasive."

"Are you?"

"And charming, too."

"Mmhmm, mmhmm. Who was it?"

"It was a joint effort between Aden in security and your PA. He's a fan, and your PA is very helpful."

I raise an eyebrow. "You been flirting with my PA?"

Wade scoffs and spreads a hand over his chest, aghast. I don't fall for his theatrics.

"I wouldn't dream of it!"

I hit the gas, speeding up to merge onto 417 West.

"Whoa, Nelly." His hands brace, gripping the console and door handle. "I can't watch this." He leans forward to unzip his backpack and retrieves a fluffy pink sleep mask with two eyelashed curves and the words, *shhh...I'm sleeping*, printed in swirly script. He quietly slips it over his eyes, wiggling his hips and shoulders to get comfortable.

I mouth a *wow*.

Wade snaps his fingers and points in my direction. "I saw that."

"When you said passenger princess, you meant it."

"You bet your sweet ass I did." The power seat whirs as he reclines. "Wake me up in thirty, Freckles."

"Sorry, do I look like your mother?"

"Not even a little bit," he snipes back, unperturbed by my snark. "You can keep mouthing off, but in half an hour, both of us are gonna be in the backseat, and only one of us will have this over our eyes. I have no qualms about traumatizing Frosty with whatever happens back there."

I seal my lips.

The four-and-a-half-hour trip takes six because...*activities*, and night falls by the time we reach the property in the middle of nowhere Ontario.

Radek's family farmhouse is picturesque, like the Christmas scene printed in a Thomas Kinkade calendar for the month of December, snow-topped rolling hills, and glassy iced-over lakes reflecting moonlight while we follow the gravel driveway.

"Sorry we missed dinner." Wade puffs out a breath and sways his head when Landon greets us in the foyer. "The holiday traffic was something else this year."

"That's okay. Glad you could make it, man." Their hands clap together before they hug. "You two hungry?"

Wade doesn't miss a beat and pats his belly. "I'm stuffed."

My mind sweeps away to three hours ago when Wade sucked my clit so hard, I mashed Frosty's face into the window and turned into a soprano.

Landon clears his throat, throwing a discerning glance between the two of us.

"I'm famished," I say, straight-faced.

"I bet. Your boyfriend is an inconsiderate snack hog." Radek shakes his head and pulls his mouth into a disappointed frown. "C'mon, I'll show you to the guest house, then make you a plate. Babi made dessert to have while we open prezzies. Get me anything good, Boehner?"

"Yeah, a decent wrist shot. You've been flubbing those recently."

They horse around on the brief walk, shoving each other until Landon curls an arm around Wade's neck.

Why do they call men grown if it never happens?

I roll my eyes and imagine Indi would be doing the same if she were here. "Hey, where's Indi?"

"She's inside, keeping her feet up."

"She okay?" I point my thumb over my shoulder. "Should I go back in there?"

Landon pshaws. "Nothing to worry about. Normal pregnancy stuff. They ache after standing for a while." He tuts. "My gorgeous wife played sous chef with Babi, Mom, and Delaney all day. And she won't take a break and sit while coaching either."

The car beeps, trunk rising with a whish as I hit the remote key.

"I've been working with the league to hire an assistant in secret. Your friend is unbelievably stubborn."

"You're telling me," Wade chimes in. "It's basically the reason they're friends."

Landon tosses him the sticks and grabs our bags while I trail behind them, empty-handed. A small, matching cabin stands to the left of the main house, donning a festive holly wreath on the door.

Our gracious host punches in the key code and explains how to reset it to whatever we want.

"I already had my dessert," Pretty Boy mumbles from the corner of his mouth against my ear. "Three times."

"Quiet, you."

"What's that?" Landon pries.

"How about we meet you back at the house in a few? I need to freshen up."

"Alright, see you in a bit."

I switch out my grungy, beat-up jeans and flannel top for a maroon sweater and leggings, and use the washroom mirror to untwist my delicate gold chain. Wade brushes aside the waves draping my shoulders and dots kisses on the cusp of my neck. We share a lazy hum.

"You doin' okay?"

"Yeah. Why wouldn't I be?"

He palms my nape and turns me to face him. "Your dad's in India."

"Tell me something I don't know."

"Gabe." His voice is stern, cutting through my defense mechanism like a hot knife through butter.

My head sags but stays supported by his hold. "I'm fine. He wanted to go and I wasn't ready yet. What do you want me to say?"

His stance widens and pins me to the vanity, cradling my jaw between his strong hands. "I want you to tell me the truth."

The truth?

That I'm more attached to him than I thought was possible in three months? That I might be as obsessed with him as he is with me, but if I show it, he'll freak out, and my heart won't be able to take losing anyone else? That I'm more afraid of the loneliness waiting for me beyond New Year's Day when we're not together any longer?

I give him another truth instead.

My arms circle his waist, cinching him to me. "I've got everything I need right here."

"*Oh, Freckles,*" he intones, tipping up my head so our mouths bump.

I smile where the seams of our lips meet. "I meant Indi."

———

The extended Radek family fills the hearth room of the farmhouse. I'm familiar with a few from past interviews. His parents, grandparents, sister, and her kids. Others look similar enough to tell they're related.

Some sip hot toddies and nod at us in mutual recognition, stopping Wade to chat. A couple of his nieces and nephews fish marshmallows from their hot cocoa. Indi stretches out on a couch where Delaney, Landon's sister, massages her feet. A fire flickers in the fireplace next to a twelve-foot tree.

Landon unexpectedly pushes her off the cushion and jumps into her spot. "Get lost, Laney. This is my job."

His sister rolls her eyes. "Cool it, caveman. I'm not looking to 'steal yo girl' or anything."

Landon scowls at his sister, then melts to kiss Indi's feet. "I'm sorry, she's a beast."

"I think we both know who the beast is—"

"Laney…" a woman's voice warns. I can't tell if it came from his mom or grandmother.

Indi and I make eye contact. She waves me over. "Don't mind them. Come hang out."

Wade doesn't let go of his clasp on my hand, and I snap back like a boomerang.

"Let go," I say through a chuckle and make a second attempt with the same outcome. "Cut it out."

"Need my kiss first." His gaze floats to the frame of the opening above us. Mine tracks after, ending on the mistletoe.

My jaw sidewinds, tongue poking through my cheek at the smartass, but let him cup my face with his free hand and pull me towards his bowed, gleeful mouth.

"Haven't you had enough?" I whisper against his lips.

"Of you? Never."

We giggle through the playful smooch, keeping it clean for the sake of the children. Our audience cheers and applauses.

"You're the worst kind of trouble," he groans, fluttering those thick, dark lashes.

"Why?"

"Because I wouldn't mind getting into you again and again."

"You're such a turd." My open palm lands on his shoulder as his child-like grin widens. "Now unhand me, you brute."

Sometimes, I forget that in big families, there's almost no privacy. I sit down next to my friend but am being touched by at least three other women. One sandwiches me to Indi, and two on the back of the couch continue a conversation over us.

One of the smallest kiddos rubs their eyes and whines. Delaney goes over to collect her and leads her up the stairs amidst whines of wanting to stay up until Santa comes.

Indi seems to understand my growing panic. "I know. It's a lot." Her hand rests on my arm. "You get used to it."

"You fit right in."

"I do, don't I?" Her eyes go round and glossy, hand on my arm returning to its spot on the swell of her lower belly. "Who would have thought?"

As much as I love the smart-mouthed, snippy Indi, this Indi is so joyful, so comfortable. So herself.

"*D'oh*!" I facepalm. "I didn't get you a Christmas present."

"Who *cares*?" Indi inflects. "You being here is what matters." She extends her arms for a hug, and I give it to her.

"Your boobs are getting so big," I say in her ear.

"It's a sweaty curse I wish upon no one. This is probably what Bea feels like 24/7. Poor thing. She's struggling so hard right now. I miss her and won't see her until..." She pauses, her eyes brightening with a thought. "Would you make garden-themed cupcakes for the baby shower in March?"

"*Um*, duh."

"Oh, thank God. Anjali Davé is already in planning mode. We're all suffering under her iron fist."

Delaney returns with a large album. "Look what I found," she sing-songs. She wedges herself between Indi and me as everyone on the sofa scoots over to make space for one more. Others hover from behind.

It's Landon and Indi's wedding album.

Stunning photo after photo is *oohed* and *aahed* at as she flips through the pages.

They tease Landon for being bricked up in all of the pictures, posed or candid.

I stifle a giggle at the series of groomsmen poses.

Landon tears through the loosely forming memory of that night by shooting his arms in the air. "I couldn't help it! My wife is fucking *hot*."

A raspy voice draws my attention away. It blends with the sweet pitch of a young child. I escape the clutches of the couch by crawling away and find Wade in the kitchen, seated on a bay window with Landon's nephew on one knee, his overgrown blond curls bouncing as they sing the lyrics of "Beggin'" by Måneskin. My shoulder bites into the wall where I lean, needing all the support I can get, considering my ovaries are spontaneously combusting.

Wade peters off when he notices me. Landon's nephew pouts. "No stopping!"

Delaney rushes in. "There you are, ya lil stinker. Come on, Gunnar. Time for bed." She picks him up with a grunt and waves. "Goodnight, Uncle Wade. Night, Miss Gabe."

When we're alone, my neck swivels to the little liar. "You sing?"

His shoulders lift and drop. "I sing all the time."

"Not like this. You can actually *sing*." An exhale hurls from my windpipe. "So what? You're pretending to be the NHL's worst singer?"

"Better than being the worst goalie."

"You got me there. Hey," I nudge him with my knee, "that was pretty cute."

"I know."

That dimple in his cheek is a menace to my swooning reproductive system.

"You don't even know what I'm talking about yet."

"That's okay. I'm always cute."

"And annoying. Don't forget annoying."

His elbow digs into mine before the same arm squeezes our shoulders together.

"I'm not used to saying nice things about you, especially not *to* you, but..." My nose kisses his stubbled cheek. "I think you'd be an amazing dad someday."

The smirk on his face dissolves. "I don't know about that."

"Well, I'm pretty sure I'm always right, so..."

Wade tosses his head back and laughs, the three quick *ha ha ha*'s enveloping my heart in their warmth. He slopes toward me and drops a lingering kiss in the corner of my jaw. "You're the best."

In bed later that night, Wade addresses the massive elephant in the room. We stare at one another from our pillows.

"What's the game plan for after New Year?"

"*Um.*"

"It ends."

"Yep." My tucked hands shift under my head.

"Do you wanna stop?"

"No," I admit, cheeks flaming.

Wade beams. "Neither do I."

My eyes screw shut. "We're idiots."

"Yeah, we are." The crook of his finger cradles my chin. "Hey."

"*Mm?*"

Excitement and relief peer back at me. "Let's not stop."

"Okay."

He snickers at the eager reply. "Merry Christmas, Freckles."

"Merry Christmas, Pretty Boy."

CHAPTER 25:
ALL THE OTHER MESSY PARTS OF ME

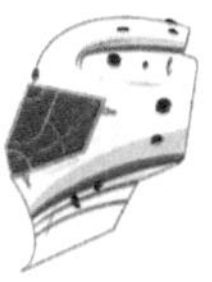

WADE

"DO YOU MIND IF I ASK ABOUT YOUR RELATIONSHIP with Gabe Finch?"

The question comes from James Bollinger, a clean-cut, middle-aged reporter from the Ottawa Daily's sports section, toward the end of the postgame press conference.

My eyes search for permission from management and PR. Jules and Elliot nod.

"Go for it."

"I noticed she's not here. Is there a reason for her absence?"

Jaeg closes his eyes with a deep sigh next to me. Landon's knee bounces. Fletch lifts his cap, rubs his forehead, and pulls the bill down to hide his eyes. They know the truth and also that I'd murder them in their sleep if they spilled. Or worse, Gabe would murder me, and then my ghost would come back to terrorize them.

"*Uh.*" My finger scratches the itch on the tip of my nose. "I don't believe she's covering this game." Soft chuckles and snorts echo in the press room. I call to another reporter from CSN, "Hey, Adrienne."

She laughs and waves back.

Bollinger's face flames, and he shakes his head while typing on his phone. "Does that mean you're still together?"

I flip my baseball cap backward and relax into the chair, arms crossing with a shrug. "She's incredibly busy."

"So you're no longer dating?"

"I thought 'a question' meant *one* question."

Jules motions for me to explain further, but Gabe and I agreed to lay low. The contracts we signed expired, and we told PR teams that we parted ways but didn't want some big press release about the breakup.

It's a win-win situation. We don't stop seeing each other, and the press is off our backs.

I lie, this time, to protect our privacy.

"Miss Finch and I have equally demanding schedules—"

The nosey prick keeps pushing. "So, you confirm you're still together?"

Coach cuts him off. "Does anyone here have questions about something other than Boehner's love life?" It would come off as rude, but he's smiling and his tone is playful, hands drawing circles over the table. "His consistency, maybe? Or extraordinary stats this season? Or anything about hockey?" There's more chittering. "If not, I think we're good," he confirms with Jules and Elliot. "Good night, everyone."

The rustle of backpacks and shuffled footsteps fade as the press exits one way, and we exit the other.

We change out of the pullovers and back into suits before leaving the arena. Fletch kicks me in the shin for cutting a hole in the blazer pocket where he usually stores his phone. I almost pissed myself watching him drop it in the hallway again and again.

"You're a douchebag." He glares as I pass him on the bus.

"It's a *joke*."

"So's your reading speed, but you don't see me breaking your Kindle over it."

Guess he's still mad at me. "I'm *sorry* I didn't finish reading Kingdom of the Feared, okay?"

He harrumphs and slaps on his headphones.

"I said I was sorry!" My index finger jabs into his neck between the bus seats. "You're a pain in my ass."

Fletcher returns an angry whisper. "No, that's the butt plug lodged up there."

I curse myself for mentioning last week's exploration and prepare to beat the living daylights out of him when Jaeg growls.

"Move and die."

"You heard what he—"

"Maybe you shouldn't have yapped about all the 'glorious backdoor action' you're allegedly getting from your not-girlfriend."

"That was the pain meds talking after I dislocated my shoulder! Wouldn't have happened if *someone* wasn't wanking off against the glass instead of—"

My defense falls on deaf ears. Our captain remains shut-eyed, cozied into his travel pillow. "Let that be a lesson to you."

"'Let that be a lesson to you?' What are you, eighty? Who says that anymore? Am I right?" I seek validation through a high-five, but no one's paying attention. Except Theron. The dude would high-five for any reason. I accept it with a resigned sigh.

I lean past the aisle and whisper toward Derrick. "And that was private information."

"Then stop screaming it from the rooftops. Now go away." His hand grips my shoulder and jostles me back to my seat. "And stay there."

The drive to L.A. from Las Vegas gets us to the hotel around 3 a.m., and I text Gabe my room number in case she wants to drop by.

Two hours later, my eyelashes tangle with hers.

What a way to wake up.

I groan happily and roll until she's on her back, gripping my biceps for support. She flexes her thigh twice against my boner.

"Well, good morning."

"Hi." My voice rattles—dry and gravelly from sleep deprivation— against her smooth skin as my lips greet her freckles.

"How's your shoulder?"

"Better now." We share lopsided smiles. "You get some rest?"

"Not really," she says. "You know how redeyes go. Nothing caffeine can't fix." Her hands glide across my bare arms and back. "Got you a cup, too. It's by the TV."

"You're a genius." I steal a coffee-heavy kiss and balance on my elbows, getting a better look at this absolutely angelic creature. It's the first time I've seen her in black and gold, and my body retreats, surprised. "What are you wearing?"

Gabe lifts to her knees, uncrumpling the number twelve plastered over her tits.

No!

She rotates slightly to show off the back. "Cute, right? I got the updated one that says Davé-Radek."

Not cute. It's not mine.

A possessive fire burns a hole in the feral part of my brain. I press my tongue between my bottom lip and lower teeth. "Nah. It's no good."

My fists catch the hockey sweater, yanking and yanking until my fingers bore holes into it.

"*Wade!*" she chides. "This was brand new."

I poke through two of the holes and tear through the knit, ripping a slash into it. "Trash the jersey."

The little brat notches her hands on her hips. "We're not even fake dating anymore."

Ouch. That's gonna leave a mark.

"You're right. We're *dating*-dating now." I hop off the bed and dig around my suitcase, recovering a practice jersey and chucking it to her. It lands on her face. "Put it on." My hands tuck the front into her jeans. "Unless you're fucking Indi and Landon, the only name on your body is mine."

She rolls her eyes, but the smile she's wearing radiates pride. "Did *not* think you were the jealous type."

"I'm all sorts of things when it comes to you." I grasp the small of her back and wrench her closer by the torso, mirroring how she kneels atop the mattress. "Jealous." Our hands intertwine. "Greedy." I bring her fingers to each closed eye before kissing them. "Obsessed."

My heart lurches in my throat when she nuzzles my forehead.

"Gabe?"

"Yeah?" Her expression is soft, yielding.

Somewhere along the way, the pretending switched spots for the real thing. Or maybe it was always the real thing, and the only people who pretended it wasn't were us.

Now we're all in, but without the label, and there's that pesky feeling that craves it. The ownership. To publicly belong to her and only her.

"What are we?"

The crinkle in her brow deepens. "*Hmm?*"

"What am I to you?"

She slots her nose next to mine, speaking into my mouth. "You're my needy little bitch."

"Gabe." I pout, whining.

"Sounds like my little bitch needs a blowjob."

I resign to the deflection. She's not ready to address it.

She said she's yours, fucker. What more could you want?

I can be patient, I repeat internally.

Mischief twinkles between us. Freckles dance along the planes of her high cheekbones, enigmatic smile fighting to break free.

"Wouldn't hurt."

———

Getting sucked dry cleared my head for the game against the Suns. Donovan breaks the tie and clinches the win by scoring in the penalty shootout. Gabe stays level-headed during his on-ice interview, but once we're in the hallway, she runs up and leaps into my arms.

"White women can jump," I tease. The skates give me enough height to tower over her.

"I'm not white," she corrects.

"Apologies, my desi queen."

A throat clears behind us.

"Hey, Wade."

The volume of Gabe's hair blocks my view, and I loosen my hold around her waist. She slides to stand on the cement floor.

Vanessa tucks a thick chocolate curl behind her ear. "I thought that was you."

"I—*hey*." My heart drops into my churning stomach imagining what's going on in Gabe's head right now. I find her hand and squeeze. "*Um*, this is Vanessa..."

Damn. I don't know her last name.

She extends a hand. "...Dearborn. Vanessa Dearborn."

"Gabe Finch," she answers back.

"Oh my gosh, I'm such a fan!" Vanessa gushes. "Loved watching your coverage of the season so far. It's been a good season, huh?"

The paddle handle twists in my grip. "It has been."

There's no malice or deceit in her voice or eyes. "You look really happy."

I pump Gabe's hand twice, hidden behind the panel of her wool coat. "I am."

"That's good to hear."

An awkward lull passes. "What are you doing here?"

"Just waiting for—"

"Hey, babe." A suited boy-next-door type sidles up and winds an arm around her waist. Sun-bleached blond waves I once yearned to touch hover over his broad shoulders, framing a tanned face. His familiar ocean-blue gaze throws my heart rate into a tailspin. "*Yooo*, Boehner!"

Memories I cast away years ago resurface as he pulls me into a hug. They curdle in my gut, buried so deep I almost don't recognize them. I'd managed to avoid the thought of Malcolm Montgomery for as long as I could.

"Hey, Mal."

"It's been a while, man. Just got traded from Dallas two weeks ago."

"Oh, yeah. I heard about that."

"Just in time to be able to play in the postseason."

"You two know each other?" Vanessa cuts in.

"Know each other?" Malcolm guffaws. "We played at Harvard together." His playful glance goes serious when it reaches mine. "This was my boy."

A shiver gallops down my spine.

My boy.

"Oh, my God! That's right." Gabe looks between us. "Weren't you two roommates at one point?"

"Yep, until I got drafted. Crazy times, eh, Wade?"

"Yep," I echo through a nervous chuckle. "Crazy times."

All those unsure, fleeting glimpses during practices that turned to longing late at night. The countless moments of tentative contact pulled away too quickly. A year of unspoken tension where nothing had happened, but everything had bloomed, waking something only to be tucked away like so many other pieces of myself.

"Where are my manners?" Mal bounces the heel of his hand off his forehead. "Have you met Vanessa?"

"Yep. Yeah." Gabe and I confirm in chorus.

"Isn't she great?" He goes gooey-eyed looking at her, then kisses her cheek. "Best thing to ever happen to me."

She blushes pink in response. "We should get going." Vanessa's suggestion is met with relieved breaths from all of us.

"For sure. Good seeing you, man." He waves goodbye and curls an arm around her neck before kissing her forehead. They disappear down the hall and through a set of double doors.

"That was...interesting." Gabe slices through the silence on our walk toward the locker area.

"Or something."

My heart wants to rip from my ribs and bare itself in her hands. But there are too many watchful eyes and eavesdropping ears surrounding us.

"Meet you at the hotel?"

"Yep."

She beats me there and waits at the foot of the mattress, rocking her foot from where it hangs over crossed legs.

I toss my coat and suit jacket on an armchair, then undo my tie. "I'm wiped."

Gabe perks an eyebrow at me. "Did you sleep with her?"

Right to the chase.

"Yes. Long before you."

There. That wasn't so hard.

"Ahh, *now* it makes sense." Her head moves through a series of nods, and I relax. She's not upset. "You're jealous she's with someone else."

The truth is more complicated, but it's the truth. Gabe deserves that much.

"No," I confess softly, untucking my shirt and slipping out of my Oxfords. "I'm jealous of *her*."

The bobbing foot stills. She straightens, placing both feet on the flooring. "What do you mean?"

I lower until my knees take up the space between her boots, running my hands up and down her thighs in wide strokes.

"Malcolm and I...we weren't close because we played together or lived together." Shame fixes my eyes to the ground. "We're close because..."

We share the same secret.

Why can't I say it?

"Go on," she encourages, lifting my head to catch my gaze. "You can tell me anything, Wade."

The admission is more for me than Gabe. "She gets to have Malcolm in a way I never did."

Her throat tenses with a swallow before a mousey murmur breathes out. "Holy crap."

"I thought I could forget he existed." My head hangs, unable to face her. "Was doing a decent job, too."

A gracious hand sweeps over my cheek and latches to my jaw, forcing my head to tip back. "Does he know?"

"What I felt about him?" I deny it. "Subconsciously? Possibly. But we never talked about it." I lean into her touch, savoring every second. Afraid it'll evaporate, and I'll lose it forever.

"Do you want to tell him? Do you still want him?"

"No. I only want you. But..." The words evade me. "It's like, the attraction is still there. This is the first time I think I've said it out loud."

Her thumb moves across my lower lip. "You can keep going, if you want."

"Oh."

She means say *it*.

Say it.

"Gabe."

Solemn encouragement glimmers in her dusky eyes. "Yeah?"

I grip her forearms, clinging to her. My heart thuds in its cage. I can't lose her, but I can't lie to her either. She knows all the other messy parts of me. She might as well know this one. Maybe I'll get to know it better, too.

"I'm bi."

Water floods her bottom lids.

One weight swaps for another. The first, a secret. The second, a fear of loss.

Both lift when her arms raise me, hauling my body onto the mattress until we're lying across it face-to-face.

"You're incredible." Velvet lips dote on my cheek, temple, forehead, and nose, peppering my face with the gentlest of kisses and dispersing my panic once and for all. "I'm so grateful I get to see all of you. I understand why you don't share yourself fully with others, but don't hide from me, okay?"

"Okay."

With the finality of the last nail in a coffin, my heart decides.

I am never letting Gabe Finch go.

CHAPTER 26:
YOU BROKE MY DICK!

GABE

BEING TRUSTED WITH WADE'S SOUL FEELS LIKE winning a gold medal.

After months of feeding me slivers of himself, witnessing the overlays peel away to reveal a gorgeous, well-crafted mosaic—*instead of the no-brainer four-piece puzzle I assumed*—is a marvel.

The rest of cuffing season allows for a routine as we bounce from city to city between short stints in Ottawa. We pay for room damages in Denver, Minneapolis, and Edmonton, defile hotel washrooms in Tampa Bay, Buffalo, and Raleigh, and ruin bedsheets in Pittsburgh, Dallas, and Newark. We sneak off to shows and make out in the theaters of Chicago, New York, and Nashville.

I thought I didn't miss any sort of commitment—*it hadn't served me in the past*—and convinced myself that Wade and I were better off defining our relationship on our terms without being stuffed into a suffocating box by societal norms.

But today, as I'm frosting succulents onto cupcakes for Indi's garden-themed baby shower, doubt fuels my unease.

Kurt Vaughn and I were together for seven years. We prepared for *years— or maybe it was only me*—for a life together, and it imploded so easily.

While Wade is the opposite of him in the most important ways, it's only been six months, and two of those were spent hating his guts. I'd handed over my broken pieces, but what if it isn't enough? What's stopping him from waking up one day and saying *fuck it* and never talking to me again?

Being my fiancé didn't deter Kurt from cheating. How would being my not-boyfriend convince him to stick around?

With that thought and a heavy sigh, I finish piping a Mexican snow-ball, admiring how the rosette pattern turned out, proud of the bluish sage color miraculously created by mixing blue and green spirulina into a cream cheese icing. A new text message from my father interrupts the complicated train of thought.

DAD

There is a landscaping company at the nursery?

Finally.

The cupcake joins some hen-and-chicks, mini aloe vera, pinwheels, mother-of-pearls, and a couple of Burro's tails on the other end of the counter before I wash and dry my hands to reply. More messages appear.

DAD

Sorry the question mark was supposed to be !

DAD

And a contractor measuring the driveway

ME

Very nice.

DAD

You shouldn't have, bala

ME

I didn't!

DAD

But they have a list of issues to correct specific to Terra Bella

He sends a picture of a printout from a place called GreenLeaf, showing an itemized five-year estimate of field care and greenhouse maintenance but without prices. Biweekly mowing and edging services, seasonal weeding, fertilization, and aeration. Replace current clear greenhouse cover with infrared thermal film. New hay bales.

Another printed estimate from Star Paving shows the steps, labor, and materials needed to convert the gravel parking lot and driveway to asphalt.

DAD

They're adamant about completing their projects

DAD

Saying they already got paid a deposit

I narrow my eyes into the air, doing mental gymnastics while guessing the cost. Who cares about the nursery and could afford to—

Wade bursts through my front door. The answer strikes like lightning. "Honey, I'm *booooome*!"

He loses his coat and sends a suitcase rolling across my condo like a bowling ball. When it bounces off the casing of the bedroom door, he hisses. "*Oooh*. So close!"

There's no point stifling my smile when Pretty Boy jogs over in a Regents hoodie, face dimpling. He squeezes me in a side hug before flooding my face and neck with plucky kisses. "Missed you, Freckles."

A laugh bubbles from my throat at the tickle. "We saw each other yesterday."

"That's too long," he whines. "Tell me you missed me, too." My low ponytail earns a few tender strokes from his fingers, molten eyes panning across me in awe, searching for validation. I give it to him.

"Yeah, I missed you."

Wade releases an extended breath from his nose. "I can't wait for this season to end."

Somersaults roil in my stomach. "Is that so?"

He confirms with a hum. "I'm tired of pretending I don't wanna hang out with you every moment instead."

"Please. You'd be bored watching me do stuff like this" —I motion around the kitchen, to the bowls of batter and frosting, the strewn-about muffin pans, cupcake liners, icing bags and piping tips— "all day."

"Sounds perfect." One final kiss is placed at my temple as he lets go, then swipes a botched Pacific opal from the countertop. He settles into a barstool facing me.

"Speaking of perfect," I remind myself. "Did you hire someone to fix up my dad's nursery?"

He freezes mid-chew, guilty as the day is long. An audible swallow follows. "Yes."

"Why would you do that?"

"Because I wanted to." His shoulders shrug. "I know your dad means everything to you," he adds between bites, "If he's happy, you're happy. And that's all I care about."

Don't cry. Don't cry. Don't fucking cry.

My doubt about his commitment dissipates to wonder and hope.

"This is delicious, by the way." It's an off-the-cuff statement as if he didn't simply admit he only cares about my happiness. "Would you ever bake professionally? 'Cause you'd crush it."

I shake away the surge of emotions. "Nah. I enjoy baking—*don't get me wrong*—but it's a creative outlet. Figuring out new flavor combos, baking a batch from scratch, and learning new decorating techniques. It's a stress reliever. But on a small scale. Mass production stresses me out. I would not be having a fun time if I had to churn out dozens of cupcakes every morning, in exactly the right amounts that would ensure profits."

"Understandable," he agrees, sucking a daub of frosting from his thumb. "I'm still waiting on this supposed life-changing grilled cheese of yours."

"As soon as I'm done making these..." I point to the two dozen unfrosted cupcakes cooling on a rack. "I'll do whatever you want."

His expression lifts, gaze dropping from my face to my flour-smattered apron and back up again.

"You look good behind that counter."

I lift a coy shoulder and accept the compliment. "Thank you."

Wade reclines and stretches, the hoodie lifting enough to show off the deep arches forming a v and flanking his abs. Drool collects in my mouth. I chew on my lower lip as he props an arm on the back of the barstool, running his eyes over me again. "You'd look even better bent over it."

He's right.

I look pretty damn good with him pounding into me from the back, hands crushing the cupcakes that didn't meet the quality standards, nipples smothered with the pale green and pink icing. Wade looks even better, panting and groaning, the sinews of his neck taut with restraint. Veins bulge atop his hand wrapping my throat, handsome face heavy with lust.

The phone screen fogs with my humid breaths. It's not recording, but I wish it was. Could've used it for cold, lonely nights.

My eyes bolt shut when he slams his hips against my ass, sliding in and out of my wet pussy at a pace that has my thighs burning from holding steady. I cry out a pitchy laugh.

"Give it to me," he orders, tilting my hips until whimpers dribble from my mouth. The angle is delicious, jarring. "Give me what's mine."

"Fuck me right, and I will," I throw over my shoulder.

Wade growls, circling his wrist with my ponytail and yanking *hard*. My head tosses, and my back arches, tight like a bowstring, as he fucks me harder and faster. "Like this?"

"Yes." I see-saw at the edge of a cliff, ready to be thrown off. "Yes, yes, *yes*."

When his movements go sloppy, I'm afraid I'll lose momentum, but one mild squeeze around my windpipe and I'm gone. I clamp down, pelvic walls nearly cramping as my cursing turns to nonsense. He finds a rhythm once more, pushing in to stretch and fill me so deeply that cartoonish stars mar my vision. My jaw locks open, and a barbaric noise accompanies the peaking orgasm. As a flash of light blinds me, Wade stuffs part of a cupcake into my mouth, muting my screams. He bottoms out with an inhuman bellow.

His grasp on my neck remains as the moist crumb of the cake and icing sticks to my swallow.

"Goddamn, Boehner." The counter cools my overheated skin as his cock twitches and softens inside me. "A heads up about choking me with the cupcake would have been nice."

As if that stunt wasn't unhinged enough, this man pulls out, rips off the used condom, and dips two fingers into it before lobbing it into the sink. His cum paints my parted lips. "Suck."

I lap it up, humming through the aftershocks and the pleasant mix of his salty release and the sweet, tart frosting. Wade tremors as I leave his fingers clean.

"I don't know how you do it," he huffs. His tight slap against my right ass cheek makes it jiggle before he pulls my gray sweats over my hips. "Being a top is tiring."

Wade spins me to face him, swaying into a tongued kiss before he bends to pull down the front panel of my apron, exposing pebbled nipples through my white shirt. "I'd much rather be on my knees, mouthing your glorious rack." He wets one, licking and nipping until my core throbs, and I'm fisting his hair and tearing him away.

I snap when he mewls. "Get in the bedroom."

Clambering to his feet while abandoning his sweatpants, he runs there with a goofy gait, zipping open his luggage and rooting around, naked except for a T-shirt like Winnie the Pooh. "We need more condoms."

"What're you using this for?" The sleek handle of the HyperVolt massage gun removed from the bag feels heavy in my palm.

"It's nothing." Wade swats his hand in the air. "My thigh was tight after yesterday's game, and the PT made me pack it."

"*Hmm.*" My imagination runs wild. "Want me to use it?"

His eyes sparkle.

The devilish smile splitting my face almost hurts. "I have an idea."

"Wade, come on." The man cannot be appeased.

"No!" He stomps away, hiding his flaccid dick and rosy asshole, respectively, with each hand. Upon reaching the washroom, his foot smacks the door shut.

I trail after him, tapping against the wooden door to be let in. "Wade?"

"Go away!"

I ignore him. The handle turns under my touch. "Listen, it's totally natural—"

"Natural?" he yells from his seat on the toilet, skin streaked in an angry red. "No one is supposed to come like Old Faithful more than once, Gabe, much less six times!" He tosses his penis in a hand, as if trying to revive it and mourning its inability to respond. "It's *not* natural. You broke my dick!"

"It's not broken," I coo, attempting comfort with long sweeps of my hand across the bulky rounds of his shoulders. "I meant having that response to your prostate massaged was natural, you big baby. And I'm sorry." My lips find his sweaty brow. "I didn't know you could come *that* hard *so* many times."

He sniffles. "I didn't either! My balls are empty. *Empty*! I may never come again." His head totters in dismay. "Oh, *God*. No more orgasms." His gasping sobs echo off the tile. "I might never have kids." He continues wailing, covering his eyes. "Goodbye, fatherhood!"

"Okay, that's a little—"

Fat tears stream down his raging cheeks as he accuses me with a pointed finger. "I would have made a *great* dad! You said so!"

I won't say I like seeing him cry, but I kinda do. Makes him more human and less like a young sex god who's bewitched my mind, heart, and cunt.

"Oh, sweet boy. *Breathe*." I make room for myself in his lap, draping his arms around my torso as I clutch him to my chest. We rock to and fro. I pepper kisses at his hairline, kneading into the tense muscles at the base of his skull with my fingers and thumb.

He calms. I purse my lips, pleading for a peck. "Do you forgive me?"

Wade nods and hungrily returns a kiss.

"Come on, I know what will make you feel better."

And then I make him a grilled cheese.

CHAPTER 27:
THIS IS MY BABY NOW

WADE

GABE'S GRILLED CHEESE MAKES ME WANT TO WIFE
her up. Amongst other things.

The sourdough brushed with olive oil was crisped to perfection. And
the gooey stretch of cheddar, the optimal cheese-to-bread ratio? One million percent better than Meltwich.

I could be biased, but her hands are magic. Whatever she touches turns
to fucking gold, like King Midas. Basketball? It's raining threes. Grilled
cheese? Chef's kiss. Sideline reporting? Viewership and ticket sales are
higher than ever. Cupcakes? Four different aunties at Indi and Landon's
baby shower asked if she took orders for special occasions.

And me? I'll never be the same.

Usually, the postseason doesn't change my day-to-day, but the first
two rounds of playoffs thoroughly kicked my ass. Luckily, being top seed
meant home-ice advantage. Which means more time with Gabe.

Tonight, like the nights we'd stayed together in the last two months,
I'm a forlorn creep, staring at her sleeping form beside me. Her expression
is peaceful. Angelic, really. A lengthy breath exits my nose as I weave three
rogue strands of her hair into a loose plait so it's out of her face.

I want everything from her. Every scarred, healing shard, every sniping
comment, every devious smile, every sweet reward and doled-out punishment. They say, 'When you know, you know,' and *I* know, but I don't
know if *she* knows I know or even if Gabe knows how she feels about that.

Fuck, I make no goddamn sense, even in my own stream of consciousness.

Her hesitation is valid. She's been hurt, and I'm not sure how else to convince her, apart from admitting to every questionable, heinous act I've done for her attention.

Yes, Gabe, I destroyed each guest room in my home so you'd have to sleep in my bed. Yes, I sold my Lamborghini because it reminded you of your ex's beloved car. Yes, I built you a basketball court in the penthouse because I don't want you to ever leave. Yes, I took care of things for your dad's business because you're my family now.

Actually, that's not a bad start.

She could either be terrified and ghost me or shove a ring on my finger.

Maybe I'd get a love confession. Maybe even an angry one like they do in the movies. If someone is gonna tell me they love me, I want it to be her.

Whatever happens, it has to be big. Public. Everyone will know about it. I'm sick and tired of hiding—

My internal monologue is cut short by a ding from my phone. Then another.

Jesus. Who the fuck is it at this hour?

LANDY

IT'S BABY TIME

DONOVAN

Now?? I was so close to falling asleep.

O JAEGER MY CAPTAIN

It's 2 a.m., for fuck's sake.

My feet thud against the mattress as I kick off the covers in a panic.

Freckles groans. "Quit that."

"Wake up, Gabe!" Pants are already being pulled on my legs, adrenaline rushing through my veins. "THEY'RE HAVING A BABY!"

"Who is?" She is way too sleepy. I'll have to drive.

"Our friends, sweetheart. Come on, we gotta go!" I leap onto the mattress on my hands and knees, bouncing her from the horizontal position. "Get up, get up, get up!"

Gabe's jaw ticks, crinkling open her bloodshot eyes. "I'm gonna kill you."

"You can do that later; now up!"

ME

Where am I going??

LANDY

Ottawa birthing centre

LANDY

But in a few hours

The man has got to be kidding me.

I throw my phone onto the nightstand.

"False alarm, Freckles. We'll get to meet Baby Davé Radek in the morning."

A pillow slams into my face before Gabe burrows under the comforter.

"Remind me to smother you in the morning."

"Yes, ma'am." I salute and simultaneously drop my pants before sliding into bed again, this time being sure to spoon this feisty cuddlebug. "I'm all yours."

"*Mm.*"

Nestling into her neck is like coming home. "And you're mine, all mine."

———

Fletcher's beady eyes follow me back and forth around the room.

"Will you sit down?" Gabe asks over her coffee cup, eyes hidden behind large, dark sunglasses. "Your pacing is making my headache worse."

"Sorry." I stop and park my ass between her and the other grump. "I'm on edge."

"Nervous to meet the baby?" Fletch chimes in.

"Meeting is fine. I'm good with meeting." My right knee bounces. "It's holding it I'm worried about. What if I break it, snap it in half?"

"I'm no expert, but I don't think babies do that." Freckles and her sass. I love it, but not right now.

Ginger eyebrows rise in confirmation. "She's right."

Jaeg yawns and bobs his head. "They're resilient little shits."

"Easy for you two to say. You have the experience of, like, a million nieces and nephews."

The lounge door opens with a creak. Four ruddy-face grandparents exit.

Congratulations are shared through handshakes and hugs as they sigh and gush about the newest addition to their world.

"Go on, guys." Landon's dad, Leon, holds the door open. "They're waiting for you."

Gabe sneaks a kiss in the seam of our interlocked hands as we stroll down the hallway.

Pale green walls line the dimly lit room.

Our chorused gasps echo through the silence at the sight of Landon outstretched alongside Indi on the bed, a cloth bundle cradled between them.

"Hi," they whisper in unison.

"Hiiii," we parrot back.

Landon beckons us with large swoops of his arm. "Come meet our daughter."

Gabe hands over her coffee to me and lifts her sunglasses to reveal brimming tears. "*Oh*, Indi."

The murmur sets off Indi's tears, too.

Landon scoots to one side of the bed to make space.

Soft looks so good on my girl. Her forehead meets Indi's before Gabe places a palm over the miniature maroon toque and joins her on the bed. The rest of us gather around. My head dips for a closer look.

Black wisps peek from the rolled-up knit, her head a perfect sphere. Pinked skin and a tiny button nose. Dark brows and a lash line that looks painted on.

"This is Akhila," Landon announces. "She's our everything."

I can't hide my awe, my voice dropping even lower. "You made her."

Gabe and Indi breathe giggles.

"Congrats, you two." Jaeg slaps a hand onto Landon's shoulder. "She's perfect."

Landon looks at Akhila, then to Indi. "Yeah, she is."

"Wanna hold her?" Indi asks Gabe, who immediately nods.

What was once my chest cavity is now a deluge of warmth. My heart skips. Not a beat, or two, but down the street and off into the horizon, never to be seen or heard from again.

Her freckles glow impossibly as she rocks Akhila against her torso. "Hi, my love."

No. I can't possibly be jealous of a newborn.

Gabe swings a leg over the edge of the bed and rises. "I'm your Aunty."

I spot her, holding up both hands. "Careful."

"Masi," Indi corrects. "You're her masi, because you're my sister."

A tear escapes and tracks down Gabe's cheek. I catch it before it lands on the baby.

Akhila gurgles and strains within the swaddle.

"Your turn."

"Me?"

The encouraging scrunch of Gabe's nose is unbearably cute.

"Make a little oval with your arms," she directs, "fold them over on your chest." With a slight jostle, Akhila's small burrito body transfers to me. "Relax your shoulders, Wade."

They drop slowly from my ears, the insignificant weight settling across my forearm and barely covering its length. "Can I walk?"

Landon snorts. "Yeah, you can walk with her."

My feet make their way toward the window, the morning sunlight blurred by opaque privacy film. The conversation behind us quiets as my eyes widen to focus on this brand-new person.

"How are you feeling?" Gabe asks Indi.

"Better after a shower," she replies. "I could use a nap, though."

"You worked so hard, baby," Landon praises her with an audible kiss. "She did so good."

Teeny nostrils flare through an inhale, followed by a soft squeak and a wiggle.

Uh oh. What have I done?

Akhila's petite arm shakily emerges from the blanket. When the fist expands, I count five fingers, five tiny fingernails. She's unbelievable. The hand spreads, and by instinct, I offer her the tip of my index finger. Her tight grasp makes me lose my breath. But when she opens her eyes with a squint, jet-black pupils encircled by a pale blue ring? My face is wet.

"Oh, my God. Are you crying?"

Leave it to Donovan to call me out.

Indi hums. "What happened?"

I shift to face them. "Look at how her tiny little hand holds my finger."

"Aw, *Wade*."

Shuffling over to a couch, I take a seat, clutching her close. Akhila falls asleep again but doesn't let go.

"I'm never giving her back."

Landon's tone goes stern. "*Excuse* me?"

"This is my baby now." I protect her from him, rolling her closer to my heart. "You two can go make another one."

"That's enough, buddy" —he makes grabby hands at the end of arms extended toward me— "Gimme back my girl."

"Nuh-uh," Fletch intervenes. "I was in line first."

"I'm her dad!"

Fletcher doesn't budge. "Then you can hold her when we go to practice."

"I'm bringing her with me to practice," I confirm. "Donovan, you can have a turn then. But only two minutes."

"Baby hog," he snaps back.

"By the way," Gabe pokes Radek in the shoulder, "Can I be the first one to report her birth? Fans wanna know!"

"Alright, alright. Everyone out." Landon shrugs her touch away and steals the baby from my arms. "I thought this was gonna be a nice, wholesome moment. Leave it to you useless goons to fight over my f—" He stops the obscenity under Indi's narrow gaze. "My daughter."

Gabe flips her hair over her shoulder and *hmph*. "I'm taking that as a yes to announce her birth."

"Yeah, yeah. Whatever. Shoo." He waves us off.

"Wade, we need to get outta here," Gabe hisses through her teeth, digging her nails into my bicep as we book it out of the building.

"Why? What's wrong?"

"Listen, Pretty Boy." In a swift, aggressive swing, she slams my back into the Ranger Rover and curves her hand around my throat. "My ovaries just high-fived each other. We. Need. To. Go."

———

We won the last game of the conference finals without Radek.

It didn't hurt that he bought a drink for everyone in the arena that night, in celebration of Akhila's birth.

Adrenaline buzzes in the locker room after, but when it dies down, my mind fixates. Seeing Landon and Indi bring their love to life has me in pieces. I'm dying to know what that feels like. To love and be loved so sincerely and deeply.

I corner Jaeg as we kick off our skates.

"Hey, Derrick. Can I ask you something?"

He grunts.

"Why'd you marry Skylar?"

A rare smile paints his face. He puffs his cheeks and blows out a hard breath. "Because I love her more than anything else in this godforsaken world."

My head hangs. "How do you know?"

"Know what?"

"That you love her."

"Oh, buddy," he says, patting my back.

My lip curls into a cringe. "I'm gonna get the speech, aren't I?"

"What speech?"

"The 'the right woman changes you' speech."

"Fuck no," he spits. "That's bullshit. A woman shouldn't have to change you. You'd be a coward to put that responsibility on someone else." His meaty finger jabs into my pec twice. "You have to figure your own shit out."

"*Ow*. Yeesh. Okay. I'm starting to think I asked the wrong guy."

Derrick peers up at the ceiling and shakes his head. "It's not the person that changes you."

"But Sky changed *you*."

He tilts his head and glances back with a side-eye. "Did she?"

I shrug. "Maybe not. I guess you're still a grumpy bastard."

"The thing is..." Jaeger grumbles and pulls his hands down his face. "I'm not good at this crap, but...it's not the person. It's the world of possibilities they open your life up to."

Oh.

"If you're lucky," he continues, "you meet someone that makes you wonder if things could be different. That *you* could be different. And they're so amazing, so breathtaking, you want to be who they deserve. You want it so badly you start imagining an entire life with them. You dream about talking late at night and breakfast in bed, living together, mowing the lawn on weekends, barbecuing in the summer, building a family, growing old together…"

A movie montage of an alternative reality with Gabe plays before my glossy eyes. Big wedding, my ring on her hand and hers on mine. Good luck kisses before games. The house overrun with kids, me making meals for everyone, but only feeding her with my hands. Late-night laughter with friends and family around backyard bonfires. Countless mountain-top sunrises and beach sunsets. Night after night in a shared bed as we age. A lifetime of joys and triumphs and love and support. The short glimpses of a future that could be forms a hard lump in my throat.

"If you're *really* lucky, she'll realize your love, your trust, is what she wants, too. And then she'll help make your dreams come true." Jaeg releases a sharp breath. "At least that's how it happened for me."

"Do you," I start, dawdling my thumbs between my knees. "*Um*, maybe, think I could have that with Gabe?"

Derrick hums. "Can't say for sure, but if you're asking, you might already know the answer."

In my heart, I do. I think I've known.

"All I'm saying is I see who you are, how you are when she's around. You're at your best."

"*Jaeg*," I sing, bumping our knees together. "That's really sweet."

He shoves me back harder, and my betraying feet nearly slide out from under me.

"Don't screw it up by being less than what she deserves."

We share a knowing, easy smile.

"I won't."

GABE

"SO LET ME GET THIS STRAIGHT."

On-screen, Indi finishes three gulps from the straw of her giant water bottle, exhales audibly, and shakes her head. "Neither you nor Wade have said 'I love you' yet?"

"No."

"Why not?"

"I don't know."

"Yes, you do. Don't you trust him?"

More than anyone.

"With my whole heart."

"Then what's the issue?"

A whiny groan vibrates in my throat. "Words are hard."

She responds with her signature eye roll, then winces, adjusting her focus to the squirming baby below the view of my phone camera before glaring at me. "You know what? I actually don't blame you. You've been through enough. He should say it first. Like, what's his deal?"

My shoulders shrug.

"Chicken."

A grayed-out rectangle labeled BI comes to life with Behraz's face. "Who's making chicken? What'd I miss?"

"No one," Indi replies. "Nothing to note here, other than figuring out why two people clearly nuts about one another are unable to admit they're in love."

"Pot, meet kettle," Bea says. "You were the same with Landon."

My fingers snap and wag at the little hypocrite. "Hey, that's true. The rest of us knew pretty early on while you hung back in a deep state of denial."

"*Shhh,* you." Indi's lips purse. "You're disturbing the baby."

"Anyone wanna ask me how I'm doing?" Bea's lower lip juts in a frowning pout.

"Sorry. How are you? It's been a while." I wave. "I was so sad that we left before you made it to the birthing center."

"Oh, God. What a disaster of a day." She lowers her head as the heels of her hands find her temples before she whips up suddenly. "Not because of the baby. We love baby Akhila." She makes tickle fingers toward the camera. "I wanna squeeze our precious girl. That's the day I found out I didn't pass the bar."

"What!" Indi straightens.

Mouth pulling into a cringe, she groans. "Did I not tell you? Oops."

"That sucks. Can you retake it?" I ask.

"Yeah, but not until the fall."

"Bummer."

Behraz slaps the air and sputters. "Nah, it's not a big deal. I'm not the best test-taker, but still. It's open book and multiple choice. How hard could it be? I'll study harder, better, faster, stronger..."

Indi and I stare in awe as she trails off, singing the lyrics to Daft Punk's "Harder, Better, Faster, Stronger" and doing the robot in her seat.

Whenever she loses the plot like this, we don't interrupt, and she usually circles back to it.

Sometimes, I wonder what's going on in her head because, from the outside, it seems like a dozen hamsters run in their wheels at different paces. Or maybe I can't keep up.

"Anyway," she returns. I expect more of an explanation about her plan, but it's left hanging. "Oh! Sorry, my brother's calling. Talk to you guys later!"

"She's something else."

"Tell me about it." Indi adjusts the claw clip in her hair with a single hand. "Hold on." She leans forward, this time pulling Akhila into view. "Hi, Masi!"

"Move your big head; it's casting a shadow on her!" Cute aggression wins, and I gibber nonsense at the milk-drunk, sweet angel. "There's my cutie baby."

"I need to burp her but wait…" She tilts her ear toward Akhila's mouth. "She wants to tell you something."

Indi intermittently tugs on my niece's tiny chin so her mouth moves as if talking, using a high-pitched tone for a baby voiceover. "Gabe Masi, if you don't tell Wade Uncle you love him *very* soon, I'll make sure to have a naaaaasty diaper blowout every time you hold me."

"Gross." I frown.

"Do it! Or else!" Akhila commands.

"I love you, kid, but you're kind of a dictator."

"And don't you forget it!" With that threat, her eyes close and head lulls.

Indi turns Akhila onto her shoulder and pats her back at a rhythm. She raises an eyebrow. "You heard what she said. When you love someone, you tell 'em. I don't make the rules."

———

Wade and I wait for Doug as he stops to investigate every fallen tulip petal along the Rideau Canal's path. Their peak bloom has passed, and the colors have faded, but even in the early morning air, there's a brightness between us, a warmth shared in our clasped hands.

It's the perfect moment.

Say it, Finch. Three little words.

Doug whines.

"You hungry, buddy?" Wade rubs the top of the golden retriever's head. "Me too."

"Me three."

"Hear that, Dougie?" Doug woofs back softly. "We gotta get our girl fed before I take you back to your parents." Dimples flank his upturned lips. "There's a bakery I've been meaning to try."

The smell of coffee and fresh-baked goods wafts past as we approach the door.

"Here it is."

"A cafe named *Freckles*?" My eyes narrow at the storefront's window signage. "Is that why you brought me here?"

"Maybe," he says through a smile. "It's cute, right?"

I try not to give him the satisfaction, but it's impossible. My comeback doesn't match the heat on my cheeks or the width of my smile. "You're so cheesy."

He opens the door with a bow. "After you, m'lady."

I step through.

Baskets of various breads line the back wall, baguettes alongside loaves of rye, and brioche. A selection of croissants, pain au chocolat, and eclairs are organized in neat rows. Mille-feuille, madeleines, cream puffs, various tarts, and macarons join non-traditionally French items: donuts, Danishes, and cupcakes in a glass encasing.

"Figured I'd bring you somewhere you understand the French language."

I lob a playful smack against his solid bicep. "Rude."

"Monsieur, mademoiselle?" The young woman behind the counter addresses us. When Wade answers, and they continue in French, I zone out.

We take our mugs of coffee and croissants over to a table across from the display case. Doug noisily scarfs down his complimentary doggy treat, a sugar-free peanut butter cookie, then places his crumby snout in my lap.

"You and Doug get the same look in your eyes when you beg."

"Are you calling me a dog?"

I stay tight-lipped. "I'm saying there are similarities."

"Oh, for sure. We're both adorable, loyal—"

"Needy—"

He ignores my addition to his list. "And don't mind begging for a worthwhile meal."

"How do you manage to make everything about sex?"

"It's a gift."

"Truly."

"On that note, what do you think of this place?"

"Yeah, it's nice." I eye the cupcakes. "Ticks all the boxes for a French bakery; the cupcakes are pretty basic."

"You could help them with that."

"Oh, *sure*." Sarcasm laces my inflection as I lodge a bite of croissant into my cheek. "It won't be presumptuous at all for me to go up there and offer unsolicited advice."

"It's your bakery; you can do whatever you want."

Croissant flakes fall from my mouth, mid-chew. "It's what?"

"It's yours."

"Since when?"

"Since I bought it for you."

My hand covers the lower half of my face. "You *bought* me a bakery?"

"Yep." The unbothered shit sips on his coffee.

"That's..." I recline into the seat, mind reeling. "...this is nuts."

"You like baking cupcakes but don't want to deal with it en masse. This place is already well-staffed and has a lead baker, so you can be as involved as you want. Consider it your testing ground."

"*Ahhh,* now I see," I tease. "You want me outta your kitchen."

"Well, I tried to be nice about it, but you leave behind the biggest mess."

This guy.

"Be serious." My shoulders drop, and my head tilts to him before my gaze drops. "It's too much."

Wade places his coffee on the tabletop and retrieves my hand from where it strokes Doug's soft ear. "It's not enough. But if you don't like it, I'll get rid of it—"

"No, don't do that. I like it."

"And me, Freckles? Do you like me?"

My heart sinks. Forget about love; I've never told him I like him. He has to know, right? How could he not know? Or maybe he knows but, like me, needs to hear it.

"Yeah, Wade. I like you."

The stupid beating organ curses itself at the yearning in his eyes, so starved for the affirmation. It wants to tear open and reveal everything, but trips.

"Will you take me home, Wade?"

After a quick stop at the Kincaid-Jaegers to return Doug, Wade, and I wordlessly walk back to his penthouse.

Tension seethes as our eyes lock.

I lead him to the ensuite of his bedroom and prepare the shower, turning the handle until the water gently splashes to the floor.

My head tips up, reaching for a kiss, the contact slow and intentional. His warm mouth invites my tongue and returns drawn-out, dizzying swipes.

We part for a moment, but I don't stop, kissing his brow, his eyes, his angled cheekbones. Adoring him. Air staggers out from the seam of his pinked, damp lips.

"Can I undress you?" I murmur.

"Yes."

I peel away his leather jacket while resting my forehead against his chin. The worn cotton of his tee heats my flattened palms as I run them down his chest, then curl my fingers under the bottom hem. "Arms up."

We detach so he can lift them over his head. I toss it aside and shed my shirt, exposing a simple black bralette.

"Wow," Wade whispers, admiring as he slips his hands over my hips, then below the elastic of my sweatpants. "I'll never get enough of you."

I hush him with a finger on his lips but let him drag the pants over my ass and down my thighs to help me step out of them. His jeans unbutton easily in my grasp, and I ignore the hardened bulge in his soft boxer briefs as I remove everything below his waist. Impatient hands rid me of the remaining thong and bralette.

Tentative steps draw us into the steaming shower, the temperature ruthlessly hot.

We shift between the dual shower heads, sighing as the cascade washes over us. Wade throws a hungry look my way before stepping into my stream and latching his mouth to mine. Water sluices between our bodies, lips and tongues ravenous, feasting.

I get swept away for a moment, then remember.

"Wait." My hands surround his cheeks. "I need to tell you something."

He catches his breath and leans into my touch.

"I know I'm not innately nurturing or maternal…I've always craved the care of others to fill the void after losing my mom, but it either felt like I was asking too much or that whatever little I got was good enough because it was better than nothing." Salty tears join the water wetting my face. "I've never really thought of caring for anyone else."

Wade wipes away the saline mixture from my cheeks.

"Until you. I wanna take care of you, Wade. I want to be gentle, and tender, and rough if that's what you need."

His forehead kisses mine, sandwiching the drenched strands of his hair between us.

"Get on your knees."

Brown eyes question, but he says nothing before kneeling between my feet.

I pull a bottle off the shelf and pump.

A foamy lather builds as I work the shampoo through the dark waves of his hair, like the ocean at midnight. He sways at the pressure of my fingers against his scalp.

"Gabe. Oh, my *God*." Relief mutters through his throaty moan. "This is unbelievable."

His grip around me tightens until his mouth collides with my lower belly, spreading short, open-mouthed kisses across it.

I cherish the feeling of his tongue gliding over a sensitive stretch of skin and hum while rinsing away the suds and replacing it with conditioner. The second scalp massage elicits the same response.

Melting at my touch.

The sharp, woodsy scent of his soap coats both of us as we wash and rinse one last time.

Rising to his feet reveals white and pink blotchy knees. I keep him still on a dry mat, running a towel over him, then myself. His cock bobs, the head a glossy wine red.

I position him at the edge of the bed and angle forward.

"Do me a favor?" His firm hand on my shoulder stops me from kissing him. "Fuck me like you love me."

My head lolls to one side, so disappointed that I've still not told this endearing soul what he means to me. "Wade."

"Pretend, Freckles," he says, the sad lilt in his tone breaking my heart. His finger draws a spiral in my palm. "I wanna experience how it feels to be loved by Gabe Finch—just once."

Every cell in my body screams at me to show mercy, to end his agony and mine.

Like a magnet, my mouth meets the smooth line of his jaw, the rigid column of his neck, the bone of his collar, the strong slope of his shoulder. Goosebumps and his content noises trail after every touch.

He relaxes into my encouraging push into the mattress, and I descend onto him, streaking fastidious, wet kisses across the firm squares of his chest, down the ravine of his sternum, and licking my way to one taut, mauve nipple.

My tongue lashes and lightly sucks, worshipping and worshipping until he writhes beneath me, hands balling the sheets. Then, I move to the other tightened peak.

Breathy groans of my name pool arousal between my thighs and glide the length of his cock between them with ease.

"Oh, God," he whimpers as I use the ridged underside of his dick to rub my clit and spread a combined wetness up and down. His eyes skewer shut before snapping open again. "Condom?"

I hunch toward him, gasping as we lose connection. "If I loved you, I wouldn't use one."

"Fucking fuck. I get to feel you?"

I motion for him to straighten so a pillow supports his head, then straddle his torso once more.

"Please." My hands seek his, fingers lacing together when they find them. "I want you to feel everything."

A pair of our woven fingers jointly enter my soaked core, languid strokes prepping my walls. I watch his pupils blow wide and relish how his cock slaps against my ass. "How's that?"

He mewls.

Setting his hands on my hips, I lie back, pumping his rock-hard shaft. It grows impossibly, leaking clear pre-cum into my fist.

Muscular thighs tense and shudder under mine as he strains for restraint and control. My knees lift, angling him over my desperate clit before lining up with the entrance. Wade's vision struggles.

"Keep your eyes open," I demand. "Watch me."

The simultaneous gasp when the swollen tip stretches me. My nails bite into his chest, thighs floundering to take every inch. I rise until only the tip remains, then sink down, hoping for more. Wade says a bunch of bad words mashed together.

Sweat trickles down my back as I repeat the motion, slicing off and then piercing myself with his cock, again and again until I can bear the fullness, the thick curve inside my throbbing pussy. Pleasure sears through me, arching my spine and tossing my head, loose, wet ends of my hair shaking across my lower back.

Rocking my hips only builds it higher, an uncontrolled high keen launching from my throat.

His head sways side-to-side as I continue the lazy-paced ride. "Am I dead?"

I jolt through words, holding myself in place and laughing. "I hope not. Why would you say that?"

Wade's teeth chatter, his fingers dimpling the flesh of my ass. "Because you feel like Heaven." He urges my hips forward. "Don't stop."

I don't.

Our hands shift, winding together once more. I press them against the pillow, our chests flush. It's a stark contrast to last fall when I wanted distance and numbness. Now, I want to feel everything, too.

Heavy-lidded eyes stare back. I want him to know.

"You're beautiful."

His upper lip curls. He's surprised.

"What? Has no one told you that?"

Wade denies it. A drumming pulse runs between our palms, the heated skin slippery. The caresses across his abs seem to take effect. His hips stutter below mine. I gasp again and fall forward.

"You're beautiful," I repeat, drawing the words against his full lips, "So, so beautiful."

My mouth takes his, tasting his moans and swallowing every one, keeping it for myself.

The rhythm of my thrusts picks up, a crescendo into a gallop, the room all humid breaths and salty sweat. "Gabe, fuck—*fuck*, Gabe," Wade prays my name. "Oh, my fucking—*Gabe*—"

Pleasure cracks, then shatters through us, with a collective, leaden cry, hot spurts of his release filling me until it spills out. I quiver through the blistering high.

The ringing in my ears peters out, switching to Wade's quick, steady heartbeat and panting breaths. I wait a few minutes before dismounting from his softened cock, rolling us until we're a tangle of limbs.

A sniffle sounds out, rousing me from near-sleep.

Wade Boehner has tears in his eyes.

"Wade?"

"I'll be right back," he answers, removing himself from my hold and slinking off the mattress. He retrieves a pair of shorts from a drawer and skitters out the bedroom door while tugging them on.

What the fuck happened?

I burrito myself in the wayward sheets, wrapping and tucking it under my armpits before scuffling out to the living room.

He sits bent over on the couch, hands on his lowered head. I join him with a graceless plop, draping my arm around his shoulders.

"Wade, are you okay?"

"Yeah, yep. Yeah," he answers with a series of nods, scrubbing his face.

"Because it doesn't seem like—"

"You know what?" A swift launch has him off the couch and facing me, agony wrinkling his face. "No, I'm not okay!"

I gulp.

"I'm fucking losing my *mind*, Gabe. All I see is you. First thing in the morning and right before I sleep." His hands bury in his hair, tearing at the roots like a madman. "I look for you in every hotel room, every arena, every airplane and bus..." They release and extend toward me, pleading. "You're who my heart wants. *You*. All of you." He keeps ranting as I stand. "You, you, you, you, you. You live in my brain, and I don't want you to leave. And I feel insane for dreaming up a future for us and wanting things you don't, like I want to kick my own face in because I. Can't. Have. You."

"Wade," I say gently. "You have me."

Genuine shock wracks through him. "What about...?"

"What about what? I love you."

His body goes lax at the admission, legs giving out as his ass hits another section of the couch. The lifted weight has my heart soaring.

I kneel and scoot between his feet. "Are you listening? I love you."

"Me?" He points to himself. "*You* love *me*?"

My hand smacks his cheek lightly. "Yeah, you big *dope*. *I* love *you*. It's so easy, too. How can anyone not love you?" I scoff to myself, remembering how I once thought I hated him.

"Oh, thank God." He loosens further, stooping to cup my face. "I love *you*."

Our noses sidle. "I know."

"You know?"

"*Mmhm*." I nod. "I know you sold that godawful Lamborghini you loved because I hated it. I know you built that basketball court, so I'd spend more time here with you. I know you figured out all of my favorite things and offered them up to me because you love me. So yeah, I love you. Not because you did all those things but because you're *you*. And I *love you*." I let a pause break my train of thought. "Plus, you let me fuck you in the ass."

Wade's laughter rumbles from his heart, sincere and childlike. I cling to it, wanting to keep it forever. "In my defense, you let me do that, too."

"Alright, alright, Pretty Boy. You gonna kiss me, or what?"
His lips brush mine, teasing a lick across the seam.
"Only if you kiss me first, Freckles."
He's mine, so I do.

CHAPTER 29:
YOU'RE AN IDIOT, BUT YOU'RE MY IDIOT

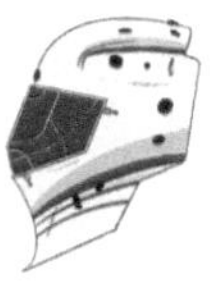

WADE

LOSING THE STANLEY CUP COULDN'T HURT ME.

Disappointing, yes. But inconsequential. I've got the love of my life by my side, giving me the happiest fucking birthday I could ever imagine.

Well, not exactly by my *side*.

Gabe leans on a sturdy headboard, hand fisting a bubble gum pink silicone cock. Her legs twist and toes squirm as I up the speed of the hidden vibrator inside her, thumbing the button on the remote. My other hand pushes a third finger into my prepped asshole. I hiss at the stretch.

She slathers the toy's length with more lube, nearly emptying the expensive tube.

"Fuck, that's so hot," I groan, removing a finger, and add more lube to pump the remaining two into my pursed opening.

Her lips shine with saliva. "How do you feel?"

"Filthy as fuck."

"That's what you are, aren't you? My filthy fucking boy."

I confirm with a whine, maxing out the vibrator speed.

Gabe's moan pitches up an octave, back curling through a wretched scream. Her torso relaxes, resting against the tufted headboard, rapid breaths slowing. A satiated smile pinches into her burnt sienna cheeks as I discard the remote.

Focused rage fires in my direction when she flicks her eyes open. "Get your ass over here."

Maroon throbs engorge my cock, strained by a cock ring at its base, swinging between my thighs as I stalk up to her.

Pulling me into a hasty, needy kiss, she strokes and squeezes pre-cum from the head, dripping it down her flat stomach. "Hands on the headboard."

I plant my feet onto the mattress, palming the top edge of the bed frame as she positions the domed head of the toy under me. My thighs wobble at the pressure.

"Breathe." Her hands surround my hips, guiding entry.

The greased tip creeps in, and I lose balance, folding to my knees.

"You're doing so good. I know you can take more."

I do, slinking down another inch before shallow breaths puff from me like a runaway train.

"Keep going," she coos. Her enamored gaze sweeps over me. "You look incredible. Like fucking paradise."

The degrading praise relaxes me enough to settle further, the smooth walls inside savoring the ridged surfaces of the silicone dick.

"Oh—*fuck*." My eyes screw shut with a quiver, stilling any motion.

"More," she demands. "I didn't say you could stop."

A final plunge impales me entirely. I cry out at the fill.

"Ride." My quads shiver, unable to assist the stutter of my hips. Gabe doles out a punishing slap to one cheek. "I said, '*ride*.'"

I obey. More fluid dribbles from my ripe-red slit as the dildo nudges back and forth. It glances off of the needy, swollen spot inside, wrenching demented, guttural moans from somewhere deep within my chest.

Gabe crushes her lips into my neck, then drops her head, grazing her teeth over a puckered nipple. They scrape as they bite down, and it's too much.

A shock of pain sets off the pleasure, and I explode, so sudden and brazen it blazes every last brain cell to ashes, save the one that controls the sound of a lengthy groan. Gossamers of thick, white-hot cum streaks up Gabe's tits and gorgeous, freshly fucked expression.

"Oh, my God, Wade." Her hands explore and spread the stickiness over her nipples and below, her mouth splitting open and webbing my release across those puffed lips. It's the prettiest sight and the last thing before my orgasm crashes and burns.

I wake up groggy and disoriented but root myself to Gabe's heartbeat. Nails lightly scratch up and down my naked back.

"You okay?"

A throaty rumble crawls out. "How long was I out?"

The goosebump-inducing scratches travel to my scalp as she shifts her spread legs beneath my resting hips. "About an hour."

"Yeesh."

"That's your fault," she teases. "You're the one who likes it rough."

The satisfied noise hums between my lips and her sternum. "The aftercare is why I like it rough." I maneuver forward, stealing a kiss from the crook of her neck. She recoils with a giggle, unable to bear the tickle. "Wait, what time is it?"

"Five."

"5 p.m.!" My elbows lift my weight from Gabe's torso. "We gotta go, Freckles."

"Three more minutes," she purrs, convincing me to rest against her chest again. "Please?"

———

"When you said birthday dinner, I thought you meant somewhere fancy." Gabe adjusts the shirred top of her forest green sundress while we wait to get seated at Cafe Jardín.

"Nah," I reply, smoothing down my denim shirt before tugging her to my side. "If I had it my way, no one would be invited, and we'd still be in bed with my hands on the headboard."

"Sometimes I worry about your masochistic side." She drops a tender kiss on the crease beneath my jaw. "If I hurt your perfect ass, I'd never forgive myself."

A host beckons us inside. "S'il vous plait."

Gabe sends a confused look my way as we skip past the seating area.

"We're sitting in the garden." I stop at the wooden door. "And don't think this is because you knocked me out with that cruel orgasm earlier."

"Why would I think—"

Her words evaporate into a gasp. Garlands of gardenia hang from the string lights, a twilight glowing against the lush green space. Decorative palms and tropical plants create walls, crawling ivy covering the entire back. It smells of her, matches her. Gabe steps into it, hands swiping at the strands as she passes.

"Hey, Freckles?" I call for her attention.

When she turns, her eyes light up at the sudden semi-circle created by our loved ones. Her dad, my mom. Indi and Landon holding Akhila. Denise and her partner. Mel. Skylar and Jaeger next to Fletcher.

"What are you guys doing here?"

I lower to one knee.

Indi points to me, and finally, Gabe notices my perched stance.

My hands reach for hers, brushing her knuckles with my thumbs. "I've done so many impulsive, reckless things in my life for attention. To be loved and cherished, at the top of someone's list. I sought it in all the wrong places. And then you showed up in that press room. Everything I thought I wanted or believed I was satisfied with evaporated into thin air. All I wanted was you, and you weren't mine to have." I swallow the knot in my throat.

"I wouldn't wish what you've been through on anyone, but I'm so grateful it was me who got caught up in you. I thank the universe for the way you hate-kissed me on New Year's Eve four years ago. How lucky was it that I convinced you to come up to my hotel room after Landon and Indi's wedding? It can't be a coincidence that our shared past—*each one of those times*—set off another chaotic series of events that led us through so many realizations about ourselves and each other and brought us here, to this point. It can't be anything but a butterfly effect cutting our seemingly well-balanced world to shreds."

Water floods her darkened lower lids.

"Maman once told me if I ever find the person who finds me as annoying as I find them, and despite that, we're able to prioritize each other above anything else, then I should marry them. Happy to announce on my 25th birthday, that's you, Freckles. You are the most maddening, infuriating, insufferable person I've ever met."

"Oh, my God." Gabe pushes out a short laugh.

"I *know*, for a fact, that I annoy the living daylights out of you. I love you, Gabe Finch. I respect you. And I don't want to live without you. Put me out of my misery and marry me."

Adoration gleams back at me from her weepy eyes.

My hands part from hers to dig the velvet box from my pocket. I snap it open. A four-carat marquise emerald and its vining diamond petals cast shadows onto my pinched-together forefinger and thumb.

"So, what do you think, Freckles?"

Gabe wipes away her sniffle with a wrist. "You wanna marry me because I annoy you?"

"Pretty much, yeah."

"God, you're an idiot," she shakes her head, "but you're *my* idiot."

"That's all I wanted to be."

"An idiot?"

"Yours."

Gabe bends forward, caging my neck between her hands as she speaks against my lips.

"Alright, Pretty Boy. I'll marry you."

EPILOGUE

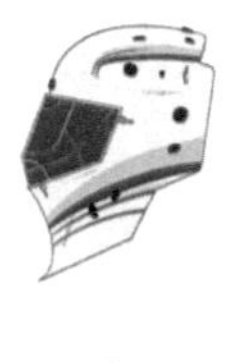

WADE

Three Years Later

I HAVEN'T SEEN GABE WEEP WITH JOY LIKE THIS since our trip to India.

We'd gone to the Maldives on honeymoon, but the surprise trip to Mumbai had been somewhat of a culture shock to us both. Every sense was overstimulated beyond limits. Being there during Ganeshotsav was part of the plan, but the pictures and videos don't do the havoc justice.

Shoulder-to-shoulder, limb-to-limb, we were two insignificant dots within a crowd of thousands headed down Linking Road to Juhu Beach, chanting and singing in chorus. A cacophony of cymbals and drums pealed out, inspiring some to throw colored powder into the air to join the smell of sandalwood and sweat. Its orange dust covered the tops of our heads, our kurtas, and cotton pajama-style pants.

The story-high Lalbaug cha Raja stood above us all, adorned in flower garlands and petals and dotted with pink and orange color brought to it by the breeze and adhered by the humidity of monsoon season. I cringed at the sweaty smear of a transliteration on my arm and repeated the cheer by ear alone. "Ganpati Bappa—Morya!"

"This is insane," Gabe yelled, securing my hand and cinching her engagement and wedding rings in our clasped fingers.

"I know!"

The procession forged ahead but unexpectedly stopped after a few loud calls.

"What's going on?" I asked.

"No idea!"

A split occurred in the crowd, allowing dozens of young men to emerge in white short-sleeved shirts peeking from bright orange Nehru jackets and topi, giant drums tied to their torsos. Women carrying the same drums joined too, decked out in traditional jewelry, sari pleats separating their legs.

"It's like the picture," Gabe stated loudly in my ear. "The one of Aai." Her rapid blinks collected tears from her waterline. "Dhol tasha."

I squeezed her hand harder.

A sharp scream garnered the crowd's attention as the drummers took their positions, heads bobbing with eight beats of light, steady clanging. Sudden, rhythmic bass notes reverberated, vibrations felt through the air, the earth, the heart. Cymbals paired in the raucous cadence, shooting energy through the masses. I wouldn't have been able to stop my body from moving if I wanted to. The throng of people roiled and jumped, throbbing with the dhol flow, rejoicing in our shared humanity.

Gabe wept and wept, streaks cutting through the powder and revealing the underlying freckles on her cheeks. I cocooned her as we pulsed together, protecting her from rowdy bystanders and selfishly wanting to experience this private catharsis with her for myself and no one else.

Eventually, the crowd spilled onto the expanse of Juhu Beach and downed the clay idol, releasing it into the ocean. We settled into a spot on the trodden, packed sand, clasping our elbows over our knees, peering off into the horizon as the sun journeyed downward. My ears rang and rushed with the slowing of adrenaline, crashing in waves like the ones before us. I was surprised to be able to hear Gabe's hush.

"I'd lost hope to ever connect with my mother. Coming here, today"
—she choked through a silent sob— "I finally felt her. Her roots, her spirit. I may never know why she left, but she remains in my heart, encouraging me to live the life she couldn't."

My arm found her shoulder. I pressed my lips into the frizz of hair atop her sweet head.

"I wouldn't have that without you. Thanks for making me come."
Dimples pursed my cheeks as she nuzzled closer, wrapping her
arms around the knees between us. "That's what she said."

Landon, his father-in-law, Rahul, Jaeger, and I sit on a sofa facing Skylar, Indi, and Gabe, their forearms linked, absolutely beside themselves. A recently unraveled gold cloth sign hangs in the background with white-outlined black text: The *Newest Addition to the Regents Roster Arriving in the Offseason!*

Congratulations and handshakes have already been exchanged, so I don't know what's going on with them. Maman and Baba clink glasses of champagne, beaming in the solidarity of forthcoming grandparenthood.

"I know why I'm crying," my wife blubbers. "Why are you two crying?"

"'Cause you're pregnant," Indi wails and pulls her loose dress taut around her belly, exposing a baby bump, "and I'm pregnant, too!"

"Way to go, buddy," I whisper to Landon. "You're really sneakin' 'em past the goalie."

Indi's dad *phews* audibly. "If it's another girl, bless you."

"They're the best." Radek was born to be a girl-dad. "I want six so they can have their own team and play puck against the neighborhood kids."

"*Six* little girls?" Rahul shakes his head. "Pass. Three was enough for me, mate."

"Skylar, what's wrong?" My ears perk at Gabe's question.

She calms for a moment between sniveling. "Jaeg and I got word this morning from the adoption agency that a child is headed our way. Our child."

Their collective weeping crescendos.

Landon and I sandwich Jaeg in a hug. "Daddy!!!"

His mouth remains downturned except for one corner, the red painting his cheeks failing to hide his excitement. "Yeah, yeah. Now get off me." He elbows us away, which tickles my ribs, and I giggle.

"Seriously, though. We're happy for you, Jaeg." Landon leaves his arm on Derrick's shoulder and squeezes before he and I exchange a look and bound from our seats, clinging to one another in a tight embrace and pretending to sob.

"We're all pregnant!"

It's a maudlin display that earns us multiple smacks from our wives and Skylar.

When she wraps her arms around my torso, I kiss the top of my best friend's head and whisper into the blonde strands, dampening them with my tears. "You're gonna be the best mom, Sky."

"Stop it, you big bully." She playfully shoves my chest and sniffles. "You're gonna make me cry harder."

Two tiny Radeks come wailing in response to our uproar, trailed by Indi's mom. Akhila and Ellora are both toddlers now, but they're still the team's first babies and are protected as such.

"Will you cut it out?" Gabe scolds me. "You scared them."

Landon and Indi pick up a daughter each and soothe them with soft coos and shushes.

Of course, they're wonderful parents. They stemmed from sets of wonderful parents. Me? I wasn't so sure.

"What if I'm not cut out for it? I don't know how to be a dad."

"I don't know how to be a mom, either." My wife, the lovely creature, held me tight. "We'll figure it out and do our best, like everyone else."

I'll believe, do, try anything Gabe says. She's my whole world.

My fingers toy with the oxidized silver chain around my neck while throwing a glance her way, unsuccessful in making eye contact. Occasionally, I stop to hook into the keyring-like circle joining the two ends.

"You've been messing around with that necklace for a while," Landon pries. "What was it, a birthday present?"

More like a commitment. It's a day collar, an everyday reminder of who I belong to.

"A gift for our one-year." I smile towards Gabe, and this time, she notices and smiles back.

———

My heart sighs, gaze tracing the delicate threaded pearls of our matching mundavalya, then the overjoyed expression we share in the wedding photo framed on a side table.

Gabe strolls up and tucks into my side, wrapping my arm around her until my hand covers the slight swell of her lower belly. Her chin rests on my shoulder, face peering skyward. I kiss her eyes.

"Good day?"

She nods, digging her chin in. "The best. You?"

"Every day with you is the best."

We share an agreeable hum. My wife turns to study the picture as well. "Look at those two silly gooses."

"That smile," I gush. "I live and breathe and die for that smile."

She says, "Romantic sap." But her arm loops through mine.

My nose scrunches, accepting the compliment. "What were you thinking right then?"

"I was wondering who forced you into dancing to 'Navrai Majhi' in the Varaat."

"Forced *me*? Pfft. I'm a naturally skilled dancer. Those TikToks aren't the brainchild of Maddie, you know."

"My apologies for doubting your ability."

"Apology accepted. I'll have you know I helped my sorry, graceless teammates learn the choreography to Landon's proposal flash mob *and* that hype song in the groom's procession."

"All those years at the barre paid off," she teases. "Wanna know what I was actually thinking?"

I nod. "Mmhm."

Streaks of hazel light up like a lamp when she peeks up at me. "That you weren't the piece missing in my puzzle. You're the deft hand who helped me find all the pieces and put me back together like one."

Who says Gabe Finch isn't a hopeless romantic?

"If you're a puzzle, I'm a puzzle."

She headbutts me for the comment, eyes heavy with sleep. "Okay, Noah Calhoun."

I never imagined I'd say such a thing, but this is better than sex.

It's the river delta of humor, comfort, and fulfillment, of the intimacy and trust we built brick-by-brick, having shed the lying and hiding under pretenses of who we're expected to be. The type of love we didn't know how to accept or maybe that we didn't truly believe we deserved. And yet, here she is.

"Wade?"

I hum as a reply.

"Carry me to bed."

An easy task, despite the long walk to the other side of the penthouse. She falls asleep before we even get to the bedroom

Of all the versions of myself, I like this one—*being hers*—the best. It always leads me home and onward to the promise of a future neither of us knew was possible.

THE END

WADE'S MATAR PANEER RECIPE
BORROWED FROM INDI'S MOM, ANJALI DAVÉ

Ingredients:
- 2 - 8 oz. cans of tomato sauce
- 4 oz. of cream cheese, melted and smooth
- One small red or white onion, diced large
- 1 cup frozen sweet peas
- 8 oz. of compressed paneer, not fried
- 1 tsp. jeera (whole cumin)
- 2 tbsp. oil
- MDH or Badshah brand Shahi Paneer masala, available at any Indian grocery
- Salt to taste
- Brown sugar to taste
- Red chili powder to taste

Directions:
1. Heat oil in a large wok-style or deep pan.
2. Add jeera.
3. Add diced onion and sauté until clear/softened.
4. Add 1 tbsp. shahi paneer masala and cook for a minute.
5. Add tomato sauce and 1 tsp. brown sugar and heat until it bubbles.
6. Transfer the sauce mix into a blender or food processor and blend until the gravy emulsifies and there's no onion or whole jeera visible. It should change from red to orange in color.
7. Transfer back into a pan on medium-heat.
8. Taste to see if it needs more or less salt, masala, or brown sugar, and add red chili powder to taste if you'd like a kick of heat.
9. Add melted cream cheese into the gravy and whisk to make creamy.
10. Add frozen peas and fresh paneer cubes until and cock until peas are cooked and paneer is soft all the way through.
11. Enjoy over rice or with paratha!

ACKNOWLEDGEMENTS

This book has truly been a labor of love. To get this story out in a way that felt like I was doing justice to the characters that have been living in my head since 2021, has been a challenge I had nearly lost hope of overcoming. Sometimes life hits hard, but I'm too stubborn to give up. I'm glad I didn't, because it's been an absolute delight to see Wade and Gabe come into their own and reveal who they truly are, what they want and how they were able to create their happily-ever-after.

I have much more to be thankful for this time around, as I've gained so many friends and supporters after releasing Snap Shot.

To Isabel and Zarin for sprinting with me constantly to get this manuscript to the finish line. Izzy, you're the best. I'm in awe of all the things you juggle and still make time for me and my silly rants and unnecessary worries. Can't wait to hug you so tight very soon!

Amelie, you're one of my first friends on this wild journey and I'm so honored that we get to do it together. Thank you for opening your heart and creative mind to me and allowing me to bounce ideas and vent and learn from you. I'll never be a whole ass aesthetic like you, but I'll die trying. You're getting a big hug soon, too!

To my alpha readers, Erin, Leigh, Reanne, Afreen, Shelby, and Nikki who patiently waited on every chapter in between long bouts of writing block or impostor syndrome paralysis.

To my beta readers, Apoorva, Bee, Nik, Carla, Lilly, Elizabeth, Carole, and Huniyah. Your honest, invaluable feedback, genuine excitement and gentle but constructive criticism improved this story tenfold.

To Lindsey Clarke, my editing angel. I've mostly conquered em dashes and paragraph structure, but may forever be bamboozled by semicolons. I may also forever abuse commas, and for that I will apologize profusely in advance. Your patience is also astounding with the delay of this release, and I hope to never put you through that again.

To the brilliant artists I've had the wonderful opportunity to collaborate with again, Allie Wygonik and Kell from Little Pluto Design: you've once more brought my characters to life and watching you grow in your craft is such a joy to witness. And I absolutely can't forget to thank Margherita, who put the work in to make the interior formatting clean and crisp.

To my desi girl author crew who inspire me every day: Ava, Bal, NM, Esha, and Anna P. I'm forever grateful for your love and support.

To Valentina, Brooke, my lovely readers and friends, who generously offered to unburden me by taking on administrative tasks I'd been putting off for so long.

To Olivia, who helped me with the French Canadian slang and French translations. Wade and Naomie wouldn't be complete without you.

To all the readers and authors I've connected with this past year and a half and beyond: thank you for seeing me and hearing my voice in a world where, now, more than ever, I'm made to feel small, unheard, undeserving and unworthy of being listened to.

And last, but in no way the least, to my husband who has sacrificed so much of our time together so that I could chase something that filled my cup. I'm sorry for the person I am when writing a book and preparing for release, haha. Love you!

ABOUT THE AUTHOR

Ruby Rana is an elder millennial who writes spicy, funny and heartfelt romance about sassy brown girls. She excels in sending messages where autocorrect has gone terribly wrong.

When she's not battling typos, you can find her explaining Midwestern slang to her East Coast-raised husband, running after her young children or experimenting with new recipes in the kitchen.

Want to connect further? You can find her on the following platforms:

Instagram: rubyranawrites
Threads: rubyranawrites
TikTok: rubyranawrites
Goodreads: rubyranawrites
Amazon: Ruby Rana

Ruby Rana is also the author of Snap Shot (Ottawa Regents, Book 1), which is available on Amazon, Kindle Unlimited and in many of your favorite independent bookstores!